LITTLE FURY

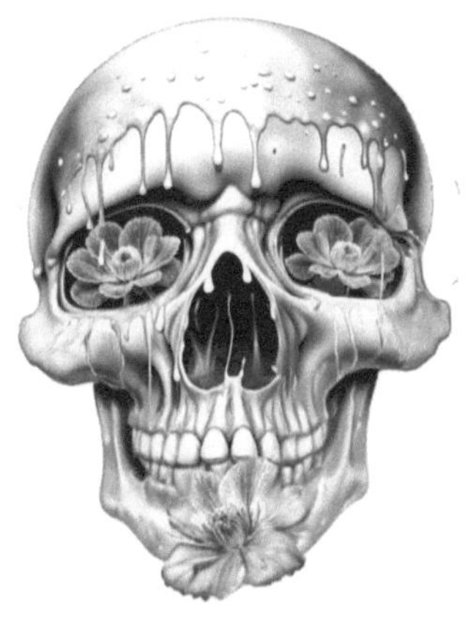

BOOK 1 OF THE DEADLY LITTLE THING TRILOGY

B. MACKENZIE

ISBN: 978-1-0690485-0-9

To all the ones who tell themselves they can't do it, I promise, we can.

LITTLE FURY PLAYLIST

Shake the Frost – Tyler Childers
5AM – Amber Run
I Wanna Dance With Somebody – Whitney Houston
Africa – Toto
One Headlight – The Wallflowers
Skin – Zola Jesus
Girl From North Country – Bob Dylan & Johnny Cash
Night Moves – Bob Seger
Crazy Train – Ozzy Osbourne
Since U Been Gone – Kelly Clarkson
Living Dead Girl - Rob Zombie
Symphony No.7 in A Major – Ludwig van Beethoven
Video Games – Lana Del Rey
Wicked Game – Chris Issak
Slip – Elliot Moss
Once Upon A Poolside – The National
These Arms Of Mine – Otis Redding
Radio Ga Ga – Queen
Miriam – Norah Jones
Fill Your Brains – Harrison Brome
California Dreamin' – Mamas & The Papas
House Of The Rising Sun – The Animals
Charleston Girl (Live) – Tyler Childers
Space Oddity – David Bowie
Stuck In The Middle With You – Steelers Wheel
Psycho Killer - Talking Heads
On The Nature Of Daylight – Max Richter
All The Debts I Owe – Caamp
Optimist – Zoe Keating
Nothing Matters – The Last Dinner Party

CHAPTER ONE

4 Days Earlier

*F*uck.

Fuck.

Fuck. Fuck!

I'm going to die in this room.

I'm going to die in this room wearing this tight fucking pencil skirt complete with slit and my favourite Louboutin black stilettos. This outfit, while hot as fuck is going to get me killed.

There are nine people in this room. Myself and eight men. Eight men who have no allegiance to me.

The room is big, with two large windows on the wall I'm in front of, and a desk that sits in between them. I'm standing in my usual spot just left of the enormous mahogany desk with my back to the window.

The room is dark in all forms of the word. The walls are a deep burgundy, and the woods are darkly stained. All the fabrics here are sombre tones of green or brown; There is nothing light in this room. The fabrics, curtains and rugs are made from thick fibres like wool and leather. The heavy fibres only add to the weight of the room. The things done and planned in this room linger here, imprints of the past that you sometimes catch out of the corner of your eye.

Wow, Ava, so poetic in the moments leading up to your probable death.

Internal Ava's voice is a sarcastic bitch today, apparently.

It's a stereotypical men's room where they retire to smoke and drink whiskey. Usually, this room is filled with the scents of cigars, bourbon, men's aftershave, and sometimes the tangy scent of iron. Today, I miss those scents. Today, it smells like nervous sweat and anxiety.

Oh, my fucking god! Focus!

How the fuck do I get out of here?

The window behind me is the most apparent exit, but it doesn't open. The things done and discussed in this room do not lend well to having windows that can be opened by anyone all willy-nilly. Extra routes of escape or entry are bad for business.

The two men between me and the door are one of the few bright spots in this situation. Lawrence, the one directly in front of the door, has just recently come back from being shot in the knee. One good kick to that knee, and he's going down hard. Ty, the one directly between Lawrence and me, is young and inexperienced. Honestly, it's the best-case scenario for me to get the fuck out of here. Once I'm out of this room, it's about 30 feet to the front door.

A plan starts to form. I'm not sure if it's a good plan, but it's a plan, nonetheless.

I start slowly inching my skirt up my thighs getting the slit high enough to give my legs full mobility. Thankful for the chair obscuring me from view, I slip out of my heels, staying on my toes so my height change and clothing adjustments don't draw attention.

Everyone here is trying to ignore me and look relaxed like it's any other day. But the usual hum of the room is missing. The guys in here are too quiet, too still.

I helped him pick and recruit almost every soldier he had. But these eight? I chose none of them. I told Marcus flat out that four of them were bad choices. They had sub par training, and none of them have the ability to remain calm, to not let the tension in their bodies give them away.

Ty is the only one who looks chill, and that's because he's an idiot of 19 who has no idea who I am and what I can do. The others know if I get out of here, I'm going to kill every last fucking one of them. The older guys have known me for years. They know who trained Marcus and me. If Ty had any sense in his head, he would realize that Marcus putting eight men in this room to kill me wasn't an error or overkill.

Marcus is anything but stupid. He doesn't waste resources.

I give my shoes one last sorrowful look, apologizing for abandoning them. And I go. Ty is on the ground before he even knows what happened. My kick to his side, stealing his breath and breaking a rib, gets him out of my way. Lawrence, however, sees me coming. The sound of surprise that leaves him is akin to a squawk or a grunt. He goes for his gun, but I'm faster. A sweep to his knee, with my leg and he's on the ground writhing in pain.

The other six wake up, yelling at each other and going for their guns. I'm almost out the door when I hear the first gunshot. A bullet hits my shoulder, and another rips into my side, but I don't stop. I can't stop. I stop, I die. And Harry would be so disappointed in me if all his training went to shit, and I stopped from the pain. But the adrenaline and the knowledge that my life is hanging in the balance keeps me going.

I'm out of the room and out the front door before even one of them has made his way from the room in pursuit of me. I don't waste time looking behind me. Sprinting across the front lawn faster than one would think this skirt would allow. I can see my car just as I hear Marcus yell for more of his men. The noise of my escape drawing him out.

Looking back for only a moment as I climb into my car, I lock eyes with Marcus. Marcus, the boy I've known since we were seven years old. The boy who I thought was my best friend. The man I shared a bed with for years. The man who just very blatantly told me I was no longer a welcome partner in the world I helped him take and rebuild.

My heart breaks for the seven-year-old girl I was. The one who came to a place alone and found someone she thought was just like her.

I floor it. Grateful for the speed of my Audi R8, I make it to the end of the block and turn just as the first car speeds out of Marcus's drive. I know where I'm heading. It's the only place Marcus won't look for me. The one place and person no one knows exists. I grab my phone, toss it out the car window, and keep moving.

Making a series of quick turns, my brain works through as many routes as possible to escape the men pursuing me. LA is a busy city, which is both good and bad. Traffic can both conceal and hinder. But I know this city; I've lived here for a while, and like the well-trained little hitman I am, there are multiple escape routes in my brain.

My R8 is far from the only one in the city, a choice I considered when I bought it. Black is my year and model's most popular colour choice, so it blends well. Ten minutes pass, and there is no high-speed chase involving myself and others I exhale a breath and give myself a mental high five for my expert driving skills, buying me some breathing room.

I reach into my center console and remove my compression bandages. Putting them on while driving will be challenging, but I don't have a choice. I still have a solid 30-minute drive till I arrive at my destination and to him. I'm able to get the first one over my shoulder reasonably quickly, putting the strap in my mouth and pulling hard to get it as tight as possible. Getting the one over my abdomen to stop the bleeding from my side is trickier. I'm pretty sure the bullet went straight through, but I need to slow the bleeding. After about 3 minutes of struggling, I give in and pull over, using both hands to get it on and done up.

Bandages secured; I grab my burner phone out of the glove box. I drive in the quiet until I'm close, and I make a call. He answers on the second ring, I can hear the smile in his voice. "Hi beautiful, I didn't expect to hear from you tonight, but this is a delightful surprise."

"Jake," I say, cutting him off mid-word. "Jake, I need you to do what I'm about to ask you, no questions asked, no hesitation. I need you to trust me and do it, and I'll explain when I get to you. Can you do that?"

I'm not sure what he hears in my voice, but whatever it is, he understands I need him to do it and do it now.

"Okay."

"Go to your garage and move your car out of its spot and onto the street, leave the door open to the side the car was in. Then go back in the house and get your medical bag. I will be there in less than 5 minutes. I have two gunshot wounds. One is a through and through, and the other, the bullet is still in my shoulder."

"Do it now, Jake," I snap at him. My voice is hard, but I need him to do what I ask right now and without question.

Wonder what the Doctor would have done had I used that tone with him in the bedroom?

Jake likes control in all things, so being told to do something without him being allowed to ask questions is probably making him angry. I hear the garage door opening and a car starting.

"Jake, I'm hanging up, but I'll see you shortly. Be ready to close the door the minute I'm in the garage." he starts to say something, but I've already disconnected the call.

I turn onto his street, slowing my speed to below the limit. As soon as I'm in, the door begins to close. Putting the car in park, leaning my head against the headrest; my hands ache from my death grip on the steering wheel. He has my door open, leaning in before I even notice him.

"Jesus, Ava, what the fuck is going on?"

I chuckle at his question. He pulls me from the car and carries me bridal style through the garage into the connected house.

Jake sets me on his kitchen counter and steps between my legs, instantly going into doctor mode. He looks over my face and chest, my side where the bullet exited. Jake moves from between my legs to the edge of the counter and gently nudges me to turn, giving him better access to my back. He asks no questions as he works, and that, I find surprising.

Coming around to my front, he removes the compression bandage from my shoulder, eyeing it curiously. "I had them made for me. I cut my leg badly one time while surfing, and I used my scuba jacket sleeve to compress the wound and to slow the bleeding until I could get to a doctor to have it stitched. It worked well, so I had some made for any future incidents."

He doesn't ask me any follow-up questions even though he wants to. He has a tight reign on himself, I think he's worried to spook me. His dominant side is at war with his doctor's side. The doctor in him needs to fix me. To tend my wounds the way he wants. The boyfriend in him is supportive and understanding, knowing that I'm not ready to talk about what happened.

The dominant alpha in him? Well, he is working ridiculously hard to suppress his urge to wrap a hand around my throat and force answers from me. He looks at me for a moment. Pausing his inspection of my shoulder, he aggressively exhales out of his nose, and I notice his left eye twitch. His carefully controlled anger is bubbling below the surface, and he is not enjoying it.

I bet his hand is fucking twitching to show my ass just how little he is enjoying this situation.

Jake is a very structured man and keeps his life very predictable. This situation must be testing every 'keep calm' technique he has.

When he was young, his temper and poor impulse control got him in trouble a lot. So, he learned that structure and predictability kept him and his life calm. He plays sports and works out a ton. He played football and was on the wrestling team in high school. A wrestling scholarship put him through medical school. Now, he is a general surgeon at one of the best hospitals in the country.

"Ava, I need to get this bullet out, and I'm assuming going to the hospital and being in an actual operating room is not something you're going to let happen?"

"You would be correct there big guy," I quip. "So how about you just take a deep breath and do what needs to be done so that I can stop bleeding all over your beautiful kitchen." The humor in my voice doesn't seem to be helping the situation. I think he's getting angrier, to be honest. I swear there is actual steam coming out of his ears.

I wonder if I lost more blood than I initially thought because I'm finding this situation funnier than I probably should.

This moment with him is so familiar to another in a different kitchen. I sigh, as thoughts of Marcus stitching up my leg years ago invade me. The memory hurts. The beginning of so many things that ended today in a hail of bullets started in that kitchen, in that house. So many things shattered today, so I decide to let this moment with this man take the place of the other one. This memory will be the one I hold onto. I close my eyes, breathe, and let that first kitchen slip away.

My emotions are under control; Jake, however, only seems to have one emotion. Severe annoyance, with a touch of seething anger. So, two emotions. He's grinding his teeth, and his eye is still visibly twitching, but he seems pretty docile. *Docile isn't the right word. Compliant? No. Resigned?*

Cutting up the back of my shirt to reveal the bullet wound, he releases another aggressive exhale and growls his words at me. "I'm going to freeze the area, but it won't do anything to stop the pain from me digging around in there to get the bullet out." I look over my shoulder at him. "It'll help with the stitches." Still looking at him, I mutter under my breath, knowing that he can hear it. "You could at least use your best bedside manner to help it hurt less," his hands pause.

"No, Ava, I can't. My good bedside manner is for patients who go to the fucking hospital when they have multiple gunshot wounds. It is reserved for patients who get in an ambulance and let the paramedics drive them to the hospital, not for patients who get in a car where they drive for God knows how long while bleeding heavily. So no, Ava. There will be no good bedside manner for you; patients like you get the bedside manner you are currently receiving and are happy about it. Besides, you aren't even in a bed. If you were in a bed, I'd be reminding you very sternly with my hand on your ass why we go to the hospital when shot and not to my house to sit on my kitchen counter bleeding all over my fucking quartz!" He chuffs at me.

I don't reply; instead, I gently nod my head about 25 times, letting him know I've been properly chastised for my behavior.

"Now, be a good fucking girl and take a deep breath because this is going to hurt, and not in any of the fun ways."

I take a deep breath preparing for the pain, but when some giant tweezers start to prod inside a bullet hole, no amount of preparedness is enough. White tinges the edge of my vision, and in that moment, I regret certain life choices. Specifically, the ones that led here to me sitting on this counter while my angry boyfriend digs a bullet out of me. I say nothing; I clench my teeth and keep breathing. Breathing is the first thing you learn with Harry. You learn that if you don't breathe through it, whatever it is will win every fucking time. Never forget to breathe no matter the pain, I hear that old bastard telling me.

"Put your hands on your knees, and don't move," Jake tells me, putting a hand on the back of my neck moving it ever so slightly to the right. I quickly realize this may be worse than being shot. Any other time I've been shot, I went to our in-house doctor. Marcus and I ensured we always had a doctor and an operating room available for our men and myself. At this moment, I'm missing the in-house operating room to have the bullet removed.

Wow, I think I miss Dr. Caine right now. Nah, I miss his drugs, not him.

Jake is quiet as he works. He's concentrating, but I think he's also ignoring me.

In one horrible flash of pain that steals both my breath and vision, I feel the bullet dislodge. Jake makes a noise of satisfaction and drops it, then tweezers onto a plate near me. He places his hand against the wound with gauze, I'm assuming to stop the bleeding. "I'm going to stitch this up now," he says quietly.

He works in silence as he stitches my shoulder. The freezing is working well to silence the pain from the stitches. I'm lost in my head, and I don't notice when he finishes until the sharp sting of a needle near the entrance wound on my side grabs my attention. I hiss at the feeling.

Jake moves around the island and stands between my legs, removing the rest of my shirt to see the exit wound. He grabs the needle again and starts to inject the area. I hiss in another sharp breath with the sting of the needle. He pauses to look at me, saying a silent sorry. I give him a slight smile. I drop my head a bit, closing my eyes, waiting for the freezing to take effect. He injects it a couple more times, then puts the syringe down. He places his finger under my chin and lifts my head to meet his eyes.

I'm always blown away by how attracted I am to him. He has dark hair that's more in line with good hockey hair than doctor hair. (*Is that even a thing, doctor hair?*) He has brown eyes that are so dark. If it weren't for the specks of hazel in them, you would think they were black. He has high cheek-bones and full lips. His nose and the scar from the corner of his left eye diagonally down his cheek to his lip are the only imperfections in his beauty. But those things only add to his allure. They add that little grit to a face that would otherwise be devastatingly perfect. The scar and slightly crooked nose first drew my attention to him six months ago.

He's tall at 6 foot 2, with a body honed by hours in the gym and time spent running. His hands are my favourite thing about him. I love how long his fingers are. I love the veins that run along the back of them. I love his rough palms from hours of lifting weights. Don't even get me started on the forearms. His choice of clothes at the hospital when outside the operating room are shirts and ties. When he gets home and removes his jacket, he loosens his tie and rolls up his sleeves to just below his elbow.

Jake's forearms are pure porn for me.

I have been drawn to this man from the moment I met him. Forearms or not he has a gravitational force over me.

"I'm sorry, Jake," I say quietly, hoping he does and doesn't hear me. "I wish I hadn't had to come here. I never wanted you to see this side of my life."

I wish for so many things if I'm being honest. I wish I were a different version of myself—a version where my life never went down the path that led me here. I wish my parents hadn't died in that car crash. I wish I hadn't been sent to Harry to learn my trade. But at the same time, given the chance, I wouldn't change it. I have a tough time wishing for that because while my life is dark and often bloody, it's led me to him, and truth be told, I'm really fucking good at what I do.

I lift my face and press my lips to his. He hesitates for a fraction of a second before he kisses me back. He grabs the back of my head, tangling his fingers in my hair tightly. His kiss is hard. More punishing than demanding. His tongue invades my mouth as if I have no say in the matter, and I happily sigh into him. It's one of my favorite things about Jake, about us. He takes control of me; he doesn't ask for it nicely; he doesn't ask for it at all. He takes it, and I yield it to him.

We somehow knew when we met that our desires and needs perfectly answered the others.

His hand slides down my arm and grabs my waist pulling me closer. But he grabs too close to my side, and no amount of freezing can stop that jolt of pain. A whimper escapes my lips sobering Jake instantly, and he glares at me, like somehow, I'm to blame for him forgetting himself and grabbing me. I hide my smirk at his glare and focus on him as he stitches the exit wound. Done with the stitches, he places his hands down on the counter, caging me in. Bending towards me, he places his head in the middle of my chest. I bring my hands up to run them through his hair, resting my chin on the back of his head.

We stay that way for a few minutes. Both of us are silent, enjoying the feel of the other being so close, a last moment of quiet before the storm. The questions Jake deserves answers to are the same ones I can't answer. I know they're coming. "Ava," he starts as he lifts his head to look at me. I tense. But Jake does something I don't expect. He kisses me softly and then turns away. He heads to the fridge, grabs a sports drink and hands it to me. "Drink that," he grumbles. I raise an eyebrow at him, twist the lid off and take a big gulp of the blue liquid, realizing how thirsty I am.

"Jake," I start to say, but he cuts me off.

"You need to rest. Sleep will help you heal and recover some of the blood you lost, and it needs to be now because we both know you aren't staying. Once you feel like it's safe, you'll be leaving me. I need you to get some sleep before that, so I don't have a panic attack thinking of you driving after what your body has just been through. The doctor in me won't allow a patient, no matter how reckless, to just take off after being shot twice." He closes his eyes for a breath and swallows. "So, let's get you down and into the shower and then bed for a couple hours."

I open my mouth to say I need to leave, but Jake stops me before I can utter a sound.

"Please, Ava. I know I'll never see you again after you leave here, so I need you to do this for me. Please shower and rest for a couple of hours, then go. Please, do this for me."

I don't believe I've ever heard him say please to me. I know I've never heard that plea in his voice before. I give him a slight nod and take his hand to help me off the counter.

CHAPTER TWO

He leads me to his bedroom ensuite and helps me undress. He takes me to the walk-in shower and steps in with me. I look at him, realizing he's only in a pair of athletic shorts slung low on his hips. He must have been in bed when he got my call. Stepping away from me he starts the shower. Steam vents, multiple shower heads, room for, I'm sure, six people. *I really will miss this fucking shower.* Turning on the rain shower head, he looks at me, nods, and turns to leave, but I grab his hand to stop him.

"I don't know if I can wash my hair by myself. Can you help me?" I'm not ready to be away from him yet. He's not wrong. The minute I leave here, I'll never see him again, and I want to keep him near me for as long as possible.

Jake slides his shorts down his hips, dropping them to the floor and steps out of them. He gets in behind me under the water and wraps his arm gently around my middle, using his other hand to tilt my head back against his shoulder and hold me for a moment. "Can I get the stitches wet?" I ask.

"It's fine; there's a waterproof bandage over the other bandages, so they'll stay clean and dry. I'll send you a bunch so you can change the bandages every 12 hours." I nod and close my eyes, enjoying the feeling of him, of feeling myself in his arms one last time.

I tilt my head back as Jake grabs another shower nozzle and wets my hair, adding the shampoo and carefully washing it for me. He rinses it then adds the conditioner to my hair, massaging it through my long tresses. His scalp massage turns me to liquid in his arms.

Removing his arm from my middle, he grabs the body wash, dumping some on a loofah. Placing my hair over my uninjured shoulder he washes my back, and over my ass in slow, small circles. He slowly drops to one knee, as he washes. His other hand slowly mimics the same movements over the same path down my body. I inhale slowly, enjoying his hands gliding gently over my skin.

Satisfied, he grabs the shower head to rinse the suds from my back. His other hand trailing along, running over it like the soap as it glides down me. His touch is firm in its caress, sinking into my skin. I lean into his touch, savouring it.

Moving in front of me, Jake grabs the body wash sans loofah. I raise an eyebrow at him in question. "Skin-on-skin contact is always better in situations like this." He tells me cheekily. I want to blame my increased breathing and pulse rate on the fact that I've sustained a fair amount of blood loss this evening. But I'm pretty sure it causes the opposite of that kind of reaction.

Jake knows my body. Never wasting a single caress when he touches me. All of his movements over my skin are deliberate, done to draw the reaction he wants out of me. The scarred side of his lip quirks up when he hears my increased breathing. He rubs his hands together, making a fluffy palm full of bubbles. The scent of my coconut shampoo mixing in the air with my tropical body wash is delicious. He places his hands on my collar bones, careful not to hurt my shoulder, as he slides his hands in towards my neck. He gently wraps them around my throat, and his thumbs push in slightly as he slides them up my neck towards my chin, tilting it up as he does. With a slow, deliberate stroke back down, he increases his pressure a bit more. I close my eyes and let him take what he wants from me however he wants. I enjoy it, knowing he will never hurt me; he will never push me farther than I'm willing to go, never taking more than he knows I can give him.

His hands begin their descent down the front of me. Rubbing in slow, methodical circles. They caress my breasts softly, still, under the guise of helping me wash. He runs his rough palms over me, my nipples hardening at the light abrasive sensation. He moves his hands, his thumbs and fingertips, grasping my nipples, rolling and pinching them gently. A jolt of pleasure shoots right to my core. I reach out for him to steady myself; he begins his circular descent down my stomach. Careful of the fresh wound there. He reaches my belly button, and he slowly lowers himself down to the floor of the shower.

Seeing this man at my feet sends a wave of desire through me. I lean my back into the shower wall, needing help to stay upright.

Anticipation is its own drug for me with Jake.

I know how his hands and mouth feel on me, what they can do, and those thoughts send another ripple of pleasure through me.

He starts at my feet, picking up one and placing it on his thigh. He begins to wash it while his other hand holds my calf and gently uses his thumb to massage the muscle. I moan from the delicious pressure of. Jake is focused on his task, his eyes on his hands as he touches me. He washes my lower leg with those small methodical circles. Every pass is inching just a little closer to my wet core.

Just above my knee, he abandons that leg, places it on the floor, picking up the other, repeating the process. He's drawing out my punishment. I'm paying for tonight. For the fear and anger I caused him. For my blatant disregard for my health and safety, for his being scared and unable to get me to comply with what he wants me to do.

I'm not mad at him playing with me like this. I deserve it.

Jake is so much more; he is worthy of a fantastic life with a woman who doesn't keep secrets from him, especially the types of secrets that have her showing up at his door shot and bleeding.

He moves his hands slowly up my thighs, kneading the muscles gently. Anticipation is making my thighs clench. Jake forces them open wider. He continues his ministrations along my inner thighs so close to where I need him to touch me but still not giving me what he knows I want. Legs clean, he rises to his feet. His hand sliding up through the suds as he drags his hand over my skin. Cupping my core as he moves over it, brushing his fingers over my pubic bone and the small patch of hair there.

He grabs the shower nozzle and rinses the suds from my body. His hand slides over my skin as it follows the path of the bubbles the same as before. Enjoying the game he's playing; he can't even be bothered to hide the slight smirk of satisfaction on his lips. I let my eyes run down the length of his body, seeing how hard he is—satisfied I'm not the only one affected by his game.

He rinses my neck and chest, caressing every inch of me as he does it. I close my eyes again, loving his hands on me. Lost for a moment feeling his hands on my thighs, I almost cum when he brings the shower nozzle to my pussy, and its stream hits my clit so perfectly. But it's only there for the briefest of seconds. I moan and reach out to grab something to hold on to. My fingers find his hair, grasping it.

He brings the nozzle back to me and holds it against me, getting the stream to pulsate over my clit, making my legs start to shake. My fingers tighten in his hair as the water drives me closer to my orgasm. He removes the nozzle again, and I let out a whimper. He stands up, looking at my face.

"What? I need to rinse the conditioner out of your hair." His grin is large. He turns me so he is behind me. I feel his cock against my ass, and I cannot help pushing back against him. I relish the feel of him, his cock in the cleft of my cheeks. He makes no sound, but I feel his pant against my shoulder. He wastes no time rinsing my hair.

The nozzle falls with a clatter, and Jake drops to the floor. He turns me to face him; his hands grip my inner thighs tightly and force my legs open wider. His tongue drags along my pussy up to my clit, flattening his tongue against me. I arch my back and push greedily into his face, and I moan as he sucks my clit into his mouth.

"God, Jake, please don't stop. You feel so fucking good. Your mouth feels so good".

The words are barely out of my mouth before Jake stops sucking and pulls back from me; looking up at me, I meet his eyes.

"No, Ava." the edge in his voice sends a shiver down my spine. "Nothing you have done tonight has granted you permission to speak and beg me to give you release. You will be very, very quiet. No moans, no begging, no pleading. No calling for a god who I assure you is not in the room with us. Our own personal demons may be here, but no God." He tells me darkly. "I will allow you to arch your back because it gives me better access to what I want, and I will allow you to hold onto my hair or shoulder. Still, I only grant you that caveat because of the blood loss you've suffered tonight, and

I'm nowhere near done with your punishment." He looks up at me, asking me to argue, but I don't. I close my mouth and nod.

With my nod of understanding, he drops his eyes back down and spreads me with his hands opening me up for his tongue to dive back in. His tongue flicks and sucks my clit as he sinks two fingers into me, causing my and I clench around his intrusion. Jake pumps his fingers in and out of me; his pace is slow and deliberate. I can hear how wet I am. The sounds from his fingers as they work me make me grip his hair even tighter and arch my back more.

"Look at this greedy little cunt so fucking wet for me. Tell me, Ava, do you want to come on my tongue with my fingers fucking your pussy or on my cock?"

I whimper in response, scared to say anything, not wanting him to stop what he's doing to me. "Answer me, " he growls.

"Both," I gasp out, "I want to come on your tongue with your fingers fucking me, and then I want to come on your cock."

"That's a perfect answer, Ava," Jake growls.

He pulls his fingers from me replacing them with his tongue working it in and out. Burying his face in me trying to get his tongue deeper. In and out, eating me; like I'm his last fucking meal.

His tongue laps at my inner walls while a hand slides to my ass, delving between my cheeks. His fingers circle my entrance there, teasing me. He grips my hips hard; he spins me to face the shower wall. I feel his hands come up and spread me wide.

Jake sinks his teeth into my cheeks, both sides getting equal attention. He rises a little higher, spreading me as wide as he can, and I feel his saliva being dripped down onto me. He drags his fingers through it, gathering it, using it to lubricate and sink them into my tight opening. Turning me back, and his mouth finds my pussy again. His fingers behind me keep massaging that tight ring, working his saliva into me allowing his fingers to slide easily inside.

His tongue swirls around my clit, sucking it into his mouth, working it fast, his finger in my ass keeping the same pace. It's almost too much, too good, too many sensations. Wetness leaks down my legs as Jake worships me with his mouth and hands. My orgasm has been building, and my legs start to shake, my muscles clench, and I cum hard, pulling his hair as I do.

When my body stops shuddering from my climax, I look down at Jake seeing his smug face. He keeps his eyes locked on mine as he gives me one last long and slow lick. Sending an aftershock through my body. A low chuckle leaves his chest as he watches me shudder again. My eyes rake over him as he stands up, his cock impossibly hard and glistening with his precum. I start to drop to my knees, but he grabs me by the throat, stopping me. Pushing me up against the wall he kisses me hard and deep. My taste still on his tongue as he finds mine, and I return his kiss, savouring it. Breaking the kiss, he leans his forehead against mine, his hand finding the back of my neck squeezing me slightly.

With a deep breath he quirks the side of his mouth up and kisses me fast on the cheek as he grabs his body wash.

"What's that look for?" I ask him.

"It's my 'that was fun, but I'm fucking hungry, so let's wash fast so we can eat' look." He dumps some in his hands, working up a lather; he quickly washes himself then turns to me and lathers me up again, but this time much more effi-ciently.

"Well, that was a very competent and serviceable wash-ing," I grumble as he turns the water off.

"Sorry, did you say something?"

"Nope, nothing," I reply.

"Because I could have sworn, I heard you grumble something about not being satisfied with the service you're receiving, and then I would have to remind you that the service you receive while in my care, is a direct result of the situation, or shall we say predicament that brought you shot and bleeding to my door." Grabbing a towel from the warmer and wrapping it around my shoulders he kisses the tip of my nose as he continues. "But you didn't grumble anything like that under your breath, so I don't need to remind you of anything." Jake grabs a towel and quickly dries himself off.

"You hungry?" he asks me as he wraps the towel around his waist.

"Yeah, I could for sure eat," I respond with a chuckle as he wraps the towel around his waist, heading out of the bathroom with a raging hard-on.

Alone in the bathroom, I gaze at myself in the mirror as I drop my towel and look over my body. A few bruises have started appearing, and I realize I have no idea how I got them. I don't remember hitting anything during my escape for my life, but who knows? Adrenaline isn't the best thing for an accurate recounting of events.

My hair hangs straight down my back, ending just above the swell of my hips. My pale skin making the black look impossibly dark. My grey eyes usually sparkle but like my skin, blood loss, fatigue and heartbreak have left them close to translucent. Even my olive skin tone can't combat that much damage.

I still look like me, the familiar splattering of freckles across my straight pert nose and cheeks. A pink pouty set of lips and a chin that is always just defiant enough completes the face staring back at me. I'm 5'4, not short or tall; my breasts are full but not overly so. My waist is trim, and my hips swell just so sweetly. I'm aware that I'm beautiful. My body is lithe and supple, the perfect package for the deadly little thing on the inside. I still look like me, except with a couple of new wounds that will leave a scar. I sigh. I don't mind the scars. I like them if I'm being honest. They are the only bits of imperfection I've ever been allowed.

I dry my body and wrap my hair in a towel. Heading into Jake's bedroom I sit on the end of his bed and breathe. I seem to be doing that a lot today, just breathing. I think it's a valid reaction to the shit show that my life became today, but it is still a lot of silent contemplation for any one person to do in a 24-hour time period.

Jake comes in wearing a new pair of athletic shorts and nothing else; they sit low on his hips. His adonis belt is on full display. I can't help admiring it.

You're not admiring it; you're thinking about all the times you've run your hands and tongue over it.

Why does he have to be so fucking hot?

Carrying a plate of food that could easily feed ninety, Jake sets the tray on the bedside table and disappears into his walk-in. I stand up as he comes out of the closet, seeing he has my favorite T-shirt of his. It's an old Queen t-shirt that has been washed and worn so often that it feels like butter on the skin. It's the shirt I always gravitate towards when I sleep here. Holding it for me, helping me slip it on so I don't hurt my shoulder.

I look at Jake, admiring his chest and the ink he has on it. It's a hyper-realistic full-colour tattoo of a beautiful cliffside with waves crashing against the rocks below. Upon the cliff is a lone figure, a woman with black hair that's wildly blowing in the wind. It's both stunningly beautiful and gut-wrenching all at the same time. When I look at the tattoo, I think the woman is sobbing, about to fling herself from the cliff. He has a few other tattoos across his body, all in colour and beautiful in their way.

There is a geometric pattern on his thigh. It encompasses the entirety of it, front and back. The pattern is so intricate that it looks like it moves. The negative spaces feed into the positive ones. It's captivating. On the inside of his left arm, there is a flock of birds that I think are starlings. On his ribs, connected to the cliffside tattoo through swirls of smoke and vines, he has a dark-cloaked figure whose hands are clasped in what looks like prayer.

He is a work of art, this man. His body, face, mind, all of him.

Jake clears his throat, breaking my drooling stare and raises an eyebrow at me with a knowing smirk. "Get on the bed." he says, still in his 'don't fucking try me' voice from the shower. I like that tone. It's the best one.

I sit on the bed and curl my legs under me as I lean against the padded headboard. Jake places the tray on the bed in front of me, then joins me, sitting with his back against the headboard, his legs straight out in front of him. We sit quietly, not talking to each other as we both eat. I grab a couple of grapes and some cheese.

Jake knows what I like, so it's full of fruit, nuts, snap peas, red peppers, hummus, pita chips, and tzatziki. It's seriously my dream spread of food.

Grabbing the remote next to his bed and turns on some music. I smile as "Shake The Frost" by Tyler Childers plays quietly over the gazillion speakers throughout his home. I'm not sure when he started playing more of my favourite music than his, but it happened slowly over the six months we've known each other.

I don't know how to be friendly and listen to music I don't like. I'm aware it's a problem, but it's not one I care enough about to change. Eventually, everyone I know gives in and lets me have my way.

It's a hill that I will die upon.

"Ava," he starts, and I look over at him, ready for the questions I'm about to be bombarded with. Instead, he hands me a couple of pills and another sports drink. I take them from him, pop them in my mouth and swallow.

"Antibiotics and painkillers," he tells me after they're gone.

We fall back into silence, both of us eating as "5am" by Amber Run begins to play. "Jake," I say, pausing to collect my thoughts before I start. I'm still unsure what I'll tell him and what I won't.

"I need you just to listen Jake and understand that there are things I can't and won't tell you. I'll tell you what I can, what I'm comfortable telling you, and what I think is safe enough to share, so no one feels like you know too much and decides you're too big a risk to be left alive." Jake says nothing. He looks at me, waiting for me to begin.

Is it odd how well he's taking all this?

CHAPTER THREE

"When I was seven, I was in a car accident with my parents. I was the only one who survived. My parents had no family, so I was sent to a family friend."

"Sent?" Jake asks.

"Yeah, sent." I sigh. "It was an odd situation. I was adopted. There was a stipulation in the adoption contract that stated, if anything was to befall my parents and they died or were unable to continue to raise and provide for me in the manner as to which was agreed upon, I would be sent to Harry."

"Harry has a last name?"

"He does, but it's not important. Harry's place was not a run-of-the-mill situation, but I was raised to be polite and do as I was told. Stoicism was the family motto." I chuckle a bit at that, remembering my parents.

"I got out of the hospital two days after the accident. I had no injuries except for some bruises and a few cuts. I think I had about a dozen stitches here and there." I stop for a moment, feeling the sadness of that day, remembering what I lost that day. Jake grabs my hand, lacing his fingers with mine.

"A woman named Beth was there to pick me up from the hospital. She took me to my home and helped me pack my things. Books, clothes, some toys, Mr. Waffle and Miss Mushroom."

"I'm sorry?"

"What part is confusing you big guy?"

"Ava." exasperation and warning in his voice.

"Stuffed animals, Jake. Squirrel and goat, respectively." He turns and looks at me, seeing if I'm joking. When he sees I'm not, he scrunches his eyebrows and nods at me.

"Anyway, after I left the hospital, I was sent to The Ranch. The ranch is not a ranch as much as it is a school of sorts. What I learned there was unconventional, but all of it useful. Just useful to a very niche market." Jake doesn't push and doesn't ask for more details. He lets my words fade out.

Why the fuck is he taking this all so well? So, in stride—like it's a story he's heard before.

Jake shifts on the bed, bringing me out of my thoughts. I take another grape from the tray and pop it into my mouth. I'm about to continue when I hear my phone. I look at Jake with a silent question. "I went to your car and grabbed your phone and bag for you while you were in the bathroom," he informs me.

"Ahh," I say. "Thank you." I rise to get my phone, but Jake stops me and grabs it for me. If I had to guess, I'd guess Harry is calling me. He's old and hates texting, so he usually calls me. Jake hands me my phone, and I sigh at the 30 or so notifications. There are three missed calls from Harry and one text from him that reads,

You better be alive, you little shit, or I'm going to drag you back from the afterlife just to kill you again myself.

As far as texts go from Harry, that one is quite lengthy and shockingly typo-free. I know instantly that Beth texted it for him; I can picture Harry handing his phone to Beth and telling her what to text and Beth cleaning up his wording and only allowing the term "little shit" because he is communicating with me.

The other messages are from three of my guys. They all say the same thing:

- *Are you alive?*
- *Harrison had to return home.*
- *The house is spick and span*
- *it's a beautiful day for a drive.*

We have a simple code but it tells us everything we need to know in as few words as possible.

Three of the four are safe and have made sure to get out of the city fast using whatever escape plans they each had in place. I feel the tension I was holding loosen, knowing that 3 of them are still alive. Losing Harrison hurts; I adored that old Englishman, and his abilities with a rifle and scope were things of beauty. He would sing some bawdy old songs when he drank too much, and we enjoyed making fun of him for it. I feel my eyes sting, so I head into the bathroom to splash some cold water on my face.

When I return to the bedroom, Jake isn't there, but I watch as the lights turn off on his path back. I'm just standing in the middle of the room when he returns. Unsure of what to do now. I know I need to leave. I need to get as far away from here as possible. No matter how careful I was, what if someone knew about Jake? Him dying because of me would break me. I know it would. That little bit of humanity I still have would completely cease to exist.

Jake comes up behind me and nuzzles into the back of my neck. He reaches up, removes the towel from my head, and lets my hair tumble over my back. He drags his hand down my arm and clasps my hand as he starts to lead me to the bed. I resist him.

"You promised me you would rest for at least a few hours, Ava."

I don't bother arguing and reminding him I never promised, but I don't want to leave him yet, and I'm exhausted.

I let him lead me to the bed and get into it as he pulls the comforter back. He pulls the blanket around me and moves towards the door to turn off the overhead light and close it. The room is cast in a soft glow from the lamp on the bedside table. He pads back to the bed and slips his shorts down over his hips, letting them fall to the floor. I watch him, enjoying how his body moves.

He gets in the bed, choosing to leave the lamp on. He moves closer to me, slipping his arm under my neck. He slides one of his legs between mine and pulls my leg to lay over top of his. He drapes his other arm across my hips carefully to avoid the injury on my side.

We're silent for a while, lying together, my face buried in his chest. I breathe him in. He smells of whiskey and citrus, always with the subtle antiseptic note from working at the hospital. I love how he smells. He smells like Jake, like everything that makes him who he is. His scent envelops me, making me feel warm.

He runs his fingers up and down my spine, eliciting shiver after shiver from me. My nipples harden more with each pass of his fingers on my back. I move closer to him, trying to feel as much of him as possible. I feel him grow hard against my stomach. My nipples harden in response to his body

I tilt my face to him and raise my hand to cup his cheek. I brush my lips softly over his. He rubs his nose along mine, and then he kisses me. It's soft. Barely anything more than a ghost of a touch. His arms tighten around me, pulling me impossibly close. His hand finds my ass squeezing it slightly when he pulls my hips to rub my pussy along his thigh.

I sigh against his mouth, getting lost in the kiss. The sweep of his tongue over my top lip, coaxes my lips to part for him. The strokes of his tongue against mine are soft, but as my tongue meets his, our kiss deepens, my hand slides up over his shoulder to his neck. I lace my fingers into his hair, gripping it tight. He growls in response to the sting and with it any calm or gentleness slips away.

Jake's mouth unbidden like this against mine makes me grip his hair tighter and grind myself against his thigh, needing to feel every inch of his skin against mine. I move to remove my t-shirt, but he isn't done with my mouth yet. He grabs my ass harder, grinding my already-drenched pussy against his thigh. This is his kiss, and he will have it as he wants. He bites my bottom lip, sucking on it to soothe the sting, and I whimper. His hands are working their way under my shirt. Smoothing over my skin, grasping and kneading.

I break the kiss to remove my shirt, he raises himself up to follow my body like it's tethered to his own. He sucks one of my nipples into his mouth and squeezes the other one between his fingers. I move onto my knees, guiding his mouth back to mine with my hand in his hair. He pushes us both so I'm straddling his hips as he leans back against the headboard without breaking the kiss.

Our kisses are slow, each one lingers on my mouth, melting into the next. I can feel how hard he is as he rubs against my ass with every roll of my hips. I reach behind me and fist him, squeezing him, feeling that first drop of precum on his tip. I smear it with my thumb and rub it back over him. He groans against my mouth, his hips buck under me and I grind against him, looking for the friction I need. Needing to feel more, I reposition myself so I am facing him and bring the head of his cock to my dripping entrance, but he stops me.

I make a noise in protest of his denial of me. "Patience, Ava. I promise your needy pussy will have my cock in it soon enough." His words go straight to my core, my clit throbbing.

Sliding his finger through my folds, my slick coating his fingers as he moves over it. I pant as he strokes me slowly, his rhythm steady as his kiss steals my breath. I gasp into his mouth when he pinches my clit. I tilt my head back, breathing in a lungful of needed air just as he slips a finger inside me, and I fucking explode. I ride his hand through my orgasm as he strokes my clit till my pussy stops clenching around his fingers.

Jake gives me no time to recover before he grabs my hips and flips us in one swift movement. He hooks one of my legs over his arm and enters me punishingly hard and fast. Driving into me over and over again. And it feels like absolute heaven.

He's large and thick, and I always feel a stretch, no matter how ready he has me. I love that stretch. I love feeling him fill me so completely.

I try to meet him stroke for stroke, but I can't. I reach my hand back and press against the headboard holding myself still so he can fuck me, burying himself deep.

"Pillow," he growls at me.

It takes me a moment for his words to penetrate my brain. I reach beside my head and grab a pillow, handing it to him. He pulls out of me, taking the pillow and placing it under my hips. My hips higher, staying on his knees he grabs my thighs, pushing my legs wide. "So, fucking beautiful, this glistening swollen cunt open for me, waiting for my cock to be buried in it again."

"Jake, please." one of his hands leaves my thigh.

"Please, what, Ava? Please finger you?" he punctuates his question pumping two fingers into me twice, collecting my slick and dragging it along me and over my clit.

"Please," I whisper.

"Please, what, Ava? Please fuck this tight little ass?" Again, he dips two fingers into my pussy, collecting more of my wetness, dragging a path of it along me until he reaches my tight hole, rubbing my wetness around the entrance and slipping a finger in just past the tight ring. Pulling it back and doing it repeatedly, sinking in a little deeper each time.

"Fucking hell," I ground out.

"Hold your thighs for me," he commands, and I obey. He sinks two new fingers into my pussy, rubbing the spot on my inner wall, instantly creating that to-die-for pressure. I feel more of my wetness slide from me as he works my pussy and ass. I know I'm making noise, crying, moaning, whimpering, grunting, groaning. "Please," I mumble when his thumb finds my clit.

He stops everything.

"Please, what, Ava?"

"Jake, I don't care, do all of it, fuck me with your hands, your cock, a fucking dildo. Fuck my pussy or my ass; I don't care. Just make me scream your name." I sob out to him. My body at a point of utter submission and need.

His teetering control snaps at my words, and his hands are back on my thighs, pressing my legs wide and back, and when he drives into me, he bottoms out. His balls hit against my ass; the noise of our skin slapping fills the room. He drags out against my inner walls, driving back into me, hitting that spot over and over again. The pressure builds and builds until the orgasm rips through me, and I scream his name as I cum. I feel his hips stutter then he is following me over that edge.

He collapses on me, burying his head in my neck, panting. He rolls off me, and I instantly miss his weight on me and the feel of him inside me. He goes into the bathroom, returns with a warm cloth and cleans me up gently. "Ava, sit up for a second. I need to check your shoulder."

"Mm-mm," I mumble and shake my head.

"Ava," He says sternly.

"Ugh, dude, stop being so bossy." I mumble grumpily at him.

I hear him chuckle, but I sit up and let him look. He says nothing, so I assume all is well. I flop back down with an overly dramatic huff. I feel him a moment later as he climbs back into bed behind me. He turns off the lamp and pulls me into him, burrowing into the back of my neck and sighing. I know I need move, but my body is exhausted, my brain can't hold a thought, and he is so warm and holding me so tight that I drift off before I can even think of getting up.

CHAPTER FOUR

I wake to the feel of Jake kissing my neck as he moves my leg on top of his and slides into me. "Oh god," I gasp as he fills me with one deep thrust. He grips my thigh tight and groans into the back of my neck, sending shivers over my skin. His movements are slow and languid. The feel of him as he slides in and out of me has me moaning his name in response. His hand slides over my hip, towards my pussy, his fingers sliding into my folds. He glides them over my clit, rubbing it slowly and methodically as he fucks me from behind.

"Jake, baby, please," He pulls out of me, and I roll onto my back. Spreading my legs for him, and he settles in between them. He kisses me gently as he pushes back into me. We both let out a shallow breath as he fills me again. I reach up and touch his cheek. Running my thumb over his bottom lip. Jake takes my thumb into his mouth, biting it gently. I lift to him, my mouth seeking his. This kiss so full of words left unsaid between us that a sadness sets in and I can't stop the tears from falling.

He doesn't say anything; he simply kisses my tears away. Kisses my neck. I realize this is what it means to make love to someone, and it just makes me need him more. "Jake," I'm not sure what I'm asking for. His pace is steady. He thrusts into me as I rock back onto him. My orgasm builds slowly with each swipe of his tongue in my mouth and thrust of his hips—the thrum of it sitting low in my belly. My breathing increases, and he knows I'm close.

"Eyes on me, Ava; I want to see you when you come. I want it burned into my very fucking soul as you come on my cock." I whimper at his words.

He moves, changing the angle so he can get deeper. His hand moving between us, his fingers finding and stroking that bundle of nerves there.

When my orgasm hits, I clench him tight. His head drops into the crook of my neck as he buries himself in me and releases a guttural noise when he cums. He lays on me for a moment, panting into my neck, kissing it, dragging his teeth gently against my skin.

He lifts his head, meeting my eyes, and I can't stop the flood of emotion that floods me. A pain like nothing I have ever felt before crushes my chest, more than my heart breaking, the knowing this is the last time my body will feel his weight on it, the last time my fingers will run over his skin, the last time his lips will meet mine, the last time his fingers will gently stroke my hair. Knowing this a crack forms in my soul.

His eyes meet mine and I can see in them the same words I wish I could say, the same things I feel but can't say.

It shatters me.

The tears come spilling from my eyes, unstoppable. He kisses me, giveing me every part of himself in that kiss. The kiss we know is goodbye. I kiss him back, hoping he feels me in it. Feels my heart and knows that if it had been different, I would have given him my very soul.

He breaks the kiss, pressing his forehead to mine. My eyes are closed as I breathe him in and out. The emotions and trauma of the day have claimed my strength, and I'm asleep before he even slides out of me.

Four hours later, just as the sun starts turning the sky that beautiful morning pink, I woke up and knew I've lingered as long as possible. Jake is asleep next to me. I can hear his ever-so-quiet snore, the one he only gets when he falls into bed after 48 hours on call at the hospital. I know he won't wake up for hours, no matter what. I could blast an air horn, and he would sleep through it.

I'm thankful for that. I untangle myself from him, another sign that he's out for the count. Jake and I are both non-cuddle types of sleepers. Sure, we snuggle in post-coital bliss, but both of us want to sleep, so we roll apart. A leg or hand or foot touching, yes. But not this tangled mess of limbs. I get out of bed and stifle a gasp at the blood on the bed from where the stitches in my shoulder opened. My side somehow held, but my shoulder was not so fortunate.

"Fuck." I mutter to myself. I head into his walk-in, find leggings, underwear, sports bra, socks, and sneakers that I had here, as well as one of Jake's black t-shirts and an over-sized black zip up and get dressed in the relative darkness of the closet. Dressed, I make my way out of the bedroom, closing the door behind me, not allowing myself to look back at him.

I get to the kitchen, find Jake's medical bag and search for what I hope it contains. Finding the glue, I quickly added some to where the stitches tore. I grab a bunch of bandages, antibiotics, and painkillers that are suspiciously sitting near the bag.

He knows me well, knew I would sneak away.

Out of the fridge, I grab water, a couple of sports drinks, and what I'm pretty sure is Jake's lunch for tomorrow. I open the front closet, grab a bag, and begin loading it with my stolen goodies.

With my bag packed, I head to the garage. I go through the cupboards and grab cleaner and paper towels. I make quick work of cleaning up my driver's seat.

This is why you get leather seats. Spills and blood clean up easily.

Going back into the house, I grab my bag of stolen goodies, go into Jake's office, and sit at his desk. I pick up a pen and paper.

Jake,

If things had been different in my life, if my parents had made one different choice, this day may have ended differently.

Do you remember that Sunday a few weeks back when we were eating in your bed, both of us reading? And you took that stupid selfie of us doing such a mundane thing? I never told you this, but that moment made me feel warm and safe. It made me feel like I used to when I was home with my parents. I knew that day that I wanted you. I wanted you for myself. I wanted the life I could see for myself with you. Realistically or not, I wanted that life with you so badly.

When I met you, I thought you would be nothing but another moment in my life—a new moment to go with all the others I've shared with someone just passing through. But that Sunday, I realized for the first time in 17 years that I wanted something for myself. Something that was mine and not tarnished by this venomous little life I lead. And for a single moment, I fooled myself into thinking it was possible. At that moment, I forgot who and what I am.

Had it been possible, I would have chosen you for myself. Forgive me, Jake, for the lies and the hurt. Forgive it of me, please, because if it had been in my power to give to you, I would have given myself to you heart, body, and soul.

–Ava

I leave the letter on Jake's desk. And make my way back to the kitchen. As I walk past the fridge, a photo catches my eye. It's that stupid selfie from that Sunday. Jake had it printed and on his fridge. My heart clenches painfully. I grab the photo, pick up my bag and head into the garage.

Backing out of Jake's garage onto the street, pausing for a breath, my hands gripping the steering wheel hard. A tear slides down my cheek more threatening to come. I wipe it away, exhale the breath I'm holding, place the car in drive and ignore the urge to look back as I leave behind a second chance, I knew I didn't deserve but still wanted.

CHAPTER FIVE

O n the road I'm out of the city within 40 minutes, grateful that even LA is quiet this time of day. Opening my navigation, I put in the address of a storage unit in Kettleman City. Grabbing a drink and a protein bar out of my stolen goodies, I turn on a more upbeat playlist than I typically listen to. "I Wanna Dance with Somebody" by Whitney Houston starts, and I make my way 3 hours to my first destination.

The storage facility comes into view, and I'm happy to be able to get out and stretch my legs. Pulling up to the gate, I punch in the code and wait for it to open. I drive through the lot to unit 18246. After punching in my code the automatic door opens.

I sigh, feeling like I have been run over by a fucking cement truck. *Of course, you do you, idiot; you've been betrayed by someone you thought of as family, shot twice, fucked within an inch of your life and broke your own heart, so yeah, cement truck sounds accurate.* I stop for a moment and cock my head to the side, wondering if maybe I talk to myself too much? But I quickly shake off the thought because who else could I talk to that would make me laugh this much.

I need to get my ass in gear. I want to be gone from here as quickly as I can. I pack up some bags with all the necessities any young woman needs to start a new chapter in her life.

Clothes ✓
Money ✓
New passports ✓
New names ✓
Guns ✓
25 books ✓
Explosives ✓

I pause for a moment, questioning if I truly need explosives. I would rather have them, just in case.

Once the truck is filled, I pat myself on the back for having such well-planned "go bags." This is one of four units I have in North America. All are equipped the same way: with a new vehicle, money, IDs, etc. Matt and Caden used to make fun of me for it. But yet again, I was right, and they were assholes.

I hop in and drive it outside, transfer my bags into it, then pull the car into the unit. Taking one last look around to see if there's anything else I should bring with me. Satisfied I see nothing else I need, I close the door, get in the truck, and return to the highway.

I'm back on the road for about 20 minutes when my phone rings. I see Ben's name pop up. "Hey," I say as I answer.

"Hey, Boss," Ben replies. "I'm assuming you've made it out of LA, with you answering the phone."

"That would be a correct assumption there, Ben. I'll never understand why Caden says you always state the obvious?" I tease him.

"Ha, you're so fucking funny!" he grumbles at me.

"I am funny. You know it; I know Caden and Matt know it as well. So, there you go again, stating the obvious thing you're so fond of doing."

I can hear his sigh of frustration at my teasing, but I also hear the smile beneath it.

"What's up, Ben?"

"Just checking in to make sure we are all still alive. I spoke to the others a few minutes ago. Everyone is on their assigned path home."

"Good," I say my tone tinged with relief.

"You know what I always wondered about?" Ben asks with genuine curiosity sounding in his voice.

"What's that?" I ask, curious because Ben is not much of a question-asker. He's my computer guy, and he usually finds answers to any questions himself.

"Why LA? I never understood why you and Marcus set up shop in Topanga."

"Ahh," I say, wondering how long he had thought about this. "Why not LA?" I ask him back. I wonder what he thinks our reasons were.

"Because Marcus was from New York, LA is a different world, and it has Hollywood and mega-rich folks who are into enough crooked and shady shit all on their own. So, it always seemed odd to me that you guys set up in LA." Ben tells me.

"Montana killed winter for me. I told Marcus I wasn't doing winter anymore. Once we left the ranch, I wanted sun and surf, oceans and sand. We were able to make it work because of the Russians. The Sokolov's wanted to be in America. Yuri wanted to be near his grandson. The last bit of his daughter that he could still touch. So, when we took out Enzo, we handed the day-to-day to the Sokolov's. And we moved to LA. I could take jobs from anywhere. And Marcus, well, we all know where he excels, so it all just kinda fell into place," I explain.

"Gotta say, Boss, you demanding no winter ever again and setting up in L.A. is very on brand for you."

"Hey! I know my worth, asshole. And I also really don't take orders very well, so it was decided before we even left the ranch. Marcus knew me well enough to know I would have walked away after a while over it. He also wasn't mad about not living in New York—too many memories for him."

"You sure you're ok, boss?" Ben asks with genuine concern in his voice.

"Better than I should be, but yeah, why?"

"Well, I've worked for you for five years, and I think you just told me more about yourself and your life than you have over the entirety of my employment with you," Ben tells me with a laugh. It's not true, but I understand his sentiment. I'm not huge on sharing.

I laugh out loud. "Well, Ben, let's do a little recap, shall we? The man I grew up with, considered to be my best friend, tried to kill me. I was shot twice, lost a fair amount of blood, found out Harrison was killed, had to say goodbye to someone I hoped to have in my life for a very, very long time, and had to implode my life. So, I think a bit of an overshare on my part should just be overlooked and never mentioned again. Yeah?"

"Ha-ha-ha, fair enough, boss. Everyone is on their way, and we will see you soon. Check the server from now on, as that's how we will update for the next little while. Be safe, Boss." Ben says to me and hangs up.

I drive for a few more hours, replaying those early days with Marcus. Looking for those moments that signalled the changes in our bond. I dial a number and hear him answer.

"Was my parents' accident an accident?"

"I don't know, Ava. I personally think it wasn't, but I can't say for sure."

"So, they set up a trust fund for me just in case? Not because they knew I'd be alone soon?"

"The trust fund and their will, how it was all set up, was part of the adoption contract with your birth family. I can show you that contract if you want, but you know everything it says."

"How did I miss it, Harry? How did I miss him plotting my death?" I ask him.

"Did you miss it? You managed to escape, and you had multiple exit strategies in place."

"Harry, all those things were because of you. You trained that shit into my head. You're aggressive, 'always be prepared motto' lives in my head rent-free.

"Even with all my training and the big IQ, I still didn't see Marcus for what he was. I didn't see when he changed. Or maybe he didn't change? Maybe I always just saw what I needed to see when it came to him. I needed him to be just like me, to be the other half of myself." He doesn't answer me right away, choosing his words carefully.

"Aye, Little Fury, he always was what he is," Harry tells me. "You two met, and both of you saw the broken in the other. You loved him, and he loved you. Don't ever doubt that, Ava. But Marcus's love was warped before he ever met you. His daddy messed him up in ways you don't ever heal from."

"I have those types of wounds, Harry," I say quietly.

"You do. But you, Ava, are uniquely equipped to deal with it. Your ability to compartmentalize, to look at and judge people and things logically without emotion, is not something Marcus possesses." Harry pauses again, having another swig of his beer. "As you got older and training progressed, it was obvious to everyone what you were. What you would be capable of. I may have balked at you coming here when you were young, but Ava, there is no denying that if anyone was made for this life, it was you. Marcus is not stupid. Intentionally or not, he recognized how valuable you were and never let you go. He saw what everyone else saw. He was made. He would be handed the power whether he deserved it or not. He, like his mother, was mafia royalty."

"So what? He decided I was more trouble than I was worth now?"

"No, I think you two made choices that irrevocably changed the parameters of your relationship, and while you were able to maintain the friendship by letting the past be the past, he wasn't. I think for that boy, you will never be his past. Only his right now and his future. I think at some point, his love became obsessive and toxic, and you always just accepted what he was offering and worked around it. I think, like always, you felt your love for him and your history with him were worth any pain and discomfort because he was worth everything to you."

"So how does that end up with me here? Shot and running for my life?"

"Ava, ego, power, drugs, money, and childhood trauma shaped Marcus. I think his fate was already sealed before you two found each other. You were the only reason he made it as long as he did before he became no better than his father." The weight of his words hangs in the air. It feels like some Shakespearean tragedy like we were doomed before we started.

"Thanks, Harry; I should pay attention to the drive. Talk soon," I say with an exhaustion I didn't know I could feel.

"Be safe, Little Fury," Harry says, disconnecting the call.

Silence comes over the car, and I instantly hit my music to start. "Africa" by Toto fills the cab. That was way too many memories and feelings to process in the last hour, and silence would only welcome more thinking, and I was not in the mood for it. *It's fine! You can deal with all that emotional shit when you have the well-deserved mental breakdown you can see looming on the horizon.* That is always a much more fun way to deal with things.

CHAPTER SIX

otels sprinkle the highway as I drive. I arbitrarily choose one to spend the night at. I need food and sleep. I pull into the hotel lot and go inside to rent a room for the night. The hotel is just like all the others on the highway. It's small, clean and has a 24-hour diner attached. I go up to the desk and ask for a room for the night. The clerk smiles at me and asks for my identification. I reach into my pocket and grab my ID. The clerk takes it and enters all my info into the computer. He hands me back my driver's licence.

"Thank you, Miss Blake. How would you like to pay?"

He asks me,

"Cash, please," I say, handing over a few bills. He takes them, gives me back my change, hands me my key card,

"You are in room 227. If you drive down to the end of this side of the building, that door is the closest to your room. The stairs are right there for you. I hope you enjoy your stay with us, Miss Blake."

I move my truck closer to the door at the end of the building and grab my stolen goodies and one of the bags of clothes from my unit. Making my way inside, I find the stairs waiting for me, and I flip them off as I begin to climb the one flight up. I'm in my room about 2 minutes later. All I want to do is fall into bed, but I have things to do before sleep gets to claim me.

Dropping my bags on the dresser and suitcase stand. I take my phone, key card and laptop and make my way back out into the hallway. Some of the most hideous carpeting designed for the sole purpose of masking all sorts of sins that land upon it greets me. The hallways have that thick ribbed wallpaper, the same generic wall art, and white sconces as all the others. It's nondescript, just like every other hotel along this highway.

Stepping into the diner, I happily seat myself in a booth at the back of the restaurant. I sit in the teal-coloured booth and look down at the chipped Formica on the table. The diner is the only non-generic thing about the hotel. It's an era-themed diner. Not the 50s or 60s, not even the wonderful neon days of the 80s. No, I'm sitting in a diner that boasts its love for the 90's. Being born at the turn of the century, I heard my fair share of 90's music thanks to having a mom who was a 90's kid. So, seeing the posters on the walls of bands like Nirvana, Pearl Jam, Audioslave, and Alice in Chains, as well as the plethora of one-hit wonders the 90's produced like Natalie Imbruglia, the Proclaimers, Aqua and Sixpence None the Richer, I can't help but think of her. Hear her singing horribly to all those songs and bands. "One Headlight" by Jacob Dylan is playing over the speakers.

Ignore it, Ava, pick up the freaking menu and decide on your dinner. The faster you eat, the sooner you will be in that shower and then unconscious in that bed.

I really do give myself the best advice. LOL. Is it odd to say the letters L O L when I talk to myself? I feel like it's a little weird. I audibly sigh, *annoyed that no one hears just how funny I am.* At the same time being grateful nobody can hear those thoughts.

I look at the menu as the waitress approaches. "Ready to order?" the waitress asks me. She is young, probably 19, wearing a Smashing Pumpkins T-shirt and an insanely wide-legged pair of jeans. Once my order is placed and the waitress, whose name I now know is Ollie, drops off my milkshake and water, I open my laptop and jump onto my phone's signal.

I quickly log into the server Ben has set up for us to speak with each other without worrying about our conversations being hacked. Don't ask me to explain it. While I can do basic computer stuff and some very rudimentary coding when Ben needs help, I couldn't begin to explain what kind of system he's set up for us.

There are five messages waiting for me. The first one makes my heart lurch.

Harrison logged on 24 hours ago.

'I'm not sure if anyone is alive or will get this in time, but Marcus's guys are here, and they aren't here for a pint. It has been a pleasure, Ava and Gents. Thank you for taking me into your fold. I genuinely enjoyed the second half of my life because of you. I'm taking these cunts with me. Cheerio, my friends.'

"Fuck" feeling my eyes start to sting from tears I won't let fall.

Ben sent two messages, telling us that he got Harrison's message but, unfortunately, was too late to help and that he was halfway home.

Caden- You will be missed, brother.

Caden- had a slow time vacating, but I'm currently on my way home.

Matt- we will have a Pint for you, Brav.

Matt - changed my flights, making a few stops. I will keep you updated.

Matt- Boss, he's going to pay for this. I don't care how long it takes, but they are all going down—every one of them.

Boss Lady- Harrison was one of the best, and I will miss his silent British judgement of our shitty American accents.

Boss lady- I'm on my way home. Slow going, blood loss is a bitch.

Boss Lady-Ben! Change my fucking name back, and seriously STOP IT!

I log off and close the laptop. Leaning my head back against the seat and take another deep breath. I am happy to know the other three are okay and that I will see them soon. I close my eyes and send a silent goodbye to Harrison. He was one of the best sharpshooters I'd ever seen. Even at 54, he could shoot the wings off a fly a football field away.

I met Harrison in a park in Germany, of all places. His wife had just died, and he was travelling aimlessly. He had sold everything. His house, all its contents, his car, everything. He told me if it had touched her in any way, he wanted to get rid of it. He could barely handle the thought of her; everything reminded him of her, so he sold it all. He told me of his time with the British Military and that he was a marksman, a sniper. He was so sad and lost and angry. For whatever reason, I asked him if he missed the rifle. He looked at me and said, "It's complicated. I miss being great at something. I was great as a sniper and at being her husband."

I told him I could offer him a job if he had questionable morals and wanted to pick up the rifle again. He chuckled at that (I instantly miss his laugh. It was big and bold). He said he had always had questionable morals but kept them in check for his wife. He looked at me, then really looked at me and said, "Well, my dear, what do you have in mind?"

My food arrives while I'm still lost in thought about Harrison, but the minute I smell that burger, I turn ravenous. If Jake were here, he would laugh at me and tell me how classy I was,

Fuck Ava! You were doing so good not thinking about him. You're such an idiot.

I sigh out loud and very quickly put the thought of Jake back in his little box and put that box in a deep and dark little corner of my mind. Fully compartmentalised, I dig back into my food. The burger is a thing of beauty, flat top cooked with melty American cheese, lettuce, tomato, and fried onions; the rings are hot and crispy and have a really nice spice on the coating. I eat every bit of it. The milkshake is fucking amazing. The pie also doesn't fucking disappoint. I'm not sure if it's just that I'm insanely hungry or if the food is that good, but I don't care. I leave money on the table with a generous tip for Ollie.

I'm barely through the door of my room when I begin to peel off my clothes. I'm in the shower fast, needing to wash the drive from me. I do my best to wash my hair and body and not get my injuries under the spray. Once I'm done, I towel dry my hair and throw another around my body. I step up to the sink, grab my toiletry bag, find my toothbrush and toothpaste and quickly brush my teeth. I put moisturizer on my face and body. Some habits are just too ingrained not to do, no matter the situation.

Staring at myself in the mirror I realise all those women in the movies and books weren't wrong. Grabbing the scissors out of my bag, I give myself a nod and cut. Five minutes later, my once waist-length hair now hangs to just below my shoulders. With one last look in the mirror, I grab up all my hair and shove it in a garbage bag with the towels and washcloths. I may not be on a job, but I still can't leave any DNA behind; it would feel wrong.

I crawl into bed and grab the laptop to check the server one last time before going to sleep.

> Ben- I've been watching our old friends, and they are scrambling, trying to find us. Our trails have yet to be found, so they're still looking. They've enlisted some police force help from their friends inside the LAPD, but so far, no one has been able to catch a glimpse of you. But that won't last forever. There are way too many cameras in LA, so at some point, they will see you leaving the city and the direction. But you chose your unit well, so it will take them a bit to find it, if ever.

> URTHEBOSS- Seriously? Change my fucking name, asshole. Sounds good. I'll be on the road early tomorrow and will update as I go.

Closing the laptop, I put it on the bedside table, turn off the lamp, and sink into the bed, surprised by how comfortable it was. I fall asleep quickly, not waking up until 8 a.m. the next morning.

I'm out of the hotel within 30 minutes of waking. Every surface or thing I used is either wiped down or in one of my bags to go with me until I can dispose of it properly. It's complete overkill on my part, but the old Scotsman would grumble at me if I didn't. I load the truck, drive to the front of the hotel, and go inside to check out.

Dropping the key off at the front desk I wait for the day clerk to print off my bill. Today, the clerk is an older lady who reminds me a lot of Ross and Monica's mom. I give myself a mental high 5 for my *Friends* reference. "All right, Elena, you are all ready to go. Thank you for staying with us, and have a safe trip," Mrs. Gellar tells me. I give myself another mental cheer for the *Friend's* reference. And yeah, Elena is going to take some getting used to.

My parents named me Ava after my mom's grandmother, and I love that name. I close my eyes and feel the loss of yet another thing that my parents gave me. And for the first time, I feel a surge of anger at Marcus for what happened and what I've had to give up because of him.

I stop at the nearest gas station to fill up the truck. Inside the mom-and-pop store is a little coffee shop. I grab a freshly baked tomato and feta pastry and a sausage and egg breakfast sandwich and order myself the largest London Fog they have.

Ben plotted my path to the meet-up spot and sent it straight to my GPS. *I must remember to kiss that guy when I see him.* I am mentally drained and physically exhausted; the thought of my vehicle telling me where to go is… well, making me tear up. *Hello, mental exhaustion emotions.* He made the route through small towns, on smaller highways, and backroads, all in the name of disappearing. I turned some music on and let my pre-set navigation tell me where to go.

"Skin" By Zola Jesus fills the cab as I start along my plotted-out path home to my guys, to what remains of my team.

My brain won't turn off, won't just let me be. No. Instead, that bitch wants to replay it all. She wants me to see it all again, regardless of us what I already having lived it. I have nothing left in me to fight her, so instead, I give in. Surrender to the memories; watch it all as it happened then.

CHAPTER SEVEN

17 years earlier

"I t'll be OK, Ava. I'm sorry for all this, for everything you have had to endure. But I promise you will be okay." Beth says to me. She tries to talk to me during the flight, but I have nothing to say. I feel like I'm slipping under the surface of some fast-moving water. Once, when I was 4, I was on vacation with my parents. We were somewhere with water, and we were playing in it, I got pulled under. It wasn't scary; it was heavy. This feels like that. Except this time, I know my dad won't be there to pull me out.

We land in Billings, Montana, a couple of hours later. Beth grabs our bags, and we make our way outside. We've been outside for about five minutes when a truck pulls up in front of us. A man gets out and heads our way. "You, Beth?" he asks. I look up at him, unsure why he sounds so angry. Our bags are lifted into the bed of the truck and strapped down.

The man opens the truck's back door holding it open for

55

me. I struggle to get in the back, as the truck is very tall, and I'm pretty small. But I manage. I get settled in the back and put on my seatbelt as we pull away from the curb. Beth tells me it's a three-hour drive.

"She hasn't eaten, so we need to get her food somewhere before we hit the highway, James," Beth informs him.

"Nothing but a fucking taxi driver, stupid mother f."

"James!" Beth yells at the big man. "There is a child in this vehicle, and you will watch your mouth while around her. Do I make myself clear?" Beth scolds James, giving the big man no option but to nod and mumble an apology.

I stare out the window, pretending I can't hear them. "There's a burger place just up ahead. Best burgers around," James grunts at us. He pulls into the parking lot, and Beth looks back over her shoulder at me.

"Let's go in and order, and you can go to the bathroom before we head out. Ok?" I don't say anything, but I nod, open my door and get out.

About 20 minutes later, we're back in the truck with our food, and James starts driving again. Beth is watching me in her visor mirror, but I ignore her and eat my food. Burgers, fries, and milkshakes are hands down my favorite meals. Whenever I had a difficult day, my dad would take me to his favorite burger place.

"When you're full, give me whatever is left over, and I'll put it in with mine."

"Oh. Sorry, I ate all mine," I tell her.

"Really?" James asks incredulously. The face he makes over his shoulder at me makes me laugh out loud.

"Well then, ah… I guess give me the garbage then." I hand Beth my garbage.

"My parents always said I could out-eat three grown men," I inform no one in particular.

"Good to know, Ava. I will keep that in mind when I feed

you."

I look at Beth and nod. Sitting back in my seat, I rest my head against the window, watching the road zoom by, and let it lull me to sleep.

The truck, coming to a stop, pulls me from my sleep. It stops in front of a house, and the man James gets out. Beth looks back at me and gives me a nod of encouragement, so I open the door and jump out.

"This way," James says as he grabs our bags. Beth waits for me to start walking before she follows behind. We walk past the house, heading towards the mountains. There are other buildings out this way I can make them out in the dwindling light. Then, as if it's just for me, lights flicker on all over the place. I pause for a moment to look around. A few people are milling about, and I hear a horse in the distance. "Come on, ladies, keep up. I'm tired and want to be home sooner rather than later." he says, clearly annoyed by having to help us anymore.

"James, just do your fucking job and shut up. Nobody here cares if you're tired or if it's past your bedtime." a voice behind us somewhere calls out. "So just keep walking and let her set the pace." James snorts and mumbles something I can't hear.

We make our way to a little house nestled amongst the trees and in front of what I think is a pond. There is a reflection from the water, but I don't pay much attention to it. I just want to be done with this day. I don't like it. I hate not knowing where I am, what's going to happen, or why I'm here.

I think my parents were odd. They always spoke to me like they spoke to any adult they came across. They always told me what was happening, where we were going and why. If friends or the people they had at the house ever questioned why conversations didn't stop when a child entered the room, my dad would simply give them a look and that was that.

I don't like not knowing things.

I miss them.

"Not sure what the fuck makes you two so special that you get this place. I wanted this place, and instead, I'm in the fucking apartment over the gym with three other guys. Harry needs to realize who the fuck I am and start showing me a little more respect." James mumbles under his breath bringing me back to the world in front of me.

"What was that, James?" I hear from right behind us. James freezes mid-movement, and I can't stop the giggle that escapes me at seeing this big man freeze like a child who got caught with his hand in the cookie jar.

"Nothing," James mumbles, just loud enough for us to hear.

"That's what I thought. I didn't think you would be so stupid that you would forget what happened the last time you ran your mouth about the accommodations."

"No sir. I'm just showing the ladies to their new home," James sneers in response to the voice.

We step up onto the porch of a little house. James opens the front door and walks in, dropping our bags just inside. He tips his head to Beth and me as he leaves the house. Apparently, the faceless voice makes James listen very well. My mom had that kind of voice.

"Beth." says the voice.

"Harry," she replies. "Let me introduce you to Ava Landry," she tells the voice.

CHAPTER EIGHT

I turn around to see who she's speaking to just as a man approaches the porch. He's a bit older than my dad is, *a bit older than my dad was. Was, because my dad is dead now.* He has a head of short red hair and a full beard to match. He's big.

Harry sinks down to one knee, bringing his green eyes in line with my grey ones. "Hello, little Ava, it's a pleasure to meet you." He says extending his hand to me. I shake it, always polite. "I'm really happy to have you here. There is a lot to do and learn, and I think you will thrive here." I cock my head to the side, finding his words odd. He lets my hand go and stands up.

He looks at Beth. "It's good to see you, Beth. You're looking lovely, as always," He says with a smile.

"Knock it off. I'm not some random woman who doesn't know exactly who you are, so just keep your smile and twinkly eyes to yourself," Beth tells him matter-of-factly.

"You think I have twinkly eyes, Bethy?" he winks at me when he says it, and I hear her huff out a breath.

"You wound me. You know I've always been on my knees at your feet, lass." Harry says it all of a sudden with an accent.

"No! Harry fuck off! Put that Scottish brogue right back on ice where it belongs. I'm not about to lose my head for you just because you think no woman can resist your charms." she tells him as she turns to grab my bags and moves further into the house.

"I think she likes me. Don't you, little Ava?" Harry asks me with mischief in his voice. "I don't know, Bethy, you did just drop an F-bomb in front of our little guest, so maybe you aren't so immune to me after all?" He calls after her, a laugh behind his words.

I pause to look at him cocking my head again, "Not sure about that sir, I think maybe she just thinks you're an ass to be honest."

Harry throws his head back and lets loose a sound that startles me a bit. It's the biggest laugh I've ever heard. When he is done laughing, he looks at me and wipes actual tears from his eyes. "Well, shit. That may be one of the funniest insults anyone has ever thrown at me."

That made me smile for the first time since all this started. "Thank you," I said to him with a small grin. It's the first real smile I've given since the accident. It makes me feel like a tiny piece of me has moved back into place.

"Ava, come this way, and I can show you your new room and bathroom. Let that jackass carry the rest of our bags this way." Beth calls from the top of the stairs.

I follow her voice. Harry picks up the bags and follows along. We find her in front of a door just down a short hall. She opens it and I get the first look at my new bedroom.

It's a lot smaller than my room in my old house, but it has

a set of doors leading out to a deck. The room is pale blue with darker blue accents. The bedding is a deep navy with light blue and white pillows. The carpet is a plush grey. A closet is on one side of the room, and a desk is on the wall by the door. The bed is large, like the bed I used to have. A chair in front of the glass doors and a nightstand on either side of the bed. There are some shelves are on the other wall, but everything is bare.

"I wasn't sure what colour you would like, so I just painted it in a colour I thought was nice. Sorry, it's not pink, but I just can't do pink," Harry says from behind me.

"I don't like pink, this is perfect. Blue is my favourite colour. Thank you." I see Beth look over me towards Harry, and I glance over my shoulder to see why. But Harry is just staring at me. "Did I do something wrong?" I'm not sure how to read the faces they're making.

"No, you didn't do anything wrong. We just weren't expecting you to say thank you. Your entire life has been upended, so we were expecting something, ah, different." she tells me.

"Well, I guess I could throw a tantrum if it would make either of you feel better."

Harry laughs again behind me, and Beth smiles at me.

"No, I think we can do it without a tantrum. There is no sense in forcing one if you're not feeling it," she laughs.

Looking at me and she pats me on the shoulder. "OK, let me show you the bathroom, and then we will leave you alone for a bit? Let you settle in? I'll be downstairs in the kitchen. So, if you need anything, or you don't want to be alone, or you need help putting your stuff in drawers or in the closet, please come and ask. I want to help you, Ava, as much as I can. So please ask me for help." she tells me, and I can see that she is being honest.

"Thank you, Beth. I will."

"All right, the bathroom is one door over. It's all yours, I have one on the main floor in my bedroom. Let's go, give her some space." Beth insists and pulls him behind her as she leaves the room.

Unsure of what to do with myself, I look at the room again and realize I really do like it. It's similar to my room back home. So that feels good.

I open my bags and start to unpack. I put my clothes in the drawers and hang the one dress I brought with me in the closet. I put my shoes in the bottom closet and place the photo of me and my parents on the table beside the bed. Just like I had it at home. I grab Miss Mushroom and Mr. Waffle and set them on the bed. I take my toothbrush and hairbrush to the bathroom and wash my face and hands.

This is home now. So be at home.

Heading downstairs to look around, I hear voices coming from the kitchen. I walk in just as I hear Beth say, "She's only 7? Why isn't she a mess? How is she so calm and composed?" I see her hands in the air as I enter.

"Sorry, Ava. We aren't trying to be mean and talk about you when you aren't in the room, but I'm concerned with how well you're taking everything," she says to me.

I shrug "not really sure how to take it differently. I miss my parents, and I think this place is weird, but I'm still me." Harry raises an eyebrow and looks at me.

"Well said, Ava. You sure don't talk like any other seven-year-old I've ever met before," He tells me.

"I turn 8 next week, so maybe I sound more like an 8-year-old, and that's why I don't sound like the other 7-year-olds you know." He isn't the first adult who's told me that. My school told my parents that I was gifted and that I would need special things. Maybe that's what Harry means?

Beth asks if I'm hungry, and I tell her I am. She opens the

fridge and pulls out cheese, butter and bread. Grabbing a frying pan from inside the oven, she gets to work making me a grilled cheese. When it's cooked, she places it on a plate before me and pours me a glass of milk. I inhale the sandwich and milk, barely pausing to breathe. When I'm done, I say goodnight. Harry says goodnight and will see me tomorrow.

Beth comes upstairs with me asking if I need any help. I tell her I don't. "Leave your dirty clothes in the hamper in the bathroom, and I'll collect them tomorrow when I do the laundry," Beth tells me as I head into the bathroom to change and brush my teeth again.

Back in my room, Beth has the blinds closed on the glass doors and the blankets on the bed pulled down, waiting for me to get in. Once I settle in, Beth pulls the blankets up around my chin and hands me Mr. Waffle and Miss Mushroom, putting one on each side of me.

"Thank you," I say to her.

"You are very welcome, Ava. I hope you like it here. It's a beautiful place to live, and Harry has a lot to offer you." Again, I don't understand what her words mean. But I smile at her anyway. She leaves, turning off the light and closing my door behind her.

I wake up the next morning, forgetting where I am for a moment, but it quickly returns to me. I do my morning stuff and then head downstairs. Finding Beth sitting in the kitchen reading a newspaper. "Morning, Ava," she said cheerily. Did you sleep well?"

"I did," I tell her, and it's the truth, I did sleep well.

"Are you hungry?" she asks. I nod my head. Opening the oven and bringing out a plate of pancakes with sausages, she grabs two plates, some knives, and forks and sets about making us each a plate. We sit together at the island and eat.

"So, what happens now?" I ask.

"What do you mean?" Beth asks me back.

"Well, why am I here? And what about my school? I like my school. Will I go there? Who will I live with?" I ask her rapidly. A little bit of panic setting in.

"Harry will explain it all. But yes, I will be staying with you if that's ok with you? I want to help you in any way I can. But if you don't want me, that is also ok, and we can find another person."

"I don't want anyone else," I say, and she smiles at me, going back to her pancakes.

"Eat up, Harry wants to see you as soon as you're fed and ready for the day."

We finish eating; and I head upstairs to get dressed. I pull on a pair of jeans and a shirt, socks and my sneakers. I grab my favourite sweater. It's a panda bear design with ears on the hood. Once I'm dressed Beth leads me to the big house we saw last night. "Harry lives here," she tells me, pointing to the large house. It's all wood and stone with huge windows and a porch that wraps all the way around. It has flower beds all along it. Beth walks right into his house through the big glass doors that are standing open letting a lovely morning breeze flow through the house.

Harry is sitting at the kitchen table with a couple other men, they stop talking when we enter.

"That's all for now, guys," he says, and they all get up together and leave. "Hello ladies," Harry calls to us.

"Morning," I call back to him, and Beth just stares at him, apparently annoyed already with the red-haired man.

"Look at you all sweet on me this morning, Bethy."

"Jesus Fuck Harry, don't call me that, I'm not 6!" she tells him with even more annoyance.

"I know you ain't Lass, but you still look like a Bethy to me, and I love it when you drop an F-bomb on us," Harry says, sending a wink in my direction.

I smile at his wink despite myself. I like how much he pokes fun at her. He makes her swear, and I think it's funny to hear her. She seems so gentle all the time until he's around.

"All right, Ava, this is where I leave you; you two have a lot to talk about, and I'm going to town to grab a few things. Give me your truck keys."

"Now now Bethy, that is not how we ask our nice friends for favours!" he tells her in a fake scolding tone.

"Harry, please don't make me hit you in front of Ava. She doesn't need to see you get your ass beat by a lady this early into her first day here." She says, her words dripping in fake sincerity.

The big man chuckles and points to the table by the door. She walks over, grabs the keys, turns to wave goodbye to me, and heads out the door.

We sit at his kitchen table facing each other. "Want something to drink?" Harry asks me.

"Got a beer?" I ask just as he takes a sip of his coffee that he promptly spits all over the table.

"I'm sorry?"

"Don't be sorry. My dad always said that to my mom when she asked if he was thirsty. Water please." Harry is just staring at me now, and I start to think my joke was not funny and that maybe I'm in trouble. I'm just about to apologize when he lets out another of his big laughs. I can't help but smile at that sound. I like this man; I feel like I shouldn't like it's too soon after losing my parents, but I can't help it. My mom would like him, I think. My mom liked to laugh, and I think Harry would have made her laugh.

He gets up to fetch me a glass of water, sets it in front of me and goes back to his chair. Placeing his hands on the table, palms down, arms straight out in front of him. "So, Ava, how did you sleep?"

"Good," I tell him.

"Good, good," he repeats back to me.

I give him a small smile, hoping to make him feel better. He seems scared, and I don't want to make anyone feel scared. He sees my smile and returns it, shaking his head slightly.

"I know this whole situation is messed up, and you have no idea what's going on. You know you were adopted, yes?"

"I do."

"Well, your birth mother had a very unique type of job. It is not the type of job that would allow her to raise you. Does that make sense?"

"I guess."

He nods at me, "So before you were born, she set up some rules and safety-type things when it came to how you were raised. She picked your parents very carefully. She wanted to make sure you had the best life possible."

I don't say anything, I look at him, and I don't know what to say.

"When your parents died, it triggered one of the safety nets she had put in place. That safety net was me, this ranch and a unique education."

"So, my mother knows I'm here?"

"She does."

"And she doesn't want to see me?"

"She does, Ava, she just cannot. It's not something she can do safely."

"Oh." The word is quiet as my brain keeps working, trying to figure out this puzzle.

"Ava, I need you to trust me. I know that is a lot to ask, but I promise you that as you get older, I will tell you more and more. I also think you are a brilliantly smart young lady who will figure things out for yourself long before I need to explain anything.

"Another thing I want to tell you is that there is a boy the same age as you, who will also be coming to live here. To learn alongside you," he says.

"Did his parents die as well? I ask him.

He sighs and shakes his head. "Unfortunately, no. His father is just a really crappy one and decided that Marcus should come here." Harry says very tightly. I'm happy there will be another kid here with me, I wonder if we will be friends.

"Ava," he says, drawing my attention back to him. "There are a few more things I need to explain to you. When people come here, they come here to learn certain things. None of those things are things I'm willing to teach someone your age. But there is no way I'll be able to keep it away from you 100% of the time, So for the next few years at least, you and Marcus will attend regular school and learn some things here on the ranch. I know you'll see stuff, that can't be helped. What happens here, what you learn is never to be used or spoken of in the world outside this place. Do you understand?"

"I do. The Ranch is private."

"Yes, that'll do."

Talking over we climb into a golf cart so he can show me the ranch that isn't a ranch. There are a lot of buildings on the ranch. There is a barn that keeps the couple horses, and Harry tells me that the barn and the horses are the only parts that are even remotely close to normal ranch things. We stop in front of one, and Harry tells me it's the gym as we go inside and take a look. There are machines, the floor is spongy, and there are two people in there clanking things and grunting. It also smells in here, and I don't like it.

From there, we head to the mess hall. We go inside and I'm surprised to see a bunch of people eating. With the name mess hall I was not expecting food. There is a cook on all the time and staff to help if you're hungry. I won't be eating here much because I have Beth. We head over to where the food is. Harry swipes a couple of brownies, and we head back out the door. Climbing back into the cart, he gives me one of the brownies, and I take it happily.

We eat in silence for a minute before Harry starts the cart, and we're off again. We drive past a few other buildings that Harry tells me house a bunch of different things I don't understand or remember. Then he shows me the best thing here.

A pool! Inside the building, there is a huge swimming pool. It doesn't have the slide or any of the fun things my pool at home did, but I'm still excited.

"That may be the first honest reaction from you since you got here. Like pools, do you?" he asks me with a grin on his face.

"I do!! I'm a good swimmer! I had a pool at home with a diving board, a slide and a bunch of pool toys! It was great!!" I tell him excitedly.

Harry is watching me, still smiling, and I think laughing at me a little bit, but I don't care. I just want to jump in there and float.

Once the tour is over, I've seen the barn where the three horses are kept, and met Bill, the old guy who looks after the horses and the yard. We see Beth has returned, so we head back to my house.

We walk inside and see Beth putting things away in the kitchen. She hears us enter but doesn't look our way; she keeps doing what she's doing." What's your favourite thing to eat, Ava?" she asks me from inside the pantry.

"Burger and onion rings and a milkshake," I reply.

"We had burgers yesterday. Do you want them again tonight?" she asks.

"I always want a burger, but mom wouldn't let our chef make them for me every day because she said people need variety in life." I smile a bit at the thought of my mom, but the memory hurts, so I put it back in its box and leave it there.

"Well, how about I make something else tonight, and I make sure we have burgers once a week. Seem like a fair plan?" she asks as she looks at me. I nod my agreement to Beth.

"There is some cheese and fruit in the fridge if you want a snack. Dinner will be in a couple of hours." I didn't realize how much time Harry and I had spent talking and him showing me the ranch.

I'm a little hungry, but. I hesitate a bit, still unsure what I'm supposed to do, how I'm supposed to behave, how comfortable I'm supposed to be.

You need to just do it. This is your home now.

I walk to the fridge, open it, and grab the cheese and fruit on the top shelf. I see juice boxes, so I grab one. I bring the food out and bite my lip, trying to decide if I should ask for help finding a plate or just open cupboards myself. I see a step stool, so I make the decision and start looking for plates.

I can feel their eyes on me as I get my search.

I open three cupboards before I find the plates. "Does anyone else need one?" I ask, turning around. They both nod, so I grab three and head to the island. I climb onto a stool beside Harry. I take one plate and begin to put some cheese and fruit on it. "Are there any crackers?" I ask.

"Yes," Beth says. I thank her, place some on my plate, and begin to eat. I have a mouthful of grapes when I look at the two of them and realize they aren't eating. I chew fast and swallow.

"I'm sorry, do we have to say grace before we eat? We never did at home, but we went to dinner once at someone's house, and none of us could eat until we said grace. It was weird, but I don't mind doing it if that's how it works here." I say, worried I didn't wait for them to tell me it was ok to eat, worried I broke a rule.

"No, Little Ava, we don't say grace here. Beth and I were just being silly. Hand me a plate, please, Bethy," Harry says, the laughter back in his voice.

Glaring at him, she puts food on her own plate, and starts eating. Harry chuckles quietly to himself and winks at me when he reaches over the island to grab the last plate. With everyone snacking, Harry asks Beth how town was. She tells him it is fine. She was able to get most of what she needed but would probably have to drive to Billings next week to get the rest. She looks at me.

"Maybe you can come with me, and we can do some shopping. We didn't really bring you a lot of toys or anything, so we could pick some up."

"Sure! I'd like that. But I don't have any money."

"You do. Your parents left money for you." Harry informs me.

"Oh. Okay."

Again, they fall silent. When I'm done, I take my plate and put it in the sink. "I'm going to my room. I want to check on Miss Mushroom and Mr. Waffle," I tell them, head up the stairs. I stop before my door and sink to the carpet.

"Fuck Harry!!! She's fucking seven, and she has more composure than most adults would after what she's been through." Beth says quietly, but not so quietly I can't hear.

"She's smart as a whip, she's observant and seems able to

compartmentalize without even trying," he says with a little chuckle, which also sounds a little sad.

"So, what now?" Beth asks him, "Shouldn't she be more upset, crying, angry, scared?"

"I don't know. She has amazing self-preservation skills. I see a lot of her mother in her. Her mother is highly intelligent and very good at her job. I'm starting to see that Ava is a lot like her," Harry replies and then Beth says something that I can't hear.

"I don't know, Beth, that's all I can tell you about why I think Ava's responding the way she is. Regardless, Enzo Rossi is sending Marcus here so there will be two of them. I spoke to the school in town, and they're both good for the fall to start. Both of them are going into third grade."

"Don't even get me fucking started on this whole Marcus shit. What kind of monster tells people they either take his son and do something with him or he will put a bullet in his head and be done with it? What the hell kind of world is this?" She asks him, her voice shaky.

"This is my world. This is the world you are sitting in the kitchen of. It is ugly, and dark. It hurts people without any care of who they are. I'll understand if it's too much and I'll make other arrangements for the kids. You do not have to be a part of this."

"I may not be one of your graduates or have ties to any of the Mafia families you train for, but my father drove for Walter English and his father for years. So, I'm not completely ignorant to this life. But I don't think what Enzo is doing has ever been done before."

"It has not. Enzo Rossi has always been a piece of shit, but he's a powerful piece of shit. Liked or not, he has one of the biggest criminal organizations in the country, and that allows him a lot of leeway without consequences."

"It's still not right," she sighs.

I hear him sigh. "I wish I had something for you Bethy, but lass I dinny know what else t'tell ye."

"Fuck off, Harry, you and your Scottish accent," she says to him, but I can hear her smile.

I open my door and walk in. Going to my bed I grab my two stuffies. Mr. Waffle is a very grumpy squirrel who only likes Miss Mushroom. Miss Mushroom is an incredibly happy goat. Miss Mushroom keeps Mr. Waffle in line. She doesn't let him get away with being grumpy. She also always convinces him to have a tea party with us. Unfortunately, I don't have our tea set here, but I can pretend. So, I do.

Unsure how long I play with the duo of grumpiness and sunshine. I hear Beth call that dinner is ready, so I head downstairs for. She grabs a plate and starts dishing out the food. She gives me a scoop of mac and cheese and a chicken drumstick. There is also salad and bread.

I wait until they have their food, and then I dig in. It's good! It's really good. We are all quiet as we eat, and I can hear my mom say, 'Well, it must be good if everyone is quiet.' I look at Harry and see him shovelling the food into his mouth, and that makes me giggle. Harry looks up at me and asks, "What's so funny, little Ava?"

"I'm pretty sure she's laughing at you for the speed at which you are filling your face," Beth says with her own chuckle.

"Is that true, Little Ava? You laughing at me?" he asks with fake hurt.

"Um, well, she isn't exactly wrong." I giggle again.

Harry is just about to say something when a car pulls into the yard in front of the big house. He is instantly on his feet and heading for the door. I see him grab something from the drawer on the table by it.

I look at Beth, who shrugs her shoulders and goes back to her food, seemingly unbothered by any of it. I see a few more people heading towards the main house. "Ava don't worry. Harry will deal with it. You should finish your dinner," she tells me.

I go back to eating, and we hear raised voices. I look at Beth, asking if she knows what's going on. "Harry's dealing with it. Nothing to worry about."

Not worried so much as curious. I nod and finish my food.

"It was really good Beth," I tell her.

CHAPTER NINE

I stand up and take my plate to the sink when all of a sudden, the front door is thrown open and a very angry Harry comes inside. *Wow! Yosemite Sam just walked in the door, anger smoke practically pouring from his ears.* I giggle to myself but quickly swallow my laughter when I see a boy step from behind him.

"Marcus, welcome. This Is Beth and Ava. You will be staying with them while you're here." Harry tells the room. I see the look that passes between the adults, and so does the boy because he is instantly mad.

"Don't fucking look at each other like I'm not in the room with you!" He yells at them. They gawk at him not expecting that to come out of his mouth.

"Sorry, Marcus," Harry recovers quickly. "We just weren't expecting you until next week, so we have been caught a little off guard."

The boy doesn't say anything else, just continues to glare at them. I'm pretty sure he hasn't seen me yet.

Wow, his eyes are super green. I cock my head to the side as I study him. He has blonde hair, and I think he is a bit taller than me. He's beautiful. *Ha! Bet he'll wanna be your friend if you tell him he's beautiful.*

He must feel my stare because his head shoots to me with lightning speed.

"Hi," I say as I get closer to him. "I'm Ava." I stick my hand out to him. He looks at my outstretched hand and back at me and slowly puts his hand in mine. I give it a large shake. "Pleased to meet you. Did you know we have a pool here? It's pretty awesome. And there are also a couple of horses. It's gonna be pretty fun here so I don't think you should be mad. We can pet the horses and swim in the pool. Did you bring any toys? I didn't get to bring much more than Miss Mushroom and Mr. Waffle but you can have Mr. Waffle. He's really nice. He's a squirrel. Miss Mushroom is a goat."

I hear Harry and Beth make a choking noise behind me. Marcus is staring at me like he's never seen another kid before. *Maybe I shouldn't have said hello?*

He doesn't say anything to me, just keeps staring. "Well ok! Nice to meet you. You can have Mr. Waffle any time you want. Bye!" I say and turn to head up the stairs to my room.

Beth collects herself, walks up to him and introduces herself. I hear her ask him if he is hungry or would rather go to his room to be alone. I don't hear any more as I close my door. It's not very late, but I'm tired, so I grab my jammies, head to the bathroom, and get ready for bed. I change and brush my teeth. I can hear voices downstairs, but I ignore them and go to my room. I crawl into bed and say good night to Miss Mushroom and Mr. Waffle.

The next morning, I find Beth at the kitchen island reading a book and having a cup of tea. "Morning, Ava" she says without even looking up.

"Morning, Beth!" She's quiet for a few more seconds then

puts her bookmark in the book, sets the book down and claps her hands.

"Hungry?" I smile and nod. She'll soon understand that I'm always hungry. "French toast and bacon?" she asks me. I nod again and go to the fridge to grab the bread and eggs.

"What else do we need?"

"Um, milk and bacon and butter, please," she says as she grabs the skillet from the pantry. "Did you cook a lot at home?" she asks, then freezes and looks at me, looking like she thinks she said something wrong.

"Yeah, my mom liked to cook but didn't do it often because she was busy. But, whenever she made breakfast or dinner, if I was home, I helped. She said it was important to know how to cook."

"Your mom was correct; knowing how to cook is important. Ava?"

"Yeah?"

"If you need to talk about anything. Or if you want to be mad about anything or need help, I'm here for you."

I look at her, unsure of what to say, or what she needs to hear me say. "I miss them. I miss them a lot. I miss my dad swatting my moms behind when she would swear around me. I miss her giggling at him. I miss her singing. She sang a lot. I didn't like it, but now I miss it. She would have music on when she was cooking and sing to the songs even if she didn't know the words." My eyes go glassy, and I blink to hold back the tears.

Beth watches me, not saying anything, and lets me sort through it in my head.

"I don't know what I'm supposed to do here, what I'm going to learn. What kinds of things Harry meant when he told me he would explain things as I get older? I know I like you. I like Harry, and I don't feel scared here. I'm alone, but I don't feel alone here." I wipe a tear from my cheek and look up at Beth, seeing her glossy eyes. "I felt alone in that hospital, till you came to get me," I whisper.

"Well, then, Ava, we will consider your liking us and not feeling scared or alone a win. Just remember, you can talk to me about anything."

I give her a big grin and nod my head. She nods back at me and we go back to making breakfast.

I grab the syrup and some strawberries from the fridge and take them to the island for us. Beth takes a bunch of bacon and wraps it in a paper towel and then tinfoil. She takes a big stack of French toast and puts it in a baking dish, covers it with the lid, and puts both in the oven to keep warm.

We fill our plates and then dig in. "You have a very good appetite," Beth muses as she smiles at me.

"I do! My dad used to make fun of me, saying my stomach was a hungry beast that no amount of food could satisfy." I laugh with a mouthful of bacon. Beth laughs with me. We are almost done eating when we hear footsteps coming down the stairs. I look over and see the boy, Marcus. He looks tired and angry. "Hello!" I say to him.

"Hi," he mumbles back at me.

"Are you hungry, Marcus?" Beth asks.

He shrugs, so she gets the food out of the oven, makes him a plate, and sets it in front of him.

"Thank you," Marcus says very quietly.

"You're welcome," Beth replies.

I finish and take my plate to the sink. I see Marcus staring at me. I smile at him; he doesn't return it; instead, he drops his eyes to his plate and eats. He doesn't eat much before he says he's done, so Beth tells him to take his plate to the sink, and he does as she asks. I go to the door to put on my shoes.

"I'm going to go explore," I yell over my shoulder at Beth and head out the door. I want to look at the horses and maybe pet one. I hear the door open and close behind me. Marcus catches up to me and settles beside me without even saying a word.

This kid is weird.

"I'm going to see the horses," I tell him and keep walking, deciding he can come if he wants, but I'm not changing my plans for him. He says nothing to me, but he comes with me, so I keep going.

Definitely weird, like say hello or ok, or grunt at me already.

We reach the horses just as someone is filling their water trough. "Hello," I say cheerily, the guy looks at me with a weird smile

"Uh, hi?" he says.

"Was that a question? Because normally, people say hello without it sounding like they're unsure if it's the right word. Hi, hello, or even hey are the right words. I've also heard people say Yo, and others don't even say Hi, but they say How are you right off the bat!!" I tell the guy who is still filling the water trough.

"Um, you know that the water is running over the edge, right?" I hear Marcus say to him. Marcus puts his hand in front of me and makes me step back. "You should be more careful next time. You almost got her shoes wet." He continues to tell the guy. The guy continues to stare at us and then says "fucking kids" under his breath as he turns and walks away from us.

"Well, that was rude," I say to myself and Marcus.

Marcus doesn't say anything to me; just nods in agreement.

"Well, well, what do we have here?" I hear from behind us. "Little Ava and young Mr. Marcus." I turn around to see Harry coming towards us.

"Hi, Harry! I wanted to see if I could pet a horse today." I tell him.

"You need to tell your employees to be more careful. That guy almost got Ava's shoes all wet." Marcus tells Harry.

"It's okay, Marcus. I don't care if my shoes get a little wet," I say.

"I care." He says like I should know it would bother him if I were uncomfortable.

Harry looks between us, "Alright, kids, let's go pet a horse."

After about an hour of us petting the horses, Harry stops. "Okay, I need to get back to work. If you make your way over to that blue Building, you'll meet Parker, and he'll find you guys something to do." We do as Harry asks and head over to the blue building, where we find Parker.

Parker is young. He's tall and skinny and pretty pale. He looks like he needs to go outside a lot more. "Hello," I say. "I'm Ava, and this is Marcus. Harry told us to come see you, and you would give us something to do to keep us busy." I spew the words out at him.

"He did, did he? "Parker says, laughing.

"Yup. "

"Well, then, let's get to it. Have either of you used a computer before? Have you guys played video games?" Parker asks us.

"Both," I say, seeing Marcus nod in agreement.

"Perfect. Then come over here, and I'll get the Nintendo going for you. We have pretty much every game, so help yourself. Do you know how to set everything up?" he asks us.

"Yeah, I had one at home, a Sega Genesis, and a PlaySta-tion." Marcus offers up.

"Perfect," Parker says. "You'll find a bunch of games over in that cupboard. Play whatever you want. I'll be over here if you need anything," he tells us and moves over to a desk that is set up with a couple screens and a keyboard.

The first month passes like that. Beth cooks us every meal. We eat together; Harry joins us often. Beth, Harry, and I talk, getting to know each other, while Marcus only speaks when he absolutely has to. He only leaves my side when I sleep or go to the bathroom. He doesn't say much, so I talk for both of us. Beth took us into town a couple of times because Marcus arrived with nothing except a bag with a toothbrush and a couple of changes of clothes.

The start of my second month at Harrys brings a couple new faces around the ranch, but really, Marcus and I spend our time with each other and Beth, or in our rooms, or swimming, or with Parker playing on the computers or video games. We see Harry all the time, but he's busy, so it's never for very long. He does try to have a meal with us a couple times a week. Summer is passing fast like it always does, and pretty soon, we are only a few days away from school starting.

Beth takes us back-to-school shopping, getting all the required things and new clothes. Both Marcus and I need an entire winter wardrobe because winter will be cold—colder than I'm used to in Chicago or Marcus is used to in New York.

I'm not going to enjoy that.

Beth drives us there on our first day of school and takes us in to meet the principal and our teacher. I don't know what they've been told about me and Marcus, but everyone seems cautious around us.

Or around Marcus

School is apparently the same everywhere. The only

difference is that Marcus' and my old school were private so here we don't have to wear a uniform. Marcus is happy about that, but I don't like having to decide what to wear every day.

Time passed, and we just were.

We were kids growing up.

We were best friends.

We were everything to and for each other.

We were lucky to have Harry and Beth; they filled the parental voids that Marcus and I had suffered.

Marcus became a fun and happy kid. We both sank into our new lives better than I think anyone expected us to after the way we came to the ranch. Birthdays, Christmas' and summer breaks marked the passing of time for us. We made friends at school, but none were ever closer to us than each other. We were starting to be truly free from the sad and harsh circumstances that formed the paths that brought us to the ranch.

We remember how we got the scars left behind from my parents' deaths, Marcus's father and the death of his mother. Those scars never go away, but for the briefest moments, we thought we might come out the other side better than we went in. We were happy.

At least until the day before Marcus turned twelve.

CHAPTER TEN

Marcus's 12th birthday is a month after mine. We had a big pool party planned for tomorrow with all the kids from school. Everything was ready for the next day. We were sitting down for dinner with Beth and Harry, talking about the party; Marcus was excited. He wouldn't stop talking.

I overheard Beth and Harry talking one night about Marcus's changes. He seemed so happy now, like a kid. When he arrived here, he was a very sad 7-year-old boy. Beth said he was broken when he got here, and now he smiled, laughed, and loved.

Yes, I eavesdrop. I'm curious by nature.

Just as we finished clearing the dishes, we saw headlights coming up the road to the ranch. It was more than one vehicle, and Harry was instantly out of his chair and heading to the door. It's easy for me to forget sometimes that Harry isn't just a father figure. Underneath his funny, larger-than-life

Scottish personality is a very smart and calculating man who could kill you just as quickly as he could laugh with you.

In the five years, Marcus and I spent here, the ranch did its best to shield us from the more brutal aspects of what people came here to learn. It was an unwritten rule among the people who lived and worked here and the guests who stayed that when it came to Marcus and me, you made sure to keep yourself under control.

Only once did we see the other side of Harry. About a year and a half ago, a guest didn't follow the rule that no guns should be allowed outside designated areas. No, instead, the gentleman thought it would be okay to threaten Parker over him, beating him in a game of cards the night before.

Harry was walking to the main house when he saw the altercation and was on the man so fast. If we hadn't seen it, I don't think either of us would have believed it if the other had told us about it.

Harry knocked the man to the ground with one kick to the knee. The guy screamed in pain and went down hard. He tried to get the gun on whoever had attacked him, but Harry was faster. Knew what the guy was going to do before he even did it. Harry grabbed the guy by the wrist with one hand, getting the gun away from him with the other, all while the dude was still trying to figure out who the hell attacked him. Harry turned the gun on him as he straddled the man's chest, pinning one arm under his knee.

"Whoa whoa whoa whoa," the man frantically yelled at Harry. "I meant no harm! I wouldn't have shot him. I swear, I just wanted him to know he can't cheat me and get away with it," the man confessed to Harry in a panicked voice.

Without removing the gun from the man's forehead, "Don't move." Harry ordered the man as he looked up at Parker.

"Boss, we were playing cards; I won," Parker tells him like it's just any other Monday. "I don't cheat. I'm just smarter than him, and the asshole has a really big fucking tell. He thinks running his tongue along the inside of his cheek is somehow less noticeable than

smirking." Parker looks at the guy under Harry, "Dude, it isn't." Parker turns his eyes away from the man under Harry.

"Well, then," Harry says, returning his focus to the man he has under him. "It looks like we need to reteach Mr. Hudson here the rules by which I run this place."

By this time, more people had come over to the commotion. Marcus and I were over by the arcade watching the whole thing happen. Wes, one of the guys who works for Harry, saw us and made Harry aware that we were watching.

"Take Mr. Hudson to the gym. I'll be there shortly." Harry starts towards us, tossing the gun at Parker as he walks by.

"Kids," Harry drawls at us as he approaches. "You two better close your mouths before you catch flies in them. Questions?"

"Not so much questions as observations," I say to Harry, cocking my head to the side as I study the big man in front of me. "First off, WOW! That was very cool for an old person." Harry raises a red eyebrow at me. "Second, no one here is stupid enough to play cards with Parker. He always wins, so the guys don't even let him play Go Fish with them." Marcus stifles a laugh. "Third, Harry, we are almost 11. We have eyes and have lived here for four years. We've seen a lot of shit."

"Don't swear, Little Ava, Bethy doesn't like it," Harry tells me.

"Well, Beth is in town picking up groceries, so she didn't hear it, so it never happened. And fourth, Harry, while we may not talk about it, Marcus and I both know why and what we were sent here to learn. So, some asshole pulling a gun, especially on Parker, barely even registers. What did grab our attention was you! Dude! You're old! And that was badass!"

That memory makes me smile it was the first time we saw that side of Harry.

Harry grabs a gun from the drawer in the table by the door and heads up towards the main house. A group of guys join him as they wait for the vehicles to make it all the way to the house.

We could hear car doors slam and hear voices but had no idea what was happening. About 5 minutes after Harry left, Parker knocks and walks in. "Hey Beth, Hey Ava. Marcus, I need you to come with me to the main house bud." Parker tells him.

"I'll come with him," I say, but Parker shakes his head.

"Sorry. I was told very clearly by Harry, Marcus only," Parker says, looking right at me. "You and Beth are to go to the arcade. That's what Harry wants. Come on, Marcus. We shouldn't keep him waiting."

I see Marcus stiffen at the mention of him. He looks over his shoulder at me and gives me a wink. I shake my head and give him the finger. It's a practised goodbye between us. One winks, and the other flips the bird. They leave, and I look at Beth. "It's his father, isn't it?"

"Probably Ava," she answers me. "Come on, we should get to the arcade. We can see and hear what's going on from there. Parker finished wiring the entire property with cameras, and some places have sound."

We head out the back door and make our way over to the arcade. We head through to the back and up the stairs. I walk over to the computer that controls the feeds, type in a few commands, and instantly, we can see the cameras up at the main house. And sure enough—there he is.

Enzo Rossi.

He hasn't seen his son since the day five years ago when he left his son here.

Marcus and I told each other a couple of years ago why we were here. Marcus's mom had died, and his dad wanted to marry another woman. But that woman wanted nothing to do with Marcus and told his father to get rid of him. So, Enzo sent him here. Gave Harry no choice. He pays for him to be here, and Harry wasn't about to turn his back on a kid in need.

I've never met the man, but I really do fucking hate him. Marcus and I have slowly been learning the ins and outs of what his father does. Over the last five years, we weren't taught per-say, it was more like osmosis. We absorbed the information from around us. Parker was the only one here who could teach us things. But I have a feeling that is all about to change. We turn the sound up so we can hear the conversation.

"What brings you here, Enzo?" He doesn't even try to hide his disgust with the man.

"What the fuck have you been doing with him all this time? I expected him to be more than this!" Enzo yells as he gestures to his silent son.

Marcus is gangly. All limbs and sinew. He's handsome and you know that he will only grow into his looks as he gets older. He has the most intense green eyes, his blonde hair is long, but he doesn't care; just pushes it out of the way. He has a straight nose, high cheekbones and an air about him that makes it seem like he is looking down his nose at you. On a kid, it's not the best look, and it's gotten him into a few fights over the years, but as he gets older, you can see the authority of the role he was born into, rising closer to the surface.

"Listen very carefully to me, Enzo." Harry says in a muffled voice, his Scottish brogue in full force, "Ye dae nae come intae my house and start yelling for any reason. Dae I make myself clear? This is ma ranch, 'n' here my word is the only fuckin word" Harry pauses to take a breath getting the Scottish in him under control.

"I seem tae remember some pathetic asshole telling anyone who would listen that someone takes him or ye will put a fucking bullet in his head. I also remember informing that asshole about how I trained or when I started the training th' bairn was at my discretion. His parental rights were null n' void. Dae ye think the asshole remembers that part o' th'arrangement?" Harry pauses, calming himself down, staring at him. "So, I will ask you again. Why the fuck are you here?"

Enzo realizes quickly he is not in charge here. He's in Harry's world and here Harry is God. "I came to see my kid and bring him home for his birthday weekend." Saying it like the Scotsman is an idiot for making him explain himself. Parker steps forward and whispers into Harry's ear.

"Or maybe," his temper finally reigned back in. "Mila's family has arrived in New York and wants to meet her son. I'm assuming you didn't tell them five years ago that you would put a bullet in his head if no one would take him. And that has always confused me. Why didn't you just give him to Mila's family?" Harry asks him.

Mr. Rossi says nothing, so he continues. "I would bet it's because you worried if they knew you were threatening to kill Mila's son, they would at the very least strip you of any standing in their family and take the boy and the money he has from Mila. Or, and I do think it's this reason more than the other—they kill you for being such a shit father. Take the boy and the money and never give you another thought,". Harry says with a smirk.

"I'm surprised it took five years for someone to finally rat you out and tell them they should check on Mila's only child. I do wish the families here had better relations with Mila's family there. But I guess even sometimes the sun shines on shit."

Marcus steps forward. "It's okay, Harry. I'll go." He tells him, not bothering to look at his father.

"You don't need tae go wit this twat."

"It's okay. I don't mind. So, take a breath; your Scottish is showing." I laugh lightly hearing the taunt we are so fond of using on Harry.

CHAPTER ELEVEN

Marcus is gone for a week, and I find myself unsure what to do with my time. We've never been apart since he came here. Even when we were younger and he didn't talk to anyone, not even me, he was still always with me. We had to cancel his birthday party, but I hope we can do it when he returns. After five days of him being gone, I was starting to worry he wouldn't be coming back. But two days later, Harry gets a call and has to drive to the airport to pick him up.

"Ava, you need to calm down, you're vibrating, it's annoying." Parker tells me as he types away on his keyboard.

"Whatever Parker, I'm excited; he's been gone for a week!" I tell him a lot louder than I need to, but my nerves make me weird.

"I'm aware Ava. I live here as well." he deadpans.

"Parker, I miss the old you who was quiet and didn't know what sarcasm was," I retort.

"Now, Ava, don't be mean. I may have been quiet, but

sarcasm and I are old friends. I just refrained from saying it out loud to people." He smirks.

"Well, can you go back to keeping it to yourself? I honestly think it would do the ranch a great service for you to stop talking." I deadpan.

Parker barks a laugh out, "Ava, I swear to god my smart mouth has nothing on yours. I can't wait to hear the venom that'll leave your mouth in a couple more years."

After spending another hour with Parker, learning some coding and doing what I am pretty sure was hacking into Wes's computer. I head back to the house.

"Hi, sweetheart " Beth calls from the living room as I enter the house.

"Hey," I say with a distinct pout as I sit down.

"They'll be here any minute, please try and relax."

"I know, but a week, Beth! What if something happened to him? It's a long time with an asshole like his father."

"AVA!!!! I understand you're worried, but there is no reason for you to swear," she scolds me.

"Sorry," I mumble.

I pick up the book I was reading last night and try to get lost in the story, but my brain is not cooperating. When I'm just about to throw the book across the room, we see head-lights on the road. I run out of the house to greet the guys.

Marcus opens the door of the truck before it even comes to a full stop. He runs to me, hugging me hard. And I return it just as fiercely. "I missed you!" I tell him.

"I missed you," he tells me with his head buried in my neck.

We turn to head to the house "Hi, Harry," I call back to him.

"Hello, Ava." Harry says as he grabs the bags from the back of the truck and follows us towards the house.

We walk into the house just as Beth pulls dinner from the

oven. "Perfect timing, guys. Sit down; dinner is ready."

We all sit in our usual spots and begin filling our plates. Once our plates are full and we've started eating, I look over at Marcus. "So? How was it? Bad? Good? Way worse, way better?"

"It was fine. But that's only because my mother's family was there so my father was on his best behavior. You were right, Harry. They had no idea he had threatened to kill me but instead sent me here."

"Did you tell them?" Harry asks Marcus.

"Nah, my dad will get his when it's time. And it will be me who delivers it, no one else," he says. The words sound like a vow.

I catch the look between the adults, but I don't care I'm just too focused on having him back.

After dinner we head up to my room to talk.

"So? How was it really?" I ask him.

"It was fine, honestly. I barely saw my dad and his new wife and son. I spent the majority of the time with my mother's family. The trip back to New York was the worst of it. My dad drilled it into me that I was to tell them I chose to live here at the ranch. Because the training Harry provides is invaluable."

"But how do they not know? How has no one let it slip that your father is a piece of shit?" I ask him, genuinely curious.

"Simple. With my mom dead and me being 12, who is going to have contact with them? The Russians here are more worried that the Sokolov's will decide to move here and take everyone out so they can run things. So, no one was ever going to give them a reason to pay closer attention to the world over here."

"That makes sense, but how does someone like your father have so much luck? "

"No idea."

"So, what did you do all week?" I ask.

"A lot of things with my mom's family. I stayed with them at the hotel, had all my meals with them. I spent a lot of time with my cousin Alexi. He's four years older than me, but he was cool. My grandfather asked me many questions about what I was doing here. If I truly wanted to be at the ranch. They also asked if I wanted to return to Russia with them."

I look over at him, panicking for a moment that he would leave me for good.

"Relax. I have no desire to go to Russia. I think the winter here is shit enough that I have zero interest in living through a Russian one." he says, "But really, I had fun. It was nice feeling like I had family again." His words sting a bit.

"You're my family, Ava, but this was blood."

I don't understand the distinction between the two, so I smile and nod. We talk for a while longer, Marcus telling me how cool Alexi is, about everything he did with his grandfather. I don't know what it is; I have no explanation other than a feeling but there's a shift with us. It's slight, and I can't put into words what it is, but our bond is different somehow.

When Marcus goes to his room to sleep, I stay up for a bit thinking about what he told me—how much it meant to him to have blood relations. As far as I'm aware, I have no blood relations anywhere. It's why I ended up here and not with them—or at least no blood relations that want me. I have no idea if I'm just being sensitive to Marcus being so happy with his family, but either way, something feels different to me.

The next morning, Harry was at the kitchen table waiting for us. Beth had made some pancakes, but she was nowhere to be seen. I knew the minute I stepped into the kitchen that I was right; something had changed.

"Eat up, guys. We have some stuff to do." His voice seems to be missing his usual undercurrent of amusement.

Once we're done eating Harry tells us to head up and get changed.

Wear things we can exercise in.

Well, this seems like it's going to be less than fun.

We get changed and meet Harry outside. "Alright, let's go," and we follow along like a couple little ducks trailing their mother.

Harry takes us to the gym, and I can't stop the sigh that escapes me when he opens the door.

Twelve years.

We got twelve years of being kids before our parents' sins catch up with us. Wes, Parker, Carter, Theo, and Sebastian await us inside. Harry's watching us; I give him a nod that he returns. My eyes go to my best friend as he greets the guys like it's any other day. He misses that the usually joking Parker is replaced with a serious one.

"Marcus shut the fuck up," Harry growls at him.

He looks at him, his tone taking him by surprise.

This is the man the others get, the one people pay for. The Harry who does bad things.

"Get on the treadmills." Theo tells us.

"Yeah, I'm not in the mood for a run today, guys. I have some insane jet lag," Marcus says to the room, still not catching on that today is a very different day than yesterday was.

Theo steps towards Marcus. He easily has a solid foot or more on him height-wise. Never mind that Theo is scary looking even when he's smiling. "Not messing around" Theo is every bit the predator I've heard Wes call him.

"Shit, man, back off." Marcus raises his voice at him.

He cocks his eyebrow and gives a low menacing chuckle. "Marcus, I'm not going to ask twice. I never ask twice. So, you can either comply, or I will force you to comply, and I promise you, if I force you, you will hate me for the rest of your days. So be a good kid and do as I ask, please." he drags a hand through his hair. "I like you and Ava a lot. What's about to happen here today and over the next few years of your stay, well, all of us here are sorry for it."

Marcus looks from him to the rest of the guys. They all nod. They all look sad and sorry but have the same determination.

Marcus realizes it now. "Who? My father or my grandfather?" he asks Harry.

"Both, son," he says quietly, "both of them feel like it's time for you to learn what you have been sent here to learn."

"And her?" he asks with a hint of fire in his tone.

"Ava is here for the same reasons. So, if one of you is starting, you both are." He tells us, focused on me.

"It's ok. I knew this was bound to happen. I thought it would happen sooner." I answer as I step on the treadmill.

"This is going to suck, Ava, but I need to get a baseline for what your fitness level is at the moment, so I know what I need to do to get you started," Theo tells me as he starts up the program.

Marcus makes his way over to one of the other treadmills and steps up.

"Same for you. This will suck today."

"I know you two are in good shape for kids, but this is a whole new world now," he tells us his voice quiet.

Our program starts, and we look at each other. I wink at Marcus, and he flips me off, and then we run.

I have no idea how long we ran. I only know I thought I was going to die. From there, Theo made us lift weights, do crunches, try to do a pull up, and so many other things that I have no idea what they were or what they were for. By the end of it, every muscle in my body is jelly. My lungs feel like they are going to explode, and I look over to Marcus and see he's fared no better.

Pretty sure this is child abuse assholes.

"What was that, Ava?" I hear Theo ask me. I realize I didn't say that in my head; I said it out loud. "I said I'm pretty sure this is child abuse assholes."

I hear Parker and Wes chuckle, and I swear I see Theo nod at me. Harry, however, didn't find it so amusing. "Oh, little Ava, you just bought yourself 50 more crunches for you and Marcus."

I glare at Harry, hating him a wee bit at that moment.

We do our crunches then slowly make our way back to the house. Beth has dinner waiting for us. Marcus and I scarf the food down so fast that I honestly couldn't tell you what it was. We head upstairs to shower and go to bed.

" You shower first." I nod, not bothering to inform him I had no intention of not showering first.

The morning comes way too early. "7 a.m., time to get up," Harry announces from my door as he flips my light on. I flop over and bury my face in my pillow, and groan. I hear Harry at Marcus's door. Marcus is less polite than I am. I hear something hit the hallway wall. "You've got a good arm there. Now please get the fuck up. Beth has breakfast almost ready." Harry calls out to us with way too much enjoyment.

I drag myself from bed, less sore than I was expecting to be. My abs hurt like I've never felt before, but the rest of me isn't too bad. I head into the bathroom to brush my teeth and pee. Marcus knocks, walks in and joins me at the sink. We have our morning routine down pretty well, so sharing the bathroom never really bothers us.

I return to my room, throw on some sweats and a T-shirt and head down the stairs for breakfast. The minute I hit the first step, every bit of yesterday's lesson comes back to me, and my legs almost give out. I have to grab the banister to stop from falling. I laugh at myself because my legs hurt so bad I can't really hold myself up. Then I laugh harder because laughing hurts my abs so much, I have tears in my eyes. *This is going super well.* I slowly make my way down the stairs, I'm almost at the bottom when I hear Marcus squeak behind me as he hits the first step. Satisfaction rolls through me at the sound. I may love Marcus, but I'm not above wanting him to hurt as much as I do.

I sit at the island, resting my head on my knuckles, watching Beth flit around the kitchen finishing up the food for us. Marcus joins me at the island and mimics my position. Harry is reading the paper, sitting in his usual spot. Today is eggs, bacon and potatoes.

Taters if you're the Scotsman to my left.

Fresh fruit and toast, as well as Beth's homemade jam. She places everything but the eggs on the table. "Sorry, Beth, I should be helping you." I move to get up, noting Marcus doesn't.

"Nope, you sit; I got this," she tells me with a wink.

We start to fill our plates, and Beth comes to each of us and puts freshly cooked eggs on them. She finishes cooking her eggs, then sits and joins us. We eat in relative silence for a bit.

"How are you two feeling today?" he asks us, no mocking in his voice.

"Oh, today you care?" Marcus asks Harry and I whip my head towards him, surprised by the tone.

"Let's get a couple of things straight right now, kids," our guardian starts. "You two have been here long enough now to have at least a small idea of what it is I do, and what this Ranch is for. Yes?"

Marcus and I nod and mumble yes, food still in our mouths.

"Good, so I don't need to explain that part to you? You are aware I train people to steal things, I train them to use guns, knives, explosives and many other things all designed to cause damage, maim or kill?" He pauses again, waiting for us to acknowledge his words. We nod. "You're aware that Parker trains people on the computer side of things? Hacking, coding, bypassing computerized locks and scanners?"

"Yes," I say.

"Yes," Marcus tells him.

"Ok, so I'm going to assume you also know people here are trained in hand-to-hand combat?" Harry says, looking at us.

Both of us nod back at him.

"Amazing. Now, have both of you pieced together why you were sent here?" Harry demands.

We're silent. Beth is just looking back and forth at all of us.

"They're only twelve. Maybe..."

Harry turns to Beth. All of his usual playfulness when he talks to her is missing. "Beth." she glares at him. "I agree they're only twelve. I had hoped to have at least two more years before training started, but Enzo fucked that up for everyone here." He pinches the bridge of his nose, something he only does when he is trying not to yell. "Enzo demanded Marcus start training now. Yuri also thought it was time. Enzo demanded that since he was paying for him to live here, he should have gotten so much more back on his investment at this point."

"I thought that you ran everything autonomously." Beth questions.

"I do. Every contract states my word is law. But Marcus and Ava aren't my typical students, so concessions had to be made on my part in order to keep him here. Enzo wanted to keep him, hire some random assholes to teach him what he was paying me to teach. I was having none of that." Harrys worked up now, and his accent is getting thicker with every word.

"We have strayed from the topic at hand. Where you two

are concerned, I'm being strongly persuaded to start training you now. The fact that Parker has been slowly teaching you guys things over the last few years is apparently not enough. So as of yesterday, you have both officially joined the program." Harry says looking resigned to all of this.

"I made my own requests and stipulations. Enzo and your grandfather accepted them. You will both still attend school like normal. You need to be able to hold normal conversations, you need to be able to hide in plain sight with the regular folk and I have no desire to teach either of you calculus, nor do I feel comfortable having a teacher who isn't part of this world here at the ranch daily teaching you. So, after school and on weekends you will train. You will train with me, Parker, Theo, Wes and Carter. You will train a bit from time to time with Sebastian, but honestly, till you guys are older, I'd rather keep that crazy fucker as far away from you as possible, and Ava, you will be seeing a lot of Miss Bennett.

"Questions? Concerns? Observations?" He asks the last one directly at me.

I smile despite the life-changing announcement he just dropped on us. "Not really an observation but more of a question: who is Miss Bennett? And why will I be spending time with her and not Marcus?" I ask with a bit of a smile.

"Because she instructs females only. She teaches them female things," he tells me.

"Well, that clears it up for me, thanks." I shake my head.

"Ava! Please don't have a piss at me right now." Harry tells me clearly not enjoying my humor.

"Ok breakfast and information hour have now come to an end. Let's go, you two. Theo is waiting." He stands, snaps his fingers like a genie granting a wish. I'm pretty sure I didn't make this wish.

Wonder if I can return it and ask for a different one.

CHAPTER TWELVE

The next week passes fast. It's the same day every day. Harry wakes us up; Marcus and I do our best not to fall down the stairs with shaky legs. We eat breakfast with him and Beth. It's a pretty quiet morning routine. None of us have the energy or strength really to hold a conversation. But when Sunday rolls around, Harry doesn't wake us up at 7 a.m. Instead, I wake up at 9. I stare up at my ceiling, confused. I'm unsure why I got to sleep in. "Marcus," I call out to him.

"Yeah?" he responds to me, still half asleep.

"Why are we still asleep at 9? Did Harry forget about us?"

"I doubt it. Maybe we get Sundays off?" Marcus questions.

"Maybe? But I got a distinct impression that the trying to kill us was going to be an everyday occurrence until we are deemed lethal." I loudly ask through the wall we share.

I instantly regret talking to Marcus when I hear heavy footsteps on the stairs. I groan and fling my arm over my eyes. My door opens, and Harry pops his head in. "Sunday is the day of rest, Little Ava. So how bout you two just enjoy it and stop being smartasses. Yes?"

"Seems like a good idea to me," I tell him all fake sweetness.

"We're going to the mess for breakfast today, so get up and dressed. I'm hungry." Harry's head disappears from my doorway, and I hear him crack open Marcus's.

"Ava," Harry's head says as it appears in my doorway again, "Hurry up, lass, Marcus is already up and dressed."

"Harry, it's Sunday; I'm tired and way too early for you to be Scottish." He chuckles and closes my door. I hear him make his way back down the stairs. My door opens again, and this time, Marcus pokes his head into my room.

"Let's go, Ava! I'm hungry."

Jesus, these two are annoying this morning.

I throw on a pair of jean shorts, a black T-shirt, and my Converse from my floor. Then I'm out my door and down the stairs. I pull my shoes on as I walk across the main floor to the front door. I can see Harry and Marcus already on the golf cart waiting for me. I hop down the steps and climb on to the cart.

"Someone's feeling very little pain this morning," Harry comments.

"Yeah, I feel pretty good, actually. I think maybe my legs are getting stronger. My abs still hate you and Theo, but it's getting better," I say as I tie my shoes.

Marcus mumbles something under his breath that I don't quite hear but I think it was something like "lucky".

We pull up to the mess hall and head inside. There are quite a few people in here today. I can hear "Bittersweet Symphony" by The Verve over the sound system. I don't know who controls the music for the mess and other buildings, but I'd assume it's Parker. Or maybe every building just plays their own? Not sure why this is something I need to think about but there it is.

We each scatter when we get to the food stations. I find Marcus and Harry sitting with Parker and Wes. Marcus is already inhaling his French toast and sausages, while Harry has toast and a coffee. I give him a look, showing I'm clearly judging his breakfast choice. "I've been up for three hours already. This is my second breakfast," he informs me.

"Ah yes Hobbits such as yourself do truly enjoy second breakfast." I deadpan.

Wes and Parker both bark out a laugh. Harry raises a red eyebrow at me in question. Marcus just shakes his head with a small smile as he continues eating.

"Ava you would think someone as smart as you would know not to make fun of the guy who decides how many crunches she does in a day. Besides, the Hobbits were onto something with a second breakfast and elevenses."

I lean over the table and offer Harry my fist. He promptly bumps it back. "Respect, old man," I tell him, then plop back down to finish my breakfast.

"What are you two going to do with your day off?" Parker asks us when we are leaving the mess hall.

"I think I'm going to go for a swim today," I announce.

I look over at Marcus; he grins and nods, confirming he thinks this is a splendid idea.

Parker and Wes both nod in agreement with Marcus. "But let's go to the pond, not the pool," Wes says. "Summer's ending, and pretty soon, we won't be able to use the pond."

"Okay, I'm going to change and grab a few things. I'll see you guys in a bit." As I start towards the house, Marcus catches up to me.

"Do we have snacks to bring with us?"

"Dude, we just ate."

"I'm a growing boy, Ava; I'm always hungry." Marcus

smiles as he nudges my shoulder. I laugh and take off towards the house in a full sprint. Marcus gives chase, and he catches me quickly. He wraps his arms around my waist and tackles me to the ground. He lands on top of me and instantly starts to tickle me. "Marcus, Marcus, stop; I'm going to pee myself," I yell at him through my laughter.

"That's the point Ava," he says as he laughs at me and keeps tickling me.

I squirm under him and manage to get a leg free that I get in between us and I'm able to push him off me. He flops onto the ground, and we just lay there looking up at the sky as our laughs taper off.

When we've stopped laughing, we get up and finish the trek to the house where we find Harry and Beth sitting on the porch talking with each other.

"Done fooling around, you two?" Beth asks us.

"It's all Marcus, he doesn't like it if I beat him. And I would have beat him to the house if he hadn't tackled me and started tickling me." I inform them.

"You wouldn't have beat me, Ava. The fact that I caught you proves that" he informs me giving me a big grin as he walks into the house.

We spend the afternoon at the pond, jumping off the dock and swimming. Wes and Parker joined us shortly after we arrived. We swim out to the floating platform in the middle, where we flip and do cannonballs off it into the water. The day is warm enough that even Beth and Harry join us. They float on tubes, having 'no interest in exhausting ourselves while climbing in and out of the water.' Their words, not mine. Harry joins us on the platform at one point, 'to show us young'uns how it's done.' Again, his words not mine.

The sun starts to go down before any of us make our way back to our homes. We're all tired after our day in the water, so Harry suggests we go to the mess for dinner so that none of us have to cook or clean up after. He heads towards his house, and the rest of us head to our place.

"If one of you wants to come to my place, the spare bedroom has another shower." Harry calls back to us.

"I'll grab my stuff and come to you. Ava can use my bathroom to shower and get ready for dinner." Beth yells back to Harry. "That work for you guys?" She asks us.

"Yup," we both say at the same time.

She grabs her things and heads to Harry's.

They're waiting for us on the golf cart when Marcus and I leave the house.

"Ready to go?" Beth asks us.

"We are. Is the water really hot at Harrys?"

"No more than ours, why do you ask?"

"Oh, just cause you look really flushed, and I know I look like that after a really hot shower."

Harry makes a noise like he's choking.

"You, ok?" Marcus asks him as he raps him on the back to help him cough up whatever has him choking.

"Yeah," cough, "I'm fi" cough. "Fine, just choked on my air there for a second," he tells Marcus, who is still hitting him on the back. "You can stop hitting me kid. I'm good. Promise." Marcus nods and gets on the golf cart with me in the back seat. Beth glances at Harry who shakes his head with an incredulous look on his face.

"Let's go. I'm starving. You hungry Bethy? Work up an appetite today, maybe? "

She groans. "Yeah, but I think maybe my exercise of choice was a mistake." Harry throws his head back and lets out a loud crack of laughter. She shakes her head and looks straight ahead.

I turn to look at Marcus, and he shrugs his shoulders. "Old people are weird," he mouths at me, and I grin and nod in agreement.

The mess always does up a huge meal for Sunday dinner —things like roast chicken, or a big beef roast, or lasagna. Tonight, there is a huge on-the-bone ham with scalloped potatoes, mac and cheese, salad, fresh buns, dilled carrots and roasted squash. I load up my plate. Harry still shakes his head at me sometimes, saying it's an impressive sight to behold, watching the amount I eat. I think it's funny. He's tried more than once to out-eat me. He has yet to do it. Theo, on the other hand, can eat three times as much as me, and I think that's far more impressive. The dessert is coconut cream pie, which is my absolute favorite. I eat two pieces before finally pushing my plate away as I lean back into my seat and give my food belly a loving swat.

"Nice, Ava." Marcus laughs at me.

"What! It was really good. I'm just showing my appreciation for the people who made the food so well."

Harry and Beth laugh at us, but my stomach is too full for me to laugh with them. So, I just give them a goofy smile.

"All right, everyone done?" Harry asks.

'Yup" Marcus and I say in unison again.

"Then let's go."

"I think I'm going to walk back," I tell them. "I ate way too much, and I feel like I need to walk some of it off before bed."

"Seems like a good idea," Beth says. "Marcus, you walking with Ava or riding with us? Like I even need to ask."

He rolls his eyes at her. "I'm walking with Ava."

"Alright, see you kids in the morning. 7 a.m. Come on, Bethy, I'll give you another ride. "

Beth flushes pink at his words.

"Seriously, old people are so odd."

We walk in silence listening to the night sounds. The mountains are beautiful any time of day, but I love them best on a night like tonight. Clear sky and a full moon. The moon is so bright tonight that the mountains remind me of a painting I once saw on TV, painted by a guy with crazy hair.

It takes us about 20 minutes to make it back to the house. Harry is still here; we can see him and Beth in the living room talking. Harry says something to her, and Beth looks up at him and bites her bottom lip. Harry drags his thumb along it, forcing her to let it go. I cock my head to the side as I watch them.

"What? "Asks Marcus.

"Oh, nothing; Harry and Beth are talking, is all." Marcus stomps up the stairs and flings open the door, kicking off his shoes and heading into the living room. He drops onto the couch, grabs the remote and turns the TV on.

"Well, I better go, don't stay up too late you two or tomorrow is going to hurt."

I groan at Harry's words and give him my best-annoyed smile, and wave once at him as he heads out the door.

"You ok Beth?" Marcus asks our caregiver.

"Yeah, I'm good hun thanks for asking. 'Kay kids I'm heading to bed. Don't stay up too late or you will regret it when 7 a.m. comes early tomorrow morning."

"I'm tired, Marcus. I'm going to go upstairs, get ready for bed, and read for a bit. Night."

"Night Ava."

CHAPTER THIRTEEN

7 am arrives bright and early, but it's easier than it was last week. I'm kind of looking forward to the workout if I'm being honest with myself. I get dressed quickly, head into the bathroom, wash my face, brush my teeth and use the toilet. I'm downstairs just as Harry enters the house. He gives me a surprised and approving look, seeing me already awake and ready to go. I move to help Beth finish up the pancakes while Harry heads upstairs to wake up Marcus. Sure, I could have woken him up, but this is a lot more fun for me.

"Wake up, buttercup." Harry happily chirps.

I laugh when I hear a thump and wonder what Marcus threw at our mentor.

"Nice! I needed a new pillow." Harry says.

I can hear Marcus groan as he gets out of bed. His heavy footfalls make their way to the bathroom.

Harry makes his way back downstairs with a grin on his

face, still carrying the pillow Marcus threw at him. "How late were you two up last night?" he asks.

"I went to bed and read briefly as soon as we got home. I have no idea how late he stayed up. I was asleep before he came upstairs."

Sitting at the island I start to dish out pancakes to myself, I'm just about to take my first bite when Marcus finally makes it to the kitchen.

"Morning," he mumbles, still not fully awake.

"Morning," I sing-song to him and I'm rewarded with the most beautiful glare I could have asked for. I laugh at him and go back to eating.

After breakfast, we climb onto the golf cart with Harry and make our way to the gym, where Theo is waiting for us. We do what we now know is our warm-up routine: running on the treadmill for 32 minutes (it increases by a minute every couple of days), followed by an ab workout and some other exercises that Theo picked for us individually.

It takes about an hour to get through this section of training. This is all to build up our muscle and stamina. Harry tells us you never know when running for your life is your only option, so you'd better be faster than whoever is chasing you. Marcus is fast, and I swear he gets faster every day.

After our warm-ups, we move into hand-to-hand training. We start with the basics: how to fall, how to fall and roll, how to block a hit, and how to throw a proper punch. So many things go into being able to fight a person and fight well. We have watched Harry and Theo spar with one another or with Wes and Parker. Every day after we are done training, they hop into the ring and show us the techniques we are learning.

The next couple of weeks pass quickly, and before we know it, school has started, and we start to divide our time between school and training. The first month of school was harder than I expected, and I cried more than once out of exhaustion and frustration. The ranch has a lot of new faces that Harry and his team work with during the day.

They keep our training closed so it's just Marcus and I and whoever is training us that day. By the time the winter holidays have arrived we are in a routine that includes school, training as well as homework and friends. Harry is adamant that we need to be able to keep friendships going; he tells us it's part of being able to blend into any situation.

Christmas was always my mums favorite holiday. She decorated the house so much that my dad would tell her that "she was lucky he loved her so goddamn much, because this level of Christmas decorating is just ridiculous." He would also tell her he was leaving her if she bought one more Christmas decoration. Then he would help her decorate the entire house. It took them 4 days or so to do the whole house. I'd only ever really helped that last Christmas with them. They were gone before I had another chance to help.

Parker takes us into town so we can Christmas shop for everyone. He has his own shopping to do, so we go our separate ways meeting up at the coffee shop when we're done. Marcus and I shop together for everyone, asking each other if something was a good idea for someone. After we had everyone else done, Marcus and I split up so we could shop for one another.

Three hours after later, we're done and sitting together in the coffee shop eating lunch while we talked about what we got for the others. Parker got Wes this remote-control car. He also bought himself one with the hopes of having car races around the arcade and gym. He got some scotch for Harry a handmade scarf and mitts and hat for Beth. He won't tell us what he got the rest of the guys, saying we were too young for that type of stuff. Marcus and I roll our eyes at him and go back to eating.

Christmas Eve is spent with everyone who is on the ranch at Harry's drinking and eating. He, has it catered so the cook staff can enjoy the party and not have to worry about feeding everyone. Pretty much all the students have gone home for the holidays to return January 3rd so it's mainly all the people we see everyday. Theo and Sebastian are in a heated debate about the names of the reindeer. So, Carter decides to sing Rudolph the red-nosed reindeer.

It doesn't go well.

The three of them argue about the names of the reindeer. Parker and Wes are sitting by the fireplace, laughing at them, arguing over something so stupid. Harry and Beth are talking to everyone and being great hosts. Marcus and I are sitting on the floor near the tree, eating and enjoying it all. After everyone has eaten everything and have drunk more than enough, Harry sits down at the piano in the corner of his living room and starts playing "Have Yourself a Merry Little Christmas."

"Ready Bethy? He asks her. She rolls her eyes at him but nods and walks over to him.

This is my favorite part. Harry plays really well, but Beth's voice is spectacular. She sings when she cooks at home, but when Harry can convince her to sing while he plays, is one of the best things I've ever seen.

Harry plays "Silent Night", "O Come All Ye Faithful", O Come O Come Emmanuel", "White Christmas", "Let It Snow," and ends with "I'll Be Home for Christmas." Everyone claps and cheers for the entertainment. After that, people start to migrate home. The caterers clean up as we sit and relax by the fireplace. Once the caterers have packed up and are on their way, Marcus and I get ready to head to our house.

"You kids, go ahead. Beth will be there shortly." Harry tells us.

"Ok," I say, and give him a hug and wish him a Merry Christmas. Marcus does the same, and Harry gives him a back-slapping bear hug that has him smiling.

Beth gives us both hugs and wishes us a Merry Christmas and a good sleep, telling us I think in case we're asleep before she gets home.

We wave goodbye to them and make the short trek to our house. Both of us quiet.

"Ava? "

"Yeah?

"I'm glad you are here with me for all this," he quietly admits to me.

"I'm glad I have you here for this as well. I don't think I would have made it this long without you. You're my best friend."

I turn and look at him, making him stop. I walk over to him and wrap my arms around his neck. "I love you. You're my family and nothing will ever change that."

Christmas morning comes and none of us are down-stairs before nine. Last night's festivities went late. Beth did not even get home before I fell asleep, so I have no idea how long Harry kept her at his place going over whatever was so important they had to do on Christmas eve. The three of us are just heading into the living room with a tray of hot chocolate and some holiday baking when Harry comes in.

"Merry Christmas," he bellows at us,

"Merry Christmas," I laugh back at him.

Beth and Marcus, both wish him a Merry Christmas.

Harry joins us in the living room, walking past Beth and running his hand down her arm as he passes her.

"All right, present time!" Marcus announces.

He digs under the tree and starts handing out everyone's gifts. Once we all have our gifts we start to open. We have never been a wait-and-see what someone else got before we open our own gift kinda group. We are a rip into our gifts and then thank and show everyone what we got. We were still opening gifts when Parker, Theo, and Wes arrive. Carter and Sebastian have family in the area. Same with all the kitchen and maintenance staff so we don't see them until the day after boxing day.

Gifts are opened, and everyone loves everything they got. Parker and Wes race their toy cars around the house. Harry, Theo, and Marcus place wagers on who they think will win the race. They are betting with chocolates and cookies so really everyone wins. I help Beth in the kitchen; we take some cinnamon buns out of the oven and cut up some fruit. We all eat a bun and pick at the treats and cookies. The rest of the day is spent playing cards and games. Dinner is early and it's delicious. Beth had the caterers also make everything for our dinner except the turkey and the gravy. All the other stuff just needs to be heated, and dinner is ready.

We sit at the table, eat, and laugh, enjoying each other's company. We play a couple more games of cards; around 9 p.m., Theo, Wes and Parker say their goodbyes and head out. Carter always has a party on Christmas after everyone is done with family things. Marcus tells the guys to take him, but they just laugh and tell him to ask again in five years.

Once the guys are gone, I thank Harry and Beth for a great Christmas and make my way up to my room. Marcus follows me up and flops on the bed with me. We turn towards each other, just relaxing.

"I have something for you."

"Why? You already gave me a Christmas gift." I remind him.

"I know, but that sweater was just an added bonus because I didn't want to give you this in front of everyone."

"Oh," I say, surprised.

Marcus reaches into his pocket and removes a small box, putting it in my hand.

"But why? We never do more than one gift for each other," I ask, still confused.

"Because I saw this and wanted you to have it," he informs me.

The box is small and wrapped in a dark blue paper with a gold ribbon tied around it. "Did you wrap this? Cause it seems pretty well wrapped, and I've seen how you wrap gifts."

"Don't be a jerk. But no, I didn't wrap it. The girl at the store did."

I laugh at him, and he looks at me, just shrugging his shoulders and grinning.

I untie the ribbon and open the paper. Inside is a small leather box.

Opening the box I find a beautiful ring inside. It's not flashy with diamonds or jewels but multiple thin cords of metals. Gold, rose gold, and platinum. They are all entwined, creating a stunningly beautiful pattern. "It's beautiful," I whisper.

Marcus removes the ring from the box. "If you look closely inside the weave, our two birthstones are encased there. I lean over to look closer and see a ruby and emerald nestled into the entwining cords.

"It's so amazing. Thank you."

Grinning at me, he grabs my left hand and slides it onto my index finger. "I wasn't sure of the size, so the jeweler in

New York advised getting it made a bit larger so you could wear it your entire life."

"You got this made for me when you were in New York this summer?" I asked him, honestly shocked that he had planned ahead.

"Ha ha, Ava, I know what you're thinking, and I do plan ahead."

"No, you don't. This is completely a fluke!" I tell him through my laughing.

"Wow, I think I need to take that gift back. You seem like you don't really appreciate it."

"No, I love it, I really do. It's one of the best gifts I've ever been given." I tell him honestly.

Satisfied, Marcus grins at me again and settles onto my bed. I lay down beside him, looking at the ring. I twist it around my finger with my thumb, loving how smooth it feels.

The next few years pass very much the same. School, training, friends, and the family we have on the ranch. Holidays and birthdays. The only thing that was ever out of the ordinary was Marcus's family requesting time with him throughout the year. Not his father- Enzo, he never bothered with him. His mother's family saw him multiple times a year. Whenever business brought any of them to the States, Marcus flew to meet them.

CHAPTER FOURTEEN

When Marcus was fifteen years old, he was gone for a week to see his family. A few days after he returned from his trip, we got word his younger half-brother and stepmother were killed in a car accident. Harry and I went with Marcus to New York for the funerals. Marcus's father didn't say much to us at the funeral. He shook Harry's hand and nodded at his son; he barely looked at me. The funeral was large. The Mafia world has customs, all families acknowledge the death of a family member.

Marcus asked for a few minutes alone with his brother before they lowered his casket, so, Harry and I made our way to the waiting limousine. We're the last ones in the cemetery while we wait for Marcus.

"So, Little Ava, what did you glean from today?" Harry asks me, with his training mode voice.

I sigh, knowing answering him isn't optional. "Enzo was sad. I think he really did love his wife and son. He has none of that for Marcus. He dislikes you a lot, and I think it's because you're respected in his world, and he is merely tolerated."

"How do you know he is barely tolerated?"

"Because while all the families were here, I'm pretty sure all the representatives were like fifth cousins. No one of any importance showed. That makes me believe the other families don't respect Enzo Rossi." I explain my logic.

Harry looks at me with the barest of smiles. "Correct. What else?"

"The Russians were absent even though we know they're in New York." I pause, walking through the funeral in my head. I close my eyes and twirl the ring on my finger. "All the families shook Marcus's hand. All of them gave him a nod. None of that was given to Enzo. The families acknowledged Enzo, but no real respect was given."

"Very good. Just a little reminder, Ava: you need to be able to do your mental walk-throughs with your eyes open. You need to be able to see what's around you if you are not someplace safe and secure." Harry reminds me. "What does all this tell you?"

I take a moment to double-check my observations and what I conclude them to mean. "First off, Harry, I don't need to have my eyes open because I have your old ass watching my back," I tell him cheekily. Harry guffaws beside me. "Secondly, it all tells me that the families want to see Marcus as the head of the Rossi family. I think that's because of how much time the Russians have been spending with him. I think that has made the other families realize that the Russians will back the child, not the father." I pause, gather my thoughts and continue, "Even though historically, the local families have had very little to do with the old-world Russians." I use air quotes for the old-world distinction. "Marcus's mother changed things. By marrying an American, she essentially opened a pathway between the two worlds."

Harry smiles slightly, telling me he's happy with my appraisal of the current situation. I feel a small bit of pride in that. Marcus makes his way over to us, and we climb into the waiting vehicle. We go out for dinner before heading back to the hotel.

Dinner is nice, just the three of us. We talk and laugh.

Back at the hotel, I make my way down to the pool and spa area, looking forward to relaxing. There are a couple of saunas. one dry and one wet.

I'd been in the pool for a little while, just floating and enjoying the quiet, when I hear a couple of voices enter the area. Looking over, I see two men in their early twenties enter. They don't see me right away, so I watch them. Setting their towels on chairs they head to the hot tub. I hear them talking but can't make out what they're saying.

Getting out I plan to head to the wet sauna for a few minutes. I make my way to the stairs and the two of them instantly track my movements. I grab my towel, wrap it around myself and head to the sauna. As I walk into the sauna, I put my hair up in a messy bun. Feeling their eyes on me as I open the sauna door. My body is tense, all the relaxation I found in the pool is gone.

I sit close to the sauna door, leaning back and closing my eyes, breathing in the eucalyptus-infused steam. I hear the door open, and I open my eyes. They take seats away from me, both making sure not to sit too close. "Intuition should always be listened to," I hear Miss Bennett's voice in my head.

Ava, just leave. You've been here long enough. I stand up and move to the door.

"Don't like our company?" one of them asks.

"Not at all; I'm sure you're great people, but my brother and father are waiting for me, and I've been down here longer than I told them I would be. I don't want them to worry and have to come down here to find me." I tell them as I open the door. I'm barely out the door when I hear them exit the sauna behind me.

If only you had been smart and told Marcus or Harry where you were going.

"Don't run off! My name's Albert, and this is my cousin Oscar," the other one says to me.

Don't do it, Ava. Just ignore the smart-ass comment in your head about their asinine names. Just keep walking.

My inner monologue audibly sighs at me the moment I open my mouth. "Albert? Did your parents want a 70-year-old cab driver for a son?" I inwardly groan. While I'm very proud of the funny thing I just put out into the world, I'm also aware that it was stupid of me. I'm a 15-year-old girl alone with 2 men, and I told no one where I was going.

"Wow, someone's a fucking comedian," guy number one, who I'm assuming is Oscar says to me.

"Sorry," I say to them. "I sometimes forget not everyone thinks I'm as funny as I do."

"Oh, don't worry. You can make it up to Albert easy enough."

"I honestly can't. I need to go meet my dad and brother." I try one last time.

I grab my key card because I can't access the elevator without it, which gives them enough time to catch up to me.

"Come on, just tell us your name. We don't bite." Albert tells me. I can smell the beer on his breath.

Why do guys think it's reassuring to a girl to tell them they don't bite? I'll never understand that logic.

Didn't they read Little Red Riding Hood when they were little? The wolf tells Red something very similar, and he still eats her.

"Guys, look, I'm sorry if I offended you, but I'm just trying to leave, so please let me pass," I ask them, doing everything I can to pacify them. I know what's coming. I can see it in their eyes, the way they're tensing up. The thoughts running trough their minds. They have no intention of letting me leave.

I drop my head back and groan out my frustration at this situation. *Such a fucking cliché. Young girl alone gets attacked by two guys when they come upon the minor alone in a hotel pool* but honestly, I'm just not having any of it.

I cock my head to the side as I look at both of them. "All right then, guys, let's do this. I'm tired, and I want to order room service before I go to sleep; there is a bacon cheeseburger here that is to fucking die for. So please, if we're doing this, can you make your moves so I can be on my way?"

Neither of them had expect the sass, so they have no idea what to say. Oscar, however, has already made up his mind. I can see it the second before he lunges at me; I punch him in the throat, and he drops, gasping for air.

Albert looks at Oscar, clearly shocked that his buddy has just been laid out. He's faster, and I would bet a thousand dollars has some kind of training. He turns his body to me in a fighter's stance, and I mirror him. I lift an eyebrow at him, tip my head to the side again slightly, and let the barest of a smile show on my lips.

I've learned over the last couple of years that because I'm small and pretty, everyone thinks I'm an easy target. When they see the cockiness in me, it makes them second guess what they think they see when they look at me.

I nod at Albert, telling him to get on with it. He swings at me, and I dodge it, allowing me to land a punch to his left kidney. He grunts at the contact, and I step back, giving him some space. He refocuses on me and attacks. He may have some training but doesn't know how to use it. He broadcasts his moves before making them, making it easy to avoid them and land my own. Albert is sporting a bloody nose, and I'm pretty sure a badly bruised kidney after a few well-placed hits on my part.

I hear Oscar start to take a few semi-normal breaths, and I see him out of the corner of my eye get up off the floor. Albert sees this as well, and an evil grin crosses his face. "Two on one bitch; let's see how well you do now."

Oscar stays behind me, effectively blocking any way for me to get to the door, but he still isn't 100% on his feet, so I know Albert is the bigger threat at the moment. Albert throws a right, and it hits me square on the cheekbone, and I feel it all the way into my eye socket. That pisses me off. I can see Oscar out of the side of my eye, so I turn to him and kick the inside of his left knee with all the power I have, and the knee gives way under my foot with a satisfying snap. Oscar screams in agony, and he is back on the floor. This time, I know he isn't getting back up. And I'm pretty sure he peed himself.

"Stop fucking with them, Ava. Just finish it." I hear Harry growl. I never even heard him enter the room. "Relax, Marcus, she's fine. "

I smirk at Albert, reveling when I see it click for him that I was toying with them. "I didn't want to hurt either of you too badly, but now I don't care. I'm going to have a bruise on my face, and that really irks me." I step towards him, and he takes a step back and drops his hands ever so slightly in what I think might have been a surrender gesture. But I don't care. I take the opportunity it produces and clock him in the temple and once more in the nose, breaking it. Albert drops like a stone.

I turn and see Marcus standing beside Harry. Harry sits in a pool chair, feet up, drinking a beer. He's bare-chested, looking like it's just another ordinary day at the pool.

"Thanks, guys, for the help," I tell them, my hand going to

my cheek, feeling the swelling and the bruise I know is starting to appear.

"I wanted to help, but Harry wouldn't let me," Marcus tells me as he approaches me.

"She didn't need help. She wouldn't have even taken that one hit had she gotten over the idea of not wanting to hurt them faster." Harry informs Marcus.

I look at Harry and stick my tongue out at him. He's right. I played nicer than I should have and have the swelling to prove it.

"Answer me this, Ava, why didn't you leave as soon as they entered? Why did you go into the sauna?"

"I don't know. I ignored my intuition, I guess," I answered without giving it any real thought.

We head to the elevator and up to our rooms.

"Miss Bennett will not like hearing that," Harry informs me. I groan, knowing Miss Bennett will make me regret doing that.

We get off the elevator and head to our rooms. I go straight to the phone and order a burger, onion rings, and a vanilla milkshake. I hop in the shower to rinse off the pool and the little bits of blood I have on me. I step out of the shower, wrap my hair in a towel, then grab the robe from behind the door and freeze.

How fucking dare, he!

I rip open my room door, walk two doors down, and bang on it. Harry answers the door with his trademark red eyebrow raised. Not giving him a chance to speak, I brace my hands on either side of the door jam, using it for leverage as I jump and swing a bit. Using the momentum, I drop-kick the Scottish asshole right in the stomach. The door frame allows me to come back to standing. "You fucking set me up??!!" I spit at him, accusing him and stating what I already know.

Harry is bent over, gasping for air, so I stand there waiting for him to answer.

It takes a couple of minutes before he can answer me, "Jesus Ava, I thought you were going to punch me in the face, nae kick me in the' tummy. Who the hell does that?" He says, his brogue thick.

"Me! I do that, Harry. I've been trained for years, that I need to do the unexpected because of my small size. And clearly kicking you in the stomach was the unexpected." I yell at him.

"Why?!" I ask him again.

"Because Ava, I test everyone. It's my fucking job."

"Do you test everyone like that? At my age?"

"You've always been so nonchalant about everything. Always just accepted everything. Since you were a little girl, you've just taken this all-in stride." Harry pauses, trying to catch his breath. "And your birth mother requested it be done now and like this."

I look at him. The shock clear on my face. He never mentions my birth mother or the circumstances of my adoption and being placed with him after my parents died. "So, you're reporting to her then? She decides how my training progresses?"

"I've always reported your progress to her. You're a minor, and when your parents died, your guardianship went back to your biological mother. She signed you over to me while you were in the hospital. That's how Beth was able to take you and bring you to the ranch."

"Are you fucking kidding me? Have you been sending her progress reports about me this whole time? And what? She sends you back notes? Tells you what training and tests?"

"No, Ava. Not once has she replied to an update, I've sent her. She's never interfered once in your eight years with me. This test here in New York, while yes, she requested it be done now, I supported the decision, or it never would have taken place."

"Fucking super. Fuck you, Harry, and fuck her."

He breathes deeply and sits on the end of the bed. "It's never once seemed to phase you. You hide behind your brain and your smartass mouth. I've seen you during training, and you're good. You've always been good. It's always felt like you were made for this life. But you never took any of it seriously." He takes a normal breath, and it's irritating right now how good of shape he's in for his age; men half his age would still be writhing on the floor. I step into his room.

"What if you were wrong? What if I froze or something went wrong? It's a fucking pool area shit is slippery!" I yell at him, and my anger begins to rise again.

"I was there. I was outside the pool area from the moment they arrived. I would never have let anything happen to you, Ava," he tells me.

"And Marcus? Was he part of this?"

'No, he just looked for you when you weren't in your room. He tried to get into the pool area as soon as he saw what was happening. But I stopped him and explained the situation. He wasn't happy about it, but we slipped into the pool area, so we were closer to you. The rest, you know."

I look at him. "Well, I hope you and her feel like you've got your money's worth from me." I sneer at him, "Fuck you, Harry." I leave his room just in time to see room service knocking on my door.

He follows me into the hall, the waiter looking between us. I'm in my bathrobe, and the Red-haired giant behind me is only in a pair of sweats. The waiter looks at me silently, asking if I need help. "Thank you," I tell him and sign for my food. "My dad and I were just having an argument about what it means to have someone's back," I inform the poor man. Opening my door, he pushes the cart inside, still looking very uncertain despite my reassurances that I'm ok.

I realize how it must look. I'm a teenager in a bathrobe with a huge welt on my cheek. And I come barreling out of this grown man's room who you can clearly see is not my father. And there is just the imposing figure Harry is. He's 6'3 with red hair and a beard; he's a bloody monster of a man. Old or not, Harry is in shape and scary if you don't know him.

The waiter accepts my answer that all was fine and heads to the elevator. Marcus pokes his head out of his room. "You guys good?" He asks.

"You know what? Fuck you too, Marcus! Fuck both of you. And neither of you fucking talk to me until we're back at the ranch."

"Not sure how Beth would feel about all the f-bombs coming out of your mouth" Harry says to me. I swing around on him and take a couple of steps towards him.

"Trust me, Harry, your relationship with her may be close, but that woman has raised me like I am her own. She is going to fucking flay you over this." I glare at him. "But go ahead, tell her what you told me, that you're just doing your job, that my birth mother requested it. I'm sure she'll be good with that."

I turn away, ignoring him when he calls my name. I step into my room and slam the door.

CHAPTER FIFTEEN

The trip back to the ranch is very quiet, neither guy was willing to risk my wrath on the plane. I sit in the back on the drive to the ranch, and the guys sit upfront talking quietly to each other.

It's not lost on me that the music is predominantly mine playing during the 3-hour drive. "Girl from the North Country" by Bob Dylan and Johnny Cash is playing. I always like this drive. Montana is beautiful in any season. But spring is on another level. Everything is turning green; flowers are blooming everywhere. I love the way Montana smells in the spring.

After the NEW YORK incident, *yes, it sure fucking was an incident.* Things are a little tense on the ranch. Beth didn't speak to Harry for a week when she saw me and heard the story. Harry just threw his hands up and stormed out. He didn't come to dinner that week either. Marcus and I went to school and continued training like we always did. But Harry was less involved. He was there watching us but was not as hands-on as usual. The ranch and everyone on it are tense, and a few people are chilly when they speak to Harry. Theo and Wes, especially. Both held nothing back in the ring with him.

By Sunday, Harry was done with the "shite" *(his words, not mine)* he was taking. He called an all-hands meeting in the mess hall before dinner.

"This week has been rough. And that stops now. This is my job. This ranch is mine. You all are here because I allow you to train, or I hired you to do a job. This will be the one and only time I will say something like this to any of you. If, after today, you still have a problem with me or how I choose to run the business or train people, you are free to leave. Is that clear?"

He waits to let people nod or say yes before he continues.

"What happened in New York with Ava is not something that hasn't happened to every single person who has been trained at this ranch since my father started this place. Every single one of you who works for me has had this kind of test administered to you, correct? " Again, he pauses to let everyone nod or say yes.

"While Ava is younger than any of you were when this test occurred in your training she was just as prepared. I would never put her or anyone in my care into a situation if I weren't 100% certain they would prevail. I will not apologize for what occurred. And I owe none of you any explanation.

"Ava and Marcus are here under very different circum-stances than any of you were or are. Ava and Marcus both have people I must answer to about them. While I think it's shite that I answer to anyone about anything, I gladly took the two of them because I believed this was their best chance. You all know the reality of their situations, so please tell me what you think was a better option."

There are a few murmurs in the room, but Harry talks

over them. "I will say this one time and one time only. How I train my students is my business. If you have an issue with something, my door is always open, and I will hear you out, but my decision is final, and you will accept it, or you will move on to a different place of employment. Are we clear?"

"ARE WE CLEAR!" He shouts. Everyone in the room says yes.

"OK then, is anyone leaving? Cause now is the time to move along. I'm hungry, and the chefs have made us a huge family dinner."

I walk over to Harry, giving him a nod. It dawned on me at that moment, something I had never realized before. My mum is part of this life. She trained here. She learned all the things I've learned and will learn here. I shake my head at myself, blown away at the fact that it never once occurred to me that my birth mom had been here before me.

You can feel the room take a deep breath, waiting to see what I'm going to do. "Well, let's fucking eat then," I say loud enough for the room to hear me, leaning in and kissing the red haired asshole on the cheek. Beth shakes her finger at me but smiles. And just like that, the bubble that the ranch was encased in all week pops, and everything feels right again. The food is brought out and served family-style on the tables, and everyone digs in.

The sound system plays "Night Moves" by Bob Segar, followed by "Crazy Train" by Ozzy Osborne. I look over at Parker. "Is this your playlist? "

"No. Why?" He asks.

"It's a little interesting?"

"Hey! It's mine. What the fuck is wrong with it?" I turn my head to see Sebastian looking at me with what I think is real hurt on his face.

"Nothing, it's great! I love how… eclectic it is. Everything flows so well," I reassure him. The table is quiet as we all eat.

But when the song changes, everyone loses it. "Since You've Been Gone" by Kelly Clarkson plays, and the entire table and room erupt in laughter.

"Laugh it up, mother fuckers. I'm here for the next two weeks, so let's see how funny you think my music is when we're in the ring or on the range. yeah?" That makes everyone stop laughing quickly, but you can still hear the odd chuckle over the din of utensils and plates.

After New York, things changed. Training was harder and longer. Pre New York-Marcus and I never sustained any injuries from training. Sore muscles, sure. After New York, though? We had bumps and bruises, bloody noses and stitches, dislocated shoulders and fingers.

I knew what I was doing here, why I was sent to the ranch instead of being adopted by another family or put into the foster system. I was sent here to learn how to break into places, learn surveillance, learn how to evade capture, drive a getaway car, steal things, kidnap people, and rescue kidnapped people.

Kill.

After New York, any training wheels we had were removed. I wasn't ignorant or oblivious to the inner workings of the ranch or why I was sent here; I was being shielded by the people here. But that was over now. Hell, even Sebastian trained us now.

We decided at the end of Grade 9 that juggling school and the ranch was too much. So, we both chose to accelerate our high school education. We spoke to the school board and were granted permission to complete grades 10, 11 & 12 as quickly as possible. The only stipulation was that we had to maintain an 80% or higher-grade average with the caveat that all classes had to have an 80% or better grade. We weren't allowed to bomb one class with a 50% and get 98 in another to balance it out.

We agreed, and our guardians signed off on it. Honestly, I think everyone in Glasgow, Montana, has an inkling about the ranch, but they all embrace the theory of willful ignorance. I think that fact had a lot to do with the school and school board agreeing to our accelerated graduation plan.

Once we got the OK, it was straightforward. All the teachers had two weeks to prepare their entire year's curriculum, assignments and tests. We finished Grade 10 in four months. We didn't do anything except school and training for those months, but it was fine. Marcus and I were used to doing what was required at this point in our lives.

Harry and Beth never asked this of us; no one did, but after New York, we decided it was time to embrace who we were. No longer pretending or choosing to ignore the paths our lives are on, regardless of what put us here.

It turns out that if you put your mind to it and have the money to hire some of the best tutors in the world, high school (well, grades 10, 11, and 12) is pretty easy and can be done in 8 months.

Once school was done, Parker started upping our computer training as well. We started learning more complex coding. We learned about firewalls and how to identify and remove them. He taught us how to hack phones and how to clone them. How to you get into CCTV systems to see what's going on, and how to you loop or delete as the situation dictates. We learned about biometric scanners and electronic password keys. Parker also taught us how to pick locks, crack safes and even how to get into the traffic light systems of cities.

The biggest difference came with guns and explosives. This was all new for Marcus and me. It started with learning what everything was and what they did best. Then we learned how to disassemble and re-assemble each item until we could do it blindfolded. We learned how to clear buildings; we learned best vantage point strategies; we learned strategic planning for hostage-taking, as well as being able to extract a target being held by others. We were taught how and where to place explosives to do maximum or minimum damage, depending on what's needed.

"Ava, Marcus, let's go," Carter calls us after lunch one day. Carter trains us daily with all kinds of firearms. Both Marcus and I are proving to be excellent shots. For small firearms, I prefer the G48. It's a slimline Glock that works for my smaller hands and doesn't lose any accuracy. The one downside is its magazine only holds 10 rounds. So, I always have to have extra magazines with me. The Glock that Marcus, Harry, Wes, Parker and Theo all favor is the original Glock 17. I can use the 17, and my accuracy is just as solid, but I can't handle it as well or as quickly as I can the 48.

Small hands are why slim lines were made anyway, right?

"How did she do?" Harry asks Sebastian.

"Good, Ava is small, but she's kind of deadly. It doesn't matter what scenario we put her in. She just fucking goes for it. She has the mentality that she either succeeds or she dies. There is no in-between with her. It's a little scary because we've known her since she was a little kid. But It's also impressive, Harry. Scary and Impressive."

"But?" Harry, pushes.

"Yeah, what's the BUT there, Sebastian?" I ask them.

"Ava, mind your own business," Harry tells me.

"Ummm, how is you talking about me, not my business?"

"Because Little Ava, we are the adults, and you are the child," he reminds me.

"I turn 18 in four days!"

"Exactly. Still. A. Child." Harry tells me punctuating every word with a tap on my nose.

"Whatever, Sebastian's just mad 'cause I laid him out."

He raises a red eyebrow at him, and Sebastian nods and bows his head.

Harry barks out a peel of laughter at Sebastian's expense. "Whatever, old man, you get in the ring with her and see how you fair. She's a little ball of fury."

"Little fury," Harry muses.

I sigh, realizing a new nickname has just been christened.

CHAPTER SIXTEEN

I sit on the couch in the gym, absently spinning the ring on my finger. I can hear Marcus before I see him. He and Parker are debating how effective some new computer program is. They have been arguing about it for the last three days. It's annoying. "Oh my god, you two! No one cares! No one wants to hear it anymore. You both have valid points. Now hug it out and move the fuck on."

"Ava!" I hear, and I groan, rubbing a hand down my face. "That is not how you have been taught to behave. Or the type of language you are to be using."

"Seriously? How do you sneak up on people in those shoes." She's wearing a stunning pair of stilettos in a gorgeous shade of navy.

"If you would practice more like I have instructed you, you would also be able to sneak up on people." She tells me using air quotes to show her distaste for the word "sneak," as it is used to describe any movement she has made.

"Miss Bennett, you know what Harry does here, right?

Like you know, he is truly teaching me, Marcus, and everyone who comes here how to kill people?"

"Yes, dear, I am aware," she says sweetly. "Let's go," she says, her words dripping in venom.

Her tone surprises everyone, and I look over at Parker and watch as he stares at her like she hung the moon. That man has it so bad for her.

"Yes, ma'am," I say as I stand up. I hear the chuckles from behind me. "It's ok; you guys can laugh all you want. But tomorrow in the ring, remember this laughter is the reason I knock you on your ass. Have a good rest of your day, gentlemen."

I make my way to Miss Bennett's office. Her office is stunning; it's white and crisp. It has windows from floor to ceiling in the back, showing off a fantastic view of the mountains. Everything about her office is perfection. To be honest, everything about her, is also perfection. That is what she teaches, after all. Perfection. She teaches women like me how to be impeccable. To be the most exquisite and beautiful creature ever created. Here, I'm taught how to ensnare. How to use my face and body to get me close to whoever my target is. I'm taught how to dress, how to speak, how to carry myself, how to do my hair and makeup. Here, I learn multiple languages: German, Russian, Mandarin, French, and Japanese.

If I'm being honest, what I've learned from Miss Bennett over the last five years will serve me better in the future than a fair amount of what Harry and the guys have taught me. Sure, I need to be able to handle a gun and knife, and I need to know how to fight and defend myself, but as a woman in this world, I must use what I have. My looks and body are my biggest advantage.

There are two facets to this world; there is the mafia side that Marcus is from. Families like the Rossi's and the Sokolov's are not quiet. They make a lot of noise in the world.

They let everyday people know they're there, and they handle the law and order the regular folks enforce. They also have very little use for women. A woman's worth is determined by what she can secure through an advantageous marriage or by what she possesses between her legs.

Then there's the side Harry is from and teaches. It's made up of people like Miss Bennett , Theo and Sebastian. They do what they do quietly. This side, my side, strives to remain unnoticed by regular folks. They are trained and work arduously to make as little noise as possible. They don't want anyone to know they were there when they kill , steal, or kidnap your grandfather.

So, while I may resent this part of my training and be pissed off that Marcus doesn't have to do any of it, I know that 75% of the time, this training will save me and make me more effective at what I do. Even today, with Sebastian, he knows me. He has been training me for years. He knows my skills and style. I was still able to bring him down because men will always underestimate me. I am, for all intents and purposes, "a small, weak woman." And Miss Bennett has taught me how to weaponize that miscalculation.

"Ava?"

"Yes, Miss Bennett?"

"Where is your head today?"

"Why do you hate me?" For the first time in five years, Miss Bennett's composure slips. For the briefest of moments, I see her shock at my question.

"I do not hate you. You are easily one of the most talented and spectacular women I've ever met. You are the most remarkable student I have ever taught." She pauses for a moment, looking me up and down. "Because of that, I'm hard on you. You pick up languages like no one I've ever taught before. You can emulate me or whatever persona I've given you in any situation I've put you in."

I stare at her. In five years, I don't think she has ever even cracked a smile at me. Maybe a few nods here or there to signal I didn't wholly disappoint her. But nothing, would have told me she liked me, or thought I was anything other than mediocre at best and inferior at worst.

Miss Bennett chuckles, and I have to sit down. "Can I have some water, please?" She nods, pours me a glass of lemon water, making sure to add four strawberry sections. She brings the crystal tumbler to me and places it on the coaster on the table in front of me.

It doesn't matter how often I see her, or watch Miss Bennett do anything, even fetching a glass of water; she is mesmerizing. Every movement is a practiced art piece, a study in beauty and grace. I sip my water and place it back on the coaster. Miss Bennett has taken the seat across from me, sitting like sculptured perfection, hands in her lap, legs crossed at the ankles, posture straight.

"Ready now?" She asks.

"Yes," I say.

I leave Miss Bennett's and head toward the house. I can see Beth and Harry through the windows. At some point, you would think they'd stop pretending that they aren't together, but for whatever reason, they seem to think Marcus and I, or the entire ranch for that matter, don't know they're together and have been for a while. They've gotten sloppy over the years. I can't even tell you how often Marcus and I have seen them through a window or around a corner. Honestly, it is easily my favourite thing about the ranch. The secret we all know, but no one will openly acknowledge.

Marcus catches up to me. "Pond? Let them have a bit more secret love time?" He asks me, eyebrow raised.

I nod and smile at him. I drop my head to his shoulder, and he wraps his arms around me. "How was your day?" I ask him.

"It was good. I finally cracked that firewall Parker created. He was happy it took me less time than he predicted."

"Well done," I tell him.

We sit on the dock, and I take off my shoes and put my feet in the water. My phone dings, and I look at the message. I smile.

"Who's that?" Marcus asks me.

"Tommy. He's picking me up in a couple of hours."

"Asshole," Marcus grumbles under his breath beside me.

"What? Why don't you like him? He's funny and nice, and his mom easily makes the best pie to ever exist."

"Ava, he's a dick," he informs me.

"No, he isn't. You guys used to be friends when we were in school. What changed?" Marcus looks at me. "What? Tell me what happened with you two."

"Nothing happened, Ava. Just go on your date with your country boy. It won't matter in a few months anyway. We leave soon. We have things to do, people to see, and debts to have repaid." Then he walks away.

I sigh. *Seriously, what the fuck is up his ass lately*? He used to be good friends with Tommy. It makes no sense to me. But he isn't wrong. We are almost done here. We turn 18 soon, and then Marcus and I will be free. Harry has a couple more things for us to do before he sets us loose on the world, but soon enough.

The next morning, Wes, Parker, and I are sitting down in the mess hall with our food when Marcus walks in. He nods at us before getting his food.

"So?"

"So, what, Wes?"

"How did the date go, Ava?"

"Ah, that. It went well. Tommy's nice. He's a good country boy with a body honed from hours on horseback and baling hay. He also started bull riding. The way he moves his hips is a whole other thing. Seriously, guys, do you want to fuck some girl's brains out? Learn how to ride a bull." A loud noise startles us all.

Marcus is glaring over at us.

"Dude, what the fuck?" Sebastian loudly asks him from a table over.

Marcus doesn't reply. He sits down, glaring at me. "Maybe we don't talk about fucking the local farm boys at the breakfast table. Have some fucking class, Ava. You may enjoy spreading your legs for anyone, but no one needs to hear about it."

I'm so taken aback by his words that I have no reply. I just stare back at him, feeling the shift at the table as it becomes awkward for everyone.

"Marcus. Man, that wasn't."

"Shut the fuck up, Parker," Marcus says, cutting him off. He stands up, grabs his tray from the table, drops it on the dish cart, slamming his way out of the mess.

"Ava?" Wes says my name. I look at him and smile slightly.

"It's okay; he doesn't like Tommy. I should've realized he wouldn't like me talking about it."

"Ava," he says again clearly not buying my nonchalance at Marcus's words.

"It's fine, really; he was an ass. He'll apologize, it'll be fine. I'm going to head to the gym." I tell the guys as I get up to leave. I see Sebastian and Theo looking at me. I give them the same smile I gave Wes and Parker and keep going. I drop my tray on the dish cart at the same time as Harry.

"Little Fury?" he says an eyebrow raised in question.

"Morning Harry. See you in the gym in a few, yeah?"

"Yup, see you there."

I step out of the mess and take a deep breath of the morning air.

What the fuck was that?

Marcus is late getting to the gym, I'm already into my run when he gets there. Once we're done with our warm-ups, we move to the ring. Today is sparring day. I love this day. I really do enjoy beating the men's asses. We draw names to see who we get. I pull Marcus.

Of course, I do.

I sigh to myself as I walk over to Sebastian getting him to wrap my hands for me. Wes is helping Marcus wrap his. Harry and Theo enter the gym just as we are finishing getting wrapped.

"They first?" Harry asks no one in particular.

"Yup," Sebastian tells him. "Okay Little Fury, you're ready. Don't take any shit in there from his bitchy ass, okay?"

"Okay."

I walk to the ring and step in. Marcus does the same. "Living Dead Girl" by Rob Zombie blares over the sound system. I glance over at Theo and shake my head at his early morning choice. He just gives me a "what" shoulder shrug. I chuckle and then refocus.

"Okay, you two, let's get a move on," Harry calls out to us. I look at Marcus and nod; he does the same, and we move toward each other.

We don't take it easy on anyone in the ring, we aren't allowed to. We need to be able to take a hit, block a hit, and return one. But the first swing Marcus throws is something else. Had I not dodged it, the hit would have knocked me to the mat.

"Jesus Marcus, what the fuck is up your ass today?" I snarl at him.

"Nothing at all Ava. Just here to spar. If this is too much for you feel free to leave the ring."

I scoff at him, if he wants to do it this way fine, let's do it. *Fuck him, and his shitty mood.*

I step toward him again, keeping my hands up watching him, letting him decide his move first. Marcus is strong and if he lands a hit, it hurts and it can break a bone or knock someone out. So, my speed is beneficial against him. I see him drop his left as he changes his stance, signaling that he's going for a kick. I drop to the mat to avoid taking the hit and sweep his supporting leg out from under him. I make the choice to let him get back to his feet.

It was the wrong choice.

He comes at me again, fast. He grabs for me, barely missing my arm. I spin away from him, landing a blow to his kidney. He grunts with the contact. I get back in front of him and land a punch to his abdomen.

Marcus responds faster than I expect and that is my first mistake. He grabs me by the neck of my t-shirt. Wearing a t-shirt in the ring was my second mistake. I know better but Marcus never usually spars with me like this. He wrenches back hard on the neck of my shirt, choking me as he flings me down to the mat. I hit hard; my breath knocked out of me. He smirks at me as he steps back. Catching my breath I get back to my feet.

"We done?" He asks me, the smirk replaced with satisfaction. I see the tension leave his body as he extends his hand to me, calling a truce.

"Fuck that," I say to him.

He smiles at me. "Ok let's keep going."

I take my T-shirt off, flinging it over the top rope and onto the floor. Looking around, I see everyone is watching us.

"Good time with Tommy last night, Ava?" Wes smirks at me.

"I guess, why?"

"Just, ah, you've got a couple love bites there," he chuckles.

"What?" He nods at me, and I look down. Sure enough, I see small fingerprint bruises and bite marks on my stomach. "Ha, look at that. Didn't realize he did that. Bull riders, ya know, strong hands." I say with a chuckle, moving the waistband of my shorts and seeing the fingerprint bruises disappear down my hips. My third mistake was taking my eyes off Marcus to talk to Wes.

"Fucking motherfucker." I hear him growl. I see Wes's eyes go wide. I turn back to Marcus just as he lets a fist fly. It connects with my cheekbone, and it drops me to the mat. My brain is rattled from the hit, and it slows me down; I leave myself open, and Marcus uses it to his advantage, getting himself on top of me.

I manage to get my arms up to block the onslaught of punches he's raining down. He's landing blows to my arms, trying to hurt me, hoping I'll drop them and allow him to hit me in the head. I fight to keep my wits about me as my head starts to clear. I hear the guys yelling our names, but I keep my focus on my best friend as he tries to knock my fucking head off. My vision clears, and now I'm mad. This is not what we do in this ring. Marcus and I have never tried to really hurt each other. But right now, he is trying to hurt me.

Marcus is always all reaction and emotion in the ring, even when he isn't trying to kill his opponent. His second mistake (his first being trying to hurt me) was scrambling on top of me so quickly that he placed himself too low on my pelvis. I bend my legs, getting my feet flat, and thrust my hips up with all my strength. It's enough to throw him off balance, and he leans slightly to the right side to place a hand down to stop himself from hitting the mat. That little bit of space is what I need. I roll to my side, allowing myself enough room to get my left leg free and thrust up again, but this time, my goal is to get my leg between us. Small and flexible is the best thing my body is right now. I get my leg between us, my foot on his chest, and I push him off me.

He falls backwards, stopping himself before hitting the mat. He recovers fast, but I'm pissed and react faster. My ass is planted on the mat, and I kick him in the face. Hard. He hits the mat, his hand going to the side of his face, and I just see fucking red. I'm on him fast, but unlike him, I pin his arms down to his side under my knees. Hit after hit, not pulling my punches; I let my fists reign down on him. I only stop when I'm pulled off him. I struggle against the arms holding me, trying to get back to the asshole on the floor.

"Ava!" I hear Harry yell behind me. I don't stop; I keep struggling.

"Little Fury, you need to take a breath. I'm not going to let you go, so I need you to breathe and hear my voice." Sebastian calmly speaks into my ear. "Calm down, Ava. Breathe. Breathe Ava."

I take in a breath.

"Good, take another," he tells me. His voice is low and calming. The red over my vision starts to abate. I take a couple more breaths as Sebastian continues to hold me. "Good, little one. A couple more calming breaths, and I'll let you go, okay? Can you do that for me?"

I nod at his words. I take a couple more breaths and feel his arms relax. My body follows his lead, relaxing even more.

"I'm okay. You can let me go."

"Yeah? no more trying to kill your bestie there?"

"He tried to kill me first."

"I'm not sure he tried to kill you exactly, but he did try to knock you out." he chuckles in my ear.

"I'm ok, Seb. I won't try to kill Marcus anymore today, I promise."

"Okay," he says, and he lets me go.

The next morning, I'm sporting a huge bruise on my cheek, and my eye is a little swollen. I didn't see Marcus at all yesterday after our fight and I have no idea what to say to him when I do. That has never happened to us before. We've had fights, sure, but never to the extent where we wanted to physically hurt each other.

Beth is in the kitchen when I come downstairs.

"Hi," she greets me.

"Hi Beth."

"Hungry?"

"I am, but I can eat at the mess. You don't have to cook for me, Beth."

"Ava, I love to cook for you guys."

"In that case, what are we having?"

"I have sausages and French toast in the oven."

"Of course you do." I laugh at her.

Beth and I sit together and eat. I keep glancing at the stairs.

"He stayed at Harry's last night. We thought maybe some space would be good for you guys." she says.

"Oh. yeah, you were probably right."

"Do you want to talk about it?"

"Nothing to talk about. Marcus was in a bad mood. I went out with Tommy the night before and Marcus hates him. I get it. I'm his best friend, and I went out with some guy he obviously hates more than I realized. When I see Marcus today, I'll tell him I won't see Tommy again."

"You don't think he should apologize to you for anything?"

"Sure, he took it way too far in the ring, but I put him down, so I think I can look past that part. I did whoop him, so it seems even to me."

"Sounds like you have it all sorted out."

"It happened. I'm over it," I tell her with a shrug. I don't miss her scrunch of her brows at my nonchalance.

Beth doesn't say any more to me about the fight with Marcus. Instead, we talk about what she has on her agenda this week. Once we have finished eating and I've helped her clean up, I tell her goodbye and make my way to the gym. I'm almost to the gym when I hear my name. I turn around to see Marcus making his way toward me. He has a split lip and eyebrow, one of his eyes is almost swollen shut, and his nose is huge. On the other side, he is sporting a bruise on his chin. I suck in a breath when I see the damage I caused.

"Marcus, I'm so sorry. I didn't mean to hurt you so bad. I was so freaking angry with you. I'm so sorry."

"Ava, there is nothing to apologize for. You didn't do anything wrong."

"Marcus, look at your face."

"I don't need to look at it. I can feel it," he chuckles.

"Jesus, Marcus, this isn't funny."

"It is. You beat my ass, Ava," he laughs again. "It's not like I didn't deserve it."

"Marcus, I didn't know how much you hated Tommy. I never would have gone out with him if I knew how much you disliked him."

"Ava," Marcus groans, running his hand through his hair and grabbing the base of his neck.

"Marcus, I'm sorry. I'd like to move past this if you're okay with it."

Marcus sighs. "Fine."

"Cool. What do you wanna do today?"

"Ice my face, Ava. That's what I want to do today."

CHAPTER SEVENTEEN

We spend our last weekend at the ranch with everyone. Our little pseudo-family all together, enjoying the time. Everyone but Sebastian was home for the weekend. He's on a job but promised to catch up with us in the outside world. That guy will just randomly pop up one day on us. Beth cooked for us the entire weekend, insisting she wasn't sending us off without making all our favourite meals.

"Little Ava." I hear Harry say as he steps out onto the porch with me.

"Old man," I say back, staring out at the night on the ranch.

"You've been here for 11 years. I honestly had no idea what I was doing when I agreed to take guardianship of you after your parents died. But I'm glad I did. This life isn't conducive for kids. So many things can go wrong. Too many times, people don't come home, and I couldn't do that to a kid. But then I got you. And I know I could never have taken

145

your father's place, but I'm so grateful to have had a hand, in the strong and beautiful young woman you have become."

"Harry, I loved my dad; he was amazing." I turn to look at him before continuing. "But in all honesty, I barely remember him. I remember that I loved him, and I remember him making me laugh. And I still miss him and my mom to this day. But Harry, not once since I stepped on your ranch did I ever feel unloved, alone, or unwanted. I may have lost my parents, and it was a shit thing to have happened, but it also brought me to you. For the last 11 years, I could not have asked for a better father. Because my dad, while great, was a great dad for a different Ava. That Ava doesn't exist anymore. She died with them. You are the one who made this Ava. You gave me a new life. Let me become who I needed to survive all that has happened and all that will. I love you, Harry, and I'm so proud to be your daughter."

Harry looks at me. "Are you crying, old man?" I ask him. He grabs me and pulls me into a bear hug.

"Don't be an asshole, Ava. You're wrecking our moment."

I laugh into his chest. I look up at him, my own tears in my eyes. "I'm going to miss ye, lass," He tells me.

"Careful old man, your Scottish is showing."

Marcus and I say our goodbyes and get on the road. We fly out early tomorrow, so Theo is driving us to Billings tonight.

When we get to the hotel, we're both quiet. We have been waiting for this day for a long time, and now that it's here, it feels a little surreal. I look around the hotel room. The hotel was pretty booked, so we had one king-sized bed for the two of us.

"I can get a cot brought in," Marcus tells me.

"Ha! I'd like to see you sleep on a cot all night," I laugh at him.

"Fine, but I don't want to hear about me hogging the blankets all night."

"Dude. I am well aware of your blanket-stealing habits. You've done it since we were kids. Housekeeping is dropping off another blanket for me," I wink at him.

"Sweet. Let's go eat."

"Food sounds good. I want pie."

"You always want pie."

"Why are you trying to make me feel bad about that?"

Marcus looks at me and shakes his head. "Let's go." He grabs my hand and drags me out of the room.

There's a steakhouse next door to the hotel, so we make our way over to it for dinner. We order a couple of beers and steaks, slipping into easy conversation about movies we want to see.

"Are you looking forward to being at the ocean for a while?" Marcus asks.

"I am. I love the ocean. I missed it at Harry's," I reply.

Our food arrives, and we order another beer as we enjoy our meals. After we finish, we head back to the hotel.

"I'm way more tired than I think I should be."

"Car rides always knock the energy out of you."

"Car rides? What the fuck am I, a dog?"

Marcus laughs at my indignation. "No, baby, you aren't. I just meant anytime we have to drive anywhere further than 30 minutes away; you're drained for the entire day."

"Don't baby me, Marcus. Just say sorry for comparing me to a puppy."

Marcus wraps his arm around my neck, pulls me in, and kisses me on the top of my head. "Awe baby, you know I meant no harm."

"Whatever," I grumble as I pass him and step out of the elevator and into the hallway.

When we get to our room, I see that there are no extra blankets on the end of the bed.

"Dammit," I mutter.

"What?"

"No blankets were delivered. I'm tired and have no desire to wait for them to deliver some now. So, I'm going to need my best friend to promise he will share the blankets." I say as I walk to the bathroom.

"Yes, Ava, I will share."

"Good," I say, closing the bathroom door.

When I finish in the bathroom, Marcus takes his turn. I crawl into bed, grab the TV remote, turn it on, and find the first "Resident Evil" playing. I settle in, getting my pillows behind me and my portion of the blanket claimed. Marcus finishes up, turns off the bathroom light and throws his clothes on top of his suitcase.

I look at him, really look at him. I don't know when it happened, but he's all grown up. He has broad shoulders and a tapered waist. The hours we spent in the gym have made him cut. He has always been ridiculously handsome. But now he is stunningly beautiful. His eyes are still so green that they always look a little fake because you don't expect them to be that color.

"What?"

"Nothing. I was just looking at you."

"I can see you looking at me, hence me asking what."

"I just don't remember when it happened, is all."

"When what happened?" he asks as he lifts the covers and climbs in.

"When did we become adults?"

"I don't know when we were ever really kids, do you?"

"I guess I stopped being a kid the day Beth picked me up from the hospital." I muse.

"I stopped when my mum died."

"Yeah, but now, we look like adults." I chuckle.

"We do."

"What are we watching?"

"Resident Evil."

"Why?"

"Did you just ask me why we're watching 'Resident Evil'? Marcus! I think maybe we shouldn't be best friends anymore."

"If that's how you feel, Ava, I'm sure we could think of other ways to stay close."

"Wow, look at you with dirty innuendos."

"Thanks, I'm quite good at them." He and I chuckle.

"Good night, Marcus."

"Night, Ava."

When I wake up, I'm instantly aware of where I am, and who has his arms around my middle; one of his hands is under my T-shirt. His hand is splayed on my sternum, his thumb resting against the underside of my breast.

Well, this is new.

Unsure of what to do, I lay there, not moving.

You should get out of bed.

Or should I lay here a bit longer? I don't hate being close to him like this if I'm being honest.

Okay, but what if he minds?

He's asleep; he probably has no idea whom he is spooning and whose underside of their breast his thumb is stroking.

"Fuck". I mutter under my breath, feeling his thumb brushing against my skin, causing goosebumps to break out.

I feel Marcus start to stir behind me. He buries his face into my neck and breathes me in. He releases a soft groan, and I feel his arm tighten around me. Fuck I need to wake him up.

"Marcus," I say softly as I run my hand over his arm. That arm pulls my body closer to his. His body, I am fully aware, is way bigger and harder than the last time we shared a bed. When we were younger, if one of us had a nightmare, we would crawl into the other's bed. But it has been years since either of us has done that.

His hand moves farther up my breast, and my nipple hardens from the contact.

Nope. Nope, Ava, he is your best friend. Get your body away from him.

What if he wakes up embarrassed? I pull out of his grasp, not caring if I wake him up. I don't want things to be awkward between us.

"No, stay," Marcus says into my neck. "You're warm, and to be perfectly honest, there is no better feeling than having a woman's breast in your hand."

"Nice. Can't say I've felt the same way about a woman's breast," I reply with a chuckle.

"That's a shame, Ava, you're missing out." His thumb brushes over my nipple, I suck in a sharp breath at his touch. My alarm goes off then, breaking the moment. I roll onto my stomach and groan into the mattress.

"We have 40 minutes until we have to be at the airport to get through security and shit," I tell him, my face still pressed into the mattress.

I hear him sigh and roll away from me. Turning my head to look at him as he stands up, relieved to see I wasn't the only one affected by our impromptu spooning, but I'm also a little unsure about what the fuck just happened. I get out of bed and head to the bathroom.

Passing Marcus on the way. I keep my eyes down, but as I step past him, his hand goes to his cock, squeezing it. I look up at him, our eyes meeting, my cheeks flush. Quickly breaking eye contact I step into the bathroom, closing the door behind me. Leaning my head against the door I take in a calming breath.

By the time we get through check-in and security, our flight is about to start boarding.

"Wow, we cut that pretty close," I say.

"Don't even. I know you like to see how close to boarding you can get when you fly."

"I hate waiting."

"I know."

We board the flight, make our way to our first-class seats, and settle in. It's a 7-hour flight to the Caymans and I think I'm going to need that time to process what happened this morning.

CHAPTER EIGHTEEN

Like all good cliches, my parents' lawyers put all the assets they left me in a bank here in the Caymans. It was here or Switzerland, so I'm glad they chose here. I love the sun and sand. We make our way to the house we rented and settle in.

The house has a cook and housekeeper, so there is a stocked fridge and bar when we arrive. Marcus lets me have the master bedroom, and I love him for it. The master is stunning, with a gorgeous marble ensuite and a huge set of glass doors leading out to the deck. I drop my suitcase and can't be bothered to unpack. Instead, I rummage through my stuff and grab a bathing suit. The ocean is calling to me, and I intend to go say hello to her right now.

I throw on the blue one-piece suit I have. It's the first one I touch, so it wins the race to be first in the ocean. I peel off my clothes and step into the suit. It's pale blue and ties behind my neck; the top covers my breasts and ties behind my back with a criss-crossing pattern, created by the strings holding the suit to my body. The bottoms are cheeky and ruched at the top of my ass.

I make my way back to the main space of the house. It's one large open room. The kitchen, dining, and living rooms are all in the space.

The floors are a glossy white stone, the walls are a pale green. So pale that they look white. The stone on the floor runs up the fireplace mantle showing the true color of the walls beside it. Accents of a darker version of the wall color are thrown around the room with pillows and décor. The kitchen is white cabinets with a dark marble countertop and stainless-steel appliances.

The most amazing part of the house is the back wall of glass. The entire back of the house is floor to ceiling glass panes that fold onto each other opening that side of the house to the outside. And the outside is sight unto itself. Straight off the deck is the ocean. Waves and sand for miles, and they are beckoning me.

Marcus comes into the main room and laughs. "I wondered how long it would take you to go to the ocean."

"And?"

"I thought maybe you would unpack first, but clearly, that is not the case."

"Nope. Ocean first." I laugh and head out of the house towards the water. The back of the house has a nice deck with a fire pit and BBQ; it's landscaped with flowers and stone. This place is stunning, and it all leads to the ocean, taking my breath away.

Once I reach the water, I put my feet in, letting the waves lap against them. The water is warm and clear, its movement is hypnotic, pulling memories from my mind. Things I work at never thinking about.

The last time I was in the ocean was with my father. So many years ago now. So many different lives ago. I wonder what they would think of the Ava I am now. Would they be ashamed of me? Scared of me? Would they still want me to come home for the holidays?

The Ava I would have been had they not died would been vastly different from who I am today. Sometimes I wonder who I would have become had my parents not died. What kind of life would I have hoped to have? I doubt my hopes for my future would have included having killed my first man at 16. The version of Ava, who had tea parties with a stuffed goat and squirrel, would never have enjoyed making grown men cry and bleed.

Are you sure about that? This, Ava, she enjoys it. She's good at it. *What makes you think the earlier version of Ava wouldn't have also enjoyed it?*

I break my stare with the ocean, pulling my thoughts back in. I take one last moment holding those memories–the thoughts of the Ava I might have been, the parents I once had–as I walk out further into the ocean and dive under its surface. I break the surface of the water, letting it cascade from my body as I stand up, and with the water falling from me, the remnants of a life that was never to be, are washed away. I let the salty water take those last bits of who I might have been out with the tide.

I let the ocean have that, Ava.

Letting her go completely.

I stay in the water, floating, thinking about nothing. Just reveling in the feel of it. Only getting out when I see Marcus coming. He has a towel for me, and I smile at him as I walk towards him.

"Enjoy yourself?"

"I did."

"I'm hungry, and I have dinner ready," he tells me.

"Yum."

"You don't even know what I made."

"I don't care; I'll eat anything, you know this."

When we return to the house, I go into my room and quickly rinse off the salt from my skin. I throw on a sundress from my closet see that Marcus put my clothes away for me. I brush out my hair and tie it into a braid, the plait falling to the middle of my back. Leaving my room, I find Marcus in the kitchen, dishing out dinner. He made us grilled salmon with veggies and some rice.

"Looks good."

"Thanks. The fridge is well stocked, so it was easy to throw this together. And the grill outside is a thing of beauty."

I look at him with a small smile.

"What? Why are you smiling at me? I've made you dinner before."

"I know. I sometimes forget how good a cook you are. I'm smiling because every single man I've ever spoken to has a solid, if not odd, love affair with grills."

He lets out a loud laugh. "It's the whole 'I cooked this with fire' thing." I chuckle at his answer and dig in. "Symphony Number 7" by Beethoven is playing overhead.

"You found the sound system," I say.

"I did. It's a nice one too. The whole house is wired, including outside." We fall back into silence as we finish eating. When I'm done, Marcus takes my plate and rinses it, placing it in the dishwasher. I stay seated at the island, pulling one of my legs up onto the seat and resting my head on my knee.

Marcus places a beer in front of me. I turn my head towards him. "Thanks."

He nods at me and opens his beer, taking a swig. His eyes are on me as he does. I grab my bottle and mimic him.

The air in here is charged. The music above us is heavy

and frantic in its pace. Marcus puts his beer down and lays his hands flat on the island. He drops his head between his shoulders, pushing against the counter. His muscles strain under his T-shirt. He lifts his head his eyes locked on mine. I watch his jaw flex, whatever he is thinking about showing there.

I don't know what the fuck is happening between us. I mean, I do know, but I don't understand what changed. When did it change, or did I even want it to?

Removing his hands from the countertop, his eyes never leaving mine. His green eyes are burning into me, causing a stir in my stomach not there before. I look away from him. The intensity of his stare is too much for me. He steps towards me, grips my chin, and tilts my face back up to his. I feel the energy radiating off him. *Is he going to kiss me? Do I want him to kiss me?* He doesn't, though. Instead, he stares at me, his thumb finding my bottom lip dragging across it.

My tongue darts out tasting his skin. The action almost involuntary. His eyes darken, and I feel his grip on my chin tighten. He leans closer, my eyes closing, anticipating his lips on mine. My breath hitches but it doesn't happen. I feel his breath on the shell of my ear.

"Not yet, Ava, we're just getting started." He whispers against my ear, his teeth nip my earlobe. I suck in a breath, at the whisper of a touch. "Goodnight, Ava," he says quietly against my ear, releasing my chin and heads to his room.

I sit at the island for a while after he leaves me, my brain unsure of what to do with what just happened. This morning in the hotel could have been chalked up to morning confusion. Bodies can respond to things without it being intentional. But this. His mouth, his words–those were intentional. And I have no idea what to do with that. I wasn't trained for this situation. Miss Bennett never prepared me to live alone with my best friend. She didn't run a scenario with me that had my best friend telling me we were just getting started. Innuendos and all received.

My body responded to his so quickly, but my brain is fighting it. My brain cannot wrap itself around the fact that my best friend just bit my earlobe, and I didn't hate it.

CHAPTER NINETEEN

The first week goes faster than I want it to. We both enjoy the house and the ocean. There's a hammock out back that is the best place to read and nap. Week two is busier. I have a lot to do at the bank, sorting out my trust funds, investments and properties my parents left me. I decided to sell most of the properties, not wanting to own so much.

I kept a couple of buildings, one in New York, because I remember how much I loved my parents' penthouse there. The building is very profitable because of its mix of commercial and residential spaces. I kept the house I grew up in and my grandfather's estate in Ireland. I instructed my lawyer to sell everything else.

Even before the sale of the properties, I was a very wealthy woman. After the sale of things, I'll be even more so. I have no idea what I'll do with all this money. I could live, travel, and not work. I could, but I won't. I'd be bored in weeks. Harry, The Ranch, and my biological mother put a lot of time and money into creating me. I don't want that to go to waste.

Sure, that's why you want to work.

I'm sitting in one of the loungers on the deck on my computer, going over a few things—currently, any jobs I take come from Parker. I haven't accepted any, and I won't until Marcus and I have dealt with Enzo, and he's in place as the new head of the Rossi family.

After that, things are a little muddier. We always said we would run things together, but I have come to learn over the last couple of years I despise the Mafia. I dislike every single aspect of organized crime families. I hate how they flaunt themselves, how they treat women and the queer community. I hate the racism they all spew. I hate the use of brute force they employ in most situations.

If the Rossi and Sokolovs were like the Campbell organization, that would be a whole other story. The Campbells seem to be a new type of crime family. Liam Campbell doesn't do things the way his grandfather did. He doesn't hold the same values as Enzo and the others. I have faith that Marcus will be better than Enzo in all the ways that matter, but I also wonder how much pressure and influence he will withstand. Will his familial obligations overtake the other influences in his life?

Marcus is on a run on the beach, and I can see him on his way back. He's tanned, and his body has a layer of sweat that makes his muscles glisten. He smiles at me as he steps onto the deck and removes his headphones.

"Good run?" I ask.

"It was. I'm going to shower quick," he replies.

I nod and go back to my computer. Instead of going inside to shower, Marcus, heads to the outdoor shower nestled in some trees back here. It offers breathtaking views of the ocean, especially in the evening after a late swim. Stepping into the shower, he turns it on. I watch as his muscles move under his skin while he sets the water temperature and grabs the toiletries from the cupboard.

With his back to me, he hooks his thumbs into the waistband of his shorts, sliding them over his trim hips and then over his trim hips and then his ass, letting them drop to the ground, and stepping out of them into the water. I watch him.

His movements are controlled and graceful. During training, I loved to watch him stalk his prey. Marcus is silent when he moves when he wants to be. He has always been light on his feet, silent in his approach with excellent control of his body. He's a sight to behold fully dressed, naked? Naked Marcus makes my mouth water.

He grabs the shampoo, washing his hair. The water rinsing the shampoo down him, over every dip and ridge of muscle in its path. I know I should stop looking, but the sight of him wet and glistening is intoxicating, I bite my lip to stop a groan from escaping.

I should look away, but no one would look away from him, soapy and wet.

Marcus is male beauty personified.

Grabbing the soap he rubs it over his chest, the sight of him causes my breath to become locked in my lungs. The soap leaves a path of lather over his tan skin, as the water cascades over him, washing it away. It runs down his body and my eyes track its path. Over his pecs, down his sternum, across the ridges of his abs.

My mind instantly conjures a vision of myself running my hands over those ridges, my tongue following behind them.

I give my head a shake and focus on the man in front of me. His hands still running the soap over his body, I catch my lip between my teeth biting it.

He likes me watching him. I have to bit3e my lip harder when I see how hard her is.

I clench my thighs the throb between he becoming intense. I can't look away from him as his hand runs over the base of his cock. Wrapping his hand around the shaft, pumping it slowly.

He grips himself hard as he works his hand up and down, over the head and back down to the base. The soap drops from his other hand, when he places it on the top of the shower wall. His knuckles white as he grips it.

His stomach moves faster as his breathing picks up, matching the rhythm of his hand working his cock. He thrusts his hips, fucking himself into his hand harder. His grip tightens, and he releases an unrestrained guttural moan. The sexiest sound I have ever heard. I look up to his eyes, seeing how dark they are as he focuses on me watching him.

I know he's close as his movements become erratic and faster. His breathing increases. "Fuck," I hear him grunt through gritted teeth. I rub my thighs together and watch him as he cums hard all over his hand. It is the most erotic thing I've ever seen. I look back up at him, seeing him looking at me with a hunger that makes my toes curl.

I need to escape from him, from this, or I'm going to do something, and I don't know if I'm ready or even want us to do it. He must see the panic on my face. "Ava," he says. I slap my computer closed placing it on the table and stand up, walking as fast as I can without breaking into a run. I get to my room, slam the door behind me, and lean against it, trying to catch my breath.

"Fuck. What the fuck? What the fuck are we doing?" I ask myself. I'm so turned on right now. I know if I slid my fingers into my panties, they would be soaked. If I stroked my clit, I would find it swollen. If I rubbed it, I would come so fast and so hard. I bang the back of my head against the door a couple of times before sliding down to sit on the floor.

I look at myself in the mirror across from me. I see my rapid breaths and my flushed cheeks, and I give in. I spread my legs as I slide my fingers under the waistband of my shorts and into my panties. I'm soaked and I groan as I run my fingers t. I shudder when I through it, skimming over my entrance, barely dipping in.

My bike shorts are too tight, too restrictive so I remove them and my panties. Spreading my legs again, I use my other hand to open my pussy for myself. I see Marcus gripping his cock and stroking himself, faster and faster. I rub my clit slowly, feeling how swollen it is and enjoying the bolts of pleasure that shoot through me as my orgasm builds.

I dip a finger into my entrance and pump into myself over and over. My hips move, and I place my other hand on the ground behind my ass so I can fuck myself harder on my hand. I let out a moan louder than I expected, wondering if he can hear me, if he knows what watching him did to me, that I'm in here making myself cum as I think about him fisting himself in the shower.

I raise my head and watch myself in the mirror. I watch my fingers in my pussy pumping in and out. I press the heel of my hand into my clit, hearing how wet I am. I'm so close. My breathing is rapid, I rub against my clit, watching myself in the mirror, and I explode. I come so hard that my eyes roll into the back of my head. As I come down from my orgasm, I wonder where he is, if he heard me. I'm unsure if I hope he did or didn't.

I stayed in my room for a bit getting cleaned up and dressed—this time in a bikini and cover-up. When I leave my room, I find Marcus lying on the couch, reading. He looks up at me, and I know he heard me. I know he listened to me as I came, thinking of him. I feel my cheeks start to heat, but I don't let them. I won't feel bad or ashamed for enjoying my body or anyone else's. He grins at me, and I return it. Then I see what book he's reading.

"Dude, are you reading Soul Eater?"

"I am. You left it out, and I was curious, so I picked it up. Gotta say, not sure what I was expecting, but I'm now invested and need to know if they get together."

"Gay monster porn for the win. Got it," I laugh.

"Going for a swim?"

"Yeah, I feel the pull of the ocean."

"Want company?"

"I always want your company, Marcus."

"Then let's go, beautiful."

CHAPTER TWENTY

The sun streams into my bedroom, and I hear the roll of the waves in the distance. I love it here. I haven't told Marcus yet, but I bought this house for us. I want us to retire here. Once we're too old for this life, I want to come back here and watch the ocean until life decides it's done with me.

I can hear someone in the kitchen, and I smell bacon. Whoever it is, they're getting a big kiss from me.

I get out of bed and make my way to my bathroom. Once I'm done, I pad my way over the cold marble floors to the kitchen looking for the magical human who is making bacon.

"Good morning, Miss Ava."

"Good morning. Miss Evelyn."

"Miss Ava, I'm too old to be a miss."

"You keep telling me this, but I disagree. Age is only a number, and I will never believe you are 76. I hope to be half as amazing as you at that age."

"Hush, Miss Ava. Now sit, I have your breakfast ready for you in two minutes."

"I'll make my coffee," I say, nodding at her before turning to the coffee maker. She nods back at me before returning to the food she's cooking.

I hear a door open and close on the other side of the house. The last couple of weeks have been interesting for Marcus and me. Since the day in the shower, there has been a level of awareness between us that was never there before. Looks are longer. Our bodies find reasons to touch each other more often.

"Morning, ladies," Marcus says as he leans over me, his chest brushing against my arm. He steals my coffee and takes it for himself. I sigh, get up, and make another.

"Mr. Marcus, good morning."

"Morning, Evelyn." She likes him. He flirts with her just enough to make her smile and blush whenever he talks to her. She places our plates in front of us.

"Thank you, this looks amazing."

"Yes, thank you," Marcus adds, kissing the older woman on the cheek. She pushes him away, telling him to stop that, but she says it with the biggest smile and blush on her cheeks.

"All right, you two, I have stocked your fridge and freezer. All the food has instructions on how to heat it up."

"You didn't have to do that. Ava and I can cook, and there are a lot of amazing restaurants on the island."

"I know, Mr. Marcus, but I miss having my kids to dote on, and Miss Ava reminds me of my daughter, so let me do this."

"As you wish," he says to her. I smile behind my hand.

"All right, you two. I will see you in four days."

"Bye, Miss Evelyn "

"Bye, dear."

Marcus walks her to the door and steps outside to speak

to the driver, making sure he takes her home and helps her into the house.

"She get away ok there, Buttercup?" I ask.

"She did. Grant will make sure she gets home and settled."

"Inconceivable." I muse.

"You keep using that word. I do not think it means what you think it means." I laugh so hard at his impression of Inigo Montoya that I drop my fork, which in turn knocks my toast off my plate, and that leads to me trying to catch it before it hits the floor, which in turn becomes me hitting my knee against the counter as my toast falls to its death.

"Ow, fuck." I yell as I feel the pain. The thunk from the contact is loud. "Ow ow ow. Motherfucking fucker, that hurt." Marcus comes over to me, laughing. I glare at him. "It's not funny. That hurt. I'm going to have a fucking bruise."

"Ava, I have seen you take a grown man down after being sliced by a big-ass knife. I have also seen you snap a dislocated finger back in place with little more than a grunt. So, maybe your reaction to banging your knee on the counter is a little dramatic. "

"Those things didn't hurt, thanks to the adrenaline pumping through me on account of the trying not to get killed by the assholes I'm trying to kill. The counter attacked me out of nowhere. I wasn't prepared." I drawl.

"Harry would be so disappointed in that. He taught you to always be prepared." Marcus tells me with a straight face.

Neither of us can stop the laughter that follows.

I move my leg and suck in a breath as I see blood on my knee. Marcus sees it at the same time, and he lifts me out of the chair, placing me on the counter so he can look at the injury. "You didn't say it cut you," he scolds me.

"I didn't know it did." Marcus lifts my leg and places my foot on my chair as he examines my knee.

"I'm going to grab the first aid kit; be right back." I want to tell him not to bother, just hand me a paper towel, and I'll be on my way, but I decide to let him fuss if he wants to. He's back quickly with the kit in his hand.

"Let's have a look." He says as he opens the case, pulling out several items. He cleans the blood off my leg with a sterile saline solution on some gauze. I look down and see its bleeding more than I initially realized.

"Ava, I don't know how you did this, but I think it needs some stitches. It's a little gapey."

"Gapey? Is that the medical term we're going with?"

"I feel like it describes your gash very well."

"Marcus, I'm not going for stitches. So, you can either find some glue, pinch the edges back together with some steri strips, or stitch it up yourself."

"Ava, I fucking hate stitching you up. It makes my stomach all fluttery."

"Marcus, you are a big scary mafia man, and you have made up the word gapey and told me I make your stomach all fluttery."

"Not big and scary yet, but soon," he laughs.

"What's it going to be?" I press.

"There is no glue in this kit, and I would bet you a grand that Steri strips won't hold it together."

"So? That means what?" I ask, raising an eyebrow.

"Fuck off, Ava."

"Fluttery tummy, here comes Marcus." He throws his head back and lets out a big laugh. I love that sound from him—that real laugh. I don't hear it nearly enough. He sighs when he stops laughing and grabs the needle, thread, and other things from the first aid kit.

He carefully rubs the area with a bit of numbing cream. "It says to leave it on the area for 6 minutes for the full numbing to take effect."

"K."

He's standing between my legs as he works, his shoulder to my chest. Once he's done applying the cream, he turns to face me. We're close like this. I'm at eye level with him for the first time. I can't help staring at his eyes up close. I have never had the right words to describe his eyes. They are a lot like Harry's green eyes, but Marcus's have these darker green flecks, and they are just spectacular to look at. They're easy to get a little lost in.

His hands are on my thighs, his thumbs making small circles over my skin. I take my eyes off his. Being this close with his hands on me as he stares into my eyes is too much. I break the connection. "Solid marks, though, for us with the Princess Bride reference extravaganza."

Marcus sighs quietly. "I'm not sure it was worth your injury, but I agree we killed that bit."

I give him a big grin. He picks up the needle and thread, "Ready?"

"As ready as I always am for stitches." He gives me another low chuckle and then starts. The first poke of the needle causes me to suck in a breath, and I grab his forearm. "You, okay?"

"I'm fine, it doesn't hurt. I was expecting it to." I look at him a little sheepishly. He ignores my embarrassment and works fast to place four stitches.

"There, all done," he says, tying off the final stitch. "Try not to fight any more inanimate objects. Yeah?"

With the stitches bandaged, Marcus lifts me from the counter and tells me to sit and relax while he cleans up. I happily listen to him and make my way outside, stopping to grab my book from the table and heading out to the hammock. The warm day and the gentle sway of the hammock lull me to sleep quickly. I wake up a little as I feel

Marcus get into the hammock with me, but he's well-practised at it, so he is able to slip onto it smoothly.

I snuggle into him, my face close to his shoulder. One of my hands finds his, and the other wraps itself around his arm. I throw my leg over his, feeling the pull of my stitches with the movement. I see Marcus reach for my book, careful to keep it open to my page before placing it on his chest, as my eyes close and I drift off.

CHAPTER TWENTY ONE

Marcus walks into my room while I'm getting ready for dinner. "Seriously, how aren't you ready?" He asks as he falls onto my bed.

"Cause my entire personality is to make your life more difficult."

"Ha! The shit part, Ava, is that you're only partially joking."

I look at him and laugh. "Go have a drink. I'll be there in about 20 minutes."

I finish doing my hair, leaving it wavy down my back. My makeup is minimal. The tan I've acquired over the last few weeks has me glowing, so I add a shimmer to the inner corner of my eyes, highlight above my cheekbones and apply a light gloss. Satisfied with my face and hair, I grab my body lotion and remove my oversized t-shirt. In only my thong, I apply the lotion all over, my skin drinking in the moisture. I'm doing my best to reach my back when I hear Marcus.

"I can do that for you," He says from the door. I hesitate

for the briefest moment, then toss him the lotion. I grab my top off the counter, hold it in front of me, and turn my back to him.

He steps closer, s breath fans over my neck and it sends a shiver over my body. He puts the lotion in his hands, warming it up a bit before placing them on my shoulders. He applies gentle pressure as he smooths the lotion over my shoulders and back. A small moan slips out at the feel of his hands on me. He stops moving for a moment, before his hands resume making their way down my back. He continues to smooth the lotion into my skin, working his hands lower and lower.

I feel his fingers dip under the waistband of my thong, his thumbs digging into the muscles there. I look at us in the mirror, his hands on my hips, his thumbs pressing into my skin. His head is down, staring at his hands on my ass.

But this. This feels different.

Marcus's eyes meet mine in the mirror, his piercing green eyes framed with dark lashes. His blonde hair is even lighter from the sun, and his tan makes his eyes more striking. He's wearing a white short-sleeved light-knit V-neck with a soft collar and navy shorts that perfectly hug his thighs. Marcus has grown into a beautiful man just as I knew he would. But now he has an air about him that's darker than when he was younger, and power radiates from him.

He holds my gaze in the mirror, I see his jaw clench. His fingers dig into me harder, hard enough that I shudder at the thought of him leaving his marks on me. That thought snaps me out of it.

"Shit, we should go. Let me throw on my dress and shoes."

He clears his throat, still looking at me in the mirror. "Yeah, I'm starving, let's go." We look at each other for another moment, and I see the hunger there, and I'm positive it's not for food. Marcus leaves the bathroom, and I close the door to get my dress from behind it. I slip the silk over my head and shiver at its cool touch on my warm skin.

It's a deep emerald green that falls to just above my knee with a slit up one side. I'm happy that Marcus removed my stitches a couple days ago. The neckline sits straight across my collarbone, with the thinnest straps crisscrossing in the back around my shoulder blades. The rest of the back is bare.

I open the bathroom door and see Marcus with my shoes hanging off his finger. He looks me up and down, saying nothing. I turn to grab my handbag off the dresser, giving him a view of the back of the dress. "Fuuuck." I hear him mutter low. A small smile crosses my lips, I smother it quickly.

I grab my gold cuffs, place them on my wrists, take my shoes from Marcus, and hold onto his shoulder as I try to put them on. They're black with a thin strap across the toes, a 3-inch heel and an ankle strap that is not cooperating. "Jesus," he says, dropping to his knee to do up my shoe, his fingers grazing the inside of my ankle. He takes the other shoe from me. "Keep your hands on my shoulders, Ava." His voice is low and rough, sending a flare of heat straight to my core.

He lifts my other foot and places the shoe on it, running a finger under my arch. He does up the buckle and runs his fingers up my calf. His touch is feather soft, sending another rush of heat through my body.

Seeing him on his knees before me is intoxicating. Him looking up at me from his knees in front of me.

Well, that's... um.

"Ready?" He asks, still kneeling in front of me.

"Uh, yeah, yes." I stumble over my words. He gets to his feet, hands me my purse and gives me a lazy smile.

"Let's go." He takes my hand, entwining our fingers, pulling me out of my bedroom.

Once outside, he opens the car door for me, waiting until I'm in before going to the driver's side. As we head to the restaurant, Lana Del Rey's "Video Games" plays over the speakers, filling the silence in the car. We pull up to the restaurant, and the valet opens my door. Marcus takes my hand, handing the valet the keys and a $50 bill.

The restaurant is on the beach and divided into different areas. There's a dining area situated at the top of the beach, and the open-air bar area with its dance floor and stage are down close to the water.

We're seated immediately, and Marcus orders a bottle of 2017 Chateau Montelena Estate Cabernet. The waiter returns with the wine and offers it to Marcus first, ensuring he approves of it. Marcus nods, and the waiter moves to fill my glass before going back to fill Marcus's. We sit quietly for a bit, enjoying the wine.

"Any idea what you want to have?" I ask Marcus as I look over the menu.

"I think I want the steak. You?"

"The same," I say with a grin.

"Not sure why I asked. No burger on the menu, I should have known steak."

"You know me so well, do you?"

He looks at me over the rim of his wine glass as he takes a sip. "I'm sure I could know you better." I feel my cheeks flame. I take a sip of my wine and notice a drop running down the side of my glass. I collect it on my fingertip and bring it to my mouth, placing my finger on my lips. I lick the drop off. He's watching me; his green eyes darken and his hand squeezes into a fist on the table. He starts to say something, but the waiter interrupts him.

"We will both have the steak medium-rare; I'll have the

oven-roasted potatoes, and she'll have the 12-hour crispy potatoes."

"Thank you, sir," the waiter says as he moves away to put our order in. My phone buzzes in my purse, and I retrieve it to see who it is. It's Beth asking how we're doing. She tells me that Harry is still mopey since we left, and that Parker and Wes won't spar with him until he lightens up. I read the text to Marcus, and we both chuckle at the thought of Harry beating them up because he's in a bad mood. The laughter lightens our mood, and we sink into a normal rhythm—a familiar cadence to our conversation.

Our food arrives, and we dig in.

The conversation flows easily, all the earlier tension seeming to have dissipated. We discuss a couple of books we've read and what movie we want to watch later. My vote is for "Blade Runner 2049". Marcus hates science fiction. It's one of the few things we disagree on. Marcus usually gives in when it comes to the movies we watch or the music we listen to. I'm grateful he does because I'm unyielding in those areas. I am fully aware it's a crappy personality trait of mine, but it's one I have no desire to change.

I've been taught and trained to be yielding and accommodating to the situations and people my work puts in front of me. If a client wants a death to look like a suicide, or I need to get close enough to drug someone, I have to be whatever they want me to be. I have to emulate whatever fantasy or impression of me gets me close to them.

My body is both a tool and a weapon. My face, my voice, my slight stature- all of it has been carefully crafted and meticulously trained to be pliable and compliant. It makes none of it mine; none of it is me. But what I watch and listen to when I'm supposed to be at home relaxing? When I'm supposed to be the real Ava? Those are mine. Those are me.

And I won't give them to anyone for anything. I will unapologetically keep that part of me for myself.

"Do you want dessert?" Marcus asks me.

"No, let's go to the bar and dance. We can order dessert later if we want."

Marcus nods, and he places money on the table; grabbing my hand, we head to the big open-air side of the restaurant. We walk down the cobblestone path towards the ocean and the already busy bar. The music is full of bass, and the dance floor is packed with people. Marcus leads us through the crowd to a table in the back corner. He leaves me there and goes to get us a couple of drinks. He's back a few minutes later with a beer for himself and a fruity drink for me. I raise an eyebrow at him.

"What?" He asks innocently. "I distinctly remember Miss Bennett telling you not to drink beer or scotch when out. She said wine, champagne or something on the fruitier spectrum."

I shake my head at him. "Really?" I grab his beer and take a big sip. He shakes his head and smiles at me, picking up the fruity drink and taking a sip.

"How is it?" I ask.

"It's horrible. How do people drink these things? "

"No clue. The beer is good, though. Thanks"

Marcus returns to the bar and comes back with a pitcher and another glass, pouring himself a beer.

We people watch for a bit—it's more of a habit trained into us than entertainment. Harry and Sebastian drilled in the importance of knowing your surroundings at all times. Take note of people and exits. Even when there is no threat or danger, you should always be able to get out. I look at Marcus. "Game?"

"Loser stops drinking to drive home?" He challenges.

"Yup," I reply.

"You go first, Little Fury."

"Alright, let's see...." I zone in on a woman with brown hair wearing a pink dress. "Pink dress," I say, nodding in her direction. I see Marcus clock her. "Just found out her husband had an affair. She booked this trip last minute, planning on fucking her way through every man she can find."

"Okay." And he heads over to the woman in question, turning on the charm instantly. He's gone for nine minutes. I see her touch his arm and make her way out of the bar.

"So?"

"How?" He asks.

I smile. "Easy. She clearly has money. You don't come here if you can't afford it. But her hair and clothes aren't vacation ready. The dress is a little ill-fitting. But it's designer, so it would have been tailored to fit her better. It's loose in places like her breasts and ass, so it's easy to guess she's had some recent weight loss. Her hair, while well-kept, needs a dye refresh. Her fingernails are gorgeous, but again, not vacation nails. You don't do a set that long for vacation. You go a bit shorter and no jewels. And her toes are not any color a woman gets before vacation to show off her newly acquired tan. She keeps moving to adjust a ring on her left ring finger, but it's not there anymore, and every time she goes to touch it, its absence startles her before she remembers she took it off."

"Your turn," I tell him sweetly while I refill my beer.

Marcus scans the bar and stops at a group of women around a high-top table. "Blonde in the t-shirt and jean shorts."

"Oh, she's cute," I tell him.

He rolls his eyes at me. "She just flunked out of school and hasn't told anyone yet because they are here for her older brother's wedding."

I look at him and then back at her. I take a sip of my beer and make my way over to her.

"I love your t-shirt," I tell her because I genuinely do.

"Thanks, it's one of my favorites."

"I'm Ava."

"Hi, I'm Cam."

"Hi, Cam. So, what brings you to the Caymans?"

"My brother is getting married." She tells me.

"Not happy about it?" I ask her.

"No, I am! I love his fiancée. She's amazing. She is a freaking pediatric orthopedic surgeon. She literally fixes little kids and babies' bones. And she's funny." I'm not getting any hint of a lie from her.

"So why are you sad?"

She looks at me and then at her family and lets out a breath that deflates her shoulders. "I just flunked out of law school and haven't told my family yet."

How the fuck did he clock that? She looks like a bored little sister wishing she was anywhere but here.

"Oh, I'm sorry that must be complicated. Have you always wanted to be a lawyer? "

She doesn't answer me immediately; her pause hangs heavy on her. "No, it was never what I wanted, but my parents are lawyers, so when my brother became a doctor, I had no choice but to follow in their footsteps."

"I see," I say, nodding at the information. "If you could do anything, what would it be?"

"Tattoo artist," she says instantly.

I look at her, seeing the spark of life in her eyes now.

"Cam, life is too unexpected and short to live it for others. You should follow your dream. Unless you don't have any actual artistic ability, then don't become a tattoo artist."

She looks at me and laughs, then lifts her t-shirt showing

me her ribs and the most beautiful tree tattooed there. Its bark has images of birds and flowers, and it's stunning.

"Wow!" I say.

"I drew this; a friend tattooed it for me."

"Okay! So yes, you should follow your dreams, Cam. I lost my parents at a young age, so I know how fast things can change, and the thought of living my life doing something I hate makes my heart hurt."

She smiles at me. "Thanks, Ava."

"You're welcome. But don't tell your family until you get home. People are crazy at weddings and experience so many emotions and all those emotions and reactions will be bigger than they probably want them to be."

"I thought the same; I'm glad to hear someone else think it." She smiles at me. "Is that your boyfriend? Because he is beautiful."

I look over at him. "No, he's my best friend. We grew up together."

"Really? He sure doesn't look at you like you're just a friend. He looks at you like he wants to devour you."

"I don't know about that, Cam. we've never been anything but friends." But that doesn't feel exactly true anymore.

"It may have been nothing but friends for you but not for him. The guys at the bar were checking you out as you walked over here, and your bestie there was having no part of it. He glared at the guys, took half a step towards them, and the three of them raised their hands in defeat and turned around."

I look over at him again. Before we arrived weeks ago, I would have laughed hysterically at anyone who said there was something other than friendship between Marcus and me. Right now? I want to say I feel nothing I haven't always felt, but that isn't the case. New feelings could complicate so much for us. We have so much to do over the next little while. Changing the parameters of our relationship could be the worst idea ever.

Or it could be the best idea ever.

I realize I've been standing there, looking at Marcus, not saying a word to Cam. "I'm sorry. I got lost in my thoughts there for a moment," I tell her sheepishly.

"No worries. I'd also get lost in those same thoughts if he were my best friend," she giggles.

"Well, Cam, it's been a pleasure! I hope I see you again. Hopefully, with a tattoo gun." I smile at her. She wraps her arms around my neck, hugging me, and I realize I've never had a girlfriend hug me before.

"Here, give me your phone. I'll put my number in, and you can text me sometime if you ever need to talk."

She hands me her phone, and I enter my number into it and then text myself, so I have hers as well. She smiles at me again, and we say goodbye.

I return to my table, where another pitcher of beer awaits. I slide into my seat beside him, and Marcus instantly puts his arm over the back of my chair and leans into me to speak in my ear. His breath against my ear sends goosebumps down my arms. His thumb finds my open back and rubs along my spine.

"So? Was I right?" He purrs into my ear.

"My only question is," I turn my body to face him, my left leg slipping between his to get closer. I know what I'm doing. I see the invitation I'm starting to offer. Will he take it or stop it? The slit in my dress rides up my thigh as I move closer. "How did you know? Hmm?" I purr back at him, leaning across to speak into his ear. "Did you overhear Cam confess to someone?" My left-hand draws small circles on the back of his hand as it grips my chair.

"I'll never tell Ava. What would be the fun of that?" he

says as he leans in more, his leg pushing in between my thighs more, forcing my legs wider to allow him closer. The slit in my dress rides higher.

"Ava." He says my name not in question but in permission.

"Marcus," I say his name, my voice sounding breathy and needy.

He leans in that last little bit. My breath stutters at the feel of his skin between my thighs. Remembering that he's wearing shorts. I let my thighs fall apart, giving him the access he wants. He slides forward in his chair, his other hand finding my chin and making me look up at him. I feel his thigh as he slides me forward ever so slightly, pressing against my core, and it's just enough to drag a breath from me.

"Tell me what you want. Tell me to stop, tell me to fuck off, tell me something. Because right now, all I want to do is take your mouth with mine while I make you come on my hand." A whimper escapes me, and then I feel his thumb sliding under the hem of my dress, moving higher. My eyes drop to his hand.

"Look at me," he demands, and I comply instantly. There is desire in his eyes, but also uncertainty.

"Let's go home, Marcus." That uncertainty in his eyes disappears with my words.

He nods at me, stands and takes my hand, leading me out of the bar. We make our way back up to the central part of the restaurant, heading to the front. He gives the valet our ticket, and we wait for the car. He keeps my hand in his while we wait, his thumb making circles in the palm of my hand. I step into him when a gust of wind comes off the ocean. His other hand goes to the small of my back, slipping slightly lower. His hands are large, and they grab my dress in a fist, pulling me closer to him. My hands rest on his chest.

The car arrives, and we're forced to separate. Marcus gets in the driver's seat and waits for me to fasten my belt before he pulls out onto the street. "Wicked Game" By Chris Issac invades the space, the song adding to the intensity inside the small space. I drop my head back against the headrest. Marcus's hand rests on my thigh, his fingers making small designs on the soft skin. I relax my legs slightly, giving his fingers more room.

He digs them into my skin more firmly as they inch higher toward my core. I gasp quietly when his fingers graze my skin, a whisper of a touch slides over my underwear. My legs shift open wider without any real intention on my part. My body wants his touch, even if my mind hesitates. We pull into the driveway of our house, and Marcus removes his hand from my leg, putting the car in park.

CHAPTER TWENTY TWO

Marcus gets out quickly walking around to my side. He opens my door, taking my hand to help me out. Opening the door to the house we step inside. Having left some lights on, the house has a warm glow. I walk across the great room to the wall of sliding glass. I slide the curtains, unlock the doors and open them. They fold into themselves and disappear into the wall at each end. I close the rest of the curtains, letting the wind blow them. Music plays, and "Slip" by Elliot Moss echo's off of the surfaces.

I walk to where Marcus is standing by the fireplace, holding a scotch for me.

"Thank you," I say as I take a sip.

He nods at me, watching my throat as I swallow. Setting his glass on the mantle, he pushes off the wall and stalks towards me. I turn just before he reaches me and walk towards the dining room. He catches me, putting his hands on the table, caging me in. I feel his breath on my shoulder and the heat radiating from his body.

He isn't touching me anywhere, but I feel him everywhere.

"Ava, tell me what you're thinking."

"I'm scared."

"Why?"

"What if we fuck it all up, Marcus?"

"What if we don't?" His mouth presses against my shoulder, his teeth lightly grazing it.

"You are my best friend. I can't lose you."

He runs a hand up my arm, hooking his thumb under my chin and tipping my head to the left. "Ava, tell me to stop, and I stop. We go back to being best friends like nothing happened," he says against my neck, his breath making my skin tingle.

He starts a slow and teasing countdown. "Five. Tell me to stop, Ava," he says. I say nothing.

"Four." He pulls me closer, and I feel his hard chest against my back. His tongue traces a path along my shoulder, and he blows on it, sending a shiver through me.

"Three. I hear your breaths coming in faster. If I ran my hand up your inner thighs, would I be rewarded with feeling your wetness there?" A wave of arousal rushes through me at his words.

"Two." He says as he drags his hand along my thigh up towards my core.

"Fuuuck, Ava, is this all for me?" He breathes against my back as he drags his up higher.

"One. Now or never, Little Fury. If you don't tell me to stop, I'm going to bury my cock in your sweet cunt and make you cry out my name." He pulls me into him and pushes against my ass, and I can feel how hard he is.

"Yes," I breathe out. "Yes."

"Finally," he growls, gripping my hip and turning me to face him as he claims my mouth for the first time.

In the years of our friendship, I have been on the receiving end of his anger, hurt, humour, and indifference. I have witnessed this man murder, maim and hurt others just to hurt them. I have felt and witnessed it all and participated in most of it, but I have never been on the receiving end of this. This claiming, this want and need, this tangible desire he has for me.

He deepens the kiss, his tongue finding mine. I moan when I feel his tongue against mine. It feels almost forbidden to me, the intimacy of it all. I open my mouth and give him more of me. Wanting to feel him take more of me. His hand snakes into my hair, gripping it tight, holding me in place.

My knees grow weak with every stroke of his tongue. His want of me makes my core clench and my wetness pool. The sounds coming from him as he claims my mouth for his own are feral. His hand tightens in my hair, eliciting a moan from me at the sting. My moan snaps the last bit of control he had. He runs his hand freely over me sending currents of electricity throughout my body.

He pulls his mouth from mine, making me whimper with its loss. Moving to my neck, biting and nipping my skin. Each one sending another rush of heat to my belly; his fingers glide over my shoulder, dragging the straps of my dress down with them. His mouth follows the dress as it slides down my body. The cool air on my breasts, and then his hand running lightly over them, causes my nipples to harden.

"So, fucking perfect," he says, teasing my nipple with his tongue, sucking it into his mouth, his tongue playing with it. I hiss at the sharp sting of his teeth. That beautiful twinge of pain delivers another rush of heat to my pussy. He releases my nipple and kisses across my chest to trap my other one in his mouth; I let out a shuddering breath when he bites down, soothing the sting with his tongue. I try to reach up and touch him, but my dress traps my arms.

"Marcus, I want to touch you."

"Not yet, Ava. I've been waiting to touch, to taste you for years, so I think I'll take my fill first." His tone is very matter of fact.

Years? He's wanted me for years.

He feels my body stiffen, feels my breathing change. "Where did you go, Ava?"

"Years?" I whisper.

He looks at me carefully considering his next words. He takes the slightest step back from me, and I see the hesitation that wasn't there a moment ago. I pull my dress back up, waiting for him to speak.

He takes a deep breath, steadying himself. "Yes, Ava, years."

He sounds exasperated, like I'm the only one who didn't know this.

"But? I, I, what?" I stammer, trying to wrap my head around this revelation.

He runs his hand through his hair, mussing his perfectly messy look.

"Best friends, Marcus," I say quietly, my brain working fast to process and remember what it missed.

"You are my best friend, Ava. You have been since I was seven, and I arrived at Harry's and met you. You shook my hand and then offered me a fucking squirrel."

"Mr. Waffle," I correct him.

"Offered me Mr. Waffle. You were mine."

Mine? His?

"But you didn't tell me."

"Why did you think none of the guys asked you out in school or the town? They all knew you were mine, so they stayed away."

"But I dated guys, Marcus. I dated Finn for like six months."

"Yeah," Marcus says, running his hand over his face. "That guy wouldn't listen to me. We got into two fights over you, but that asshole would not give up. So, when he finally got you to say yes, I knew I couldn't stop it without hurting you, so I let it be. I even tried to get Harry or Sebastian to interfere and run him off, but neither felt it was necessary. Those six months were some of the shittiest of my life. Every time you went on another date, it made me crazy."

I think back to the six months I dated Finn. Looking back, Marcus was quiet and never came with Finn and me to parties or anything we asked him to do with us. Finn was my first everything: date, boyfriend, kiss, and I lost my virginity to him. And then it hit me.

"Oh, fucking hell! Marcus! You were my best friend, and I didn't know. Why did you let me tell you all that stuff? I told you when I lost my virginity!"

Darkness flashes across his eyes at the mention of my lost virginity. "Because, Ava, you're my best friend, and I'm yours, and I never wanted to be a reason you didn't smile."

"When I went out with Tommy?"

He grabs the back of his neck, looking down to the floor. "Yeah, that was not a good look on me. Tommy knew how I felt about you. We were friends for a while. But he still pursued you. I fucking hate that guy."

I feel my heart ache for him. I think of all the pain I must have caused him, but he still just took it. "The fight a few months ago? That was because I went out with Tommy?"

"Yeah. I was so fucking mad that when we got in the ring, I just lost it. When I threw you to the mat, and you lost your breath, I knew I needed to step back. But then you took off your t-shirt, and I saw the marks he had left on you from the night before and, well, you know the rest–you were there." I don't say anything to him. I don't know what to say.

"Ava, I was so far out of line. But I couldn't stop myself. You hurt me, and I wanted to hurt you back."

"It's done. We're past it."

He's standing there looking at me like I have the power to shatter him. I walk towards him, his eyes tracking my every step. I step into his body and look up at him. He bows his head to look down at me. Reaching up I touch his face, this beautiful boy who grew up into this spectacular man who looks at me like I am his only purpose in life. He leans into my hand, and his eyes close. I run my other hand up under his shirt, over his abs, stopping over his heart.

I feel it's beat against my palm, strong and steady. His skin is molten against my own. I keep my eyes on him as I close the space between our lips and kiss him. I kiss him; I ghost my lips over his and feel his lips part a fraction, surprised at my touch—that tiny intake of breath at his shock. I kiss him harder. He doesn't fight me for control of the kiss. He lets me lead it and allows me to explore as I want.

I open my mouth to him, and he does the same. My fingers move into his hair as I pull him on harder to me. Still, he lets me drive the kiss. The kiss is deep and slow, his hands still at his side like he's afraid to touch me, worried he will spook me or wake up and realize this isn't real.

My tongue gently invades his mouth, just enough to find his. The choked noise he makes at the caress of my tongue is the only warning I get. His arms wrap around my waist, pulling me into him and I snake mine around his neck. His tongue delves into my mouth.

There is no catching our breath, no gentle touches, nothing slow and tender. Our mouths are fused as our kiss becomes greedy and possessive. Marcus's hands find the straps of my dress and pulls them down over my shoulders, letting my dress slide off my body and pool on the floor at my feet. I grab the bottom of his shirt, working it up, needing to have it off him, needing to feel his skin against mine.

Marcus breaks the kiss for a moment. His hand reaches behind his head as he pulls his shirt off in one smooth motion. Dropping it on the floor with my dress. His hand slides over my jaw, landing in the hair at the nape of my neck as he buries his fingers into it. His other one grips my ass, squeezing it before dragging his hand and fingers along it between my cheeks. Finding the waistband of my underwear, gripping it and tugging it down my body.

My hands go to the button on his shorts, undoing it, sliding my hands in, pushing his shorts and underwear down together. He growls low in his chest as I wrap my hand around his shaft, he hisses against my mouth as I tighten my hand around giving him a slow pump.

"Ava." He chokes out my name as I work my hand down and back up his cock, repeatedly, my pace painfully slow. I tighten my grip on him "fuck" he grounds out. Both his hands grip my ass, hoisting me up, I wrap my legs around his waist. Our mouths find each other again, hard and fast. Marcus carries me a few steps back to the table, setting my ass on it.

"I'm sorry. I wanted to take my time with you, but I can't; I need to be in you, Ava." He says raggedly against my lips, lining himself up with my entrance and driving into me in one hard thrust.

"A-Ah," I rasp out, my breath stolen with that one thrust. My head drops back as he enters me; the slight sting does nothing but unleash something carnal in me. His hand finds my throat and grips it, keeping me sitting up as he drives into me. I place my hands behind me on the table to meet his punishing pace. Marcus looks down between us, watching our bodies as he pushes in and out of me. His hand tightened around my throat with a primal need as he watches himself disappear into my body.

His pace slows with each thrust his hand leaves my hip and goes between us, spreading me with his fingers, mesmerized, watching himself fuck into me. The sight starts to unravel him, his motions becoming less controlled. His eyes close tight, as he stops moving inside me, pulling me closer to him and kissing me again; this kiss is slow and tender, with a reverence in it. I move my hips slowly, coaxing him to do the same.

"Ava, if you keep moving, I am going to cum." He pants out at me.

"Then make me come with you," I tell him, my voice ragged. He looks at me for a moment like he has no idea what I'm saying, and then a devilish smile passes over his beautiful face. He pulls out of me and drops to his knees his fingers still spreading me as his tongue delves in and out of my entrance before licking up my pussy and claiming my clit with his mouth. He sucks and licks my orgasm already so close. He drags his teeth over the sensitive bud, and my pussy clenches, and my body tightens as I come.

My orgasm is still rolling over me as he gets to his feet and drives himself back into me. He pounds in and out of me as he chases his own orgasm. He starts to thrust erratically into me, and I know he's close. He reaches between us and strokes my clit, pressing down on it, causing another orgasm to roll over me before the first one completely subsided. I clench around him and he lets out a strained curse as he cums in me. His last few thrusts are deep in me as he rides the last of his pleasure out.

Panting, he grabs my face and drags it to his own and kisses me. Kisses me gently, so beautifully. Kissing my lips gently, he pulls back and stares at me, looking at me like I'm the reason he breathes. He's looking into my eyes, searching for something.

I just see him.

I see my best friend.

I feel his cum sliding down my thighs and the magnitude of what we just did overwhelms my brain.

He watches it happen, watches the fear start to corrupt what we just shared, and sees the words run through my mind.

What we were yesterday, we will never be it again.

"No! Don't you fucking dare. This is a good thing. We didn't fuck anything up. It's you and me, just like always. None of that has changed." His eyes are desperately searching mine. I know what he's looking for. I also know he isn't going to see it. At least not in the way he feels it for me. I can see the pain in his eyes. He takes a steading breath. "Ava, this changes nothing. We are still us. We are still going to finish what we've started, none of that has changed."

"Marcus, how does this not change anything?" I plead, looking at him to fix it somehow.

"Because we don't let it. Ava, I love you. I have loved you since I was seven years old. I've been in love with you for almost as long. This here tonight is everything I've ever wanted. To have you like this. To know you're mine in every way. Please, baby, don't let your big brain take this from us. Don't think about the odds or any of that shit. Just look at me. See me." He takes my hand and places it on his chest, and I can feel his heart beating there. "That's for you. My heart is yours, and it always has been."

I look up at him, as the first tear slip past my lashes. "I'm scared, Marcus. You are all I have. Having you with me for my entire life is why I've done all of it. Because I knew I would have you beside me for the good and the bad. But sex, sex always complicates things, and I CANNOT lose you."

He wipes my tears away, kissing my cheeks, eyes, lips, and forehead. "Ava, we can do this. We can do it because we will always have our friendship to fall back on as a solid base. Nothing can tear that down."

I look at him, seeing the certainty in his eyes. I look at my hand on his chest, feeling it in the steady beat of his heart. I feel the truth in his words that he loves me. And I do love this man. I decided to love him when I offered Mr. Waffle all those years ago. Whatever comes now, whatever becomes of us, I'll know that this was the moment I made the choice. I chose to give him everything I could give him. His heart beating under my palm, promising me so much.

You may not be in love with him like he is with you, but you love him enough to give him all the rest.

I school my features, removing any uncertainty I feel so he can't see it there. I never want him to see it there. "Okay."

"Okay," he repeats, that one word filled with relief.

CHAPTER TWENTY THREE

"Once Upon a Poolside" by The National plays throughout the house. I'm sitting at the island having breakfast. Marcus is outside talking on the phone. He's speaking Russian, so I know he's talking to someone in his family. I finish my breakfast and place my dishes in the dishwasher. As he finishes up his call and strolls back into the house. He's only wearing board shorts, and his tanned chest and abs make my mouth water.

"These Arms of Mine" by Otis Redding starts. "I love this song," I remark casually.

"I know you do." Marcus says, "this playlist is called Ava. I made it for when I'm with you because nobody wants to deal with cranky Ava when she doesn't like the music." I don't say anything to that, but I flip him off in a playful, familiar way.

After we get dressed, I have to head to the bank to finish a few things. Marcus has some work to do finalizing a few of our plans before we head back to the States.

"I'll see you in a bit," I called over my shoulder to him.

I close the door behind me and slide my sunglasses onto my face. The morning heat from the sun is just starting to become too much. I'm wearing a simple grey dress with one side gathered at the mid-thigh. I paired it with simple black leather flip-flops, the perfect footwear for a leisurely day in town.

I make my way into the heart of town, stopping here and there to look at the flowers and pet a couple of dogs out with their owners for a stroll. I stop in a little bodega a few doors down from the bank and get a fresh raspberry mint iced tea. I sip the cold drink, enjoying the tartness mixed with the coolness of the mint.

I open the bank door, and Brynn Walters, my account manager, greets me. "Good morning, Ava."

"Morning, Brynn." I follow her back to her office and sit on the couch. She goes to her desk, grabs her laptop and some papers, and then joins me in the chair on my right.

"So, I have all the finalized paperwork for you to sign. All the properties and investments you wanted to unload have been sold. You did well, great profits across the board."

"That's great. You did an amazing job, Brynn."

"It's my job, but I'm pleased with how it went."

"You should be. This is more than I expected, to be honest. I'm adding another 5% to your commission on these sales. You deserve it. You made this the easiest process ever."

"Ava, that is not necessary. My commission is already the biggest one I've ever garnered."

"I'm glad to hear that, but I'm still doing it, Brynn. You deserve the money, and that's that."

She nods at me, and I nod at her. We both smile at each other. "I like you, Brynn. I hope we can work together for many years to come."

"I feel the same, Ava. It has been an absolute pleasure."

It takes another hour to finish signing and going over everything before we stand and shake hands. Brynn walks me to the door and wishes me well. I head out into the mid-day heat.

I walk towards home for about ten minutes when I feel eyes on me.

"Miss me?" I ask him.

"I did. I got bored waiting for you."

"Why didn't you go for a swim or watch a movie?" I ask him.

"I thought it would be more fun to come meet you. One of these days, I will sneak up on you." I snort a laugh at that. He has been trying to sneak up on me for years and has yet to be able to take me by surprise. "I stopped and had a sandwich at the little stand over there," he informs me, pointing across the street. "Then I got a beer from that pub there. Then I got an ice cream from the bodega beside the bank."

"Wow, that's a lot in a short time," I tell him, laughing.

"So, how did it go?" he inquires.

"Good. Everything is in order."

"Perfect."

Marcus's phone rings with a text notification: "It's Alexi. He will be here first thing in the morning."

"What?" I ask, genuinely surprised by this announcement.

"I was talking to him this morning, and he wants to come enjoy the ocean before we leave here. He was in New York, so he booked himself on the next flight here."

"Well, that'll be fun," I say, my sarcasm not masked one bit.

"I want Alexi as my second." I nod at that statement. I knew it was coming. I don't like Alexi and trust him even less than Enzo. I could stop it if I wanted, but I don't want to work for Marcus like that. I have no desire to be part of the

Mafia world. They're loud and messy, and women are not accepted for the most part. "So, he's going to come here so I can go over some things with him for when we return to New York. Besides, I need my team. I don't know how many will be left standing after we move on Enzo. I feel like it makes sense to have my family."

"It does. I expected the Sokolovs to fill in any spots you needed filled. But speaking of Enzo. Marcus, it really would be easier and cleaner just to kill him."

"Ava, my father is going to pay for throwing me away. He will pay with his pride and status. When he signs the family over to me, he will do it on his knees at my feet like the piece of shit he is. I want him to live, wondering if I'm going to kill him. I want him to live the rest of his days out in squalor."

"That is the plan. I just wanted to offer up an easier option one last time."

"Thanks," he says with a chuckle.

"What do you want to do for the rest of the day?" I ask as we keep walking towards the house.

"I'm open to anything. I thought you would probably want to swim in the ocean today."

I grin at him, "You know me so well! That is exactly what I want to do. I want to swim, read, and listen to music. Oh, and eat! Speaking of eating, I'm hungry. We should grab a lobster sandwich from that little dive a block from the house."

"Anything you want, Ava." He tells me his words soft.

We spend the day at the beach, enjoying the water, sun and reading. Marcus finally finished *Soul Eater* and decided to read the entire *Monstrous* series by Lily Maine. When we get back to the house, he heads inside to shower quickly and then drives to grab our dinner. He kisses me goodbye before he leaves. My fingers go to my lips, feeling them, remembering his kiss, thinking how it seems impossible to me that he kisses me now. As I dial a number, I stand on the deck, watching the sun go down over the ocean. She answers on the second ring.

"Ava!" Beth's voice sounds so happy to hear from me.

"How are you? How's Marcus?"

"Ah, we're good. Just relaxing, enjoying the sun and ocean."

"I bet you are."

"What?" I ask, puzzled by her statement.

"How long did it take him?"

"Take him to do what?"

"Don't play dumb, Ava. It's not becoming on you."

"How did I never see it, Beth?"

"I don't know Ava. That boy has been in love with you since he met you."

"Why didn't you ever tell me? Or even hint at it? Give me a heads-up. I told him all about Finn when I was dating him. Fuck, Beth, I told Marcus as soon as I got home after I lost my virginity to Finn."

"Language, Ava. It was not mine or Harry's place to tell you."

"Harry knew?" I screech.

"Ava honey, you're gonna need to accept that everybody but you knew."

"Fucking hell."

"Language." Beth scolds me again, and it brings a smile to my face.

"I still can't believe nobody let it slip for all those years. I mean, Parker has the biggest mouth ever."

"And you? Do you love him, Ava?" She asks me quietly. Like she's worried the question is out of line.

"Of course I do!" I tell her, offended that she asked me that.

"No, I know you love him. You decided he was yours years ago and never looked back. What I mean is, are you in love with him like he is with you? Marcus is charming, gorgeous, and knows you better than anyone. He always wants to make you happy and see you smile. So, falling into his bed after he tells you he loves you is easy. Anyone would, but are you in love with him?"

"Beth, if I can't love Marcus, the person who knows all my deep, dark secrets, I will probably never love anyone like that. And I love him enough and in enough ways that being with him, giving him what he wants far exceeds the life I thought I'd have."

"Oh, Ava." I hear the pain in her voice. The pain she feels for me over my own words.

"Beth, my parents died when I was seven. I was sent to a place by a biological mother I have never known. Harry trained me to hurt and kill people. Happy is not something I ever really am. I enjoy things, and I have sarcasm and snide comments down pat. But happy? I think when you have a beginning to life like I did, happy as most people see it, is not something I'll ever have or be."

Beth doesn't say anything at first. Then I hear Harry's voice, making me realize I was on speakerphone this whole time. "We know Little Ava, but we love you like our own, so we need to know you have some joy in your life."

"I know you guys. I was so lucky to have you. No matter how my life started or how it ends, I will forever be grateful that I had the two of you. I should go. Marcus will be back with food any minute and I need a quick shower. Night, you two,"

"Night, Little Fury," Harry says.

"Night, Ava." Beth adds.

I disconnect the call, placing it down on the charger and turn on some music. "Radio Ga Ga" By Queen comes on, and I turn it up as I head into my room and the bathroom to shower. I put my hair up in a messy bun, peel off my damp suit, and turn the water lukewarm, I step in. My skin is warmed from the sun, and the cooler water feels nice. I wash myself, getting the last bits of sand off my body, then step out, wrapping my body in a towel.

Walking into my bedroom, I hear someone in the house. Instantly knowing it's not Marcus, I tense. He would've come into the bathroom or yelled that he was back. I grab shorts and a tank top and throw them on quickly. I snag my gun as I head out of my room onto the patio. I click off the safety, making my way down the deck toward the doors that open into the house.

I step onto the deck, thankful for the clouds tonight. The moon can be very bright off the ocean, but tonight, the moon is hidden, so the light is minimal. I approach the open patio doors, careful to stay in the shadows. I see them then. Two men in black are quietly moving through the house. I make my way closer to the open door on the deck, keeping my eyes on them. I step over the threshold into the house my bare feet moving me silently.

Both men have their guns out as they head towards my room. They aren't looking behind them, having entered here from where I'm currently watching them. I raise my gun and shoot the first one in the head, His body hits the marble floor with a slap. The second man reacts quickly, and my shot misses him, embedding itself into the wall behind him. He raises his gun at me. We look at each other, my gun trained on him just like his is trained on me.

He slides the deadbolt into place, answering my first question about who they're here for. I see Marcus's house key on the table by the door.

Fuck. That's not great for me.

"Miriam" by Norah Jones comes on over the speakers. I can't stop the laugh and smile that song emits from me.

"What's so funny, Ava?" he asks.

I cock my head at him. "Hmm, you know my name. What's so funny, sir, is that if you knew this song, you would know it's about a man who kills a woman for cheating on him. Not saying I cheated on you, but it's still rather amusing. Out of all the songs that could have come on, this song seems slightly poetic." He just stares at me.

"NO? You don't see the poetry in it?" I pause, waiting for an answer, but none comes. "All right, are we doing this? Should we do like 3,2,1, shoot? Or do you want to put the guns down and see if you can take me? Honestly, I'm open to either. You look like a one-on-one kinda guy. Am I right?"

"You're a little crazy, aren't you, sugar."

"Aww, sweetheart, if you only knew. But really, what's it going to be? Marcus will be back soon, and then it'll be two-on-one, so your odds go significantly down."

"You sure about those odds?"

There's a tone to his voice that gives me pause. A bit of smugness that he really shouldn't have. He knows something, or at least thinks he knows something I don't.

"Pretty sure, but really, can anyone ever be 100% sure of anything?"

"Seriously, you're fucking nuts, devochka."

"There it is." I smile slightly.

He instantly knows what he did. "I'm going to fucking enjoy this," he says in Russian.

"It's good for you to believe that; confidence in oneself is key," I reply my Russian surprising him.

Putting his gun onto the side table, all pretense gone now, I do as he did and place my gun on the dining room table. I keep my eyes on him waiting for him to make a move. He looks at me and sees a tiny female. I see that little leer that enters his eyes as he looks me up and down. He likes what he sees. Small female, nice boobs, bare feet, and for him, that all adds up to easily subdued. He comes at me fast. Believing his size alone is all he needs against me.

He isn't protecting himself at all, and I audibly sigh. He hears it, his eyes flash a question. But it's too late; he realizes his miscalculation but can't do anything to change his course. Someone obviously didn't tell him about Harry.

Whatever, not my problem.

I step to the side just as he swings at me, trying to knock me out. He misses, and the force of his swing causes him to lose his balance, which in turn forces him to use his arms for a moment to regain his balance, but it's too late. I punch him in the throat, and I feel the impact of my fist on his trachea.

Punching a person in the throat is just satisfying.

He drops to one knee, gasping for breath. I grab my gun from the table and put it to his head.

"OK, so I have a couple of questions for you, and I don't have much time, so I expect yes or no answers. I will only ask once. If you don't answer pretty much instantly, I will shoot you in all the painful places that hurt like fuck and let you die slowly. If you answer, I'll shoot you in the head, and it'll be over fast. You won't feel a thing."

"Does that seem fair?" I give him a moment. He's still gasping for air. But the moment passes, and he still doesn't answer, so I sigh, take his hand, and shoot two of his fingers off.

He makes a horrible sound that I can't even begin to categorize.

"Let's try again. Does that seem fair?"

He nods his head, glaring at me with hate.

"Now I need to know who sent you. So, I will say a couple of names, and you will nod yes or no. M'kay?"

Again, he nods.

"Great! "

"Enzo Rossi?"

He's moving his head, but it's not a yes or no. "I'm going to need some clarification there."

He lifts the hand I shot and tips it from side to side.

"Alexi Sokolov?"

Again, with the side-to-side hand gesture, that's surprising. His answers imply they are working together.

"Thank you," I tell him

"Fill your Brains" by Harrison Brome starts to play, and I can't help but chuckle again. He looks at me, so I explain. "The name of this song is 'Fill Your Brains.' And since I'm about to shoot you in yours, you can see the humor in that parallel, can't you?"

He looks at me then. He really looks at me. You can see the moment it clicks. "You see it now, don't you?"

A smirk lifts the corner of his mouth. "Alexi is in for quite a surprise where you're concerned, devochka. He has no idea what you really are." He bows his head; I press my gun to it and pull the trigger.

CHAPTER TWENTY FOUR

I walk to the door and unlock it. I stand looking at the two dead bodies in the room and sigh loudly. Fuuuck, I really don't want to clean this shit up.

You made the mess; you clean it up.

"Fucking HELLLLL!"

I walk back to my room to grab my phone. "Well, hello there, Little Fury," Sebastian says on the first ring.

"Hey, how's it going? You miss me yet?"

"Oh, Ava, you know it. What do you need?"

"Why do I need to need anything? Maybe I miss hearing your annoying voice."

"Ava, I'm on a job, so spit it out, buttercup."

"Do you know anyone in the Caymans who cleans?"

"Did you finally wise up and kill Marcus?"

"Seriously, dude, not funny."

I hear him chuckle. "Yeah, let me make a call."

"Thank you, Sebastian. Oh, and please don't tell Harry or the guys."

"No promises on that, Little Fury. Try to stay out of trouble." He disconnects the call.

"Wonder how long it'll take till Harry calls me?" I ask dead guy number two.

I see headlights through the windows by the front door. Marcus is back.

"Fuck Ava, sorry that took so long. The Shanty Hut was busy." He calls as he heads into the kitchen to place the food on the counter. "Ava?"

"Here," I call as I walk into the kitchen. He looks at me, unsure of what he sees on my face. He looks me up and down, and I know the moment he sees blood splatter on my legs and shorts.

"What happened?" He asks, quirking an eyebrow at me.

I take his hand and lead him into the great room. He takes in the two dead men on the floor and chuckles. "Guess they should have sent more men."

"Fuck off Marcus. But also, yes, they should have."

"Any idea who they are or who sent them?"

"None. They were dead before I could ask them anything." I lie.

Why are you lying to him, Ava? My inner voice asks me condescendingly.

"I just got off the phone with Sebastian, and he's making a call for me. So, I expect a cleaner will be here in the next hour. Let's eat. I'm starving now."

Marcus nods his head, not looking at me. Instead, he keeps his eyes rooted on the men on the floor. He turns towards the kitchen. "Ava, did I see fingers on the floor?"

"Yeah, I shot one in the hand when he called me a bitch after I shot his friend in the head."

"You couldn't have just shot him in the head as well? Shooting off his fingers was the only option?" He asks as he grabs the food, takes it out of the bag, and lays it on the island.

I grab a couple of beers out of the fridge and pop the tops off, handing him one. "I mean, I could have just shot him in the head, but really, he broke into our house trying to kill us; he called me a bitch, and it annoyed me."

Marcus studies me, looking for a lie, but he won't see any. Harry is really the only one who can. I grab a beer-battered shrimp and pop it in my mouth. He shakes his head, and smiles, then begins to eat. "How long will it take Harry to call you, do you think? "

"Ha! I thought he would have already, but Sebastian is on a job, so he might be unable to tattle on me for a bit." There's a knock at the door, so I pop another shrimp in my mouth and head over to meet the cleaners.

There is a tiny little black woman at my door. Her greying curls and sweet smile make me want to hug her and ask her to bake me cookies.

Wow, you're never having a grandma is showing, Ava.

"Hello," I say

"Hello, dear," she says, and I melt. She called me dear. All she needs to do now is pat my hand and tell me everything will be okay, and I'll ask her to adopt me.

"I'm Mrs. Bodden. These are my sons Anthony and Michael." Both men nod at me when their mamma introduces them. "Sebastian said you needed some cleaning looked after."

"Yes. Come in, please. Would any of you like a drink? Coffee, tea, water, beer?"

"I would love a spot of tea. Boys?" Mrs. Bodden says.

"Water," both guys say in unison.

The guys start to carry in plastic bags, tape, and cleaning supplies. I lead them to the great room where the mess awaits.

Marcus brings a couple of water bottles for them. The three of them nod at each other, and then Anthony and Michael get to work.

Mrs. Bodden joins us in the kitchen, where I've put the kettle on to make her a pot of tea. Marcus pulls the tea basket down to let Mrs. Bodden choose what she wants.

She chooses a black tea. "Do you need cream or sugar?" Marcus asks

"No, I like my tea black, but thank you, dear."

Marcus puts out some cookies and crackers.

"We were just eating. Do you mind if we finish?" I ask her.

"No, dears, eat."

Marcus and I finish our meals while Mrs. Bodden has tea and a few cookies. Michael comes into the kitchen about 45 minutes later. "Done," he informs us

"That was fast," I say.

"It was a pretty clean kill site, Miss. Not a lot of splatters or damage. Whoever did it was very efficient, except the fingers. So, it made our job easy."

"All right, dears. Then we will be out of your hair. I'll send the bill to Sebastian."

"Thanks so much." I say.

We walk them to the door, and the guys pull out a couple of heavy suitcases. "Oh! Do you want to know where to find your bags should you need them again?" She asks me.

"If you could send that information with the bill to Sebastian, that would be great."

We say goodbye and close the door.

"You, ok?" Marcus asks me.

"I am," I assure him.

"I'm going to jump in the shower and clean up. Want to watch a movie?"

"Yeah, but let's watch it in bed. I'm pretty sure you're going to fall asleep during it."

"You are probably correct," I tell him as I leave him and walk to my bedroom.

I take off my clothes and place them in the garbage bin. I'll burn them later.

I step into the shower, turning the water on hot, seeming to have found a chill over the last couple hours. My mind wanders, thinking about Alexi and Enzo working together to eliminate me. Alexi is cunning. If he can get rid of me and have Enzo take the blame, he will have Marcus all to himself, well, to the Sokolovs, to be precise. I have to admit, Alexi has bigger balls than I thought.

I finish showering and wrap my hair in a towel and another around my body. I can hear Marcus in the bedroom. I leave the bathroom and see him putting a water bottle and popcorn on my bedside table. "Aww, look at you taking care of me."

"Always," He replies.

I'm hit with the intensity of what he feels for me. I haven't entirely accepted it; I walk over to the dresser and grab a pair of sleep shorts and a crop tank top. I drop my towel and look at Marcus in the mirror as I slip them on. His eyes drink me in. I am starting to love the feeling of his eyes on me; seeing that kind of want in anyone's eyes is intoxicating.

I crawl on the bed and get under the covers, propping up my pillows to be movie ready. "What are we watching?"

"What do you want to watch, Ava? I'm not the picky one out of the two of us."

"But this was your idea, so I thought you had a movie in mind."

"Ava, we have been watching movies together since we were seven. In all those years, have I ever had a movie in mind?"

"Didn't you suggest we watch *Dumbo* once?"

"I did, and how did that go? Do you remember? Because I do." He deadpans.

"Seriously, someone needs to tell a child that they are going to have their hearts ripped out over a baby elephant whose mom just wanted to protect him! And whoever decided on "Baby Mine" while his mamma was swinging him on her trunk through her cage door needs a psych evaluation. Cause that was just evil," I spew, not taking a breath. I had to stop watching it because I couldn't stop crying. And I cried for days after. It's honestly one of my worst childhood memories.

"Correct. So, you pick the movie."

"Let's watch The *Princess Bride* or *Labyrinth*. I'm in the mood for old-school nostalgia."

Marcus grabs the remote, does a quick search, and finds *Labyrinth*. He starts it up, and I happily snuggle into the bed with him and popcorn.

Marcus falls asleep before the movie ends, but I keep watching, not ready for sleep yet. When it's over, I turn the TV off and put my empty bowl on the table beside the bed. I look over and see his isn't empty; it's on the bed beside him. I get on my knees and lean over him.

Grabbing his bowl I stop to look at him. I see the boy I've always known in his face when he sleeps. All the worries that weigh him down are gone. He looks calm. I place his bowl in mine on the side table; Beth's words keep playing in my head. Maybe I need to stop this now. What if I never love him like he loves me? Is it fair to him? How do I even talk to him about it?

Looking at him, I lean over and place a kiss on his lips. Its soft and gentle. He stirs under my kiss as I grow a little bolder It's slow, but it deepens the more awake he becomes. I hear a soft moan from him, his hands finding me. He lifts me in one smooth movement so I'm straddling him. He keeps his hands on me and sits up to meet my mouth.

His hands glide up my sides, sliding under my top, squeezing my breasts, skimming over my nipples; they harden under his touch. Marcus breaks his kiss only long enough to remove my shirt. I grind against him, feeling him grow hard under me.

I'm on my back, and Marcus is looking down at me before it even registers in my brain that he flipped us. He's staring at me. We're staring at each other. His hand comes up to my face, his thumb rubbing over my bottom lip. My tongue darts out to lick it, and I suck it into my mouth, my tongue swirling around it. Marcus pulls his thumb out of my mouth and kisses me gently.

My eyes close. It's slow and sensual. His hand trails along my neck, over my collarbone. My hands glide down his back, and I feel the lean muscles there. I grip his ass, loving how firm it is. Sliding my hands into the waistband of his shorts, my hands caress his skin, feeling the heat from him warming me.

I work his shorts down over his hips. He lifts his body to help me. I use my feet to get them off him the rest of the way. Marcus's hand slides up my thigh as he rests on his other arm, staying just off my body so he can touch me. My hand slides over his body, making its way to his length. I run my fingers along the hard shaft, loving the velvety soft skin there. I grip him in my hand, feeling his hips buck. I feel his finger in my shorts, finding my wet folds and running through them before he sinks it into me. I exhale a gasp at the sensation of his finger inside me. I grab him tighter, and I move my hand up the thick shaft closing it over the head. I slide my hand back down, forcing the head of his cock to push through a tightly clasped junction of my thumb and index finger. He hisses at the sensation pumping into my hand. "Jesus," he grits out.

He takes his fingers out of me, grips my shorts, and pulls them down my legs. I grab him tighter, bringing my hand to the head of his cock, feeling a couple of drops of precum, and using it to lubricate the head as he thrusts into my tight grip.

"Fuck" he says. Pulling my hand away, he pins both my hands above my head. Settling himself between my legs, he takes his cock and rubs himself up and down my clit, forcing a needy moan out of me. He notches the head at my entrance and pushes in slowly.

"Ahh, god, Marcus fuck," I breathe out.

"Fuck, you feel so good, Ava," he says as he buries himself in me entirely. I arch my back off the mattress. He releases my hands, and I find his ass with them instantly, feeling his muscles as he pumps into me. He drops his full weight on me, and I love it. I love the pressure of his body on mine. He moves in and out of me, and I move my hips to meet him for every movement. He brings his face to mine. "I love you, Ava."

"Marcus," I whisper, bringing my hand to his face to touch him so that I can lower his lips to mine. I kiss him; it's slow and gentle, and there is nothing hurried or rushed in the kiss or the rhythm of our bodies. I realize then what this is. What we're doing. This isn't sex or fucking. This is making love. Marcus is making love to me.

I deepen the kiss between us, my tongue finding his, coaxing a moan from him in response. I run my hands down the planes of his back and over his ass. I tighten my grip on him, trying to move him faster inside me, needing to change his intention. "Please, baby. I need to come."

He breaks the kiss, moving his lips to my neck, kissing and biting that spot I love so much. My breathing starts to increase as his thrusts get faster and harder. He lifts from me, hooking my legs over his arms. Placing his hands just past my hips on the bed, the position almost folding me in half. He is so deep in me, with every thrust hitting a spot inside of me, an intense pressure starts to build quickly. Over and over, he hits that spot; his fervent pace makes it hard for me to think. "Please, please," I beg him.

"What do you need? Tell me." Marcus's voice is strained. I know he is holding himself back, trying to prolong this torture.

"It's too much; I can't." I cry out, his body never stopping driving into me, into that spot.

"I know what you need, baby." Releasing one of my legs, he forces my other leg farther back, keeping me open to him. His body and fingers find a pace driving me mad; tears running down my face, my words incoherent as he drives my body towards oblivion, and my body explodes into it.

My body shatters as I come. Marcus groans over me as I spasm around his cock, milking his orgasm from him as he follows me over the edge. He collapses on top of me, both of us panting for breath. Once his breathing evens out, he removes his weight from me, sitting back on his heels. "Fuck Ava, that was the hottest thing ever. You came all over my cock. Your cum is everywhere." Marcus bends down over me and licks up the entirety of my pussy; flicking my clit with his tongue when he reaches it. I react instantly and grab his hair. "Marcus," I gasp.

"Ava, I caused the mess, I think I should be the one to clean it up." Without even waiting to hear any protest I might have; he dives back between my legs and feasts on me. He licks every inch of me, cleaning every drop of my orgasm. He pushes his tongue into me. The sounds coming from his mouth as he laps up my orgasm are erotic and dirty. My brain is a mess from the orgasm he is cleaning up. I feel tears running down my cheeks, my mind telling me I can't possibly come again. But he is driven. His tongue is still inside me, still pumping in and out, drinking in our combined mess. His tongue leaves my pussy, continuing its path. His noises are feral as he follows my cum towards my asshole. I try to squirm away from his mouth, but my body is too soft and pliant under his firm grasp. He keeps me in place and finishes his mission. His tongue enters me, his hands spreading my ass so he can reach every spot. His tongue works in and out of my tight hole; his thumb works my clit.

I have nothing left, but somehow, he forces more from me. Pleasure and pain envelope my body as this orgasm rips through me. My scream at its release is guttural. Everything, he takes everything. I hear him moan his approval as he keeps his tongue going in and out of my ass, and he keeps circling my clit until my pussy stops clenching. "So, fucking perfect." I hear as the world fades to black.

CHAPTER TWENTY FIVE

I wake up the following day alone in bed again. But this time, I can smell bacon. I grin like a madwoman because I'm hungry this morning.

No kidding, you horn dog, anyone who got railed like you last night would wake up hungry.

I smirk at my sarcasm, grab a dress off the back of the bedroom door, and slip it over my head. It's a simple black maxi dress with thin straps and V- neck. I walk down the hall toward the kitchen when I hear a voice that isn't Marcus's. *Fuck.* I forgot Alexi was arriving this morning. I enter the kitchen and smile at the guys. "Morning! How was your flight, Alexi?" I walk towards the coffee maker; Marcus grabs me and brings me in for a kiss.

"Morning," he says, releasing me. I approach the coffee maker, select my pod and all the extras, and request a dark roast coffee with cream. I turn around and face the guys as I wait for my it.

"I hear you had a run-in with some men last night," Alexi tells me in broken English.

"Yeah, it was very unexpected, that's for sure. They must have been watching the house and waited until Marcus was gone. I'm glad for that anyway. It would kill me if anything happened to him while some assholes from God knows what family tried to kill me." I say to Alexi.

"Well, I wish I had been here because they sure as fuck would not have been let off so easy. I would have made sure to get some names from them." Marcus tells Alexi and me.

"Of course, you would have, Marcus. We have ways to make others talk. Someone tiny like Ava is better off taking them out fast instead of risking them getting the better of her," Alexi says, staring at me.

I cock my head to the side and lift one side of my mouth. Alexi meets my eyes, and I give him the barest of eyebrow lifts and a look of 'Don't bullshit a bullshitter.' "Well, I did shoot off a couple fingers of the one guy. So at least he suffered a bit of pain before the bullet to his head." I hear Marcus chuckle.

"How long till breakfast? I'm starving." I ask.

"Sit down; it's almost ready. When this is all over and we're home, we're hiring a staff to feed you 24 hours a day."

"That is the dream."

He shakes his head at me.

"We have things to discuss, Marcus," Alexi says in Russian.

Miss Bennett was a lot of things, but the next time I see her, I'm going to give her the biggest kiss on the mouth ever, thanking her for forcing me to learn so many languages. It's obvious Alexi doesn't know I speak Russian, and when I think about it I'm not sure if Marcus has any idea of the languages she had me learn. Biggest mouth kiss ever, coming her way.

He says nothing, just nods at Alexi.

"Ava, sit."

"Yes, sir."

Marcus looks at me and cocks an eyebrow.

He hands me my plate loaded with eggs, bacon, potatoes, and toast. "Sir, sounds good coming out of your mouth," He whispers against my ear, sending a shiver through my body. I give him the slightest nod, then sit down and dig in. Marcus hands a plate to Alexi and sets one down for himself. We eat, listening to the sounds of the waves on the beach.

"What do you guys have planned today?" I ask them.

"Business," Alexi tells me.

Marcus looks at him and shakes his head. "Our grandfather needs a few things," he tells me.

"Okay. Well, I have a few things of my own that I'll get done for us since we are only here for another two days." I get up and clear my dishes. I open the dishwasher, put everything in it, and turn it on. "Have a good day, boys," I call over my shoulder as I go to my room to get a few things before I leave.

My door opens, and Marcus walks in. "Thank you for breakfast. It was delicious." I tell him.

"You're welcome. What are you going to do today?"

"Just checking a couple of things for when we get to New York."

"Have dinner with me later?" he asks, wrapping his arms around me.

"Sure, text me where and when. How long is Alexi here? Is he flying back to New York with us?"

"No, he's only here for today. He flies back out at nine tonight. So, we'll have to have a late dinner so I can drop him off at the airport."

"Works for me." I look up at him and rise on my tiptoes to kiss him.

Marcus's hand slides down over my ass, feeling my lack of underwear, and he groans into my mouth. "So, fucking hot."

I smile against him. I reach down and slide the straps of my dress down my arms, letting it fall down my body, leaving me naked in front of him. He sucks in a breath and kisses me.

He flings me onto the bed, and I squeal as he lands on top of me. His mouth on mine. He rolls his hips into me, and I feel him against my core. I wriggle against him, and he curses as I rub against his hardening cock. "Ava, I need to leave."

"Oh? Really? I have a vibrating friend in the drawer who can fill in for you so it's okay for you to go," I say cheekily.

He slides a finger into me, and I moan; his thumb is on my clit, demanding and fast as he works it. "Fuck," I moan loudly.

A loud banging on the door causes Marcus to pause. He drops his forehead to mine. "Fucking asshole," he grumbles. "Better make you come fast, or else he's liable to walk in here and drag me out." He leans back from me, sitting on his heels. "Quick and dirty, Ava."

He undoes his shorts pulling his cock out and fisting it as he watches me get on all fours. I turn away from him, spreading my legs and dropping onto my elbows on the bed.

"Fuck, look at your cunt perfectly presented for me." he moves off the bed, standing behind me. I look over my shoulder at him and see him spit into his hand and then rub it all over my exposed pussy, delving a couple of fingers into me. Satisfied, his hand grabs my ass, and I feel him line the head of his cock at my entrance. His hands grab my hips, and he pulls me back onto his waiting cock, impaling me in one swift motion. I cry out as he fills me; the slight pain of the abrupt intrusion feels good.

"Jesus, Ava, your pussy was fucking made for me."

He starts pounding into me, his fingers digging into the flesh on my hips. The sounds of our skin slapping against each other as he buries himself in me repeatedly leaves me panting. I can't form any words. My sounds are hums of begging him not to stop.

"Fuck, I'm going to come," he says, pulling out of me. "Marcus," I protest, feeling the loss of him inside me. "What drawer, Ava?" he asks with a sly smile.

"That one, top drawer." I point to my bedside table. He opens the drawer, and his eyes widen when he sees the treasure trove I have in there.

"Oh, Little Fury, we will do so many dirty things with this drawer later." He plucks a purple flower-shaped vibrator out of the drawer and raises an eyebrow at me.

"Ah yeah, that'll work," I tell him, and I can feel my cheeks heat. He turns it on, and his eyes go wide. The flower sucks and licks the clit; it has a small tongue-like mechanism. I turn over, getting off all fours and sitting up. He walks back to me, his dick still rock hard.

There is another loud bang on the door. "In a fucking minute Alexi. If you interrupt me again, I will come out there and break your fucking nose. Do you hear me?" Marcus yells. It's the first time I've ever caught a glimpse of the Mafia Don he was born to be, the one he will become in a few short days. There's no answer from Alexi, but we hear footsteps as he retreats.

Marcus cracks his neck, letting the anger fall away. "Now, where were we, beautiful?" I don't answer him. Instead, I just lay back down and let my legs fall apart for him. He smiles a predator's grin at my core, licking his lips. "I want to make that fucker wait longer."

"It's not him you have business to attend to for." I see the pause in him. The Boss in him is warring against the grandson.

Someone is starting to resent being told what to do.

He closes his eyes for a moment. When he opens them, he's still not the Marcus I want. I let my hand glide down my body sliding a finger inside myself, plunging it in and out a couple of times, and then dragging my slick over my clit, working it slowly. My eyes go back to his, and I see my Marcus again. "While I could watch you finger yourself all day, beautiful, I want to see what this little flower will do to you as I fuck you." His hand goes to his cock, stroking it. He hands me the toy. "Show me," he commands. I obey.

I place the flower over my clit and turn it on. My hips shoot off the mattress instantly from the sensation. Marcus strokes himself faster, tightening his grip on his cock as he watches the toy cause me to writhe before him. With a growl, he grabs my thighs and pulls me to the end of the bed, spreading me wide and lining himself up with me, and hammers into me. Between Marcus sliding in and out of me and the sucking on my clit I don't last even 45 seconds before I'm coming all over his cock.

My pussy clenches around him hard, the ferocity of my orgasm commanding him to come with me. Marcus drives into me three more times before he releases a yell with his orgasm. He drops onto one arm on the bed, catching his breath. "Holy fuck, Ava, toys are something we will be including a lot more often." I can't help but giggle when I answer him.

"Yes, sir."

He smiles at me, leans over, and kisses me thoroughly. He rises from the bed, tucks himself back into his shorts, and heads to the door. Shooting me a wink over his shoulder as he closes the door behind him.

I lay there for a moment, contemplating having a nap, but I groan and force myself to get up. I clean up in the shower quickly, when I'm done drying myself off I throw on a pair of underwear, then walk into my closet, I stand there and stare at everything in it, not sure what I want to wear today. I see a pair of cream-coloured linen pants, so I slip those on. I grab the matching vest and slip it on, doing up the three buttons as I make my way to the dining room table where my laptop is.

Opening it, I sign on when I see an incoming video call. I don't even have to guess who it is. I hit connect, and a very large and angry Scotsman is sitting there with his arms crossed, glowering at me.

"Are you seriously glowering at me?"

"Wanna tell me what happened there yesterday?" he growls at me.

"Not overly, to be honest. And I'd bet you ten grand Sebastian already told you the gist of it. So, I'm thinking you want to hear the whole thing from me so you can get even more annoyed and angry at me, and then you get to use that Scottish glower you're so proud of for longer. And glower at me harder."

I hear Beth laugh out loud at that, and I can't help but grin.

"Careful, Bethy. You're the only one here to work my frustrations out with," he practically purrs at her.

"Oh, eww. Really? Nope, let's go back to you guys pretending that everyone doesn't know you two are together. Back when sexual innuendos were not part of our conversations. Please."

Beth laughs again. "I told you everyone knew, Harry."

"You thought no one knew?" I grin at him. "Do you know how windows work? Like, I get that you're old and shit, but still. Cause windows, they do this crazy thing where they let the people on one side see what's going on, on the other side. It's super trippy, really. It's like you're almost in the same room as the other people. Even when those people are making out like teenagers."

Harry is unimpressed with me at the moment. He is getting redder by the second. He really does do the best unintentional Yosemite Sam impression when he gets like this.

"Ava, I did nae raise ye t'back talk me!" he yells at me.

"Um, actually, you did. You raised me to take no shit. You also fostered and helped me grow my sarcastic and smart-ass mouth. So, you need to maybe look in a mirror. And to help, a mirror is like a window. Both have glass but only one of them allows you to see things through it. The other, the mirror, shows you a reflection, so chances are, you'll be looking at yourself in it."

The screen goes black.

Did Harry just hang up on me?

How much trouble am I in? Am I grounded now?

My computer rings again, and I answer the video call right away. Beth's laughing face lights up my screen. "Hi!" I say, happy to see her.

"Heya," she says back.

"Did he finally explode? Did actual steam come out of his ears this time?"

"He's taking a moment," she tells me, laughing the whole time. We both laugh for a few more beats. I have tears in my eyes, and my abs hurt from laughing. "Okay, seriously, Beth, pull it together." She laughs again and shakes her head at me.

"Ok." Taking a deep breath, she continues. "What happened, Ava?"

I give her a quick rundown of the events last night. I pause when I reach the point in the story where I told Marcus something different than what happened. "Finish the story, Ava, the whole story, not whatever shite you told Marcus." I hear Harry say.

"Um, guy number two locked the deadbolt, telling me he was well aware Marcus was not in the house with me."

"What then?" Beth asks. Harry moves into view and

studies me through the screen, so I give in and tell them all the details.

"Guy two was mad I killed his buddy. I asked him if he wanted to have an old west shootout or if he would prefer to put the guns down and see if he could take me."

"Ava, why taunt the guy? Just shoot him," Beth asks me.

"Because I needed a couple answers. He took option two, thinking he could have a little fun with me before he killed me. He came at me fast, but his training was shit. He tried to take me down with one hit, but he missed. I punched him in the throat."

"Go on," Harry prompts.

"I asked him a couple questions. He didn't answer the first one right away, so I may have shot a couple of his fingers off." I see Harry's mouth quirk up at one side at that. "Then he answered the questions."

"And what questions did you ask him, Little Fury?"

"Well, Harry, I asked him who sent him."

There is a silence between us. Harry wants me to tell them, and I want him to ask for it.

So, instead, we sit there staring at each other.

"Guess who's visiting us here?" I say, breaking the silence.

Harry turns his head ever so slightly, asking who.

"Alexi," I say very matter-of-factly.

Harry says nothing, and neither does Beth. They look at each other, and Beth gets up and leaves the room.

"Where is she going?"

"She already knows anything I might say regarding Alexi and has a few things to do."

"Okay. "

"I'm going to assume Alexi's name came up when you asked who sent them?"

I don't answer. Instead, I raise my hand and tip it side to side, just like my buddy from last night.

"What do you mean, kind of?"

"Alexi and Enzo," I say leaving it hanging there for him. I sit quietly, letting him think about it.

"Well, that's not great if they're working together."

"Not great for me, no," I confirm for him.

"Okay, Parker is back in a couple of hours. I'll let you know what we can find out."

"OK, I need to talk to Parker. Can you have him call me when he gets back to the ranch? Also, I wired you some money for Sebastian for the cleaners last night. Can you get it to him for me?"

"I can do that."

"Great. Okay, Harry, I gotta go."

"I'll let you know what we find out."

I nod at him and end the call. I sit back in my chair and look out at the ocean. I'm going to miss this place when we leave. The development of Enzo being in bed with Alexi may complicate things for me. While I'm 99% sure Alexi is using Enzo so that if he succeeds in killing me, he can lay blame at his feet, so Marcus doesn't ever find out about his hand in it.

I realized a couple of years back that my relationship with Marcus wasn't exactly something his father or the Sokolovs were particularly fond of. Marcus has always listened to advice from his mother's family except where I'm concerned and, by association, the Ranch. I was never leaving the Ranch, so neither was Marcus. Enzo never cared or even bothered to check on his son until Mila's family decided they should check on the Russian princess's only child.

Mila's father may have doted on his daughter, giving her anything and everything, but after she died, out of grief, they left Marcus with his father and left the country. I believe they honestly thought the boy's father would raise and love him. They were very wrong, but I've seen Marcus's grandfather with him. I see the way he looks at him. He sees his daughter in Marcus, and he would never have left him with Enzo had he known just what that asshole was.

We will be in New York in two days, and the minute we arrive, Marcus won't wait to pay his father a visit. Enzo will happen fast. Then, it will take a few days for the lawyers and banks to transfer everything to the younger Rossi. I find I have no feelings about the older Rossi and what Marcus and I are about to reign down on him. The only change I would make would be to just kill Enzo. Marcus wants him to suffer, I think that will be very messy; but I am here to support only.

CHAPTER TWENTY SIX

I work for a couple of hours, only stopping when my phone rings and I see Parker's name appear.

"Hey." I say as I answer, "Give me one sec." I grab my headphones and turn them on. I hear the Bluetooth click on. "You there?" I ask.

"Yup, I'm here."

"How's things Parker?" I ask as I make my way out of the house and head towards the water. It's a very calm afternoon,

"Things are good. What's up, Ava? Tell Parker what you need," he asks me. I hear keys clicking in the background, telling me he's working while we chat.

"I need you to find me some candidates."

"What type?"

"I need a you to start, as well as my own Wes, Theo, and Sebastian," he laughs.

"I figured you would. I've started a list. I have a few

names you and Marcus will each like, so you will have to decide who works best for you guys."

"Actually, Parker, I need them just for me. I have a feeling Marcus will be receiving a few of his family members to fill those roles."

"Okay, then. Let me see. I have a couple of guys in mind for each of your specifications." I can hear the air quotes when he says "specifications." As I walk in the surf, enjoying the feel of the water on my feet, I can't help but laugh.

"And you've fully vetted them?"

"Ava Landry!!!! You did not just insult me like that," he says, his voice raised, clearly annoyed. I know he would never do a half-assed job.

"Sorry, I know you wouldn't give me names if they weren't solid. Just not thinking before I spoke." I tell him, my apology sincere.

"No worries. I've worked with all of them before. I've also tried to get Harry to hire each of them. But he keeps telling me we don't need another Theo or Sebastian and that we sure as fuck don't want another Wes with his mouth." I laugh out loud at that because it's all true. The ranch would be crazy with more of the same type of guys.

"Perfect. Send me their dossiers, and I'll take a look right away. I want to video meet them all today or tomorrow and then set up in-person meetings as soon as possible when I'm back in New York."

Parker and I chatted for another minute, talking music and sci-fi movies, Dune Part 1 being the dominant topic. We hung up, and three minutes later, as I was walking back to the house, I heard a notification that the dossiers had arrived.

I spent the next three hours going over the guys Parker sent me. I like them all, but I have my top picks. Ben Williams is young and has done some impressive hacks. Parker has noted that the kid is genius-level and think-tank smart.

Next is Caden Harker. He is older than me.

Ava, you're 20. They're all going to be older than you.

"Ben isn't," I mumble to the empty house.

Caden was a ranger. He did one tour and was given an honorable discharge after his brother and half his team were killed out on assignment and his mother was diagnosed with terminal brain cancer. He's an explosives expert and excels in small firearms. Lastly, there is Matt Forestt. Matt is a former MMA fighter. He coaches now and teaches self-defense classes after his little sister was killed by a mugger when she was 17.

Parker has included psychological evaluations for all the men. I see why he chose them. Matt and Caden have strong protective instincts regarding women and children. They both also have no problem, it seems, with a bit of questionable morality. And Ben is young, brilliant, and alone. According to his file, he bounced from foster home to foster home after his mom was killed by a drunk driver when he was eight. When he was fourteen, he hacked into the child welfare database and changed his date of birth so he would age out instantly. He's been supporting himself by writing code and doing smaller hack jobs for the last three years. Parker's notes all say that they all have strong loyalty tendencies and that all three will bond to form a strong unit. None of them have any indicators that make us think they won't work for a woman. They all seem more likely to, especially when that woman is strong and intelligent.

I send messages to the three of them, and I go to the kitchen to make myself a bite to eat. I open the fridge and see a bunch of fruit and veggies and cheese. I grab it all in my arms and turn to drop it on the island. I grab a big platter and begin arranging the food on it. I open the cupboard and find some delicious roasted almonds, crackers and a couple of cookies. "Perfect," I say to the empty house… "girl lunch!" I smile down at the food. My phone goes off, and I return to the table. I see it's a video call from Ben.

"Hello," I say, smiling at the screen.

"Oh shit, you're way hotter than I was expecting." I raise an eyebrow at him but can't help but smile at his bluntness.

"Hi, Ben, I'm Ava." I look at him. He's got dirty blonde hair that he has shaved on the sides, and the top is longer, falling over his forehead. He's skinny, still in his gangly teenager body. He has a cute face, the kind girls swoon over, and a dimple to boot. "Tell me about yourself, Ben."

"I know Parker, so I highly doubt there is anything you don't already know."

I bark out a laugh. "Fair enough. Favorite color?"

"Green, but like jade green."

"Favorite food?"

"I'm not picky, but I do love Indian."

"Favorite memory?" He doesn't raise an eyebrow or miss a beat when answering my odd questions.

"When I was six, my mom took me to a fair. She let me ride every ride and eat everything I wanted. I threw up and then asked for ice cream, and she bought it for me." He smiles at the memory.

"What do you know about me?" I ask him.

"I know you and your parents were in a car accident when you were seven. You survived; they didn't. You were adopted, and the situation of your adoption is odd. From what I could see when I hacked Parker's archives, your birth mother has pull with a lot of people. Because the adoption contract between her and your parents was like nothing I've ever seen before, I also, no matter how hard I tried, couldn't find out who she was, and I looked. She paid some very skilled people to make all records of her giving birth to you disappear from existence. What else? Harry Baird trained you, and every single record I've seen or watched says you're fucking good. You were also raised by Beth, along with Marcus Rossi."

I'm impressed with his rundown of me. Parker works hard at keeping all of our digital footprints to a minimum. "Well done, Ben. I'll be in New York in a couple of days. I want to meet you in person. Can you be in New York on the 17th? I'll have a room for you at the Hilton in midtown."

"I can do that."

"Parker will send you your ticket and flight info. There will be a car for you at the airport. I look forward to meeting you in person, Ben."

"Me too, boss."

I shake my head at him and disconnect the call. I eat a bit of the food I have in front of me. I turn on the sound system and select a playlist. "California Dreamin' By the Mammas and the Papas starts playing.

I let my mind wander momentarily and hear my phone ring again. I look at the screen; it's Caden Harker.

I answer the video call, "Hello, Caden."

"Hello, Miss."

"How are you?"

"I'm well, Miss, thank you."

"Caden, please call me Ava."

"Ava," he says, trying it out.

"You were a ranger? Do you miss it?"

"I was, and I do, but only because I miss the order; I miss the regiment of it all," he says evenly.

"I'm sorry about your guys and your mom."

"All good, Ava. It's just life."

"Favorite colour?"

His lip twitches the tiniest bit, "Purple," he says, and I hear it.

"Gonna need that explained, Caden. Not many grown

men have the color purple as their favorite unless you're a Vikings fan?"

He looks at me, narrowing his eyes. "Not a Vikings fan. My mom loved purple. Obsessively loved it. It's ingrained in my DNA, seeing as how I grew up surrounded by it."

"And now, when you think of purple, you get warm fuzzies remembering your mama," I say, not looking for confirmation. But he does, nodding his head at me.

"Favorite food?"

"Fresh baked bread."

I let him see that I was surprised by that answer.

"What do you know about me?"

"You're smart, really well trained, lost your parents young and now you do bad things."

"Ha," I bark out. "Yes, that's all correct. How do you feel about doing bad things?"

It's his turn to laugh. "Parker filled me in, Ava. I wouldn't have called if I couldn't give 100% to you and our team. I follow orders well. I'm better than good with explosives. I'm trained to be calm in all situations. I know your history, and I would be happy to work for you."

"Perfect! Parker will contact you with your plane tickets and hotel information. I need you in New York on the 17th. Does that work?"

"It does. See you then, Ava."

"See you soon, Caden." He disconnects the call.

I get a text from Parker; Matt will video call in a couple of hours as he is at a U-9 jiu-jitsu tournament. Looking at the time, I still have about four hours before Marcus will be ready to meet for dinner. The ocean is calling me; I head to my bedroom and change into one of my bathing suits. It's a pink string bikini. I love the color against my tanned skin, and my ass looks great in it. I spray myself with sunscreen, grab a wide-brim hat and a towel, and head to the water.

The beach is quiet for such a lovely day, but I don't mind. I drop my towel and hat and continue to the water, walking in and enjoying the warmth of it. The crystal-clear water always makes me feel so relaxed. I wade out before I float, my eyes closed, clearing my mind. I let the water cradle me. The water is soft, and the tiny waves caress my skin. I feel some fish swim by, so I turn to tread water to watch them. I have no idea what kind they are, but they're pretty and have lovely colours. I haven't swum out to it, but there is a reef is nearby. It makes for some beautiful aquatic life.

I float and swim a while longer before I leave the ocean. The sun is about to set, so I head back to the house. I see the outside shower and decide it is calling my name. I start it and step under the spray of water. I untie my bathing suit, hanging it over the side of the shower.

No one is on the beach, so I don't bother closing the shower door. I leave it open and enjoy the stunning sunset as I wash the ocean's salt from my skin and hair. The sun is barely a sliver when I turn off the shower. I grab a towel from the outdoor stash and wrap it around myself. I ring my hair out, twist it, and pile it on top of my head. I enter the house, realizing I have left the music on. "House Of The Rising Sun" by the Animals is playing. I heard this song a lot growing up. It was one of my dad's favorites.

I walk into my bedroom and grab a towel for my hair. I head back out to the dining room, cleaning up my snack from earlier. I throw out the garbage and put the compost in the bin. I grab a beer and pop off the top when I hear my computer ring. I look down at my towel. "Fuck." I walk over to the screen and answer the call, sitting down as his face fills the screen.

"Hey," he says. "Want to call me back when you have some clothes on?" he grumbles at me.

"I'm fine, Matt, but if it bothers you, I can throw some clothes on."

"I don't care what you wear."

"Amazing, let's do this," I say, looking at him. The man is fucking spectacular. He is all muscle and tattoos. He has a full beard and long dark hair, currently in a man bun, which he pulls off very well.

"What do you know about me, Matt?"

"Your name is Ava. Your parents were killed when you were seven. For some fucked up reason, you ended up at the Ranch, and I'm assuming you learned some less-than-legal skills."

"Correct on all fronts. Do you have any questions for me?"

"Not really. I looked into you. I know Harry a little. He trains some pretty stellar fighters."

"Don't let him hear you say that. He doesn't need another reason to have an inflated ego."

"It's the truth." he says with a shrug.

"All right, Matt. I just have a couple more questions. What's your favorite color?" He glares at me, and I realize that glaring is his resting bitch face.

"Grey."

"Favorite food?"

"Burgers."

"100% on the burger. Favorite memory?"

He's quiet for a moment. And I'm not sure if he's thinking or annoyed and ignoring the question. He has a constant scowl, so it's hard to get a read on him yet.

"Teaching my little sister to drive. She was horrible at it but tried her hardest, convinced she would be the best driver ever."

"I'm very sorry about your sister. Did they ever catch the guy?"

"Nope, the cops found nothing."

"Did you, ever find the guy?"

He sighs before answering, "No, unfortunately, I also couldn't find out who it was."

"Well, Matt, I like you. If you're interested in working for a morally challenged soon-to-be 20-year-old, I would love to meet you in person."

"Just like that? That's a pretty fast decision," he questions me, and I smile.

"Parker vetted you a lot before he passed your file onto me. Harry also teaches other skills than just MMA."

He nods, satisfied with my answer.

"Perfect. Parker will contact you with your flight and hotel information. I need you in New York for the 17th."

He nods at me, all the confirmation I'll be getting.

"Super. See you in a couple days."

He grunts at me and disconnects the call. I close my computer, stand up and head to my room to get ready for dinner with Marcus.

CHAPTER TWENTY SEVEN

It's 8 p.m. I still haven't heard from Marcus, so I text him. My phone rings, and I see it's a video call.

"Hey," I say as the call connects. It's not Marcus on the other end; it's Alexi.

"Ava! Marcus is just a little held up at the moment. We had to change my flight to a later one."

"Why do you have his phone, Alexi?"

"Because, like I fucking told you, he's busy at the moment."

"Actually, you said held up. So, Alexi, what is he busy doing?"

"Not any of your fucking business."

"You really don't like me, do you? I've always kinda wondered why. Is it as simple as Marcus listening to me? Or is it that I am a woman and you have no use for us? Or maybe you're just a small, insignificant man who feels threatened by someone like me."

"Fuck you, you stupid cunt. Soon enough, Marcus will wake up and realize no matter how good your pussy is, you're not worth it."

"Hey, you may be right. That could happen. Hell, it could be happening right now. But you want to know a secret, Alexi? When men break into your home to kill you, if you shoot one in the head and blow a couple of fingers off the other, the one missing the fingers will tell you things. And if you're really lucky, he will call you such pretty little names. Things like sweetheart and devochka." That word lands. I see his breath catch; I see that slight tick in his jaw.

"Anyway, Alexi, let Marcus know I'm going to eat without him. Please stick him in a cab after you guys are done. Please don't let him OD on the coke. Also, make sure he wraps his dick up if he's going to stick it in anyone. The last thing your grandfather would want is a bastard Marcus running around." I smile sweetly at him and end the call.

I stare at my phone for a moment and question my own words. Was my nonchalance to Marcus fucking another woman real or fake? I'm unsure. I have always been in control of my emotions, feelings and reactions. I have a great poker face. It wasn't something I had to be taught. I wonder if I have buried too many emotions too deeply for too long, and now they're not something I can access. I wonder how I would react if I saw him with another woman. Marcus is mine. And now with the change in our relationship he is mine in every way. But my confusion, the pause I feel myself taking is that I don't know if I'm his, or rather I don't know if I have, or can give myself to him like I've taken him for myself.

I hear a car pull up in front of the house. Glancing at the clock, I see it's a little after 2. I get out of bed and go to the door to help him. I have no idea what condition he's going to be in. I open the door and stand in the doorframe, leaning against it, watching the driver help a fucked-up Marcus get out of the back.

"Ma'am," the driver nods to me as he helps Marcus to the door. "Do you want me to help you get him inside?"

"No, I've got him. This isn't the first time. Thank you for bringing him home. Do you need me to sign anything?"

"Nope, already paid for."

"Thanks again."

He hands Marcus off to me. "Hey, baby!" He calls to me as I get my arms around his middle.

"Hey, baby. Marcus, I'm going to need you to help me get you to the bedroom, okay?"

"Yup, I can."

"Great," I chuckle. "Let's go, dude."

I don't know how we manage it, but I get him to the bedroom and onto the bed. I get his shirt off him easily; his pants are a bit trickier, but with some assistance from the man himself, we complete that task as well.

"Ava, I didn't feed you!"

"No, you didn't. But it's ok. I fed myself."

"Dats goo."

"It is goo." It's taking everything in me not to break out in laughter at him. I'm happy he's more drunk than high. Drunk Marcus is soft and usually pretty sweet. High on coke, Marcus is not nearly as nice; high on coke, Marcus is unpredictable and violent.

"I love you, Ava."

"I know you do. It's sleep time now, Marcus."

"K."

"K," I mimic him. I throw his clothes in the laundry in the bathroom; they reek of smoke, vodka, and weed. At least he had a fun night. I get back into bed now that he is settled and passed out.

I wake up a little later as I feel the weight in the bed shift.

Marcus gets out of bed and heads into the bathroom. I drift back to sleep quickly in his absence.

I wake up suddenly to the feel of a hand on my throat. For a moment, a single heartbeat of panic engulfs me. I open my eyes, the light from the bathroom hurting them for a moment. Marcus is above me, and I quickly realize I'm in trouble. He's squeezing harder than he ever would if this was a kink. My hands grab his, my nails digging in, trying to get him to loosen his hold.

As my eyes adjust to the light, I can see him better. One look, and I know he's high. His pupils are nowhere near normal size. Alexi likes coke, and he has been feeding it to Marcus here and there for the last couple of years whenever they were together.

About a year ago, I went to New York with Marcus. I wanted to do some shopping and get some Christmas gifts for a few people, and since he was already going to see his family, I figured it's always more fun to travel with a friend.

I spent very little time with them. I don't like the Russian cousin—I never have—so I stayed busy in New York. But on our last night, Marcus convinced me to join them at a club.

It was fun until it wasn't. Drugs, alcohol, women in tight dresses, and young men who believe they own the women on their laps are always a bad combination.

Alexi had a girl in his lap and his hand up her skirt; her boyfriend took exception to this. *Fair enough, dude, some guy had his hand in your girl's pussy right in front of you and your friends.* The guy tried to take his girlfriend off Alexi's lap, but the Russian was not going to let that happen. No, instead, he finger-fucked her in front of him, making her come, then showed the boyfriend her release on his fingers.

The guy yanked her off Alexi and then took a shot at him, landing a punch to Alexi's jaw. Marcus reacted instantly, jumped on the guy, and beat the ever-living shit out of him.

Bouncers tried to pull him off, Alexi and the other guys tried to pull him off the guy, but Marcus was high as fuck, so he felt and heard none of it. The only way we got him to stop beating the guy was by me grabbing a gun off one the Russians and clocking Marcus in the back of the head.

Now, he has one hand around my throat, and the other is trying to get my sleep shorts down.

Fuck this shit.

My vision is starting to go a little fuzzy, so I release his wrist and slap my hands on either side of his head, hard. It hurts like a mother fucker when you get a person just right on the ears. Marcus howls in pain and rolls off me. I shake my head and suck in a massive lungful of air. I scramble up and get my knees onto Marcus's chest instantly. Using all my weight and strength to push one of my knees into his sternum. I wrap my hand around his throat.

"I will put up with a lot of shit, Marcus. I will accept the coke problem and being stood up for your fucking piece-of-shit cousin. But what I will not accept is you laying your fucking hands on me while you're coked out of your head." I squeeze his neck harder. "I will not accept you trying to fuck me when you have no fucking idea where you are, or who the fuck you're trying to stick your dick into." I squeeze tighter, seeing his face go red. "If you ever do this again, I will put a fucking bullet in your head and never look back."

"Time to go to sleep, asshole." When he passes out, I let go of his neck and get off his chest.

I get out of bed and head to the other side of the house. I go into Marcus's room, close the door, lock it behind me, and pull the dresser in front of it. I don't bother with any lights; I pull back the covers on the bed, get in, and sleep.

I wake up the next morning to Marcus knocking on the bedroom door.

"Ava?"

"Yeah?"

"Baby, I… I'm so sorry. I don't know what the fuck happened. I have no idea how to tell you how sorry I am. Please, Baby, you must know that wasn't me."

"You watch the surveillance video?"

"Yeah."

"So, you saw it all?"

"Yes."

"How much do you remember?"

"Enough that I made myself watch the video to know what I did."

"I'll be out in a while, Marcus."

"Okay," he says and leaves the other side of the door.

I go back to sleep, waking up three hours later. I move the dresser, unlock the door and open it. I head to the kitchen, not hearing any movement. I'm surprised to see Marcus sitting at the island. His back is to me, but I see his body stiffen when he hears me enter. He turns in the chair, and I see how wrung out he looks. I see the tears in his eyes and the stains on his face.

Walking over, I take his face and make him meet my eyes. "Never again, Marcus. You want to get high with Alexi in the future, go for it. But stay at his place or a hotel. You don't come home to me. Do you understand me?"

"Yes."

"Once, Marcus. What you did and tried to do last night happens once. I will kill you if it happens again." My voice is calm and quiet. "Look at me and see if what I'm telling you is the truth."

"I know Ava. You should have killed me last night."

"No, I shouldn't have. Everyone makes mistakes, but you don't get to make this one again."

He nods and closes his eyes, more tears falling from them.

I bend toward him, my lips to his, kissing him softly. He startled at my touch, and then I felt him sink into the kiss. Marcus has more than a few issues. What I've learned over the years is that he needs physical reassurance. I can tell him we're good, but he won't believe it. He needs to feel it.

I deepen the kiss, running my tongue along the seam of his lips. He opens for me, letting me run my tongue along his. I step into the space between his legs and wrap my arms around his neck. He doesn't return the embrace, not entirely trusting yet that I forgive him and that he should accept it. I step into him more, my breasts against his chest.

I let my hand run through his hair. Finally, I feel his arms wrap around me. I remove my shirt, pressing myself into his bare chest, crushing my breasts against him. His hands tighten on my skin, and he starts to kiss me deeper.

I moan into his mouth at the feel of his tongue against mine. He loves that noise and responds with a groan of his own. I feel his cock hard against my thigh, and I reach down and slide my shorts off, letting them fall to the floor. Marcus's hands move to my ass, gripping it. My hands slide under the waistband of his shorts, grasping his cock. I feel his hips thrust when I tighten my grip on him.

His mouth moves to my neck, and he drags his teeth over my sensitive skin, sending a wave of pleasure to my core. His fingers stroke their way down the cleft of my ass, finding my pussy wet and waiting for him. He slides a finger into me, and my head falls back as I gasp, feeling him push his finger further in.

"Ava." He groans.

I release his cock and tug his shorts down. Marcus lifts himself up to help me remove them. I step on the rung of the chair he is sitting on and raise myself to straddle him. Marcus's hands find my hips and I place a hand on his shoulder, steadying myself; I move him to my entrance, and I sink onto him, and we both let out a long sigh.

I rise again, letting him slide out of me to the tip, and then I drop down on him again, torturously slow for both of us. I do it again, sinking onto him even more slowly this time. I hear his breath hitch the slow torture of my movements, pushing him to his breaking point. I rise again, this time staying with just his tip inside me. I clench my pussy around his tip and draw a curse out of him. It's the only warning I get before he grabs my hips and slams me down onto him.

"Oh, fuck." I ground out.

"Fuck baby, you grip me so well." His hands are on my ass, lifting me off his cock only to bring me back down hard over and over again. Both of us are panting now, desperate for the other. I place my hand behind me on the counter and arch my back so he can fuck up into me, hitting that spot inside that has me begging him to make me come. He moves me on his cock as he thrusts his hips up to meet mine. The force of him slamming into me and pulling me onto him is bordering on being too much. My needy sounds are just spurring him on. "Come on my cock, baby, soak me with your cum."

My hand goes to my breast as I watch Marcus bury himself in me over and over again. Releasing his bruising grip on my hip, he shifts one of his hands, bringing it to my pussy, finding my clit. "Your clit is so swollen, baby. You are going to come so fucking hard, aren't you." I whimper, unable to form a real word. He rubs faster and then pinching it, and I come. Marcus keeps plunging in and out of me, my orgasm pushing him over into his own.

When we finally come down, I'm physically and emotionally drained. I have no coherent thoughts, only tears. Marcus wraps me in his arms and carries me to the bedroom. He lays me in the bed, crawling in with me. He wraps his arms around me, pulling me into his chest. He strokes my hair, telling me he's sorry, loves me, and it'll all be okay. He keeps repeating those words over and over, stroking my hair and kissing my forehead and hair. I fall asleep in his arms, tears still washing over my face.

CHAPTER TWENTY EIGHT

We arrive in New York on the morning of the 17th. Marcus heads to see his grandfather and Alexi, and I head to the Hilton Midtown. "Good morning," the hotel clerk says.

"Morning, I have a reservation under Landry."

She types on the computer, finding my information. "I see you have a suite booked, correct?"

"That is correct. I slide her my credit card. She takes it, does her stuff quickly, and hands me my key cards. "Welcome to the Hilton Midtown. You are in room 38465, 36th floor. Enjoy your stay."

A bellhop is beside me instantly to carry my bags. Once I'm settled in my room I grab my laptop. Checking my emails, I reply to a couple of questions from Brynn at the bank and talk to a realtor in LA who is trying to find us a house. Once I have that done I look at my phone and realize the guys will be here any minute.

Needing to get out of the yoga pants and T-shirt I wore

for the flight, I quickly rinse off in the shower. I throw on a pair of dark skinny jeans and a deep green oversized knit sweater with a matching green bralette underneath. Happy with the amount of bralette that shows through the holes of the large knit, I slip on my Jimmy Choo combat boots. I blow dry my hair fast and then run a straightener through it quickly. Hair done I quickly do my eyebrows and throw on some mascara. Ready for the rest of my day I leave the bedroom.

In the main room, I pick up the food menu to order room service, and wait for the guys to arrive. I don't wait long before the first knock at my door. Caden is the first to arrive. It's no surprise; military folks are always prompt.

"Caden," I say, opening the door to let him in. "The flight was ok? How's your room?"

"Flight was good. Short, I was only in Philly. My room is good."

There's another knock at the door, and Caden turns to open it. "Help you?" he asks, directing the question to who I assume is Matt.

"Matt Forestt," he says, with irritation in his voice, confirming once again that grumpy is his baseline.

Caden looks over his shoulder to me, and I nod; he allows Matt into the room.

"Matt, meet Caden. Caden, meet Matt." I bite my lip to stop laughing aloud as these two men size each other up. Matt has a strong stay-the-fuck-away vibe. Caden has more of a size-you-up-and-find-you-lacking vibe. I'm not sure exactly how men their age make friends, but apparently, for these two, it's a staring contest followed by a couple of grunts and nods.

"We good, gentlemen?" I ask. Both men look at me, nod, and say, "Fine." "Good."

"Great to hear it because that wasn't weird at all. Make

yourselves at home. We are expecting one more and some food and drinks."

Matt stands by the window, looking out over Times Square. Caden leans against the wall near the door. We hear a loud knock. Both men look at me.

"Room service," I tell them.

Caden goes to open the door and lets the concierge bring the food in. He sets all the food on the dining table and places the beverages in the fridge. He puts an ice bucket on the bar near the glasses. "Will there be anything else ma'am?" He says, looking only at me, clearly not intimidated by the two large men watching him.

"That's it for now, thank you." He nods and steps towards me, and both Caden and Matt move to get between him and me.

"Easy there, guys. He needs my signature." The concierge hands me a leather folder. Not even blinking at the behavior of the two large men glowering at him. I remove the pen, fill in the tip, and sign, then hand it back to him.

"Thank you, Miss Landry. I'm Robert, and I'm the concierge for this floor. I will be happy to accommodate you with anything you need." With that, Robert leaves us, taking his cart with him.

"I wasn't sure what you guys would want or if you were even hungry, so I ordered a bunch of different things. Please help yourselves to any of it." I watch them both, waiting to see what they'll do. Matt is the first to move and lifts a cloche, finding a couple of sandwiches. Lifting a few more, he finds soup and a burger. He looks over at me and gives me the slightest nod. He places the burger in front of a chair at the table, goes to the fridge and grabs a bottle of water.

"Anyone?" he asks.

"Me, please," I answer.

"Same," Caden says.

Matt comes back to the table, water in hand. Passing us each one, he sits down and devours his food.

Caden finds a salad and soup, sits down, and eats. I grab the turkey BLT on rye and sit in a chair between them. The room is quiet, and I can hear people chewing. Picking up my phone, connecting it to the audio system, I scroll looking for something I want to hear. Then I remember the two men in the room with me. "Do you two have any music you absolutely despise?" They both look at me. Matt raises a single dark eyebrow. He shakes his head and goes back to eating.

Caden takes a sip of his water and says, "Jazz."

"No jazz it is. I also despise jazz, so you were never in any danger of hearing it." I select a playlist, and "Charleston Girl" by Tyler Childers fills the air.

We've just finished eating when there's a knock at the door. I look at the time and smile. Right on time, only 54 minutes late. Caden gets up to open the door. "That'll be Ben, 17, skinny and has a dimple," I tell him. He walks and opens the door.

"Well fuck you're big," I hear Ben say, and I realize his outburst when he saw me on the video call is his normal.

Ben enters the room, sees me, and grins, "Yup, still hot." He turns and sees Matt. "Well fuck, you're even bigger than the other one. You also look really angry, but I bet that works well for you with the ladies, eh? Tall, dark, tattoos, the ability to grow a beard."

Matt looks at the kid, and if I wasn't sitting down, I'm pretty sure I'd have fallen over because he looks at Ben, and lets out a throw-your-head-back laugh. I shake my head, amazed that this may work out well.

"All right, gentlemen. This is Ben. Ben, that's Matt," I introduce them. Matt gives him a small smile, "And that's Caden."

"Hey, kid," Caden says.

"All right, the gang's all here. Let's figure some stuff out."

The guys head back to their rooms about four hours later. I was able to fill them in on what's about to go down here in New York. Ben is already running a program to monitor Enzo's banking, ensuring no big moves are made. He also tapped into the security system at the house to monitor him until we pay him a visit. The visit to Enzo is set to take place in 48 hours.

I got a text from Marcus telling me he'll be another hour. I tell him to take his time. Taking my Kindle I head down to the lobby. There's a cute coffee shop, and I find an empty table in the back. I order a large London fog and a cheesecake pastry. The waitress brings me my order and I sit there for over an hour reading and drinking two London fogs. I know it's been over an hour because I hear the chair pull out across from me, and Marcus sits down.

"Well, hello there," I say without looking up from my Kindle.

"Babe, what would Harry say about you sitting out in public so engrossed in a dirty book that you're unaware of your surroundings?" Marcus asks.

"First of all, the spice in this book is fucking impressive, so I feel like he would understand. Seriously, it's given me a few ideas." I hear him chuckle at that, but it sounds a bit forced. "Secondly, there are nine people in this coffee shop. The waitress, the barista, the dish boy in the back, you, me, the couple behind you to your left who just decided they want to adopt a cat. The man to my right has an Americano and is very deep in thought. It's a little remarkable. The dude hasn't stopped staring off into space for 23 minutes. And the young lady over by the door is studying for a class. I've been here for an hour or so, and 11 other people have come in, got coffee, and left."

Marcus laughs hard at that, a real laugh, "One of these days, it'll sink in just how good you are, Ava."

I close my Kindle and look at him. It will never stop shocking me how beautiful he is. His eyes and mouth are exquisite, even with the pulled expression marring them. Something happened today with Alexi and his family. I wonder if he will tell me what it was. I won't ask, its not my place to ask about his family things. "Did you eat?"

"I did. Did you?"

I nod and stand up, moving to stand beside him. I grab his hand. "Come on, then, let's go up."

We get to our room just as the sun is setting over New York. The city lights are starting to come on, and the view is magnificent. "Want a drink?" he, asks.

"Scotch, please," I reply, watching him walk to the bar. I bend down to undo the laces on my boots, kick them off and remove my socks, enjoying being barefoot.

He grabs a couple of glasses and pours a drink for each of us. Marcus walks to the window, looking out over the city. "Do you miss New York?" I ask him.

"You know, when I was young, when I first came to the Ranch, I did. Now it doesn't feel like home anymore."

"Where will home be for us when this is done?"

Marcus looks at me. "Someplace warm? I know you hate winter."

"I do. Montana killed any love for winter I had." I say with a laugh.

"You're home for me, Ava. The address isn't important. It just has to have you there. The rest is just background." He genuinely believes that. I can see the sincerity in his eyes. But his body—is it anger? Is that what I feel coming off him?

He moves and sits in the armchair in front of the window, placing his scotch on the floor by his feet. He leans his forearms on his legs, undoing his tie and a couple of his shirt buttons. He rolls his sleeves up, folding them below his elbow.

Fucking hell, how is he that attractive?

He sits there, elbows on his knees, chin resting on his thumbs, fingers clasped together, watching me.

Typically, that look goes instantly to my pussy, but right now, it causes me to pause ever so slightly. I feel a prickle at the back of my neck—a warning. I look at Marcus, watching him watch me. Something has changed, shifted. I don't know what happened. I'm not even sure why I'm so convinced something has happened to us that I wasn't privy to, but it's there all the same—a crack in my trust in him, in us.

I stand across from him, both of us considering the other. He sits there, only his eyes moving as he watches me. Marcus shifts, letting one hand dangle between his thighs and using his other hand to rub his chin. He drags one of his fingers over his bottom lip. His eyes never leave mine.

I feel like prey under his gaze.

There's something different tonight.

He's, different tonight.

I bite my bottom lip, watching the man in front of me try to contain something within him that wants to come out.

"Ava," he says darkly, there's a warning in my name.

"What? Do you want something from me?" I ask with my own warning.

He meets my eyes, leaning back in his chair. "I don't think I'm in the mood not to have what I want tonight, Ava."

Well, that doesn't sound threatening at all.

He's so tense; so many emotions roiling over him. He's clenching and releasing his fist. His jaw has a tick. Whatever happened today with his family has him ready for a fight, and that fight seems to be directed at me.

I take a step closer to him. Then another, until I'm

standing between his legs. His fist still clenching. The tension in him is palpable standing this close.

"Where are you tonight Marcus? What happened when you were gone?"

His eyes roam over my body, not meeting mine. "What happens after?"

"After what?"

"After I end my father, and I have control of the family." His eyes haven't left my body, still not meeting mine as he collects his thoughts.

"Ask what you really want to know, Marcus." He finally looks at me, raising a single eyebrow. There's a challenge there.

His voice is low, "how about you tell me, Ava, what is it I really want to know."

There it is.

I cock my head as I study him. Listening to the words he isn't saying.

I take a breath before I answer. "You want to know, or you want me to tell you that I will happily work only for you," I say. He says nothing. Instead, he takes a hand and runs it up my inner thigh, cupping me and grinding the heel of his palm into me. I widen my stance for him, still willing to play this game for the moment.

He pushes into me harder, rubbing the heel of his hand roughly against my core. The scrape of the fabric against my sensitive skin causes me to inhale sharply, not entirely from pleasure.

He likes that sound. I see his cock jump in his pants. "And will you, Ava? Work just for me? For the Rossi's and, by extension, the Sokolovs? Will you take orders from me? From my grandfather Yuri?" He asks me these questions as he pushes into me harder.

My inner voice tells me not to push him, but I'm not listening to her. Miss Bennett's voice echoes in my head, "Always listen to your instincts," but I'm not listening to her either at the moment. I grab Marcus by the hair and force him to look at me.

"Are you still my best friend?"

"Yes," he replies.

"Have our end goals changed?" I ask, tightening my hold on his hair.

"No," he hisses.

"When have we ever said I would work for you? When have I ever said I would work for the Sokolovs in any capacity?" He says nothing.

"When?" I ask, pulling his hair tighter.

"Never." he grounds out.

"Then what the fuck are you asking me?" I gesture to the position we are in.

"Alexi," Marcus starts.

"Fucking Alexi," I mutter, releasing his hair and taking a step back.

"Alexi and Yuri think that you would do better working for us."

"Us? "I say.

"Yes. You don't even need to work, Ava. You have more money than you could ever spend. So, we were talking, and we feel it's stupid for you to take risks when you don't need to."

"So, what will I be doing with my time then?"

"Whatever you want. Travel, start a charity. A charity is a great way to launder money." He informs me like this is the best idea ever.

"So, ok." I take another step back from him. "Let me work through this. You, your grandfather, and your cousin, feel I would be more useful to your organizations by using my money to open a charity, so it can launder money for both of you?"

"Yeah! I mean, think about it. You and I could get married, fuck, we could have kids!" I find myself searching his face for the punchline. But there isn't one; no, he is wholly serious.

I drop my head back and look up at the ceiling. "Fuck, Marcus. You're with your fucking family for like one day, and they already have you thinking like them. I will not work for the Sokolovs." I look at him again. "Ignore their voices in your head for a minute. Think about me. Think about all the things you know about me. Think about all the years we've been together; in any of that, do you see a moment where I would have been open to working for the fucking Sokolovs?"

" Well, I just thought–"

I cut him off. "No, you didn't just think. They told you what to think." I see a flicker of anger in his eyes, but I push on. This moment is going to define us going forward.

"Marcus, you're fucking smarter than this. They don't care if I live or die. Honestly, their lives would be a lot easier without me in yours. They want my money and to be the only ones you listen to in your life."

"And what Ava?" He gets up and stalks toward me. "I should listen to you and you only?"

"No, you fucking asshole. You should listen to your own fucking mind. We made all our plans together. Since we were seven, we worked with each other. Neither of us trying to manipulate the other. Partners, Marcus."

"Ava, I have family obligations!" he snarls at me.

"No, actually, you don't. You are about to be the head of the Rossi family. You are about to control a huge criminal organization. Enzo is the least respected Don out there. But he has so much clout, so much power, so many soldiers and connections that no one fucking messes with him or his turf." I yell back, throwing my arms into the air.

"You don't need the Sokolovs for a second! They fucking need you! They don't have a foothold here yet. The Russians already here will do everything they can to stop the Sokolovs from gaining any traction in the States. But if they have you!? The others will bow down if they have the Rossi family with them. The Sokolovs will absorb every other Russian Bratva in this country. If they're allowed to amass that kind of power. they will be the biggest Bratva anywhere."

The anger running through me is electric. Anger I work very hard to control and I never let out. Harry's voice rages in my head, "Anger will get you killed every single time. Anger makes you stupid; it makes you miss the little things. And the little things, Little Fury, are usually what you need to see." The anger that this jackass just caused.

I wait, letting my words sink in, giving myself a moment to slip the anger back into its little box. "They're my family, Ava," he says, the fight leaving his voice.

"They are, so I get you deciding to back them. But Marcus, they are not my family. You are. Only you. Do you understand what I'm saying? I'll pull jobs for you; I'll kill anyone you need removed. I'll kill anyone you want me to; your gardener did a shit job? Fuck that guy; I'll kill him if that's what you need. Fuck, I'll steal the Mona Lisa for you if you want, but I won't work for them. I won't sit at home and open a charity. I will do what we have always planned for me to do. If you need to change your side of the plan, I will respect that and do my best to adjust or accommodate the changes, but I will work. I will take jobs from whoever and whenever I want. I won't check with you or them. You running my life or me running yours was never part of our plan. Our plan was always for me to help you achieve your goals and for me to do my own thing. Still together, still us, but me independent from the Mafia. In no world will I ever be part of a made family."

Silence hangs in the air for a few heartbeats. I see Marcus working through everything I just yelled at him. I know this man so well I can see the thoughts running through his mind. The moment he has his words collected, I brace myself. I want to be wrong. I want him to surprise me with the answer that is about to leave his mouth.

"I know. I'm sorry. But I'm not going to lie, Ava. The thought of you home safe, maybe pregnant with my baby, or just knowing you're there for me when I get home is intoxicating." He rubs his hands along the back of his neck.

I sigh. "I get it. But I can't give you that."

"Can't or won't?" A touch of bitterness lances through his question.

"I won't, Marcus." I won't lie to him. He nods his head at me. He knew the answer before he asked the question. "You need to decide, baby. You and me just like we always planned. Or you and them."

He looks at me, holding my gaze. "You and I, Ava. Always you and I." And there it is. The lie. *Fuck.* I smile at him because while I know it's a lie, I don't know if he does. I step into him and press my lips to his just as his phone rings.

"Yeah?" He listens to the voice on the other end. Nodding, he says "OK" a couple of times. "Yeah, pick me up in 30."

He turns to me. "Ava, I need to help my family with some things."

"I heard."

"I don't know how long I'll be."

"It's fine, Marcus. It's family, I get it."

"You seem mad."

"Marcus, you've seen me mad. Wanna rephrase that?"

"Ok, you seem annoyed that your boyfriend is going out."

I can't help but smile at that. "My only concern is tomorrow and you being ready for it."

"I've been ready for it for five years," he reminds me.

"That's not what I mean, and you know it."

"Ava, I have been waiting for this for a long time, and there is nothing I would do to jeopardize it. Family or not, if I thought for a moment it would fuck things up tomorrow, I wouldn't go."

"And boyfriend, really Marcus?"

"You aren't my girlfriend?"

"No more than you're my boyfriend," I inform him.

He looks at me, very unsure what the fuck is going on.

I sigh. "Marcus, we aren't kids, nor are we college students. Boyfriend/girlfriend seems so juvenile to me. You are a grown man, and you make your own choices. Does calling me your girlfriend somehow put ownership on us? Cause for me, it's just us. Fucking or not. It's us. We just are."

His eyes are locked on me. "Take off your pants, Ava." I quirk up an eyebrow at him, and then I take off to the bedroom, but he's faster than me; he's always been faster than me. He has me by the waist and throws me onto the bed. He grabs my ankles, dragging me to the end of the bed. His hand grabs the waistband of my pants and in one rough tug he removes them and my underwear with them. I turn to get away, trying to scramble higher on the bed, but he catches me again.

He gets me to the edge of the bed, and holds me down as he buries his face between my legs. He drags his tongue along me. One long. slow, strong, lick. "I have to go to Release tonight," he tells me before he sucks my clit into his mouth stopping just as quickly.

"So, I'm going to make you come on my face before I leave." He finishes his sentence punctuating it with a slide of his tongue between my folds, Working up to my clit, his tongue flicking it before continuing.

"I'm going to walk through that place, watching all the dirty and debauched things they do to each other there." He drags his teeth over it, before closing his lips over me, using his tongue to drag a moan from me.

"I'm going to watch as men fuck the women hard, making them scream and writhe for release." He pushes a finger inside me, twisting it as he draws it back out. Sliding it back in, his mouth closes over me again, this time sucking and flicking my clit making me moan. My hips raise off the bed as he works me with his finger, as his mouth takes pleasure in teasing me. Taking from me but not quite giving me back what I need.

"I'm going to stop and watch the women on their knees, letting the men fuck their faces." His tongue presses against my swollen clit, I whimper, ready to beg him not to stop.

"I'm going to stop and watch as some gorgeous man gets topped by another. I'll watch him fuck him hard and fast, his ass gripping his thick cock so tight as they both explode for the other." He slams two fingers into me my core quivering. His words make me ache. He works his fingers in me. The sounds of my wetness on his fingers as they fuck me fill the room.

"I'm going to see all this, all those writhing bodies." His fingers are stroking that spot inside me as he speaks. "Skin on skin, the slap of bodies as one person ravages another's." His fingers are moving in and out of me faster now, my breathing picking up with his pace and his words.

"My cock is going to be so fucking hard, but I won't do a thing about it. I'll just endure the pain of it." His Tongue and fingers find a punishing rhythm, My thighs are shaking as my release starts coming fast. just for him to stop again.

"Marcus, please, please let me come; I can't. It's too much."

"It's not too much; just breathe, baby." His fingers haven't stopped working me. His thumb slowly circles my clit, just slow enough to keep me edged.

"Then Ava, I'm going to walk into a back room and put a couple of bullets in the heads of a couple of guys who thought they could steal from my grandfather." My breaths are coming so hard and fast now. My legs won't stop shaking. Marcus continues his demanding, sweet torture of me. "Then I'm going to come back here, and I'm going to find you asleep in this bed naked." I'm just panting now, and mewling noises are leaving my mouth. My pussy is dripping from his words and his touch.

"Tell me what you think I'm going to do when I find you naked in this bed in a couple of hours?"

My body tenses when he sucks on my clit again, dragging it into his mouth as he slides his fingers out of me only to add another, stretching me while he strokes me, and then he stops. "Jesus fuck, Marcus, I'm going to fucking kill you if you leave me like this."

"Answer my question, Ava, and I'll let you come."

"What was the question?"

"What will I do when I get back here and find you naked in this bed?" He repeats. "Answer quickly, Ava; my ride will be here soon."

"You're going to fuck me," I say matter-of-factly.

"Tsk tsk," he taunts me. "You can do better than that. Tell me what you want, and I'll give it to you." His tongue swipes along my pussy so lightly it's barely there.

"You'll come home and find me naked, still wet for you." This gets me the smallest circle from his tongue against my clit. "Then you'll climb onto the bed slowly, careful not to wake me." His fingers pick their pace back up. In and out of me, dragging against my inner walls. "Then you'll lift my hips just a bit, line yourself up with my entrance and bury yourself in me. It'll be hard and fast, and I'll wake up having you in me ravishing my needy cunt."

This must have been the correct answer; he pushes my

legs wide. "Hands, Ava," I give him my hands, and he places them on my legs. "Keep your legs there for me, baby. Keep this glistening pussy wide open for me."

I don't reply; I hold myself open for him. His face comes back to me, his mouth on me fast. He eats me, licking and sucking my clit in his mouth again, two fingers inside me, plunging them into me. His fingers fixate on that spot inside me, and his tongue moves against my clit. He works me so expertly, making my body sing for him. My orgasm is building fast.

"Fuck. Your pussy is dripping wet, running down my hand," he tells me with pride. He seals his lips around my clit sucking hard, and it pushes me over the edge. I can't keep my hands on my legs anymore. I grab Marcus by the hair, and my legs clamp around his head as I fuck his face. Taking everything, I can as I ride out the orgasm. I feel my come running out of me, dripping towards my ass. Marcus eats and eats, cleaning up every last bit of it. He shoves his face into me harder, and I know he's rubbing my juices over his face. It's so fucking dirty, so fucking depraved, and I love it.

I release my hold on him, letting my legs fall open. "Fuck, Ava, if I didn't know better, I'd think you like the idea of me going to Release wearing your cum as my cologne." I hear him chuckle. I look at him and roll my eyes. "Go away, Marcus. I just fucked someone's face so hard I saw stars." I crawl up the bed, flop onto my stomach, and close my eyes. I feel a blanket placed over me, and I hear the door to the bedroom close, and then I'm asleep.

I feel the bed shift, but none of it registers until he plunges into me. He pulls out and drives back in and I moan.

"Fuck." I feel him pull my hips higher, so I get my knees under me, giving both of us a chance to move against each other. His hands grip my ass as he pummels into me over and over. I feel the sting, as he slaps my ass, then he rubs it before he smacks it again. The sting is more intense this time. I groan into the mattress. My hands grab the sheets, and I thrust back into him, meeting him over and over again. "Work yourself, Ava; I want you to come with me."

I do as he asks, and I start to rub my clit; it's swollen and throbbing, so ready for my fingers. "Marcus, I'm not going to last. Baby, please, I can't stop." The words are barely out of my mouth before I feel my orgasm hit. I feel my pussy clench his cock so fucking hard.

"Jesus," I hear Marcus' groan, and I feel him drive into me harder and more frantically. "Fuck!" he yells out as his own orgasm tears through him.

We both collapse onto the bed, and Marcus falls to my side so he doesn't crush me. "You're good. Everything went okay?"

"Yeah," he laughs. "It went fine. Not as good as that, but still fine," he tells me through laboured breaths.

I mumble something incoherent, my eyes already closing, as sleep takes me.

CHAPTER TWENTY NINE

I wake up with Marcus wrapped around me as I hear the door to the suite click. I grab my gun from the table beside me and get out of bed, careful not to make any noise. I'm just about to open the door to the bedroom when I hear Ben say, "We should order food. I'm hungry, and Ava is always hungry," he says, with emphasis on always. I smile, slide the safety back on the gun and go into the bathroom. I get cleaned up and dressed quickly, throwing on a one-piece romper and making my way into the main room, leaving Marcus to sleep a bit longer.

"Gentleman," I say as I close the bedroom door.

"Boss Lady," Ben says, not looking up at me. Matt slaps the back of his head. "Ow, what the hell, man? Oh. Right. Hi Ava."

"Ava," Matt and Caden both grunt at me.

"I ordered breakfast," Ben tells me.

"I know I heard you say that. It's the only reason I didn't shoot you guys."

I hear Matt snort out a laugh. Caden looks at Ben, shaking his head. "The kid will learn some manners. It's just going to take Matt and me a little time to drill them into him," he informs me.

"I'm what?" Ben asks, only listening to half the conversation as he types away. "OK, so I have all the cameras at Mr. Rossi's house linked to my system. No one will even know you're there. I looked into the guy who he has working for him in the cyber area of his criminal empire, and he's shit. So, we're good."

"Perfect. As long as he's shit," I repeat his words to him.

Food is delivered just as Marcus comes out of the bedroom, all sleep-tousled hair and grey sweats. "Guys, this is Marcus."

Caden makes his way over and offers Marcus his hand, and both men shake. "Nice to finally meet you. Ava has mentioned you a lot. I'm Caden. The kid is Ben, and the grumpy fucker over there is Matt."

Ben waves, not bothering to look up, and Matt nods at him from his spot at the table.

"Hungry?" I ask Marcus.

"I am," he answers. A sleepy smile spreads over his face.

We all sit down and start to eat, and I make it 47 seconds before I turn the music on. "Space Oddity" by Bowie drowns out the eating noises. Marcus laughs at me, shaking his head and kisses me on the cheek.

"OK, so it will be perfect if we are in place and ready for 8 p.m. tonight. He will just be getting home from his dinner. The housekeeper and cook will both be gone home for the night." Ben lets us know, obviously not having heard the conversation. Caden and Matt shake their heads at the kid and return to eating.

"The cook and Housekeeper won't interfere or care even if they were there. They will probably want to come to work for us, Ava. They were my mom's and stayed for her and me for all these years." Marcus adds.

"Sounds good to me. You did promise me a cook," I remind him

"I did," he says, grinning at me.

After eating, we review everything again, ensuring everyone knows what they're doing. Essentially, Ben will turn off the cameras and open the front gate for Marcus and me to walk through—or drive.

We arrive before 8 to watch the house. The cook and housekeeper leave for the night just as Ben predicted. Marcus and I sit in the truck quietly for the next hour or so, talking about nothing important. Caden and Matt are in Matt's car, parked a few houses in the other direction. Ben chose the spot because he liked the reception of signals from the house.

A little before 8:30, we see Enzo's car approaching the house. His driver punches in the gate code and heads up the driveway. Enzo and his bodyguard, Hank head into the house. We wait another half hour before we move.

According to Ben, Enzo and his bodyguard are the only ones in the house. Hanks's room is on the first floor, and he will need to be dealt with quietly so we don't alert the man of the house. Ben confirms that Enzo has retired to his area for the night. The entire left side of the second floor is his. His office, bedroom, bathroom and walk-in closet are all located there, making it easy for us to find him even without Ben telling us he's in the office.

I look over at Marcus. "Ready?"

"Yeah."

We drive up to the gate and see it flash green and open. "That kid's not bad," Marcus says.

"Yeah, I like him. He's smart, and Parker hand-picked him, so... " We stop in front of the house and get out, not fully closing the car doors.

"The gate or sounds of the truck didn't alert anyone," Ben tells me over my earpiece.

"Great, now get the front door."

"Yes, Boss." Then I hear the deadbolt disengage. "Your wish is my command, Boss Lady."

"Ben, if you keep calling me that, I will have to reconsider your employment with me." I hear Marcus chuckle.

"Yeah, kid. Ava loves her name. Her parents named her after her great-grandmother," Marcus tells Ben with a smile.

I look at Marcus, wait for his nod, and then open the door. The house is silent except for a grandfather clock in the entranceway.

That's such a cliché. Of course, this asshole has a grandfather clock.

Marcus takes the lead; I follow along, staying out of his way. I'm only here because Marcus wants me here. He doesn't need me here to do this. He could have done this all on his own.

We reach Hank's door. I step to the side and put my hand on the doorknob. I wait for his nod again and open it. Marcus steps into the room, and Hank doesn't even get a chance to make a noise before Marcus shoots him in the head. I cock my head to the side, looking at Hank. "Have I met him before?" I ask Marcus quietly.

"At the funeral."

"Ah, yes. He looked good for his age."

Marcus shakes his head at me and starts out of the room. I follow him again, and we head up the stairs this time. We pause once we're in the hall at the top of the stairs. I step up behind him and put my hand in his, squeezing it to let him know I'm with him. He squeezes my hand back, lets it go, and starts towards his father's office. "Still in his office," Ben tells us through the earpieces.

We walk up to the door, and I move to the side, placing

my hand on the knob and waiting for the nod from Marcus. He takes a breath and then nods at me. Turning the knob I open the door, letting it swing inside the room. Enzo sits behind his desk, looking at some papers. The sound of the door opening alerting him that someone entered his space. "What do you need Hank?" he says without even looking up.

"Dad." Enzo's head shoots up, locking eyes with his son.

"Marcus."

I step into the room, moving to the side and leaning against the bookcase. I look at the two of them, waiting to see who'll make the first move. It's Enzo—his overinflated sense of worth kicks in. "You can't kill me; people won't stand for it." He says with a smirk.

"Possibly? But I think it's more likely no one is going to care that you're dead. Besides, we aren't here to kill you. There's no need. You're just going to sign it all over to me."

"And why would I do that?" Enzo laughs.

"Because I'm a Rossi and a Sokolov and people don't like you. Sign it all over, or Ava will put a bullet in your head."

Enzo looks at me now, realizing I'm in the room with them.

"Hello, Mr. Rossi," I say, smiling and offering him a little wave.

Manners at all times.

"Dad, just get up. Let's go."

"You think I'm going to make this easy for you?"

"You have two options, Dad. Get up and come with us. Show some class. Or two, I hit you in the head and then drag you out of your house."

"I like number two personally," I tell them.

He stares at me. "Who the fuck asked you?" he snarls.

"Wow, someone is a little testy."

Marcus doesn't turn to look at me, but I see his head shake

a bit. I'm not sure if that's frustration or laughter, but I will choose to believe the latter.

"Fine."

Marcus steps up to his father, clocks him, and Enzo goes down.

"Matt, can you and Caden come help us carry something?" I ask over the comms in my most pleasant voice.

"We're already coming up the stairs, Ava."

"Wow, you guys are killing it on your first field trip."

"Do you always talk like this?" Matt asks.

"Like what?" I ask, cocking my head to the side as they enter the room with us.

"Yes, she always talks like this when she's working. Just wait until she starts humming the Muppets fucking theme song." Marcus tells them.

Both men look at me. "Trying to decide if my level of crazy pays well enough?" I ask them.

"Something like that," Matt smirks.

"It does," I assure them.

A couple of hours later, we're safely tucked away in one of Mr. Rossi's buildings. We're sitting around a table in the little kitchen. "Go fish," I tell Matt.

He grumbles but takes one from the mess of cards in the middle of the table.

"Caden got any fours?" Ben asks him.

"Fuck kid, how!" Caden tosses his four at him.

"Do you have any kings?" Ben asks Marcus. Marcus says nothing; he just hands the king to him.

"Got any aces? Boss lady?"

"Go fish, asshole." Ben looks at me like he doesn't believe me.

The sound of a chair moving makes us all look to the door leading downstairs. Marcus looks at me, and we lay our hands down, standing up we head downstairs.

The room off to the left at the bottom of the stairs has one occupant. The man tied to the chair has hate rolling off of him, and it's directed right at Marcus.

Moving behind Marcus, I go to the counter against the wall and hop up on it to sit.

"Fucking pathetic. Can't you do anything without her holding your hand? Had I known how much of a pussy you were going to be, I would have just put a bullet in your head instead of wasting time and money sending you to Harry."

Marcus doesn't engage him. He waits quietly, letting the man spew his vitrol. Once the older man quiets again, Marcus talks to him. "Uncle Sergi told me a story." I see the muscles in Mr. Rossi tense at the mention of Sergi's name. "Do you know what he told me?" Marcus waits momentarily, letting his dad decide if he will answer.

"How the fuck would I know?" He spits out.

"Did you kill my mother?" Marcus asks bluntly.

That question shocks me. Marcus has never said Yuri, Alexi, or Sergi told him that. Enzo stares at his son, deciding what he wants to say, weighing his options, and determining if the truth or a lie will save him.

When he makes his choice, it's the smile that fills his face that tells me he is choosing a painful death. "It was so amazing killing that fucking cunt."

"She was your wife. She was my mother, the mother of your child." Marcus tells his father.

And then Enzo laughs. He laughs at his son. He laughs at his son's words.

"Fuck," I mutter to myself. I see the look of pleasure on Enzo's face. And I instantly connect the dots.

"You're not even my fucking kid, you dumb cunt. Your whore of a mother was already pregnant when we got married. She tried to pass you off as my own. But blood types don't lie."

I look at Marcus, watching as both shock and relief pass over his face. I'm proud of him for being able to swallow it down and stay calm.

"Thank fucking God I'm not your son. You have always been a fucking piece of shit, and I was ashamed you were my father. Such a useless dumb cunt." Enzo, unfortunately, is anything but dumb. He knows he's going to die in this room now. So, he doubles down and makes sure to hurt Marcus as much as possible with his last bit of time on this earth.

Enzo glares at Marcus, and I see a glint of malice there. Malice and pleasure. "God dammit," I say under my breath, knowing the asshole is about to drop another bombshell.

"She told me his name, you know." I see Marcus stiffen. "At the end there, she was pretty beaten and broken. But she still had some venom in her. I loved breaking her. That Russian princess. Thinking she could make a fool out of me. Thinking she could make me look stupid to our world by trying to trick me into raising someone else's bastard.

"She thought she was so fucking clever, so fucking untouchable," Enzo says quietly. Marcus is standing there, barely breathing; he is so still. "But I fucking touched her. My guys fucking touched her for hours. One after another. They treated her good, treated her like the whore she was. And oh, how she begged for me to kill her at the end. It was so beautiful hearing her whimper; the pain in her cries is still music in my ears. She was in so much pain only speaking in Russian. The tears and the blood were a spectacular sight to behold."

I know what he's doing. He's trying to push Marcus to get him so angry that he just kills him. But I won't let that happen. I won't allow him a fast and painless death after all the hurt he has caused my best friend his entire life.

I slide off the counter and walk towards Marcus. I grab his hand, but he doesn't look at me. I force him to turn and look at me. Force him to break his line of sight with the man tied to the chair. "Marcus," I say, but he doesn't meet my eyes. "Marcus," I touch his face, but he still doesn't meet my eyes. I tilt my head up and brush my lips against his. I brush them across again, firmer this time. I find the bottom of his shirt and slide my hand up underneath it, placing my hand on his abdomen. The muscles under my hand are so tense.

I move my hand up to his heart, feeling it beat under his skin. I deepen the kiss, sweeping my tongue over the seam of his lips and coaxing him to let me in. His mouth opens slightly, but it's enough. I slide my tongue into his mouth, touching his. The slightest noise leaves him. I feel a hand grasp my waist. Marcus kisses me back then, pouring his pain and anger into the kiss and giving it to me. His hands slide down and grab my ass, lifting me.

I wrap my legs around his trim waist, bringing him closer. He walks us backwards until his boots hit the bottom of the counter, and he drops my ass on it, embedding himself between my legs. His kiss is hard and desperate. His hands still gripping my ass, he pulls me forward and grinds his hardening cock against the seam of my jeans, pushing the stiff material against my core.

I break the kiss, bringing my hands to his face and forcing him to look at me. He's panting and staring at me. "Marcus," his eyes focus on me finally.

"Let me do this for you," I beg him. "He deserves to hurt just as much as he hurt you and her. Let me inflict that pain. Then when he's broken, crying and bleeding, you can put a bullet in his head." He's staring at me intensely; I can't read him. I think maybe he's going to say no, that he will do it himself, but instead, he blinks and nods.

"Make it fucking hurt, Ava."

"Baby, I will have him begging for you to kill him."

He drops his forehead to mine and breathes for a moment. He kisses me quickly, grasps my waist, lifts me off the counter, and places me back on my feet. Then, without glancing at the man who was once his sorry excuse for a father, he leaves the room.

I watch his back as he leaves. I stare at the door until I hear him on the stairs waiting for the other door to open and close. I grab my phone and text Matt, asking him to bring me some things. I may as well kill two birds with one stone. I need to know for sure Matt can stomach this shit, and I want a bottle of water, my speaker and my bag of goodies. I hop back up on the counter while I wait for Matt to bring me what I need. I sit there looking at Enzo. I remember the day Marcus came to the ranch. I remember hearing Harry and Beth speak about him and how he had threatened to kill Marcus rather than raise him.

I hear Matt on the stairs about five minutes later. "Oh, thank god, he's a mouth breather, it's a real trigger for me." I grab the bag, find the speaker, and connect it to my phone. "What do you want to listen to, Mr. Rossi?" I ask the older man because I was raised with manners. I lean to my right to peer past Matt to see if Mr. Rossi has any requests.

"Fuck you, Ava." Matt tenses at Enzo's words. I'm starting to see Matt is not a fan of men who speak poorly to women. "You are just as fucking useless as every other woman. Your dripping cunts are the only things about you that have real worth."

"Mr. Rossi," I say as I lean back to my centre and start scrolling through my phone to find a playlist that feels right. "You really shouldn't insult the woman who is about to start hurting you." I show Matt my playlist to see if he likes it. He raises one side of his mouth and shakes his head. "I think it's in bad taste and stupid on your part," I tell Enzo. Matt takes my phone and scrolls, finding something he likes because he smiles and nods his head.

I almost laugh out loud at his song choice. I look up at him with a smile I can't fully contain. "You're kind of funny for a grumpy asshole," I tell him quietly as "Stuck in the Middle With You" by Stealers Wheel plays in the room. He doesn't say anything. He just gives me a wink. "That wink probably drops a lot of panties for you, doesn't it?"

"Panties and boxers. They all melt for it, and I don't discriminate."

"I bet they do. All right, Matt, will you be staying or going?" I ask him as I get off the counter.

"Is there a wrong answer for me to give?"

"No. I'm just wondering."

"Wondering if I have it in me to watch or help you hurt a man who threatened to kill his seven-year-old son? Wondering if I have it in me to help or watch you hurt an asshole who had his wife raped repeatedly and then beaten to death?"

"Pretty much."

He doesn't say anything. He looks at me and nods. "I'll be back. I need to get something from my car." He then heads up the stairs. I turn to the man in the chair, and I cock my head to the side, letting the smallest of smiles cross my lips.

"So, Enzo, just us girls for right now. Are you excited? I don't think we have ever really talked, you and me. I have a question for you. Would you indulge me while we wait for Matt to return?" He nods at me. "Great. Did you and Alexi really think two idiots would be enough to kill me? Eight. Eight would be a good number of men to have sent. Eight would have probably got you guys the desired outcome." He glares at me.

"My son is too weak to do this himself, eh?"

I sigh audibly, needing him to hear how much he exhausts me. "1. Not your son, and you telling him he's not your son directly led to you being here alone with me. 2. He's not weak. He's just man enough to understand that his hate for you will overpower his want to make it hurt. Bloodlust is a real thing, dude." I nod at him, hoping he understands how sincere that statement is. "3. He loves me and knows I kinda enjoy this part of things. He knows I won't lose control and break my promise to him."

I nod at Matt as he enters the room. He puts a bag on the counter and starts to put on gloves.

"Enzo?" My voice is no longer playful as the older man looks at me. "I'm going to hurt you now. And when I'm done, you will be begging and crying for Marcus to kill you. Just like his mother begged you."

"I know who his father is," he blurts out. "I'll tell you if you let me go."

"Mr. Rossi, nothing will make me let you go. Nothing is going to save you from this. And besides, I know who his father is. It's all in the eyes."

He looks at me, and genuine fear blanches his face for the first time since we entered his office. I smell something, and I groan, "Fucking hell, did you just piss yourself?" And sure enough, a large wet spot has appeared between his khaki-clad legs. It runs off the seat of the wooden chair he's tied to. "That's fucking gross, man." I sigh. "You need to get it together, Mr. Rossi. I haven't even started yet."

Would it be really horrible of me to place a wager with Matt on how long it'll take Enzo to lose his bowels?

CHAPTER THIRTY

I emerge from the room with Matt an hour later. Wiping my hands on a towel, I go up the stairs and see Marcus sitting at the table with a bottle of scotch and two glasses. "One of those for me?" I ask. "Where are Ben and Caden?"

"Outside. Ben said you have shit taste in music."

I look at Matt, and he glares at me. "Find them. Get a read of the room." Matt nods at me and goes to find Caden and Ben.

"Marcus."

He looks up at me and nods. "Whenever you're ready," I tell him.

"Stuck in the middle with you?"

"Whoa, now. It's a really good song. And Matt selected the music. So, he gets the credit for the homage to Tarantino playlist."

"How'd he do?" he asks.

"Good. he enjoys hurting bad men."

"I'm not sure Caden will make it," Marcus tells me.

"Yeah, I'm not sure, but I don't need Caden if I have Matt. Matt and I can do the dirty work. May as well leave it to the ones who enjoy it. Caden is fucking loyal and protective as hell. I think he will be perfect for bodyguard duty with training from Harry and Wes. I don't need both of them to be able to inflict pain. As long as he can pull the trigger when it's needed, I'll keep him."

"And Ben?" Marcus says as he stands from his chair.

"Ben needs some self-defence and basic firearms training, but for the most part, he'll never be in the midst of it. And he's too good with computers for me not to make it work somehow."

Marcus nods to me, and we head back down.

He says nothing as he walks into the room. He simply walks up to the bloody man moaning in the chair, pulls his gun out of its holster, puts it against the man's skull, and pulls the trigger.

Theo, Wes, and Sebastian join us in New York. They are here to help clear out anyone who wasn't feeling the management change in the Rossi organization. In the ten days that followed, 17 didn't make it through the transition. The funniest part was that 11 of the guys turned us down because we took out Hank. They didn't care that Marcus was in charge or that Enzo was dead.

Marcus apologized to them all. He told them he understood and wished he could have spared Hank, but Hank was never going to bend to Marcus, and he was too much of a liability to leave alive. All 11 understood, and it was unnaturally civilized for people of our nature.

When the guys return to the ranch, they will take Caden, Matt, and Ben.

We booked an entire restaurant so we could enjoy ourselves with a family dinner. After the last ten days, I'm happy to sit here to drink, laugh, and eat. I'm so very done with people at the moment. The men at this table are the exception to that. I love every one of them, and I know how lucky I am to have them.

We have just finished our meals when the door opens, and in walks Frank Campano and Walter English with a handful of their men. I do my best to hide my surprise as Thomas Murphy follows them in with a few of what I assume are his own men.

I turn into Marcus, rubbing my hand across his abdomen so I can pull his gun from his holster. "Now, Ava, if we didn't want to speak, we would not have come ourselves," Thomas tells me, his Irish lilt bringing a blush to my cheeks like it did when I was a child.

"Still blushing, I see?" He laughs lightly at me.

"Only for you and that accent, Thomas. You look good for an old man. I was sorry to hear about Anna. Cancer is heartless, and Anna was a spectacular woman."

"Thank you, Ava."

The guys have already gotten up from the table, leaving Marcus and me sitting. They have placed themselves around the room close to the other men standing. Frank, Walter, and Thomas join us, sitting in the vacated chairs. The restaurant staff has cleared off the plates and cutlery. The three men sitting with us look relaxed as if this is just any other day for them.

"It seems you made some changes the last few days, Marcus," Walter says.

"Yes, sir. My father's time had come to an end."

"Did he see it that way?" Thomas asks.

"Of course he did, Thomas. It just took Ava a moment to convince him."

I slide my hand onto Marcus's thigh, squeezing it and telling him he needs to relax. He rubs the back of my hand and takes a steadying breath.

"And will the new head of the Rossi family be expecting a seat at the table?" Walter asks.

"What table would that be?" I respond.

"Mind your fucking mouth, girl." Frank snarls at me.

"No, she's just fine like she is, Mr. Campano," Marcus tells him. His voice is low and rough. "And you will remember who she is to me before you speak to her again like that. Understood?"

"And who the fuck is she exactly? She has no family or has ever been part of one of the families. So, I will speak to the bitch any way I please."

"Frank, Ava may not be a member of any made or criminal family, but I promise you, getting on her bad side is a mistake," Thomas replies, surprising everyone.

"Thomas, just because you may want to get your dick wet in that–" Thomas sighs, interrupting Frank before he can finish that thought. He looks over at Frank; he doesn't stand, doesn't raise his voice, but whatever the look on his face is, he has the older man shrinking back into his seat.

"Frank, you will do well listening to me. You have no idea who that young woman is. You have no idea what she is capable of. If you want to keep breathing, I would suggest you shut the fuck up and refrain from speaking to her again in such a manner. Because while we may be here together to speak to Marcus and Ava, I promise you if things go badly and Ava decides to kill you for insulting her, I will not interfere. Fuck, I'd happily let her use my gun to do it."

Frank doesn't reply, but he also doesn't say anything else. These three men are here to see how Marcus is going to conduct business now. They want to know if things will be the same or if he will be making changes. They can't come out and ask him outright, so instead, Thomas speaks to me.

"Ava, I'm sure it's a wee bit of a surprise seeing me here."

"A bit, yeah."

"I knew your dad very well. We did business here and there and became friends. But your parents were not part of this world. They were more adjacent to it. I don't know how much of their life was above board, but I know some was down here on our level."

"I've been wondering that since I got a look at the bank accounts and investments and such."

"Enough Thomas! Just ask them the fucking questions so we can leave," Walter commands. Thomas turns to the older gentleman and, in a low voice, barely audible, tells Walter to shut the fuck up. And Walter does. I look at Thomas, cocking my head to the side a bit. That Irish bastard has something on the other two. Thomas looks at me and winks, and I sigh at the wink. I can't help it. I still have such a crush on this man. Marcus laughs at me. "Fucking hell, Ava, get it together, woman."

"I'm trying, Marcus, I am, but that Irish lilt is my fucking kryptonite."

Marcus and Thomas both let out a big laugh at my admission. I see Matt and Sebastian both chuckle as well.

"Ava dear, what is the plan for the Rossi family?"

I look at Marcus, seeing if he wants to do the talking. He nods at me, so I speak. "Well, Thomas, the new head of the Rossi Family, plans to make no changes. Unless something glaringly bad comes to his attention, he sees no reason to change anything. That being said, Mr. Rossi is open to changing certain deals if both parties would like. Mr. Rossi understands some of his father's deals were unfairly one-sided. So, in a show of good faith, he would discuss new and more equal terms." That gets their attention.

"Why would he do that?" Frank asks me.

"Because he isn't Enzo."

"No one willingly renegotiates terms like the ones Enzo had. It would be stupid on his part. He runs the risk of losing out on millions," Walter tells me, confusion lacing his words.

"Right. So, I'm going to speak very bluntly, ok?" I look at Marcus again, and he smirks at me. "Dude, you could do the talking. I'd be thrilled to sit back and stare at Mr. Murphy while you fine gentlemen figure shit out." Marcus smiles at me again.

"Fine," he says. "Gentlemen, my dad was a piece of shit. I'm not him. I also have zero interest in having to keep a fucking eye on you guys all the time. Do you know how much fucking manpower he wasted watching you three? And the best part? He still fucking missed pretty much every single deal Thomas did in the last three years. Sir, you are impressive. I understand Ava's crush on you a bit," Marcus tells Thomas. Both men chuckle.

"Happy to share some tips if you need, Marcus."

"Thanks. I may take you up on that offer, but not around Ava because I'm not sure what she's liable to do to you if she is forced to spend a lot more time with you."

"Piss off. I've got myself under control. Just get the fuck on with it."

"Very well, gentleman, speak to your lawyers, draw up new offers, and we will sit down and work it out. I don't want your business. I don't want to have to babysit. I just want to move the fuck on from everything Enzo Rossi was."

Frank, Walter, and their men leave after a toast to new deals. I look over at Thomas. "What do you want, Mr. Murphy?" I ask him.

"Nothing, Ava. I want to make sure you're good. Your dad was my best friend, so I wanted to see how you fared."

"I fared well. Harry was good to me. He loves me like a daughter. The only thing that would have been better was if my parents hadn't died. I promise, Thomas; I'm happy, I'm good."

Thomas smiles at me, and I know I'm blushing, but the man is magnificent. He's about six feet tall, with black hair sprinkled with grey. His eyes are a cornflower blue, framed with black lashes. His jaw is strong, and he has a close-cropped beard that, like his hair, is black, speckled with grey, He gets this tick in his jaw when he's mad and trying to keep his temper in check. His shoulders are broad, and he has a slim waist. His ass is juicy, and his thighs are a whole other level of insanity. The man plays rugby. Even now, in his late forties, he still plays. I want to play rugby with him. I'd happily let him lift me to catch the ball like they do.

"Ava," Marcus squeezes my leg to get my attention.

"Yeah? Yes? "

"You are in so much trouble when we get back to the hotel, Little Fury," he whispers into my ear, his teeth skimming the shell of it. It sends a shiver through my body straight to my core.

"Seems reasonable," I reply.

Thomas shakes Marcus's hand, kisses me on the cheek, collects his men, and heads out.

"So that's what hearts in the eyes look like," Caden muses.

"Haha. You're funny, Caden," all the guys laugh at my expense. "Don't you assholes have a fucking plane to catch?"

"Yes, Little Fury, we do," Sebastian says. "All right, guys, lets go. The car is here to take us to the airport."

We say goodbye, and the boys leave me and Marcus.

"Well, Ava, I think we should head to the hotel. My palm

is itching to teach my woman a lesson about openly flirting with an older man in front of me."

I look up at him and smile back at his smile. I reach up on my tiptoes and kiss him. "I will gladly accept my punishment."

CHAPTER THIRTY ONE

PRESENT

I'm so lost in my thoughts that I almost miss my turn-off. Thankfully, my navigation is set and I see the airport up ahead. It's small, used mostly for planes bringing in fishermen who takes boats from here to many of the surrounding islands.

I see the hanger Ben told me to go to, and drive right over, marveling at the lack of security. I pull into the hangar and see my plane, and I notice Matt standing, talking to the pilot. He looks in my direction as I pull in and park my truck beside his Charger. Once in park, I let my head fall back and breathe. One flight and a two-hour drive, and I'll be able to collapse.

Matt opens my door and looks me over. "I'm fine, Matt. I need food, some painkillers and sleep." His grumpy ass glares at me, then takes my hand and helps me out.

"Ava?" I hear Caden from behind Matt.

"I'm okay. I'm just exhausted." Caden takes my hand and leads me to the plane. He helps me up the stairs and into a seat. Then brings me pills and a drink along with some snacks. "I love you, Caden. You always feed me, and it's like the best thing ever."

"You're welcome, Ava. Please eat and drink the sports drink as well. We will be taking off right away."

"I didn't see Ben."

"He's here loading his computer equipment, and you know he won't let anyone else do it."

I let out a little chuckle at that. "Ben needs to learn to relax more."

"I think we all do."

"Caden. You can stay. You don't have to come with me. None of you do. I'll give you all the money you need to disappear."

"Ava, my place is with you and those other two assholes. And look at it this way, Costa Rica will force us all to slow the fuck down."

"Ha! I hope so. You and Matt should make babies." He gives me a look, and I realize how that sounded. "I mean, find someone who makes you happy, settle down, and make some babies. Or, even, hey–settle down with Matt and adopt some babies. I would seriously love being an aunt to the babies you guys got."

"Ava, honey, I'm going to just back away now. You should recline and get comfy and get ready to sleep." I hear him chuckle as he heads out into the hangar.

"Whatever, he knows what I meant. But Matt and Caden would have cute babies if it worked like that."

"Talking to yourself, boss lady?"

"Always, Ben, I have the best advice and stories." I deadpan.

He gives me a huge smile, that dimple still there. He has

grown into his height and looks, that's for sure. Ben has never had issues with the ladies. None of the guys do. Even older now, Matt is still a freaking smoke show, and that guy pulls men and women of any age. It's pretty impressive to watch. Caden is still Caden. He doesn't do random hookups and never has. He dated a few women over the last five years, but once he decided to stay in my employ, he would never bring someone into this life. I hope he doesn't stick with that promise; that man needs someone to come home to.

Matt and Caden enter the plane, as does Gus, the pilot. "Hey, Ava, we are ready to take off. It should take us about eight hours to get to Costa Rica."

"Thanks, Gus."

The guys find seats. Matt sits beside me while Caden goes into the cockpit with Gus. Ben sits further back so he has a table to set up his laptop.

"Did you eat? "

"Yes, Matt, I ate; Caden gave me snacks." He rolls his eyes at me.

"What?"

"I'm sorry about Jake."

The mention of Jake brings a pang of sadness, but I try to push it away. "It's fine." I tell him. "Really, who in our business gets to have something like that? I had him for six months, and I wouldn't give that up for anything."

"I know, Ava, but after all the shit with Marcus when you were together, I worried that maybe you would never fall in love again."

"I loved Marcus, but I was never in love with him like he was with me. I thought I was. But after meeting Jake, I know now that I wasn't. Or, at the very least, I didn't love him enough. That was ultimately what did us in. He was in love with me, and one day, he woke up and realized I would never love him that much. Well, that and the drugs and the other women and Alexi."

"So what? He started plotting your death after that?"

"Ha! No. He stayed with me for a while after he realized it. I think he wanted to make sure he was right. Or he hoped to prove himself wrong. It all changed once Marcus realized that his feelings for me gave me power over him. Alexi was finally able to get his claws into Marcus. He was able to influence him and finally drive a wedge between us."

I take a sip of my sports drink as we start down the runway, getting up to speed for takeoff.

"No, I'm pretty sure he didn't start plotting my death until about nine months ago." Matt looks at me and raises an eyebrow.

"I've had a two-day drive to think about it," I say.

Caden comes out of the cockpit and sits beside Matt.

"What are we talking about?"

"I was just starting to fill Matt in on when I think Marcus started to plot my death."

"Ahh yeah, that's a story I'd like to hear as well," Caden says, and Matt grunts back, looking out the window.

"Can I listen as well, or is it an adults-only story?" Ben calls from behind us.

"It is going to be so great living with him. I honestly can't see me wanting to kill him for being a smartass," Caden tells us.

"No killing the kid; we need his skills. I don't want to have to train a new one," I scold him. "Anyway, as I was starting to tell Matt, nine months ago, I had a meeting with the Irish. They needed a couple of people taken care of, and they couldn't do it themselves. They also wanted it to look like an accident. Thomas Murphy sent them to me. Marcus wanted to tag along because he had been trying to get a sit-down with Liam Campbell for a while. We met in Vancouver.

Liam was cordial to Marcus but wouldn't even pretend to discuss business with him. He told Marcus that he had no interest in doing business with him. He said that while he does have his hands in some drugs, heroin is not one of them and never will be. Liam made sure Marcus understood that he considered him less than." I sigh, remembering the shit show that night was.

"Once Liam told Marcus flat-out no, Marcus got pissed off. He stood up from the table and started to walk away. When he saw I wasn't following, he snapped his fingers at me. He snapped his fucking fingers like I was a fucking dog or one of the whores he fucks. Before I could call him on his shit, Liam stood up and walked calmly over to him. Have you ever met the Campbells?"

They all shake their heads. "Well, Liam Campbell is all man. You guys are men, but Liam Campbell is something else. He's six foot four. Black hair and blue eyes. Dark lashes and brows. He has a jawline that should be illegal. Liam Campbell demands your attention. He is devilishly attractive. I say devilishly because Liam looks like how you'd picture the devil. Oh! And shoulders that make Matt look small."

"You and Irish men, hey Ava?" Caden laughs at me.

"It's so true. I can't even explain what the Irish accent does to my lady parts." We all laugh, remembering every single time I had to interact with Thomas Murphy.

"Anyway, Liam stood up, walked over to Marcus, and got right in his face. Marcus is tall and in good shape. But next to Liam Campbell, Marcus looks like Ben."

"Hey! I've put on a ton of muscle. Don't be mean."

"Sorry, Ben, yes, you have." I chuckle again and keep going. "Anyway, Liam got in his face and calmly told him never to speak to me like that again. And that 'he should learn some fucking respect for the woman who is probably the only reason he was still alive and that anyone still does business with him." I close my eyes, taking a breath. "Liam said some things to Marcus I couldn't hear, and Marcus said nothing, just nodded and looked at me, then turned and left with Alexi. Marcus called me about five minutes later. I told him I would take the job from Liam and talk to him the next day. That night still pisses me off."

"That went over well with Marcus, I'm assuming?" Caden asks.

"Caden, it really didn't," I reply.

"Will you have dinner with me, lass?" Liam asks me.

"I think I could be persuaded to do that."

"What will it take for me to persuade you?"

"Honestly?"

"Yes."

"Very little. Just keep talking to me, and I'll do pretty much anything you ask me to."

He looks at me over the rim of his whiskey glass as he takes a sip, never breaking eye contact. "Let's start with dinner and then see how we feel about dessert."

The conversation flows easily between us. We talk about a few of the more interesting jobs I've done over the years. I tell him about a couple of hits that went awry and about stealing a 200-year-old book for some recluse collector. Before long, we had been sitting talking for a couple of hours.

"You should come up to my room with me, Ava."

"Hmm, I don't usually visit clients in their rooms. Doesn't seem safe to me."

"I'm not safe, Ava, but you'll be safe with me."

He stands up, moving closer; bending down over me, I feel his breath on my neck. I smell the whisky he's drunk tonight and a deep, warm spice that I'm sure is just him. He smells so good I close my eyes as his lips graze the curve of my ear. I can't hide the shudder that his closeness elicits from me.

"Say yes, Ava, come to my room and let me taste every fucking

delectable inch of you. Let me bury my tongue in you." I feel his hand on my leg, his fingers brushing across the flesh on my inner thighs. "While you come on it, whimpering my name."

I don't speak; I can't. I just nod and stand. He takes my hand, pulling me into his side. We walk to the hotel lobby, leading me to the elevator, where one of his guys has it waiting already. His men check that the elevator's empty, and Liam pulls me into it with him. None of his guys join us, and when the elevator doors close, Liam is on me.

His kiss is possessive and hungry. He wraps my hair around his fist, tugging it. The slight twinge of pain causing me to gasp against his mouth, giving his tongue the access it wants. His tongue slides against mine, and he grabs my bottom lip with his teeth, biting. I moan into his mouth, and he takes that from me like I owe it to him.

And maybe I do.

I feel drunk as he kisses me. Like my lips and body are his to control and use, however he pleases. My entire body is alive from his kiss. I feel him everywhere, and I want him to take more from me. Take all of it.

His hands are on my ass, and he lifts me; I wrap my legs around his waist as he pushes me into the wall of the elevator hard. I feel him against my core; he is so fucking hard already. My skirt is up over my hips, and his hands have my ass in their grasp, and he kneads it as he rolls his hips into me. The movement rubs him against my core, against my clit. I break the kiss and drop my head back against the wall of the elevator as he rocks his hips into me again. I moan out my breath as he drags his pant-covered rock-hard cock against me.

Liam groans in response to my breathy moan, "I think I'm going to make you come like this first before I even get my fingers or tongue into your sweet pussy." He punctuates his words with another roll of his hips, and I answer with another needy gasp.

"Yes," I say as the elevator doors open, and Liam walks us out of

it, his hands holding my ass firm so he keeps me pressed against him. The steps he takes rock him over my clit, again and again. He takes another step into the suite, pushing me against another wall. His mouth finds my throat, and he drags his teeth over my sensitive skin, his hips rolling into me over and over.

My hips start moving to meet his, every thrust causing my panties to drag along my clit, spreading my lips, allowing the material of his pants and his rock-hard cock to drive me closer and closer to an orgasm.

"Fuck, Little Villain, I can feel how sopping wet you are for me; you are soaking my cock right through my pants." My eyes close as I let my orgasm grow. "Look at me, Ava," his words are said low and huskily. "Eyes on me every time I make you come tonight. Do you hear me?" My eyes open to meet his.

"Yes," I reply to his command.

His mouth is back on my neck, one of his hands is grabbing my breast, squeezing and pinching my nipple; the overload of sensations through my clothing is making me dizzy. He doesn't even have me naked yet. Fuck. I think to myself.

"You going to come for me?" he asks as he grinds himself into me.

"Yes," I reply, and a strangled, needy cry leaves me.

"Good girl. Now, let's see you come all over my pants; let's see how wet you can make them." He rolls into me harder and bites me where my neck and shoulder meet, and I cannot stop the orgasm as it hits. I throw my head back, banging it against the wall as I let out a cry. My nails dig into the back of his head; pulling him closer so I can ride my orgasm out against him. My breathing is fast and ragged.

"Fucking hell," I mumble. Liam chuckles at me.

"Oh, Little Villain, we are only getting started; that was the single most fucking beautiful thing I have ever seen. I cannot wait to watch you come while my cock is buried so far into you." He

looks down to where my skirt is over my hips, and he runs his knuckles over the lace.

He presses one against my clit.

"Liam," I whimper.

"That's one."

I look at him, confused. "I told you I'd make you whimper my name, lass. I'm keeping count."

"Ahh," I say, laughing at him.

"Put your purse on the table, lass."

"Huh? What table?"

"This one." He drops my purse onto the table beside the elevator doors.

We're staring at each other, and he growls low in his chest. His mouth is back on mine, and he starts walking down a hallway, carrying me with him as he ravishes my mouth again. My phone starts ringing just as we reach a door. "Can you ignore it?"

I drop my head against his. "No, probably not. No one calls me unless they actually have to speak to me. And very few people have my number, so I need to answer it."

I unwrap my legs from him, and he sets me down on the shiny black stone floor. I walk back to my phone, my shoes clicking with each step. I see Liam from the corner of my eye. He's standing in the hall, his arms braced against either side.

"Hello …. Well, why the fuck would you let him do that? Jesus fuck, Alexi, what fucking use are you?" He starts yelling at me in Russian, and I pull the phone away from my ear. Liam grabs it from me and puts it on speaker.

"You will watch your fucking tone with her, asshole, or you and I will be having a very direct conversation," Liam growls at him in Russian. Alexi stops yelling at me and switches back to English.

"Ava, I had to take a fucking call from Yuri. I was gone from him for about ten minutes. I came back, and he was already half a vile in."

"I fucking hate you, Alexi. Marcus never tried a fucking drug

before you. If I get the chance, I'm going to kill you so fucking slowly and painfully for what you did to him. I'll be there in ten."

Liam looks down at his phone. "My car is waiting for you downstairs. My driver will take you wherever you want to go. Is there any chance I can persuade you to take me with you?" Liam looks up at me, asking.

"I wish, but you, unfortunately, are the reason for this little temper tantrum," I reply.

"I assumed. Colin will go with you and stay with you until he is certain you are safe."

"I could probably give you like four minutes," I say, waggling my eyebrows at him.

He lets out a laugh at that. "Ava love, the first time I bury myself in you, it will be after you have already come on my tongue and hand."

"A girl can dream." I step into him just as the elevator doors open. A guy steps out, who I'm assuming is Colin. I grab Liam's shirt, pull him down to me, and kiss him hard.

"Goodnight, Liam."

"Goodnight, Little Villain."

"Marcus hung up on me. A couple of hours later, I got a call from Alexi–Marcus was fucked up, and there was an escort who had been hurt. So, I had to cut my evening short to deal with that." I shake my head at the memories from that clusterfuck of a night.

"After that, Marcus was different with me. After I completed the job, Marcus was distant the next week. He stopped confiding in me. Even after we broke up, we were still us, you know? We were still the other person's person. But it was all different when I chose to do the Campbell job. I knew it was different, but I figured it was a tiff, and we would get past it like we always had. Guess I was a wee bit off about that." I laugh without humor. "Anyway, that is when I think he started to plot my death."

"Well, fuck, Ava."

"Pretty much, right, Matt?"

"You need to sleep, Ava," Caden tells me. I nod and recline my seat. I pull my legs up and snuggle into the pillow. Matt leans over and covers me with a blanket. One of them dims the cabin lights, and I'm asleep. I don't wake up until Caden tells me we have landed.

CHAPTER THIRTY TWO

The guys get off the plane and start loading the truck, waiting for us. I make my way slowly off the plane, the stiffness in my shoulder is a little concerning, but it's not something I can deal with for another few hours. As I step off of the plane, the heat greets me, and I smile. Matt has been to Costa Rica multiple times, and he's the one who bought the property here for me and built the homes. It's incredible how fast things get done when money is no issue. I realized then that Harry was right. I had an idea or a clue that this would or could happen. Matt did all the groundwork here. I asked him to do it a week after I met Liam. Everything is in his name, well, not his real name, but Ben made sure to bury any trace of Costa Rica so deep that no one would be able to find a connection between here and us.

"Told you the heat would be everything you wanted," Matt says with satisfaction.

"You didn't lie, Matt."

Once the guys have loaded the truck's bed and everything strapped down and covered, Caden helps me into the back seat. "Ava, are you sure you don't want to sit up front?" Ben asks me before he slides into the passenger seat.

"I'm sure Ben."

I know my voice sounds tired. I'm exhausted, and I feel warm. There is a tingling suspicion that it's not just the tropical weather making me feel this way. I rummage through my bag and find the antibiotics and painkillers Jake gave me. I take two of each. We aren't on the road long before I'm asleep again.

I wake up to the sounds of Matt and Caden discussing what to do with me. "You don't need to do anything with me. Just help me get into the house and show me where my room is. I can do the rest," I inform them. I don't miss the look that passes between the two of them. "Boys, be aware, even in my current state, I'm pretty sure I could take both of you." Caden rolls his eyes at me.

"You keep believing that, princess," Matt says, taking my hand and leading me into the house.

"Fuck, Matt! This is spectacular!" I am awestruck by this house. You enter into a wide-open space. The stairs lead to the second floor, but the main floor is a glass masterpiece. The main room has a large U-shaped sectional. Everything is white and wood accented with grey and a deep navy throws and pillows. The kitchen has granite countertops, and the lower cupboards are a deep navy. The appliances are stainless, and the upper cabinets are white and have simple, clean lines. The main floor is open, and you can see all the way through to the back of the house. The back wall is just glass that I assume opens up to nothing. "I want to see the backyard."

"Ava, the backyard will still be there tomorrow after you clean up, eat, shower, and sleep."

"I'm aware, Matt, but I want to see it now."

I hear what I believe is a grumble from him consisting of words like "stubborn," "fucking woman," and "do what's best," and I think, "It drives me crazy." But he leads me through the kitchen and opens the back of the house for me. I audibly gasp. There is jungle around us, but an oasis is directly out the back of the house. It has an outdoor kitchen and seating areas; fire bowls are all along the walkways, and what looks like a fire-burning pizza oven, gas barbeque, and flat-top grill. All this leads you to the largest infinity edge pool I've ever seen. And the edge of that pool continues right out into the ocean.

"Matt, this is better than I ever could have asked for. I don't know how you did it, but it is so close to the house in the Caymans, yet so much better. Thank you. Thank you." I throw my arms around him to hug him, but it pulls my shoulder and side, causing a lot of pain. I school my features, and Matt doesn't notice, his gaze still locked on the ocean before him. "Point me in the direction of my room?"

"Yeah, let me carry your bag up for you."

"Nope, I got it." I swing my bag onto my good shoulder, showing how fine I am. I hit my side and bite my tongue to stop the cry of pain that's about to bubble out.

"You are upstairs. The entire upstairs is yours. Ben is in the blue house over to the right. Caden and I are in the guest rooms as we wait for the last few things for our places. So, you will have us with you for a few weeks in the main house."

"Works for me. Again, thank you, Matt. This is the most beautiful place I've ever seen."

He nods at me, not one for compliments, and I make my way inside and up the stairs. My last bit of strength is quickly draining.

I enter my room, and again, it's like Matt stole the images from my head and made them real. I don't know when it happened, but over the last five years, Matt has quickly become probably my best friend. Marcus hasn't been that for a while, but I didn't notice when Matt took over that role.

The first thing I see is dark wood floors. The stone from downstairs is not up here. The walls are dark grey, and the bed is covered in a black bedding set woven with a deep jade green thread.

I carry my bag with me into the bathroom and close the door. I start the shower and let it run while I peel off the clothes I've been wearing for two days. "So gross," I tell the empty room. Standing in front of the mirror, I carefully remove the bandage on my side, instantly knowing it's infected. It's red and hot and leaks less than appealing fluid. I reach behind me to remove the bandage from my shoulder, and I smell the infection there when I pull the bandage off. Jake would be so mad. He would slap my ass to remind me that this is why we go to the hospital when we get shot.

I shake my head, not letting thoughts of Jake in. I'm too tired and drained to let him invade my thoughts; if I do, I know I'll break.

I climb into the shower. I know I shouldn't get my stitches wet, but I need to clean the wounds more than anything. I have a bar of antibacterial soap that I stole from Jake and use it to clean both bullet wounds. I hiss, and a few tears fall because it hurts worse than I would like to admit. "Ava?" I hear Matt as he enters my bathroom. He looks at the bandages I left in the sink. "You could have asked for help, you know."

"I'm aware! But what's the fun in that? This way, I can inflict more pain than necessary to wash my hair and clean the infected areas."

"Fucking Hell, Ava!" Matt pulls his phone, keys and wallet out of his pocket, toes off his boots and removes his socks, t-shirt and jeans. He steps into the shower with me. "Turn around."

I do, and he grabs the showerhead and helps me wash my hair so that the shampoo doesn't run over my shoulder and side. He then runs a bit of conditioner through it, quickly rinsing it out.

"Do you need me to wash your back?" he asks me cheekily.

"Matt, you'd be so lucky to be able to wash my back. I mean, you're still super hot for an old guy." I laugh back at him.

"Shut up, Ava; we don't make sex jokes about each other; let's try to remember that."

I can't help the laugh that escapes me. "You sure? Cause I am pretty sure we both just made one." I tell him amusement lacing my words. "I washed my body before you came in."

He reaches around me and turns off the water. He steps out, dripping wet, and hands me a towel. I wrap my body, taking another towel and wrap my hair in it. I step out of the shower and head towards the vanity. Matt towels himself off quickly, drops his boxers, and steps into his jeans.

There is a level of familiarity with Matt that I have never had with another. We have always been at ease with each other. He rummages in the bag, finds everything he needs, and cleans my shoulder. I can't help the hisses of pain or the whimper here and there. It hurts badly, and I have no energy to hide it. "Ava, I'm going to remove the stitches. I need to clean everything better."

"Matt, I don't think I can handle being re-stitched with how bad it hurts right now."

"I know. I won't restitch you if you promise me you will move around this place like a 90-year-old who just broke her hip. I can bandage you. But if you do anything that causes them to bleed, I'll have to stitch them back up."

"Okay," I say quietly. I feel the tears stinging my eyes. I suck in a breath and bite my cheek until they pass.

Once he's done and my shoulder has a new bandage, I grab a pair of panties from the bag and slip them on. I hold a tank top, and Matt helps me slide it on, careful not to jostle my arm.

"I'm going to go change. You good?"

"Yup, thank you. I'm going to go to sleep. Thanks again for all of it, Matt."

"It's why you pay me so well."

"A bit, yeah." I laugh. I follow him out of the bathroom, and he walks out my door.

"The switch on the bedside table will lower blackout curtains for you," he calls to me over his shoulder as he makes his way back to the stairs. Once I'm in bed and the curtains are drawn, I sleep. I sleep for 18 hours. I get up to use the bathroom and go back to sleep for another 12. I know Matt and the guys woke me a few times to take painkillers and antibiotics, but I don't remember much.

When I finally wake up, I feel a lot better. My side and shoulder still hurt, but the pain from the infection is gone. I head into the bathroom to wash my face and brush my teeth. I see clean clothes laid out for me, so I change and pull my hair into a ponytail.

I open the blackout curtains, and I see the patio doors for the first time. I step out in the mid-morning sun. I can hear the waves up ahead, knowing this will be one of my favorite spots. I sigh, not wanting to go in, but my stomach is being terribly rude and won't settle down for me to enjoy the view a bit longer.

I leave my room and carefully go down the stairs. I remember Matt's threat about the stitches, so I won't do anything that will make him think he needs to restitch them.

I enter the kitchen, heading for the fridge. I open it and

start pulling things out. I see breakfast sausage, so I get that in a pan on low. I grab a couple of potatoes, quickly chop them up, add them to another pan and put the lid on them, leaving them to cook. I grab a brick of cheese out of the fridge and cut off a slice, then I see a loaf of fresh bread and cut a piece off, slathering it in butter. I'm pretty sure I moan when I bite into the bread. It's so fluffy, and it's still a bit warm. I silently thank Parker for finding Caden for me; the man makes good bread.

"Hey, boss lady, look at you up and about," Ben says as he walks inside.

"Have you eaten?" I ask.

"No, I have not."

I nod and grab another couple of potatoes. I chop them up quickly and put them in the pan. I add water to the pan to steam the potatoes before I get them crispy. "I'm just doing scrambled eggs. Is that okay?"

"Yup, I'm not one to complain about food someone else makes me," Ben says, watching me.

"What?"

"Nothing, it's just good to see you up and about."

"Worried about me, were you? Where are the other two?"

"Town to pick up more groceries. I was voted to stay here and keep an eye on you."

"Well, now you get food, so it's win-win."

"How are things? "

"Marcus is still looking for you. But we got out fast enough that we're nice and lost." Ben smiles to himself, clearly pleased with his ability to outsmart Arthur. Arthur is the tech guy Marcus has. Marcus felt Ben was too young and mouthy—his loss. Ben is one of the best there is. Parker will tell you Ben is better than him now, so there is no better compliment than that.

"Are you going to miss showing him up?"

"No, it got very boring. But Marcus is pissed, so I think, unfortunately, Arthur will be finding himself with a hole in his head very soon."

"Fair. You can only take so many fuck-ups before it's time to cut your losses."

"Is that what you would have done with me? Cut your losses?"

"Yes," I say matter-of-factly. "If you or any of you three had turned out not to be as good at your jobs as you are, I would have cut my losses. But I wouldn't have waited two years like Marcus. I would have done it the first time any of you fucked up. That also would have meant the likelihood of you guys getting a bullet in the head was significantly less. You knew way less sketchy shit about me back then."

Ben laughs. And I smile at him. I love to hear the guys laugh.

"Did Matt mention a sound system?"

"Pay up, Caden. She's been up for less than 40 minutes and is already asking about the sound system," Matt says as he and Caden come into the house.

Caden puts his bags down and digs into his pocket, dropping $50 on the island for Matt.

"If I knew you were cooking, we wouldn't have eaten in town," Matt says.

"I'm sure it was better than what I'm throwing together."

"Ava, your phone is hooked up to the house systems already. You can talk to the system, and it'll respond." Ben informs me.

"Like Alexa?" I ask.

"Yes, but your system name is B.O.B.," Caden says with a grin.

"What am I missing?"

"Those two old men think they were funny naming the system BOB."

"Ava, ask him what it stands for."

"What does it stand for, Ben?" I ask as I turn back to stir the potatoes.

"Fuck off, I'm not telling her. It's not even funny."

"Can't you just change the name to whatever?"

"No, he can't actually. He lost a bet."

"Hey Bob, can you tell us what your name stands for?"

"Good morning, Caden; my name is an acronym for Ben, only better. BOB"

I look at the three of them, and I can't stop my grin. I look at Ben and roll my eyes because he's right. It's not nearly as funny as Matt and Caden think. I also realize how lucky I was to find them.

"Hand me my phone, please." Ben slides it over to me, and I open it and connect it to BOB. I select a playlist.

"Psycho Killer" by the Talking Heads fills the house, and I smile. Caden barks out a laugh.

"It seemed fitting," I say, going back to cooking.

Once the food is ready, Ben and I sit down to eat. Caden and Matt have gone to talk to the guys working on the property and finishing up their homes. I got a text from Matt saying the woman he hired for housekeeping and cooking would be here at 1 to meet me and go over what I would need from her. That gives me a couple of hours, so I grab my headphones and head out to walk along the beach.

My ears are filled with "The Nature of Daylight" by Max Ritcher as I walk along the beach, letting the water lap at my legs. I need to decide what my plan is. I must decide if I want to retaliate or just let it be. Just walk away, let the hurt and the anger go, and let Marcus go. I know he's been gone for a while, but until a few days ago, I still hoped he would snap out of it. Or Yuri would die, I would kill Alexi, and Marcus would be Marcus again.

I sit down in the sand and stare out at the waves. Water

has always calmed and centered me and it does so for me now. I realize that I don't want revenge. I want to be. I want to wake up in the morning and read. I want to sit on my balcony and watch the waves roll in. I want to let Marcus and that life just be. I don't need the money; I have more than I can ever spend. I don't want revenge. I want Marcus to find some peace. And maybe me disappearing from his world will do that for him.

I know I will never stop loving Marcus. Our bond will outlast anything he puts me through. I will always want that seven-year-old boy I offered Mr. Waffle to, to find peace, to find a place in himself that his demons both inflicted upon and caused by him to no longer torment him. That beautiful boy with those intense green eyes flecked with gold, who grew into a man with a shattered soul, grew into a man whose past traumas won the majority of the battles that shaped him.

I know I made a mistake when I let our relationship progress from friends. But back then, I would have done and given Marcus anything. He was my family, and I loved him more than anyone. When things started to shift between us, I honestly thought we loved each other enough that we would make it work.

I head back to the house to tell the guys what I've decided and meet my new housekeeper and cook.

Marguerite is a lovely older woman who had her only child later in life. She has raised her daughter alone her whole life. Her daughter, Anna, is 17. I loved Marguerite the moment I met her. I'm excited that she will start tomorrow. I asked her if she and her daughter would like to live on the grounds, but she said no, they have a small apartment in town. I introduce her to Caden. She had already met Matt, and I let her know that either of the guys would be happy to pick her up in case of bad weather as she drives a little scooter, and we are a solid 30 minutes from town on that thing.

We say our goodbyes, and then I wander. I wander around the house looking and learning it. There are three guest bedrooms. Two are occupied with Matt and Caden. There is also a home gym with sparring mats and heavy bags, a treadmill, a rowing machine, free weights and a few other things. It's a well-stocked gym. I did give Matt free rein, and he has his priorities.

Matt BBQs us all steaks with grilled veggies and sweet potatoes that evening. We sit outside enjoying the breeze off the ocean, laughing and talking about nothing and everything. The guys clean up after dinner, and I say good night and head upstairs. I sit on the balcony in an overstuffed chair that makes me feel like I'm sitting in a marshmallow. I grab my Kindle and read for a couple of hours.

Marguerite shows up the following day before I'm even awake. She gets started on many things I never would have thought to ask her to do. When I go downstairs around 10, she smiles and tells me to sit, and she will feed me. Her English is broken, but I know more than enough Spanish so we have no trouble communicating. I like her even more. She is the kind of person everyone should have in their lives. She is just genuine and open and kind. And in my life, that is not something I'm used to. It's pretty much trained out of you by Harry very quickly.

The following four months pass fast. Caden's house gets finished, he moves out leaving me and Matt in the big house. I like living with Matt. He's quiet but is always up for a workout buddy, or to play crib, or another board game. We share very similar tastes in music, so that's a massive plus for me as far as roommates go. Action and sci-fi movies every Thursday night. The guys and I have found a good rhythm. Ben still works, but because of the nature of his work, he does it under a different name. Matt and Caden have decided to open a gym in town. They need to be busy. We all need to be busy.

The sun is starting to go down as I make my way back to the house. Ben is on a date, and Matt and Caden went into town for a beer with some locals they met surfing a couple of months ago. No one should be in the house. So, I find it a little odd, seeing a guy in there.

What is with men breaking into my beach houses and trying to kill me?

It seems ridiculous that this has happened twice in my life.

I make my way towards the house and in through the glass doors. This situation is too close to what happened in the Caymans a few years ago. I reach into my bag and grab my gun. When Caden gets home, he owes me $100. I told him it was necessary to carry a gun to the beach with me. Pretty sure I said, "Fuck that; you never know," but the point is, I was right.

I slowly make my way towards my intruder. Once I'm close enough, I move at him fast, sweeping his legs out from under him. He goes down hard. He recovers quickly, but I expect it. No one is going to send a half-ass hitman after me again. My gun is against his head before he can get back to his feet. The guy raises his hands, and I run mine along his sides, checking for a weapon.

"Ava." I'm not done checking him for weapons yet when he says my name. Ignoring him, I finish checking when he repeats my name. This time, I'm 90% sure I heard what I thought I had heard.

"Ava, could you put the gun down? "

I stop moving. I stop breathing. I press the gun harder into his head.

"Jake?"

CHAPTER THIRTY THREE

I press my gun into his temple. Knowing it hurts. "Who the fuck do you work for?" I demand.

He raises his hands, showing me that he has no weapon. "Ava, please, love, can you put the gun down so we can talk?"

"Who, Jake? Who the fuck do you work for?" I pause for a second, realizing what I heard. I move in front of him and take a step back so I can see him better.

"Is that a fucking Irish accent?"

"Ava. Ava, please let me explain."

"No. You need to shush for a moment." I cock my head and really look at him, searching for what I had missed for months. I study him for a moment, running scenarios through my head and only one makes any sense. Pain shoots through my heart as I realize who he is.

"Fuck, I'm stupid. You played me for months. You and your fucking brother. Was fucking me a part of the plan for both of you? Liam couldn't complete the task, so it was your turn?" Confusion crosses his face, but I ignore it because I am ignoring his face.

"You're a fucking Campbell! Liam has a brother. What the hell is his name?"

"It's…" he starts to say, but my gun is back against his skull, pressing harder as I contemplate.

"No, Jake. You. Do. Not. Speak. What the fuck was his name… Declan. You're Declan Campbell. Liam is your older brother." He nods.

I take a few steps back and sit in the chair in front of him, my gun on my thigh as I stare at him. The man I never thought I would see again. The man I would have given anything to see again. And here he is. And my heart is breaking all over again.

"You have two minutes, Jake–I mean, Declan. Explain yourself with as few words as possible." I see him flinch at the hurt in my voice, but I can't seem to care at the moment. I want him to hurt.

"Ava, I'm so sorry."

I cut him off. "No, Jake, keep your fucking apologies. You will either explain the how and the what and all that, or I will put a bullet in your head and bury you in the jungle. Those are the only two options for you, so explain well and explain quickly."

He's looking right at me, but he's unsure, he has never seen this side of me. He's never been face to face with this Ava. So he is trying to gauge how serious my threat is. "I will shoot you, Jake. I won't risk what I have here, and I won't risk the guys' lives. Not for anyone, not for any reason." I say with a resigned sigh. I see him nod slightly and then take a calming breath. A twitch in his eye tells me he is close to losing his temper. He isn't enjoying the gun pointed at him or the fact that I am not doing what he wants.

"The night we met; I didn't know who you were. You

were just a beautiful woman on the side of the road who had a flat tire. When I got close to you, I recognized you pretty quickly." He pauses to take a breath. "You smiled at me, and I made a choice in that moment. I gave you my cover name and story."

"Jake–ah Declan–I met you in the hospital. For lunch."

"My backstory is true. I was a smart kid; I went to university on a wrestling scholarship and became a doctor. The family needed a doctor, and I had always wanted to be one. My father was shot when I was 15. I was with him, and he bled out while I sat there, unable to do anything." He closes his eyes and breathes out. "I was working in LA. I had a one-year contract to cover for a friend while they did research when I met you. You were not part of a plan. You were a fluke meeting, Ava. I didn't even know you had met with Liam when I met you. I told Liam nothing about you. I knew he would have an issue with us dating because of who you are. I didn't know you and Liam had a history. Apparently, neither Liam nor I wanted to share you with the other," he says with a clenched jaw. I see his hand flex at the mention of my history with his brother.

"Our meeting was purely by chance. Starting a relationship with you was risky. I knew that, but I also didn't care. I wanted you. I have never wanted someone as much as I wanted you from the moment I met you."

The front door opens, and Matt walks in. "Honey, I'm home." he bellows.

"In the living room, sweet cheeks," I yell back. Matt looks over at me. "We have company."

"So, no movie night then?" He deadpans.

"I mean, this one's time is up, so I'd be open to a movie."

"Need help with anything, Ava?" Matt asks me.

"No, I got this. Jake, or should I say, Declan Campbell, was just leaving." I catch Matt's look of surprise at the name.

"I'm not done talking to you, Ava," Jake says with gritted teeth as he starts to get to his feet.

"You're done here, Jake. I mean Declan. We're done." I click the safety back on and stand. "Just go. There's nothing here for you." I feel exhausted.

"Matt, can you start the BBQ? I made some burgers earlier." I turn my back on Declan and head towards the kitchen. He grabs my wrist to pull me back, but I'm on edge, so I'm ready for it. I get an elbow up as he pulls me back and nail him in the cheek. He sucks in a breath at the impact. I get my hands on his arm, twist it behind his back, place my other hand on the back of his head, grab his hair, and push his head forward, forcing him to bend.

"Need any help there, Boss?" Matt asks, concern in his voice.

"Nah, I'm good; the younger Campbell is leaving anyway."

"I'm not done talking to you, Ava," Declan hisses at me.

"You are, though." I start moving us towards the door. I let go of his head to open it, but Declan twists in my grasp, forcing himself into my body and breaking the hold on his arm. He shoves me against the door.

"Ava," I hear Matt say tensely.

"It's fine, Matt. He isn't going to hurt me. It turns out the doc has a few moves I didn't know about."

"Ava lass, please, I need you to listen to me." That Irish lilt in his voice is sexier than I want to admit. It's also distracting because I find myself staring at his lips and remembering how good they feel.

"And I need you to let me go and get out of my house."

He pushes me into the door harder. "Little Fury, please listen to me."

I freeze at that name and hear Matt stop doing whatever

he is doing in the kitchen. "How the fuck do you know that name?"

"Because Liam went to see Harry. He's how I found you. "

"Harry would never have given me up. What the fuck did you do to him." I seethe, but I'm done with this shit now. "Matt, call him right fucking now." Declan has me pinned between his body and the door; my arms are between us, his hands on my wrists. I only have two options here: headbutt him or option number two. I go with number two, and I crash my mouth to his.

Declan is startled by my kiss and freezes for a moment. I hear him growl and return my kiss. I open my mouth and allow his tongue to invade. His hands let go of my wrists and instantly go to my ass, and that's all I needed. Once my hands are free, I place them on his chest, sinking my nails into his muscles, and he rocks his body against me in response. I bend one knee, getting my foot flat on the door, and push off as hard as possible.

The force and surprise are enough to make Declan step back, allowing me to clock him. He grunts at the contact, but I don't stop. I kick him in the chest, sending him sprawling to the floor. He has no time to catch his breath before I'm straddling him. I get my knees on his fingers beside his hips and rise, putting as much force as I can on them. "Matt! Give me my fucking gun." Matt is already in the room, phone to his ear, passing my gun to me.

Looking down at Declan, I cock my head to the side. He's watching me intently, trying to figure out a way to make me listen to him. None of this was going the way he hoped it would. His eyes go wide as he watches me. He sees the change, whether he knows what it is, is a different question. But it's not fear. I see it in his eyes; it's wonder and awe.

"Mr. Campbell, you and I are going to have a chat now," I

say. Matt stiffens in my peripheral vision when he hears that tone. He turns and starts walking toward me.

"Ava, maybe you need to take a step back. You don't want to do something you'll regret when you are more, ah... you again." I turn my head to look at him, letting "her" look at him. Matt puts his hands up in surrender. He glances down at Declan. "Sorry, man. It's your bed, apparently."

"I know it is, and I'll take it." Matt nods and takes a few steps back.

I turn back to Declan. "Did you speak to Harry, Matt?"

"I spoke to Beth. Liam went to see Harry two weeks ago. She isn't sure how they found you, but Liam was there. Harry is out fixing a fence. Buck got out. Parker and Wes are figuring out how Liam found you, and she will call me back."

"I'm having a hard time reasoning out why I don't just put a bullet in your head," I tell him, exasperated with myself.

"You can put a bullet in me, Ava; I'll understand. Liam may be annoyed, but I'll understand."

Still looking at him, I roll my eyes. "Mr. Campbell, do you know who I am? Do you know what I do?"

"Yes."

"Do you think your brother scares me?"

"I don't know Ava. There are things about you and him that I was not privy to, apparently."

"Guess if you leave here, you'll have to have a few words with the older Campbell brother. I should have known, though. Thinking back, you both kiss the same, and you both are ass men." Declan growls under me, not enjoying my words. I snap my fingers, my brain clicking.

"Matt! Tell Parker to sweep for bugs. That's what Liam did. When I spoke to Harry four days ago, he greeted me with, "Little Fury, have you learned to make any good Costa

Rican foods yet?" I don't need him to confirm it for me. I know I'm right.

"Ava, I'm not going to put up a fight, but I really do need my hands for work. If you let me up, I'll go."

I nod then get off him. I turn, dismissing him, and walk into the kitchen. I grab the burgers and head outside to cook them. Declan tells Matt he is staying at the Casa Flora in town. But I keep walking. Matt joins me outside a few minutes later, handing me a beer and taking the flipper from me to take over cooking the burgers. "I'm going to make a salad." I start to go back inside.

"Just sit, Ava. We can throw a salad together when I take the burgers off the grill."

"How am I not dead, Matt?" he looks at me, trying to figure out my thought process.

"Look at the last year of my life. How did I survive as a fucking paid killer for years when in the last year, two of the biggest parts of my life lied to me. One tried to have me killed, and the other one played me for six months. Matt, I wanted to walk away for Jake. I wanted to sign everything over to Marcus. I wanted a white picket fence life with Jake. And it turns out that Jake doesn't even exist."

"Ava, you're very good at your job. You're one of the best in the world. The jobs you did over the last few years and the amount people paid you prove that. But you loved Marcus since you were seven. No one with a history like yours would have seen what Marcus had planned. You trusted him. You guys had each other's backs for a long time. We all missed it, Ava. I've known Marcus a while. I never liked him, but I also never questioned his love for you."

"I think maybe you knew. You did set Costa Rica up without any question."

"No, that's more of a 'we follow Ava's orders kind of thing,' and I wanted to be here. We didn't see you and

Marcus grow up together. We came in in what turned out to be closer to the end than the middle. And as for Jake Ben ran him multiple times. Nothing was ever even remotely off.. There was no way you would have known unless he slipped up, which he never did."

"Ben is going to be so mad when you tell him he missed that Jake's whole life was a fake."

"I'm telling him?" Matt asks me as he flips the burgers.

"You're telling me you aren't going to enjoy his little meltdown when you tell him he fucked up?"

He doesn't say anything, just smirks and sips his beer. "What are you going to do about the Irishman?"

"I have no fucking clue, Matt."

CHAPTER THIRTY FOUR

The next couple of days pass quietly. Declan has been out to my place every day, managing to make friends with Caden and Matt. He's been helping them build a pergola. Ben won't speak to him, furious that the Campbells have someone better than him. He's been obsessively trying to figure out who it is. Declan won't tell him anything, making Ben even more obsessed. I told Caden to give him one more day before stepping in to force Ben to stop.

"Ready, Matt?" I ask as I come out to where they are building.

"Yeah, let me just get this last screw in."

"Have you beat him yet?" Caden asks me with all seriousness.

"No, Caden. I have not. Once he has me under him, I can't move him, so I will keep trying."

"You'll get it. Then you can Pin Matt."

"He likes that position, so I don't think he'll mind too much." I cackle at that.

"Fucker," Matt says and punches Caden when he walks past him.

"Ava," Declan says, but I just walk by, ignoring him. I hear his sigh, but I keep walking like I didn't.

"Sorry man, she'll come around," Caden says to him.

"No, she won't. She's done with men who lie, or try to kill her," I throw back at him.

We head into the gym and start stretching and warming up. Matt has been trying to teach me how to get out from under a man faster. I'm small, which makes me quick, but I'm always at the mercy of my size if my opponent gets the jump on me. That's why I'm always on the offensive when fighting or killing. I need to take them out or incapacitate whoever they are faster than they can get a hold of me. I can get out of a lot of holds, but once I'm pinned, like I had Declan pinned, I'm fucked.

It's happened to me twice. The first time, the guy tried to teach me a lesson by showing me the only thing he thought women are good for. When he went for my pants, his center of gravity shifted, and I bucked him off, hitting him in the head with a nearby rock. It dazed him enough for me to kick him in the balls, retrieve my gun, and shoot him in the head.

The second time, unfortunately, the guy was smarter. He knew who I was and my record, so he just wanted to kill me. He got me down fast and hard, cracking a rib with the impact. Once he was on top of me, the combination of his size and the broken rib made it impossible for me to regain my breath. He had me. I knew I was dead. But that's why I never go alone on a job.

Often, it's only me doing the job, but I always have someone with me in case shit goes sideways. Shit went sideways, and Marcus saved me. He shot the guy in the back of the head and got me the fuck out of there.

"Okay, Ava, let's try to get one arm free today. I know you have enough skill with pressure points and such that if you can get one arm free, you should be able to inflict enough pain to change the attacker's position slightly. I'm not sure if it will be enough, but I think it's a good idea to try."

"That sounds good," I say as I plug in my phone. "What do you want to listen to?"

"I don't know. Whatever you're feeling works for me."

"Death metal it is," Matt gives me a dirty look. I settle on a bluegrass playlist instead. "All the Debts I Owe" by Caamp fills the gym and the rest of the house.

I crack my neck and shake out my hands, watching him, waiting to see when he'll decide to strike. He's fucking fast for a big guy, so I can't take my eyes from him. I manage to avoid his initial grab and go for his legs, but he knows that's what I'll do and it allows him to grab me by the leg and tosses me gently, so I land on the mat. He wastes no time getting on top of me. His larger than fuck body has me locked down underneath him. He makes no mistakes about his body placement on mine. I fight a bit, but I need him to pin me, so I eventually swallow down my need to win and let him.

The goal is to get one arm free. The only thing free for me is my head and legs. My legs are the better choice. I need to get his balance to shift before I can get my arm out from under him. I bend my knees knowing he is expecting me to thrust my hips up. This move works well, but he knows it's coming and counteracts it. I've whined that my attackers won't know my moves like he does, and he tells me to suck it up and figure it out without the hip thrust.

I've been talking to Harry, and he has sent me a few videos: one on how to do a modified outside heel lock and another showing me how to hook my legs under his arms and push him off. I'm going to try both today.

The heel lock is first. I scoot my foot back towards my ass until it's lined with his toe on that side. Then, I get my other foot against the inside of the heel. As quickly as I can, I force his ankle to bend to the floor and twist simultaneously. It works, and I have his lower leg twisted at an uncomfortable angle, and I pull myself out from under him, hitting him in the head, or in a real situation, shooting him in the head or stabbing him in the throat.

I do enjoy a good throat jab or stab.

"Jesus, Ava, that fucking hurt. I think you pulled the ligaments in my ankle."

"Sorry, I wasn't sure how much strength I needed to make it work."

"It's ok. I'm happy you got out of the hold. But I think I need to stop for today. I need to ice my ankle."

"I really am sorry, but I'm also super proud of myself." I can't help but smile at him as we leave the gym. Matt is limping, so I get under his arm to take some weight off his ankle.

Declan and Caden are still outside working. I sit Matt on the couch. "I'll go get your buddy, the doctor, to have a look at you."

"No, that's not needed." But I've already started to walk towards the guys building the pergola.

I stopped to look at the progress of it. I need to hire less attractive men because, seriously, it's beyond ridiculous when you throw a shirtless Jake/Declan into the mix. I shake my head, and I can't help the smile that forms on my lips.

"Doctor Campbell, Matt had an accident in the gym, and he was hoping you could take a look at him?"

"Doctor Campbell? Really, Ava?"

"Doctor Campbell, is that a, yes?"

"God dammit woman." He mutters, resignation, or maybe

a touch of defeat in his voice. My stomach does an involuntary flip of fear for a moment, then I remind myself who he is. "Yes, I'll come and take a look at him."

"Great, he is on the couch. I'm going to get my suit on, boys. The ocean is calling my name."

"Did you take him down, Ava?" Caden asks me.

"I sure did!"

I change quickly into a bathing suit and grab my hat, sunglasses, gun, book, headphones and beach mat. I spray myself down with sunscreen before tossing the bottle in my bag. I stop in the kitchen where Marguerite is making cookies. "Hello, Miss Ava."

"Hi! Those look yummy."

"Yes, Dr. Declan said he likes peanut butter chocolate chip cookies, so I thought I would make him some. Welcome him to your family." Her Spanish-accented English always makes me smile.

"Umm, that is not necessary. He will not be staying." She eyes me like she doesn't believe me.

"Oh, come on now, Little Fury, we both know I'll crack you soon enough," Declan says with that strong, Irish accent.

"Fuck off, Dr. Campbell."

"Here, dear, I made you a sandwich and a few snacks," Marguerite says, handing me a small cooler bag. "Your mug is already filled with ice and water. You go now. Relax," she says and sends me on my way.

I walk down to the beach and find my usual spot. I set my stuff down and lay out my beach mat. I get myself settled. "Fuck," I say, realizing I forgot my beach reading chair. It's this stand-on-its-own armchair pillow thingy. I sit there trying to decide how lazy I am. Do I go back and get it? Do I just make do? Do I text one of the guys and offer them a thousand dollars to bring it to me? If I thought for one moment they wouldn't be dicks and send Declan with it, I would for sure take door number three. My aggravated sigh is more like a toddler whine than a grown woman's.

"Ughhhhh," I grumble as I grab my bag, because it's not like I can leave my gun unattended on the beach.

A shadow crosses over me, and I know who it is without even looking. "Fuck Jake–I mean Declan–why are you here?"

"Caden said you forgot this thing." I look at him, and he is holding my thingy.

"You brought me my thingy?"

"You call it a thingy?"

"I have no idea what to call it. Caden made it for me. He took one of my reading pillows and gave it a hardback and a small stand part that sinks into the sand for stability. Then he had Marguerite cover it in a more beach-friendly fabric. So THINGY!" I raise my hands, gesturing for him to figure it out. "If thingy bothers you so much, you fucking rename it."

I hear him sigh again, and my heart clenches, and my stomach flips again. Thinking that I might have hurt his feelings.

Fucking body is a traitor just like the guys. Then I remember his name is Declan. He's Irish, and his brother is the head of the Campbell Family. And I don't feel bad anymore.

"Bye, Declan," I say, dismissing him. I watch his shadow retreat as he heads back to the house.

Maybe he won't be there when I get back this time. Perhaps he's had enough. I'm not mature enough to dissect the pang of loss I feel thinking he won't be there when I get back to the house. I put him out of my head, put my headphones on and open my book. I've been reading for about an hour when a commotion out of the corner of my eye catches my attention. I put my book down and remove my headphones, and I hear a woman screaming.

CHAPTER THIRTY FIVE

I'm off my spot and running to the woman to see what is happening. She is holding a baby of about six months and pointing out to the water. I see what she is screaming about. There is a little boy out there, way too far out and going under the water. "Fuck." I look at the teenagers standing and staring as this kid drowns. "Hey!" I grab the girl closest to me. She looks at me. "You see that house there? The white one with blue trim?"

"Si."

"Run there and tell Jake to come fast." She doesn't move, so I scream at her, "Run!" She and her friends snap out of it and take off toward my house. I run into the water, seeing the little boy, and he's gone again. I dive into the water and swim out to where I saw him go under. I can't see him, so I dive deeper searching for him. I can't find him and have to come up for air.

I submerge again, this time going deeper. I keep swimming down not finding anything until I see a mop of brown hair. The saltwater is hurting my eyes, but I keep them open. I swim down more, and more, my lungs burning. Just when I think my lungs will explode, I can reach him. I grab him by the arm and start our ascent. I feel like my lungs are going to explode. I break the surface, sucking in a massive lungful of air and getting my arm around the little boy to keep his head above the water. He isn't breathing; I know he isn't.

I swim as fast as I can with one arm towards the beach. I can still hear his mother screaming. Then I hear Caden. He is swimming out to meet me. "Caden," I call out to him. He takes the boy from me and starts swimming to shore with him. He's so much faster than me.

Caden makes it to shore with the boy, and I see him lay him down as Declan arrives and performs CPR. I roll onto my back, needing to catch my breath. I have a horrible cramp in my side. I'm floating for a few minutes before there are splashes as someone swims out to me. "How's it going here, Boss?" Matt asks as he treads water beside me.

"Well, Matt, I definitely didn't have the relaxing afternoon at the beach I had planned on."

"I see that. Ah, Ava, Is there a reason you're out here floating?"

"Oh, yeah. I have a cramp, and I'm trying to catch my breath."

"Ah. Well, you feel up to going into shore now?"

"I guess."

"Good, 'cause the doc is starting to look a little panicked."

We make our way to shore slowly. The cramp in my side is not any better. Breathing hurts. Matt helps me out of the water just as the mother places her son into a car pulled onto the beach. I give Caden a look. "They're taking him to the hospital just to get him checked over, and this is faster than calling an ambulance."

"He's ok?" I look to Declan, meeting his eyes.

"He's going to be fine. He was completely responsive, and his breath sounds were clear on both sides."

"That's good. Thank you for coming. I don't know if he would have made it without you."

I step away from Matt to grab my stuff, but that pain in my side will not let go. It takes my breath away, and I stumble; Matt catches me by grabbing my side, and I think I might have hit him in reflex to the pain he caused me. "What the fuck is wrong with me?"

Declan is beside me before I can protest. He lifts my left arm and touches my ribs. "Fuck!" I yell, "Don't, that hurts."

"Shut up, Ava, and let me look. I've fucked you with fresh bullet wounds, so I know you can withstand a fair amount of pain for a moment."

Matt and Caden laugh at that, not even trying to pretend they didn't hear it. "Asshole," I mutter under my breath. But I do as he asks and stay quiet as he checks my side out. "Okay, so good news, it's nothing serious, just a dislocated rib, and it's an easy fix."

"That's good. So, what's the bad news?"

I miss the look he gives Matt, but suddenly, Matt holds me firm, and Declan puts his hands on my ribs and pushes in and up, and I scream. I've been shot, and this hurt more. I think I pass out for a second, or at least see stars, grateful that Matt has me. "That's the bad news. Ava. Hey, look at me."

I look up at him, blinking my eyes rapidly. "Fuck, Jake, that hurt. Why didn't you warn me?"

"It's worse if you know it's coming, Ava; trust me." Matt says. "Are you good now?"

"Yeah, I'm ok. You can let me go. Thank you."

"All right then. Caden and I will grab your things, and you and the doc can make your way back nice and slow.'

"Why can't you walk me back?" I plead with my friend to save me.

"Because, Ava, the man helped us build a pergola and saved that kid's life after you saved his life. And as much as I want to throat punch him for hurting you, I can't help but like the Irish bastard," he says and then leaves quickly with Caden as I stare after them.

"Go with them, Declan. I'm fine."

"Someone should walk back with you."

I glare at him for a moment before relenting. "Fuck, fine."

We walk back slowly; neither of us says anything. We reach the house, and I go to the outdoor shower to rinse off, but pause when I remember I'm not alone. Showering in my room seems like the safer option. I look at him and give him a small smile. "Thank you."

"Nothing to thank me for. I should go, the restaurant at the hotel; it gets busy at night. Goodnight, Ava."

Fuck, fuck.

"You could join us for dinner. Marguerite is an amazing cook, and she made tamales for us. She makes them with shredded pork and this red sauce we all fight over." I smile, thinking about the last time we had that sauce. "The last time we had the sauce, Ben stabbed Caden in the hand with his fork when Caden tried to claim the last bit. It's that good."

"Sure, I think I would like that. As long as you don't stab me." That fucking accent is an unfair advantage.

"I can't promise no stabbing, but I will try to be on my best behavior. I'm going to go up and shower. You can use the outside shower if you like. There are towels in the box on the side of it," I tell him as I head upstairs.

Once clean, I open my closet, throw on a pair of underwear, grab a racerback tank maxi dress, and put it on. Looking in the mirror, I try to decide if I love how much side boob it shows.

I do, yes.

I grab a couple of things out of my closet and head downstairs. I bunch up some of the skirt material to about mid-thigh on one leg, letting it lay longer on the other. I left my pin upstairs, so instead, I tuck it up under the leg of my underwear.

I step into the kitchen, and I see Jake–Declan–standing outside with a towel around his waist, looking at the ocean. "Hey," I say as I step up beside him. "Enjoying my view?"

"Yeah."

"It is pretty spectacular," I say.

"It is." He says no longer looking at the water.

A slight blush creeps up my neck, under his gaze. "Oh, here, I stole these from the last guy I slept with, but they should fit you," I say, shoving some clothes in his arms. He glares at me.

"Relax, they're yours, you jackass. I thought you might want them instead of putting your shorts back on. I know they were pretty wet after the beach."

"Bloody Hell, woman! I have been looking for these fucking sweats for months!" Declan roars at me.

"Sorry?" I say with a cheeky grin as I go into the house.

"I'm not sure you understand how exactly an apology works."

"Ha! I'm going to text the guys for food. I'm starving."

"Matt and Caden decided to go into town and meet Ben for a couple of beers and some food," he informs me.

I shake my head. "Of course they did. Fucking traitors."

I turn on music because, God knows, I need the distraction. "Optimist" by Zoe Keating fills the space.

I grab dishes and things, as well as a bottle of wine. I lay everything out, pull the tamales from the oven, and throw a salad together quickly. Declan returns to the kitchen as I put the last fixings into the salad bowl. I look up at him as he enters. The man is trying to kill me. He's only wearing the grey sweats. "Fuck my life," I mutter. "I can grab you a shirt from Matt's room. Give me one minute." I start to leave the kitchen.

"I don't need a shirt Ava, sit."

"Don't use that tone with me, Declan."

"What tone is that?"

"You know exactly what tone."

"Hmm, not sure I do," he says, well aware of the tone. It's his 'doctor dominant' tone.

"Do you want wine?" I ask, changing the subject.

"I'd love some wine, thank you." He says, chuckling at my discomfort. This man knows me too well.

You're so fucking fucked, Ava.

I hand him his wine and food, make my plate, and we dig in. "Holy shit, that is good."

"I told you." I laugh at him.

"You did. What does she put in this stuff?"

"I have no idea why she won't share the recipe with me; we've all tried, but she just says no."

We finish eating and start to clear away our dishes. "Nothing Matters" By The Last Dinner Party plays. The chorus hits, and I can't help but look at Declan, waiting for his reaction. He looks at me questioningly.

"Yeah, it's a little aggressive, but I love this song. It reminds me of Abba but with an unhinged twist."

"That is a pretty accurate description, actually," he laughs.

We look at each other across the island. I close my eyes, feeling the need to center myself. "Don't look at me like that."

"Like what, Ava?"

"Like you haven't eaten in weeks." I say as I open my eyes.

"I haven't." He says low. I can't help the noise that statement elicits from me. He takes a step towards my side of the island. I take a step in the other direction. He takes another step towards me, and I take another away from him. "Ava." The threat in his voice is unmistakable. "I would stop moving if I were you." His voice is still low but with a rasp now to it.

He takes a couple slow, deliberate steps towards me, trying to not engage my fight or flight response. I stay still, letting him get closer, unsure if I'm going to let him catch me or not. If I'm going to let him have me or if I'll run. He takes two more steps. He's close enough now to be able to touch me.

My feet are moving before I even realize I made a choice. I bolt from him, getting past him and running for the stairs. "This'll be fun," I hear him say, and then he's after me.

I make it halfway up the stairs before he hits the first step. His legs are longer than mine, and he gains on me fast. Adrenaline is coursing through me, spurring me on.

I reach my bedroom door, but he's there before I can open it. He slams against me, his arms on either side of me, elbows bent, forearms trapping me in. "I told you not to move, Ava," he says in my ear, his teeth grabbing my earlobe.

A shiver runs through me. I can hear how weak his control on himself is and I revel in it. I push back against him, grinding my ass into him. I feel his cock against me, already so fucking hard. "But you ran from me," he drags his nose up my neck, scenting me. "I caught you though, didn't I?" When I don't answer him, he pushes himself into me harder, smashing my breasts against the door. "I asked you a question," his mouth against my ear, his teeth grazing over it.

Jesus, fuck, what did he ask me? "Yes, you caught me." His right-hand leaves the door, running over my thigh, over my ass and up my ribs until he finds the skin along my side that my dress leaves exposed. I hear a low growl from him before his hand snakes into my dress and cups my breast, squeezing it to that beautiful point of almost too much. Another sound escapes me, this one is needy.

"I think you missed my hands on you. Didn't you, lass." That voice with that Irish lilt sends a wave of heat through me, making me clench my thighs so tightly. A low chuckle sounds in my ear. "Instead of clenching your thighs, you should spread them wide, let me between them, and you can fuck yourself on my hand until you come."

"Please," I beg him.

"Please what, Ava?"

I push my ass back into him, making him suck in a breath. "Please what, Ava," he demands and squeezes my breast again to emphasize his request that I answer him.

"I don't know," I answer him honestly, squirming.

"Stop moving, woman. My cock is so fucking hard. If you keep squirming against me, I'm going to come in my sweats like a fucking teenager." He turns me, so I'm facing him.

I look up and meet his eyes. He wants to unleash himself on me, but he's holding back, trying to take it slow. He doesn't fully trust me to not shut him down before he even gets started. He drops his forehead to mine, his breaths are ragged, his eyes are darker than I have ever seen them. He stays like that for a moment, closing his eyes for a breath, his heart rate calming. He lets out another breath, it sounds like a surrender almost, "Mianach," he grits out and claims my mouth.

Months of want and frustration, pain and uncertainty, anger and hope. All of what he felt over the last few months is in this kiss. He me to know I'm in trouble for leaving him, his mouth is punishing me. His tongue and teeth brand me as his. I grab his waistband, pulling him into me, needing to take his punishment just as much as he needs to inflict it upon me.

He crushes himself against me as he rocks his hips into

me. Everything I feel from him is that of a starving man, a man who has been denied the only thing that can save his life. I part my lips, gasping at the ferocity of his possession of it. Needing air but not getting any but the air he gives me. My head is spinning; the sensations running over me from having his mouth on mine again are almost too much. He swallows that gasp from me, claiming it as his own. I have nothing to anchor myself to. His possession of me is rough and reckless, nothing soft and gentle. It's all savage and punishing.

His lips leave mine, kissing my neck, going to that spot he knows will undo me. His teeth sink into that spot, and I moan. My hand finds his hair, grasping it. I pull his mouth back to mine, a hunger of my own unleashed. I rock my hips against him, and his hands find my ass, lifting me. My legs wrap around his waist, tightening around him and pulling him in as close as possible.

Our tongues tease and sweep against each other. I bite his bottom lip, and he groans into my mouth and drives his hips forward, dragging his cock against my wet centre. My dress is around my waist; my panties are soaked. "Oh God," I whisper as he rocks into me again. His cock dragging against my core, the fabric of my underwear slick against me.

He reaches between us, pulling my underwear to the side as he drags a finger through me. I feel my slickness rub against his skin. I shiver, sending another rush of wetness to my pussy. He slides a finger inside me, and I lean into the door, angling my hips harder toward him. His finger plunges into me, his thumb circling my clit. I gasp as he pulls me closer, his mouth on mine again.

His need for me is a living thing between us and it invades every inch of space. It leaves very little of me in its wake

He works his pants down, freeing himself, lining up with my entrance and drives into me in one hard thrust. Both of us moan out a filthy sound of pleasure when he's fully seated in me. He starts to move inside me, his hands roaming over my body. He's touching me everywhere, everywhere I thought his hand would never touch again. Even when I dreamt about him, I knew in my dreams he was lost to me.

"Fuck, you feel so good around my cock, Ava. I missed you so much." His voice is heavy with lust.

His hands on my body are familiar, they haven't forgotten an inch of me. My skin remembers him as well. It sings back to his touch as they slide down to my side, grazing over the scar there, and he runs them absently along it as he drives into me.

Memories of the day I got that scar take over my thoughts, almost like they're sitting on top of this moment. I feel him moving inside me, and I know it's Jake, I can feel his fingers on my side, running over the scar that's still so fresh. I feel it, that first slip, but I don't recognize it for what it is.

Fighting to focus back on him, on this moment here, not one from the past. I concentrate on his skin, his scent, his breath, the feel of him inside me, his fingers caressing that smooth patch of skin on my side. The memory of that day crashes in, until it's the only thing I can see, or feel—the day my entire world crumbled.

"Stop," I whisper so quietly I don't know how he hears me. I barely heard me. But he stops instantly, his eyes finding my face. Concern washing over him.

"Ava? "

"I need… please… please let me down." I hear the same pain in my voice as he does. He slides out of me, placing my feet gently onto the wood floor. He steps back from me, putting himself back in his pants. He steps forward to touch me, but I flinch. Seeing the flinch he takes another step back from me. "Ava? Please, baby, tell me what's wrong."

"Don't call me baby," I whisper. Staring at the ground,

mentally trying to shake off whatever is happening in my head.

"I'm not your baby. I'm not your anything. I left you. We broke up." I don't understand what is happening. How is he here? It doesn't make sense to me. My brain can't focus. I can't reconcile this Declan here with Jake from that day. "Why the fuck are you here?" I feel fear building in me. I hear my voice get louder, but I can't stop it. "Why are you here? What did you come here for?" I yell at him. I feel the break nearing the surface. "Why, Jake? Declan, whoever the fuck you are."

"Ava, please let me help you, baby."

"Stop fucking calling me that! I'm not your baby! Fuck, we didn't even really know each other. We were both lies!"

"Ava," he says again. There's a plea in his voice for me to hear him, but I don't.

"Except you knew who I was; you knew everything about me! You fucking played me, Jake! Fuck–Declan! Why? Why? Why did you do it? Why? Why not tell me who you were? What did you want from me?" He says nothing. He can see me unravelling in front of him. He understands I don't want his answers. I need to get this pain out of me, and he is the one in the vicinity of the explosion.

A thought runs through me, and I turn cold, my body going preternaturally still. "Are you here to kill me?" The understanding of him being a Campbell finally hits me. I ask him, my voice quiet, "Are you here for that? It's okay; I won't fight you so long as you don't hurt the guys. They did nothing but place their loyalty in me. You can have me; just don't hurt them."

"Fuck. Ava, no. I'm not here to hurt you or them. I love you; I am so in love with you. I was so lost when you left. I worked and came home. That was it."

I charge at him and push him with all my strength. "NO!

NO! You don't get to say that to me. You don't know me! I don't know you!" I keep pushing him until I have him against the far wall.

I don't see him anymore. My rage and pain have taken my sight.

I can't separate that day's memories from today's reality. It's all too much. It all blurs. I lash out at anything. I know my fist hits something. So, I keep hitting. The feeling of something solid, a small anchor point for me in the haze of my mind. Minutes or days could have passed in that haze. The days all one big jumble in my mind.

I'm being lifted off my feet then, my arms trapped against my body. I fight like a wild animal, as I was trained to do. I fight like my life depends on it. I hear voices; someone yells for a bag, and I hear my name being said repeatedly. But it all seems so distant. "Let me go!" I keep fighting whoever is holding me, but they have me so tight. I feel a sharp sting in my arm. Then everything starts to go fuzzy. My body starts to feel heavy. I hear Matts voice break through the static in my ears, but my eyes keep closing, and I can't find him. "Why, Matt? When did he stop loving me and start hating me?" I hear someone sobbing, but I can't keep my eyes open to find them. "Why did he want me dead? He broke us, Matt."

My pain from that day and the destruction of my life shatters over me again and again. A blackness is quickly taking over and I welcome it. I feel my body get heavier. I can hear Matt, but he sounds so far away. I can hear that woman sobbing again, but I don't have it in me to reach out and help her. I can hear the breaking of her soul, and it crushes me. It crushes me and drags me into oblivion.

CHAPTER THIRTY SIX

I wake up in my bed, unsure how I got here. It's dark outside. "You're awake?"

I roll over and see Matt lying next to me. "I think so. But you being in bed with me is new, so maybe I'm still dreaming?"

"You're awake," he grumbles as he sits up and grabs a bottle of water, handing it to me. "Drink that," he commands. I pull myself up into a sitting position, my back against the headboard. My brain is fuzzy as hell, but it only takes a moment before it all starts coming back to me. I go to put the water bottle on the bedside table, but I miss the table and drop it on the floor. I scramble off the bed, falling on the floor, trying to get to the door.

"Ava," Matt calls after me, but I'm already on my feet and heading down the stairs. Caden and Ben stand up as they hear me barreling down the steps.

Caden is on his feet and at the bottom before I reach the last one.

"Where is he?" Caden doesn't answer; he watches me, looking to see if I'm okay. "Where is he?" I repeat, letting him know I want an answer.

"I'll take you," Caden says, taking my hand and leading me outside. He leads me toward the ocean, and then I see him. Declan is standing in the water, looking out at it. I shake my hand from Caden's grasp and take off running.

I'm still wobbly on my legs, and I lose my footing in the sand as I run to him. My feet scramble under me, and I get back up. "Declan!" I shout. His head whips around when he hears me call him. His eyes find me, and he starts towards me. I crash into him, wrapping my arms around his neck.

"I'm so sorry, I'm so sorry. I don't know what happened. Are you okay? Did I hurt you?" My hands are all over him, looking for any injury I might have caused. I see a shadow near his eye and reach up to touch it. "Oh fuck, I hit you." I step back, looking at him and seeing where else I might've hurt him. "I hit you," I repeat, but he stops me, careful not to grab me and instead taking my hand lightly in his.

"Ava, I'm ok. I've had way worse; I promise."

"But I hurt you. I don't understand what that was; I wasn't even in control of myself."

He intertwines our fingers and kisses my knuckles. "It's been five months since everything with Marcus happened?"

"Yeah, pretty much." I answer.

"I'm going to go out on a limb and use my big doctor brain and say you never really dealt with any of the emotional fallout from it?" Declan says.

I don't respond immediately, giving him a look as if I don't understand.

Declan shakes his head at me, "Everything that happened to you that day was both physically and mentally traumatizing. I understand that you think you're above dealing with trauma, but your mind didn't feel the same. So many things happened to you that day, and you couldn't stop to process any of it because you were fleeing for your life." He brings our entwined hands to his mouth, ghosting his lips across my knuckles. "All of it–the stress of the actual getaway, the stress of starting over and constantly monitoring that he hasn't found you, me showing up here and dropping my bombshell on you, the stress of saving that little boy, you and I getting physical–it all just finally broke the dam."

"One minute, you were inside me, and I was there with you, and then I was back in that day. You were Jake, but I knew you were also Declan. It was like both things were happening at the same time. I couldn't separate the past from the present. None of it made any sense. It was a jumble of pain and confusion. Then you touched the scar on my side. You ran your fingers along it; it was too much."

Declan nods his head, not pushing or asking any more questions.

"You'll be fine, Ava. Your brain just forced your hand. It said, 'no more stress or hurt' until you acknowledge the past ones."

"I guess I need to work through a few things," I say with a chuckle. "I'm tired."

"Of course. I'll walk you back, then be on my way."

"Could you stay?"

He looks over at me. "I can stay."

We walk back in silence, our hands still entwined.

I get inside and drop his hand, running to Matt and throwing my arms around him. I give him a kiss and tell him thank you for staying with me. I walk over to Ben and Caden, wrapping both in a hug so tight they have to tell me to let them go. "I don't deserve you guys, but I'm so grateful I have you."

"Go to bed, Ava. You're being sappy."

"Hush, Matt, I get to say this tonight because I had an

emotional breakthrough. Breakdown? And because I do love you guys."

"We love you too, Boss Lady. "

"Shut up, Ben," I laugh. "We're going to go to bed. You guys should head home and try and get some sleep."

Ben and Caden tell me good night before heading to their houses. Matt looks me up and down, then sets his eyes on Declan. "She'll be ok. I'll call you if anything happens."

"You better." He says as he heads to his room.

Declan turns off a few lights and then follows me up the stairs. My room's lights are still off, so we just close the door behind us. Still in my dress, I slip it off and crawl into bed. Declan takes his shirt off and removes his sweats, crawling in behind me. I turn to face him, and he drags me into his arms. I burrow into him, breathing in his scent. I missed his scent. He smells like I remember him–citrusy, like his body wash, mixed with leather. There is an added scent of salt from the breeze off the ocean tonight.

"Sleep. We have all the time in the world now." He tells me softly.

I wake up the next day snuggled up to a very warm Declan Campbell. I enjoy the feel of his arms around me for a moment. Looking up at him and realize I don't care anymore. I don't care that he lied to me; I also lied to him. I'm just happy he's here with me and that his arms are around me again. The rest is all just background. It matters so little how we started. How we started is how we got here. Sure, having that perfect meet-cute story would be great, but would that even be us? My life isn't exactly a rom-com-type story. We're both born of worlds covered in blood and death. So, a lie for a lie seems very poetic for the story of our beginning.

Looking at him–*no, you're actually creepy stalker staring at him*–I drink in his features. He has always been one of the most attractive men I've ever seen. Marcus is stunning to look at, almost angelic in his perfection. But Declan is something else. Both Campbell boys have an air about them. It's like shadow is part of their DNA. I think it comes from being near dark men and deeds their entire lives. Add in the fact that Declan is a doctor who saves little kids and that scar, and there is no escaping how attractive he is to me.

The blanket is down around his waist, and he's on his back, so I have my fill of looking at him. He looks leaner than he did five months ago. His muscles are still hard and defined but just leaner–*the last few months took a toll on him type of leaner*. I run my fingers over his stomach; the sensation of him under my hand is familiar. He's on the cusp of waking up as I drag my hand over his chest. The smooth skin and muscles there beg for me to bite them. I lean over, careful not to wake him. I kiss his chest, dragging my teeth ever so lightly over his nipple.

He makes a noise, a rumble in his chest, and I like that sound. I want to make him do it again. I kiss his skin, making a path to his neck to that spot just above his collarbone where neck and shoulder meet, letting my tongue taste him as I bring my lips to his. Softly, I sweep my mouth over his. I run my fingers along his bottom lip and see a shiver over his skin. I kiss him again. Soft and gentle, my tongue grazing over his lips. As the final hold of sleep lets him go, his mouth opens to mine, deepening the kiss.

Welcoming my tongue with a swipe of his own, and I am rewarded with that rumble again. This kiss is slow and sensual, neither of us in a rush. I bite his bottom lip, and the groan from him is my only warning before he has me settled on top of him, my legs straddling his thighs. I feel him hard beneath me as I settle on him. Leaning forward, I trace a finger along his scar, letting my fingers run over his mouth when I reach it. "How come you've never told me how you got this?" I ask absentmindedly, continuing to explore him with my fingertips. I run them over the column of his neck to his chest, where I trace over his tattoo.

"The story of that scar is not a story I tell. One day, which isn't today, I'll tell you about it."

Sitting up, he shifts us backwards to rest his back on the headboard. Kissing my mouth, I feel a hand on my throat, his thumb dragging along my jaw, forcing my face up more to meet his. His tongue opens my mouth, seeking mine. He slides his tongue over mine, and I moan.

His hands grip my breasts roughly, and I arch into them. Rolling my nipples between his fingers, tugging them, pinching them, sending little shocks of pleasure through me. His mouth is everywhere. His mouth, teeth, and tongue claim every piece of exposed skin. Every nip or swipe of them sends shivers across my body, all of them pooling between my thighs.

My underwear is a flimsy barrier between us, Declan has nothing on, and I can feel him hard between us. My wetness has long since soaked through the lace, leaving me to drench him.

I place my hands over his on my breasts, tightening his grip on them and wanting that bite of pain to go along with the other sensations. I roll my hips over him, dragging my wetness along his hard shaft. His mouth is back on mine, and his kiss is hungry; his need is palpable. His tongue in my mouth is unyielding.

Declan's last threads of self-control snap; there are no more gentle or tender touches. A hand slides between us, cupping my pussy and lifting me off him slightly; his fingers push my underwear to the side as he sinks two into me. A sob breaks free from my throat at the intrusion. I move my hips, grinding myself onto his hand.

"Fuck, you're gripping my fingers so tight," he grounds out through gritted teeth. Raising me a little higher, I feel him fist himself. I watch him as he watches his fingers as they enter me, as he pulls them from me only to plunge them back in. I can see my wetness on his fingers dripping down his hand.

He tears his fingers from me and lines his cock up with my entrance, slamming me down onto him. I throw my head back and choke out a strangled cry when he fills me so violently. "Fuck, Jake again." He lifts me from his cock, and just when I think he might slip from me, he slams me down over him while he thrusts up into me. I cry out; the pleasure and agony of him driving into me so callously sets my body on fire.

My orgasm is building fast as I watch him. He's lost in his punishment of me. His fingers dig into my flesh harder with every thrust of his hips. I slide my hand down my body, my fingers stroking my clit. Declan watches my hand as I work myself, bringing my orgasm closer. He keeps fucking me, his eyes locked on my movements. A deep noise rumbles in his chest as my pussy clenches around his cock; that noise is the last straw. My orgasm explodes over me.

My pussy is still clenching him when he grips my waist and flips us so he's on top of me. A hand digs into my hip while the other wraps around my throat. Declan fucks me hard, hammering into my body, his hands grasping me tighter. The pressure on my throat and the pummeling of my clit against his pelvic bone rips another orgasm from me. Declan cums hard, his voice scratchy as he says my name.

He releases me, and I suck in a full breath of air. He collapses on my chest, his breathing is ragged and panting. I bring my hand to his hair and run my fingers through it as I catch my breath. He lifts his head from my chest and looks at me. "Are you ok? Was I too rough?"

I can't stop the laugh. "I'm fine. That was intense. It was good."

He rolls off me and pulls me into him. He kisses my face, then kisses my mouth sweetly, humming as he does. "Why Jake?" I blurt out, and he stills against me.

"Umm? What?" he asks.

"Why the name Jake?"

"Oh, Jacob is my middle name." I nod at his answer. "Why was that something you needed to know right now?" he asks, amused.

"Because I can't seem to call you one name in my head. I'm pretty sure when we were in the middle of fucking, I called you both."

"You did. But I'll respond to either. So, feel free to call me Jake or Declan. I understand that I will probably always be Jake for you. I'm good with that."

We lay wrapped up in each other. I fall asleep with his scent on my skin and all around me. He is intoxicating to me —he always has been. From the moment I met him on the side of the road, I was enthralled.

I'm unsure how long I sleep, but Declan is staring at me when I wake up. "What's wrong?"

"Nothing," he says, rolling onto his back and staring at the ceiling. "Just needed a second to remind myself this was real, not a dream. When you left me, I dreamt about you every night. When I couldn't find you, I thought I'd lost you for good."

"You're here. You found me." I sit up and move over to kiss him gently, putting everything I feel into that kiss, hoping he can feel what I can't say: that I'm so happy he found me, that I feel complete again, that I love him. I want to tell him, but I have never uttered those words before, and the thought of them scares me.

I bring my mouth to his, no rush to my intention. His eyes close as my lips brush against his. Declan's hand cups my cheek, and I nuzzle into it, placing a kiss on his palm as he runs a thumb along my bottom lip.

He slides his arm around my waist hugging me close, as he rolls us and lowers me onto my back. His care of me in that simple movement is heart-stoppingly gentle. I open my legs for him, and he settles between them. We both let a breath loose, our eyes locked on each other as he slowly pushes inside me. Our movements are intentional, full of purpose and reverence.

Declan entwines our fingers, pressing our hands into the mattress, his other hand grips my hip. My legs wrap around his, and I trail my fingers up and down his spine, feeling his muscles moving under his skin as he makes love to me.

That's what this is. My heart and body feel it, but the words still elude me.

"I love you, Ava." He breathes the words out against my lips.

"Declan," I gasp against his.

Our kiss goes from tender to urgent and raw in the space of a single breath. Our bodies move against each other. Both of us driving the other closer to their peak. He reaches between us, rubbing my clit slowly, pressing down on it just enough. He knows my body, knows how to make it do what he wants.

"You're going to come with me," he tells me.

"Yes." I gasp, not being able to do anything different even if I wanted to. It may be my body, but he owns it just the same. He slams into me hard and presses down on my clit at the same time. The most exquisite fire floods my body when my orgasm hits. I feel him thicken as he cums and my body tenses as we tumble over that sweet edge together. Still inside me, he places his forehead on mine.

"Mianach." he says and then he kisses me lightly on my lips before he slides out of me, rolling beside me and pulling me onto his chest. His arms surround me as his fingers run up and down my spine.

"What does that mean?" I ask him. He looks at me, confused for a moment.

"Mianach?"

"Yes." I answer.

"It's Gaelic for 'Mine'."

I can't help but smile at that. The thought of him claiming me as his makes me feel warm inside.

"Good morning," he says against my mouth.

"Morning, Declan.

"I like hearing my name on your lips. Ava?"

"Hmmm?"

"I love you." He says to me. A tear slips down my cheek. "Why are you crying?"

"Not sure," my voice breaks, "but I promise they are happy tears. I was sure I would never see you again when I left you in LA. And it broke my heart. I broke my own heart when I left you. I could see a whole other life with you, but I had to leave you instead. And now here you are, telling me you love me, and I don't know how. I don't understand how I got you back. I don't deserve you. I'm a bad person. I do bad things. I enjoy the bad things I do."

"Ava, I love you. You. The good and the bad, all of it, all of you. So, it doesn't matter if you think you don't deserve it because it's mine to give you, and I give you my love freely. No restrictions, no strings, no rules, no demands. Bad deeds and all."

I nod at him. "Bad deeds and all." He smiles at me.

"All right, woman, we need food."

CHAPTER THIRTY SEVEN

The next month passes quietly. Declan stays, helping at the local hospital several days a week, while the guys finish Matt's place.

"I'm going to miss living with you, Matt."

"Ava, I love you, you are fucking spectacular, but I need to get out of here. When it was just you and I, it was great. No offence, Doc, but the amount of sex you two have all over this house, and loudly, is frankly astounding. I'm seriously starting to get a complex. I used to think I was good at sex. I make my partners cum, it's a priority for me to make sure they do. But listening to you two, I've never felt more inadequate. I question everything I have ever done for a partner. Any chance your brother is single?" Matt asks looking at Declan.

"He is, as far as I know."

"And just as hot, Matt. Seriously, if you get a shot at Liam, fucking take it. And then let me know how it is." Declan glares at me. "What? I'm not wrong." I laugh as I walk away from them.

We're all outside around the pool, having a few beers. Ben and Caden are arguing over some video game. Matt is at the grill making lunch. Declan and I are just watching them, enjoying the sun.

"Dec?"

"Yeah?"

"I love you."

He freezes beside me. His beer is midway to his mouth, frozen there. I don't even think he's breathing. After a beat, he nods and takes a swig of his beer. The smallest pull of his lips is visible. I get off the couch, stand between his legs, bend down and kiss him. I break the kiss and turn to the rest of them.

"I've decided I want to return to work," I announce. "I miss it. I miss being good at something. So! As for the three of you, I will leave it up to you to decide what you want to do. This is your home, and nothing will change that. If you want to get back to work, great! If not, also great. I'll start looking for new team members. Good? Ok! Let me know when you know." They are all silent as I sit back down beside Declan.

I start to smile at him when I see movement out of the corner of my eye. I sigh. He quirks an eyebrow at me. "Just remember I loved you before I decided to go back to work. I loved you about four days after I met you. It was a hassle, to be honest. Please remember that." He gives me a questioning look just as a shadow comes over the top of us. I see Matt step towards the gun he has by the grill. Caden rises to his feet slowly, tense as they see a man step onto the deck from the house.

"Liam, just say hello. Don't look at them all grumpy; you're making everyone tense. And Matt shoots people when he's tense," I sigh.

Fucking hell, this is going to be interesting.

"Hello," he says. His accent is thicker than Declan's. He walks over and drops himself down on the other side of me. Pulling my feet into his lap. "Dearthâir Beag."

"Seanfhear," Declan replies, taking another swig of his beer.

"You're early," I tell him.

"I like to be unexpected. It's how I'm still alive. I assume you haven't told them yet?" I give him a look saying no, asshole, I haven't, and you know it. Declan takes a deep breath, gets up, and heads to the fridge, grabbing another beer. He hands his brother one as he drops back to his seat on my other side.

"No, I was just starting to. You weren't supposed to be here until tomorrow."

"Ava, why is Liam Campbell here?" Ben asks.

"Because Ava needs someone to back her," Declan tells Ben, with a slight undertone to his words.

"Correct. I want to return to work, but I can't do that without some protection. I have no desire to go after Marcus. I want to leave it alone. He tried, he failed, and that's the end of it as far as I'm concerned. The Campbells have one of the biggest reaches and are one of the few families or groups almost everyone takes very seriously."

"That's one way to put it," Liam says, smirking as he drinks his beer. I shake my head at his arrogance.

"So, you want to return to work under the Campbell banner?" Matt asks.

"I do. And Liam has already agreed. He's here to go over

some fine print. If you guys don't feel like it's a good fit, that is understandable. You all have the freedom to do whatever you like. This is your home no matter what."

"I'm in. It'll be nice working for you again, Ava. You are way more fun than the assholes I've worked for the last few months."

"I was hoping you would say that, Ben." I look over at him and smile. I look at Matt and raise an eyebrow at him.

 "Knock it off. You know where you go, I go."

"Awe, Matt, you big softie."

 Caden is quiet. "Let's go for a walk?" I ask Caden.

"Sure."

We head towards the ocean, walking in the water once we reach it. "Caden, you don't have to come back to work. I see how happy you are here. So, stay. Open the gym and keep working with the kids. I would rather come home to you happy here between jobs than have you out there when you don't want to be. I know you took the job because I was 19, and your protective instincts kicked in." He looks down at me beside him. I put my hand in his, wrapping my other hand around his forearm. "Caden?"

"What if something happens to you or the kid, and I'm not there? What If Matt tries to take on a guy and finds he's too much for him?"

"Oh my god, please tell him you worry you'll need to save him because he may have to fight a guy bigger than him. But let me be there when you do."

"Ava."

"Why do all the men in my life say my name like that?" I ask, looking at him.

"Like what?" he asks with a grin.

"Like I'm the most vexing person ever."

"Vexing, maddening, frustrating," he deadpans. I look at him and crack up.

"Fuck, part of me thinks there may be truth to that." I laugh.

"I'm retiring," Caden tells me quietly.

"Thank God!" I laugh. Caden picks me up and runs with me, screaming into the ocean. He crashes us into a wave, taking us both under. I come up sputtering and laughing. I wrap my arms around him and bury my face in his neck. "Thank you for taking such good care of me all these years. You were always too good for this life."

We splash around a bit more before heading back to the house. My dress is heavy with water. Caden removes his shirt, wringing it out as we walk. There is a quiet between us. Caden has always been a big brother to me. His retirement makes me happy. I should never have hired him; he was never meant to be part of this life. He met me, saw a young girl, and decided that I was his next mission. As time passed, we found a rhythm, and I'm selfish; he, like Matt, has always made me feel safe and looked after–things I was lacking in my life.

When we get back to the house, Caden heads to his place. Ben and Matt look at me; I shake my head. They get up and follow Caden home. The three have a bond, and this will hurt them as well.

I stand looking at the brothers sitting on the couch. They stop talking as I walk up. "Guys?"

"Yes, Little Villain?" Liam says.

"You've landed on that as my nickname, then?" I ask.

"Yeah, the others are more for behind closed doors… don't want to make anyone blush."

"Liam, is there a reason you're flirting with my woman?" Declan asks.

"Does 'I had her first' count as a reason?"

"You had me first? Did you really just say that?" I ask in disbelief.

"I did, and I did. Both statements are true." Liam responds with confidence.

Declan looks at his brother. Liam looks back at him.

Well fuck, this isn't going to go well.

"Liam, be nice. Or I will ask you to leave and won't ask nicely."

"Well, that's just foreplay for me, Little Villain."

"Liam, she isn't one of the others for fuck's sake," Declan tells his brother.

"And if I wanted to have that discussion about her?" Declan and Liam are staring each other down, and it isn't them just dicking around. The tension between them is palpable.

"Liam, be nice," I yell, and the big Irishman sighs and nods.

"This is nice for him, Ava." Declan tells me.

"Gentlemen, tell me if I'm right. I assume Liam never told you about our previous encounter?" Declan grunts in confirmation. "I'm also assuming, Declan, you never told Liam about me until after I left?" Again, he grunts at me in confirmation.

"Dec, why didn't you tell Liam about me? We were together for a while."

"He didn't tell me because he knew I would have stopped it. You're a dangerous person, Ava. Your life is dangerous, and I work hard to keep that shit away from him." Liam explains.

"I didn't tell him I met you because I wasn't risking losing you for anyone or anything," Declan tells me, confirming what Liam had said.

"But why would you put an end to it? Declan is a Campbell. He knows about all that shit." I asked Liam.

"Because, Ava, while Declan is a Campbell and very good with a gun, a sniper rifle, and has an above-average right hook, he is not a part of the world you and I dwell in. He is a doctor. And yes, he repairs a lot of bullet wounds, stabbings, and beatings that my men and I sustain in our work, but he is not part of it."

"That explains why you had everything you needed to patch me up when I came to you after escaping Marcus," I say. He doesn't reply; he just tips his beer to me. Declan still hasn't looked at me, his eyes trained on his beer.

"So, what now, Dec?" I ask.

His eyes snap to mine. "What do you mean, 'what now', Ava?" Declan gets to his feet fast and stalks toward me. I find myself backing up from him until I hit the wall of the outdoor shower. Declan keeps walking until his feet touch mine. His hand goes around my throat, pressing lightly.

"Declan," Liam warns from behind him.

"This doesn't concern you, Liam, so you would do well to shut the fuck up, Seanfhear. Now, Ava, I will ask again. What. Do. You. Mean. What. Now." He cocks his head to the side ever so slightly. "Do you think because my brother touched you first, it changes that you're mine? That I love you?"

"Ah, well–"

"Nope, I'm not done speaking yet, Ava," he tightens his grip on my throat slightly. Over Declan's shoulder, I see Liam take another step toward us. "I don't care if he tasted you first. I don't care if he made you come first. I don't care if he fucked you first. You and I are not fucking around, Ava. You are my fucking endgame. If we need to have a conversation about my brother, we can. I can accommodate almost anything for the people I love, but listen to me very, very well." His hand tightens slightly with every very. "You are mine. Do you understand me? I am not leaving you again; you are not leaving me, again. There will never be a time when you and I are not together. How that looks down the road where the asshole behind me is concerned is a conversation we'll have to have at some point, judging by the way he's holding himself back from ripping me off of you. But none of that, none of his bullshit can or will change us and what this is. Am I making myself clear, Ava?"

"Yes," I tell him, swallowing against his hand.

"Good." He kisses me hard and fast, then lets go of my neck. He turns to his brother. "Do we need to have a conversation, Liam?"

Liam runs his hands through his hair, then grabs the back of his neck and looks up at the sky. "Fuck," he grunts, then turns on his heel and leaves us standing there.

Declan looks at me, shaking his head. "Goddammit, Liam," he mutters and heads into the house, leaving me alone outside to wonder what the fuck just happened.

About an hour later, I'm lying in my favourite chair on my balcony when Declan opens the door and steps out. I put my book down, sit up, and cross my legs. I don't know what to say, so I just blurt out, "We didn't fuck. He made me come, and we were going to, but Marcus got fucked up and almost killed a prostitute because he was angry. I chose to stay with Liam instead of leaving with him and Alexi after your brother insulted him. Our night got cut short since I had to deal with Marcus and Alexi and the almost dead prostitute."

He looks at me with many different expressions on his face. "Jake, I'm sorry; I can find someone else to work with. Or I can work alone. Or–" he places his hand over my mouth, stopping me from spewing more things at him.

"Ava," he sighs. "Please stop talking. Liam, you, and I will figure shit out when we need to. As for you working under the Campbell name, I won't even discuss you working alone or under another family. Liam, no matter what will protect you with all his reach and resources, so I don't want to hear any more of that shit. As for the not fucking and him making you come and Marcus almost killing a prostitute, that was probably shit I didn't need to know, at least not tonight. But alas, here we are. So, I vote that we table all this talk until you or Liam make it an issue, okay?"

I look at him, about to ask what he means, but he places his hand over my mouth again and shakes his head. "But I don't understand," I mumble against his hand.

"Ava, stop talking. It's fine."

"But I need you to know," I say into his hand that is still covering my mouth.

He drops his head back with a dramatic sigh. "Enough Ava, I promise it's fine. I'm fine . Don't make me tell you again, please."

"But," I start to say against his hand.

"Ava, three." He says to me, and I look at him, confused. "Three times I told you to stop talking about it, but you didn't. Apparently, I'm going to have to make you stop. Now, get on your knees and open your fucking mouth." I hesitate for a moment, He's all dark and stormy, but I uncross my legs and slide off the chair onto my knees. He lowers his shorts and grips his hardening cock in his hand. I open my mouth.

He leaves me like that for a minute while he works his hand over his shaft slowly. He steps closer, placing the head of his cock on my tongue. "Lick," he commands, and I comply. I lick my tongue over the head of him, then trail my tongue down his shaft to his hand at the base and back up. "Now suck, Ava, just the head and suck hard."

I follow his instructions, taking the head of his cock into my mouth and sucking hard. Jake's hand goes to my hair, wrapping my ponytail around his hand. I can't suppress the moan that escapes as he pulls my hair. "Again. Suck again and take more of me this time," he commands.

I take him into my mouth until my lips meet the hand, he's using to stroke himself. "Keep going," he tells me, tightening his grip on my hair. I moan again, the vibration sending shivers through his cock, making him groan at the sensation. He pushes me further down on him, my hands bracing against his thighs for balance.

"Wrap your hand around my cock and work me while I fuck your mouth." I do as I'm told, wrapping my hand around his impressive shaft. He grips my hair with both hands now, holding my head steady as he thrusts his hips, driving his cock deeper into my mouth. He hits the back of my throat, and I breathe through my nose, trying to control my gag reflex, but I still choke on him, tears springing into my eyes. He thrusts again, going even deeper this time. "Now swallow my cock down your throat," he commands. I moan around him, his dominance sending a jolt straight to my pussy, and I swallow.

"So, fucking good," he grits out, pulling out of my mouth. I take a couple of deep breaths before he thrusts himself back in. "Again." He forces my head closer to him, and I take all of him. "Swallow the rest," he grunts, and I do, bringing him all the way into my mouth. He stays there, his head thrown back, legs shaking.

He pulls out with a drawn-out hiss, dragging his thumb across my bottom lip, I respond playfully by tonguing his finger. "Stand up, Ava." I follow his command. He slides a hand along my neck, grasping the back of it. His lips find mine in a sweet kiss, and I hum against his mouth. The contrast between his dominant side and his sweet side always undoes me. I open my mouth, sliding my tongue against his. He growls, his hands moving to my ass. He picks me up and lays me down on the lounger, his hand sliding between my legs to pull my underwear down.

His kiss deepens as his fingers run through my wetness. He shivers at how wet I am from his use of me. He pulls his shorts off, freeing himself, and drags my dress up as he settles between my legs, sinking into me. His fingers find my clit instantly, working that bundle of nerves as he fucks me. He's close; I can feel the stutter of his movements. He stops moving his hips but keeps working my clit.

I sigh as he works my clit faster, my orgasm building quickly. Jake feels my body tensing.

"Good girl," he says, driving into me again with a fervor. His breath hitches, and then he presses on my clit, and I come as he unloads into me.

As we come down, Declan slides out of me. We make our way into the bedroom and fall into bed. He pulls me against his chest, and I sigh with contentment, drifting off to sleep.

CHAPTER THIRTY EIGHT

A few days later, Liam is back at the house, going over things for my reemergence into the world's seedy underbelly. Liam, Declan and I are all actively ignoring the awkwardness from a couple of days ago. Like adults, we pretend it didn't happen. Declan, however, seems to find it amusing, which pisses me off and annoys the hell out of Liam. Our discomfort entertains him even more.

"How do you want to do this? I can put the word out that you are available for new jobs. Or Ben could make a post on the dark web? Do you have a preference?"

"Honestly, I don't. Your call."

"Works for me, Little Villain. I had Ben put the announcement up three days ago." I look at him, scrunching my eyebrows, trying to decide what to call him, but instead, I just shake my head.

"Are you always going to do things first and then tell me about them after?"

"Probably. Why?"

"Because while I'm working under you, I don't work for you."

"Oh, Little Villain, if only I could work you under me."

Declan enters the room, leans over me, and lifts my chin up to his face. He drags his lips across mine softly. Liam clears his throat. "Hello, brother." Declan says as he winks at me and gives me a quick peck on the lips.

"Love you. See you later." Declan says, shrugging at his brother.

"Love you. Save lots of lives!" I call after him as he heads to the door. The door closes behind Declan, and I turn back to Liam. There's a tick in his jaw that wasn't there a moment ago. "Sorry."

"Sorry for what, Mo Ghrá?"

"I don't know," I tell him honestly. "I just feel like I should apologize." He doesn't say anything, staring at me momentarily before refocusing. I choose to do the same, not willing to open the can of worms Liam being here is causing within me.

"There are four jobs available. Three are legit. One is Marcus."

"Well, fuck, that didn't take long now, did it?"

"No, he pounced on it. It was up for six hours before Ben got alerts it was being opened and responded to."

"How do we know it's Marcus?" He shows me the message.

~~~ It's time to come home, A. I'd hate to have to paint the ranch in red.

~~~~~M

"He's threatening Harry."

"Yes. Harry and I have been talking. Beth is on her way here. He forced Parker to leave with Beth. He told Parker it was his job to keep her safe. Sebastian won't leave. Wes and

Theo are out on a job and cannot be reached for another 36 hours."

"I need to call him." I take my phone and head outside to call Harry.

Liam follows behind me quietly.

"What? Why are you following me? I can talk to Harry just fine on my own." I see his jaw tick again. "What!?"

"My guys tell me Marcus got on a plane this morning with 25 men. Their flight plan was Billings."

"Why the fuck are you only telling me about this now? What the fuck? I can't do anything from here! There's no time for me to get to him! Why would you wait so long to tell me?" I go after him. My anger turned physical. I punch him in the face, connecting with his jaw. I throw another, and he blocks it.

I keep going after him, hit after hit, kick, punch; some he blocks, others land. "What the fucking hell, Liam? How the fuck am I supposed to trust you? I could have got there in time. I could be there right now to help him." He blocks my last hits; I'm panting, my anger alive under my skin. He says nothing and stands there panting, blood dripping from his lip and eyebrow.

Matt and Ben have come to see what's happening. Liam raises a hand to stop them from getting involved.

"FUCK!!!" I scream.

I picked up the phone from where I had dropped it and dialled his number.

"Little Fury," he answers.

"Harry, I'm so sorry I didn't find out until right now. I can't get to you in time."

"I know, Ava. I asked Liam not to tell you. I asked him to keep it to himself, so don't be mad at him. He owed me a few favours. It cost me all of them to get him to agree to hold off telling you. He didn't seem keen on making you mad at him.

Even with all the favours, the Irish asshole still told you before I told him he could."

"Why, Harry?"

"Because the idea of my son trying to kill the woman I consider my daughter is not a sin I want weighing on my soul when I meet my maker, Ava."

"How long have you known?"

"Since he killed Enzo. Enzo had a couple of bombshells delivered to a few folks upon his death. Marcus's parentage was one of them."

"Cars coming up the lane, Harry," Sebastian says.

"Tell him, Harry! Fucking tell Marcus you're his father. Please tell him."

"I can't, Ava. I can't and won't put that on him."

"But he won't kill you if he knows."

"Ava."

"Harry, don't! Just fucking tell him!"

"Ava, he wouldn't believe me if I did. Or he would, and then he would realize how I was never there for him. I can't put that on him, Ava. I did nothing good for that boy. I won't make my last act one that causes him more pain."

"Goddammit, Harry."

"Six cars, Harry," Sebastian tells him. I hear a couple of guns cock.

"Ava, I need you to promise me something."

"Fuck you, Harry. I'm not promising you that. The minute he pulls that trigger, he's fucking dead."

"Ava! I will never find peace if I know my daughter killed my son out of revenge for my death. I need you to promise me."

"Harry–"

"Promise me, Ava!" He yells at me.

"Fuck you, Harry. You're a son of a bitch. You have no right to make me promise this! He deserves to die for all of it."

"Maybe he does, Ava, but then so do we all. We've all done enough bad in this life to warrant our deaths. But I will not have his death be because of me. Promise me."

"Please, Harry." I sob.

"Ava, I'm sorry it lands on you. I'm sorry it's always been on you, so much of the shit of this life. As much as I wish your life had been different, I can't seem to make a wish to change it. Raising you and training you was the best thing I ever did. I love you, Ava."

"I love you. Thank you for the life you gave me."

I hear the screen door open and close.

"Promise me."

"I promise," I tell him as another sob leaves me. Liam's arms are around me as I crumple to the ground. He takes my phone from me and puts it on speaker. He holds me tight, rocking me slightly in his arms.

"Hey, Harry," I hear Marcus shout in the distance.

"Marcus," Harry says.

"Where is she, Harry? Tell me where she is, and we'll turn around and head back home," Marcus tells him. His voice gets louder the closer he gets to him.

"I can't do that, Marcus. But you feel free to go back home anyway."

"I wish I could, Harry. But you gotta understand something. She won't engage with me. She's decided to go back to work, and just let bygones be bygones. While I'm sure that sounds like a great plan to her, I disagree. I started something, and I will finish it even if I have to burn the entire fucking world down to find her. She's mine. She has always been mine, and she will always be mine. And she will die how I want."

"Why Marcus? You loved that girl from the moment you met her."

"I did. I loved Ava. I still love her. But she never loved me back. Sure, she fucked me. She let me use her body however I wanted for years. But she never gave me her heart."

"You were her best friend, Marcus. She loved you so much. She only wanted you to be happy and find peace in your life."

"Ha! She moved on from me, Harry. I didn't want to move on from her."

"Marcus–"

"Enough. It's done. Tell me where she is." He notices the phone in Harry's hand.

"Is that her on the phone, Harry? Has she been listening to us this whole time?" Marcus sounds giddy, knowing I'm right there listening. "Put it on speaker."

Harry puts the phone on speaker. "Ava, Ava, Ava. Tell me where you are. Tell me where to find you, and I'll let the Scotsman live. You for him. Fair trade. One for one."

"Marcus, please don't hurt him. He fucking raised us. Loved us!"

"I know that, Ava. I was there. I know he raised us. He loved you; he raised me out of obligation, not being able to just let Enzo put a bullet in my head. Sometimes I wish he had just let him kill me." That last part is said barely above a whisper. "But none of that matters. You tell me where you are, or he dies. It's that simple."

"Why Marcus? What happened? When did you decide you hated me so much?"

"See, that's just it, Ava. I don't hate you. I fucking want to hate you. I want to hate you so badly, but I don't. I still fucking love you."

"Then why are you doing this? This will hurt me, Marcus. This will break my heart."

"Why? Aren't you supposed to have a genius-level IQ? How are you this stupid? The day you caught me with that woman in our bed, you just looked at me and her. I figured you would kill her when you caught us. It's why I fucked her in our bed. I wanted you to kill her for fucking what was yours. But you didn't. You just walked in and watched her ride my dick for a minute, looked at me, and left. It was the look you gave me, Ava. That look? That look started all this."

"What fucking look did I give you that could deserve all this as payback?"

"Relief Ava. You looked relieved when you saw us. And then you left me. No fight, no argument. You just left me."

"I didn't leave you, Marcus. I just stopped fucking you! I was still there with you every day. I was still there talking with you every day. The business was still us. Nothing changed except you could no longer stick your dick in me. That's it!" My anger is so overwhelming right now that if Liam wasn't holding me, I think I would have passed out. I can feel Liam breathing. I can feel his breath in my hair. I can feel his heart beating against my hand. And it's keeping me here, keeping me grounded.

"You changed after that, not me. You stopped talking to me. Alexi was the only person whose opinion you cared to hear after that. You started using all the time. Fuck. Marcus, do you realize that you sent me to a job that didn't exist? There was no target. It was never a contract. And another time, you sent me on a job alone where I almost died because the intel you gave me was so bad that there were an extra eight guys on the property! Eight! Fuck, Marcus! But sure, I stopped letting you cum in me, so it's all my fault. My body was no longer yours to use whenever you wanted; that's what fucked us."

"Enough Ava! Tell me where the fuck you are, last warning."

"Ava, remember your promise."

"Fuck you, Harry. I love you."

"You did this, Ava. Remember that when you tell Beth why Harry is dead, tell her you decided your life was more important than his. You let the man she loves die because you were a fucking coward."

A sob leaves me that is full of nothing but anguish. Liam tightens his arms around me like he's trying to give me his strength. Tears are running down my face, and my breathing is painful and ragged. "Please don't, please don't, please," I whisper like a chant in Liam's arms as he rocks me. I hear him murmuring. I feel him kissing my head. I raise my head to him, looking into his eyes, pleading for him to stop it.

"I'm so sorry, Mo Ghrá," I hear him whisper as a single gunshot goes off, and a thud follows as body and phone hit the ground.

AUTHORS NOTE

Well, shit. I wrote a book, and apparently, you read it.

This book was written and mapped out in my head over a year when my husband lived in Alberta and my daughter and I were still in Manitoba. Meaghan, our daughter, was in her last year of high school when my husband took a job in Alberta; we didn't want to move her. So, we stayed here, and he went there. This book was the product of those 11+ hour drives.

The most curious thing I learned during this process was how much a character or plot drives itself. So many things in this book went is directions even I didn't see coming. I didn't expect the characters to decide for themselves where they went on their journey. It was a remarkably interesting experience.

I have a philosophy or, at the very least, a direction I know my books will always take. And it is simply, and I apologize to any of you this hurts—If it's not a romcom, none of the characters are safe.

ACKNOWLEDGMENTS

I have very little faith in my ability as a writer. I don't say this so people can tell me I'm wrong. I say this with nothing but complete honesty. Like so many, I am my worst critic, and I am in no way a champion or cheerleader for myself. I am unkind to myself, if I am being perfectly honest.

However, I have an amazingly supportive and caring group of people in my life.

Isis Te Tuhi, this book is literally here on these pages because of you. You told me to do it, told me, "What did you have to lose?" So, I put ideas to the page, and 5 weeks later, I had a very rough, erratic, and messy 115,000-word manuscript. I profusely apologize to you for asking you to read it before I did an initial edit. That was mean of me.

My BFF Sarah is easily one of the smartest, most talented, and all-around beautiful humans I know. She is a lot like Miss Bennett in her ability to make everything look effortless and artful. She spent hours of her life editing this book for me, and there is no way I can thank her for that. She is also one of my biggest supporters or cheerleaders for any idiotic idea I get, and writing this book felt like an idiotic idea. No matter how far down the rabbit hole I went (June 1), she either helped me out of it or joined me in it.

EJ. Lindell, thank you. Just thank you for all of it. All the advice, the help, the questions you answered, the dos and don'ts you provided. Thank you. I am so grateful to have found you and come on! "MB for life"

Lori and all my beta readers, you guys are amazing.

When I wrote this and decided to publish it, my only goal or hope was for 1 person who didn't have a vested interest in my happiness to read it and like it. So, you being here? Reading this is easily one of the most incredible things that has ever happened to me, and hopefully, you liked it.